The Guardian's Playlist

2nd edition

by

J. Powell Ogden

www.JPowellOgden.com
Read it. Play it. Believe.

SPARKSTREET Media, LLC.

Cover Design and Artwork created by Tony Mauro Illustration and Design
Copyright © 2012 by Tony Mauro
www.tonymauroillustration.com

Cover Tattoo Art created by Eric Adkins
Copyright © 2011 by Eric Adkins

Latin Translation in Chapter Twenty-six provided by Dan Foley
Editing Consultant: Erin MacLellan
Character Art created by Koa Beam; http://koabeam.wix.com/koabeam
Cover and Interior format Specialist: T.C. McMullen of Star Publish LLC
www.starpublishllc.com   www.tcmcmullen.com

ISBN#: 978-0-692-59281-6

Published by Spark Street Media, LLC.
PO Box 3155, Dublin, Ohio 43016

Author Website: www.jpowellogden.com

Printed in the United States of America

10 9 8 7 6 5 4 3 2 1

For my Mom and Dad

And for all the songwriters in the world
You are the great poets of our time.

Table of Contents

The Guardian's Playlist

a novel

Prologue

THE BRILLIANT LIGHT *faded, and the bedroom was soon dark again, but not peaceful.*

"You know I'll be back. I can't let this one survive," said the beautiful demon standing next to the bed.

The Guardian on the bed looked down at the small figure tucked securely against his chest. The child was asleep, finally. It had been a long night.

The demon creature eyed the child curiously with black eyes that seemed to expand within his face. He moved a millimeter closer, but found his nose instantly breathing down the scalding tip of a slow-burning sword. The light flashed anew in the room.

"One step closer, and you'll fly apart like the rest of them!" the Guardian growled. He was young, but he'd already brought down creatures such as this one who were millions of years old. "Bring an army," he taunted, flipping his blade up and under the creature's chin. "I'll take them all down."

The demon smiled and backed up, his thorny black veins revealing themselves through his incandescent skin.

"Ah...but it's not you who needs to make the choice to resist, is it?" he said.

The Guardian's jaw twitched, and his eyes flicked down to the face of the safely sleeping child. When he looked up again, his eyes flashed silver. "She has ten times more faith in her pinky than you have in your entire soul."

The smile on the creature broadened. His eyes grew larger. "You're right," he said, a sinister laugh slipping out from between his lips. "But she won't see me coming next time." Then he became like smoke and faded away like the light into the night.

The Guardian sighed and bent his head to kiss the child's smallest finger. He smiled down at her and then tipped his head back against the headboard and closed his eyes. He knew he needed to take his rest when he could. He needed to be ready. Always ready.

Part One:
The Real World

Chapter 1
Lullaby

GOD SPEAKS TO me through the radio. Right. Sure. That's crazy. Which is why you'll never hear me admit that out loud. My family may be Catholic, we may go to church every Sunday, and we may even be known to pray the entire Rosary when someone dies, but I know without a doubt that an admission of this sort was certain to earn me an extended vacation on a therapist's couch.

Nonetheless, my Playlist grows. And it never...ever...ceases to amaze me. I don't ask for the song selections, don't pray for them, but just when it seems like my whole world is crashing down, and I'm ready to hide under my bed–that is, if there's not too much stuff under it–a song will come on the radio that's the perfect antidote for whatever is plaguing me. Between you and me—*sometimes I think an Angel picks them.*

For instance, this morning I was dreading the first day of school, because I knew I would finally have to face the fallout from my hugely embarrassing public fight with my boyfriend, Jason. I still couldn't believe I'd done what I'd done to him. I'd managed to avoid him for the last seven days, but today that ended. Today, Jason would be waiting for me in the honors courses we were sure to share. And the rest of the kids? They'd be waiting to see what happened next. Yeah. I was front-page Facebook news. Top Tweet of the week.

I was yanking a brush through my hair, working myself into a fit, worrying about what people would say and what Jason might do, when my sister, Cici, turned on the radio we shared, and I heard Shawn Mullins' "Lullaby."

Everything's gonna be alright
Rockabye, rockabye
Everything's gonna be alright
Rockabye, rockabye, rockabye

She still lives with her mom outside the city
Down that street about half a mile
And her friends tell her she's so pretty
But she'd be a whole lot prettier
If she smiled once in a while
'Cause even her smile looks like a frown
She's seen her share of devils
In this Angel town

Everything's gonna be all right…Rockabye, rockabye…

I turned and stared at the radio. Coincidence? Delusion? Chill pill from God? My perception mostly depended on my mood, which often changed every five minutes.

Faith is a slippery thing.

Okay, okay, I thought, calming my frenzied stroking, and then: *hopeless.*

The more I brushed my hair, the frizzier it got. I looked sideways at my sister who was carefully putting the final touches on her shiny blonde-streaked bangs with the flat iron. Cici was a freshman this year and wanted to look perfect for her first day. What was the point? Identical gray plaid skirts and white blouses. Not much you could do to improve on that. I surrendered, set the brush on the dresser, and pulled my thick, honey blonde hair up into a ponytail. Cici smiled at herself in the mirror.

"Ready?" she chirped.

"Sure," I said, leading the way down the worn, blue-carpeted stairs to the kitchen. My dad was already there with the newspaper spread out on the table.

"Good morning, girls!" he said, spooning his last bite of oat bran cereal into his mouth. He looked much younger than his fifty years. Because of his family's history of heart attacks, he'd been faithful to his heart-healthy diet for the past twenty years, and it showed. He folded his newspaper and stood up to leave. "Are you girls sure you don't want a ride?"

Cici and I exchanged a look, and then we both said, "Um…" My dad worked at the auto repair shop near our school, and the car in the garage was his latest "project" car. He'd just gotten it running. Cosmetic improvements were always the last part of his restoration efforts.

"Thanks, Dad, but we want to talk to our friends on the way to school," I said.

His face fell a little. "Well, if you change your mind…" He pecked my mom goodbye on the cheek. "Goodbye, Claire!" he called up the stairs to my older sister before ducking out the door. Soon we heard what sounded like a chainsaw revving up in the garage. Cici and I rolled our eyes, relieved we weren't in the car with him.

My mom turned and got to the business of coercing us to eat breakfast.

"Eggs?" she asked.

"No," I said.

"French toast?"

"Sounds great!" said Cici.

Mom handed Cici a plate and raised her dark eyebrows at me. "French toast, Catherine?"

"I don't know…"

"You have to eat something. You'll starve by lunchtime."

"Okay…Rice Krispies?"

She went to the pantry to grab the box of cereal. While she rummaged, my older sister Claire finally made her appearance. Mom knew better than to ask *her* what she wanted for breakfast. Instead, she deftly stepped out of the way as Claire grabbed a slice of bread from the pantry and slapped half with peanut butter and half with honey. She folded it over, slung her backpack onto her sturdy shoulder, and shot a cursory glance at Cici and me. Seeing we were nowhere near ready to leave, she said, "See you at the bus stop." Then she disappeared out the front door, her long, wavy brown hair bouncing behind her.

Cici's mouth dropped open. Claire was a senior. Being a sophomore, I'd already spent a year coming to grips with the fact that I wasn't on Claire's priority list. Anywhere.

"Does she *ever* wait for you?" Cici asked.

"Only if Mom lets her drive the Honda and refuses to give her the keys until I'm in the car." I smiled, remembering I would be getting my license in October, but my smile faded when I realized Claire wouldn't relinquish the keys easily.

"Come on," I said. "We'd better move. Claire loves it when I miss the bus." There was only one city bus that picked up kids in Fairview Park and took them to our Catholic high school. If we missed it, we were S.O.L. We gathered up our things and headed for the door. I took one last look at myself as I passed the hall mirror. Not bad. My hair needed work, but at least I'd lost the glasses and braces in the past week.

"Bye, Mom!" I called.

"Did you take your asthma medicine, Catherine?" she called after me.

I pretended not to hear her and continued toward the door.

"Catherine Alexandra?" she called sharply.

I sighed, dropped my bag and hurried back to the kitchen counter.

"I'm fine," I said irritably.

"You don't want to have an asthma attack on the first day of school, do you?"

Cici gave me a sympathetic look. I glanced down into my mom's face as she dropped the pills onto my palm. Her face was pinched with worry, her eyes ringed with dark circles. I sighed again, berating myself for not asking earlier.

"How's Mina?"

My Grandmother Philomina had been getting sicker and weaker over the last few weeks, and it was tearing my mom up inside that she lived so far away.

"Not well. She slept on the sofa last night, because she couldn't make it up the stairs. I really need to get down to Bluefield to check on her soon."

"I'm sorry, Mom. I hope she does better this week." I gave her a quick hug, and then Cici and I hurried down the front porch steps and out into the pink morning sunshine. We arrived at the bus stop just as the city bus pulled up to the curb. The folded door swung open, and the stale smell of street grime and fellow passengers washed over us. We climbed up the stairs behind Claire, who sat down with her friends near the front. I guided Cici to a seat about halfway back.

The bus lurched ahead. Minutes later, it ground to a halt at the Thomas Avenue stop where my friends, Meri and Grace, waited with Meri's older brother, Leo. Off to the side stood Shawn Fowler, a waifish, mousy-haired sophomore I detested, and with him was a boy I hadn't seen before. The two were smoking, and a bluish haze wafted away from them in the late summer breeze. They casually flicked their cigarettes to the ground, not bothering to stamp them out.

Leo shot them a disapproving look before ushering Meri and Grace up the steps. As soon as Shawn and the new boy cleared the door, the bus lumbered forward again, and the two boys grabbed the backs of the seats as they stumbled past us on their way to the back. I glanced furtively up into the new boy's face, trying to puzzle out his identity. He was of average height and build, with dark blonde hair that waved haphazardly well past his ears. His slate gray eyes remained focused on the back of the bus as he passed. He looked familiar, but my attention was abruptly broken when Meri, who had plopped down in the seat across from mine, turned and shrieked, "Where are your glasses, Cate?"

Almost everyone but my mom calls me Cate—with the exception of my dad who calls me Caty, sometimes adding the endearing but embarrassing "Bug" to round out my name. Feeling self-conscious, I blinked at my friends while they showered me with compliments and questions about my new contacts.

"When did you get them?"

"Why didn't you tell us?"

"Your eyes are so blue!"

"Jason will be kicking himself."

"What's with your hair?"

"Why didn't you do something with it?

"Because she got up only thirty minutes ago," tattled Cici.

All three of them stared at me, flabbergasted.

"This will *not* do," Meri said. "Break out the first aid kit, Grace."

"Here," Grace said, shoving a white plastic box onto Meri's lap. Meri dug through it, her glossy black hair obscuring her face.

"Who am I trying to impress, anyway?" I whined. Meri stopped pawing to glare at me with her almond-shaped eyes.

"You never know who you're going to meet," she replied. Then she leaned in and whispered, "Like that new kid who just got on the bus."

"You have *got* to be kidding!" I said. No friend of Shawn's would be a friend of mine. He'd hated me ever since I'd gotten him in trouble for smoking on the bus freshman year.

"Whatever," she said. "You never know." She pulled out a sable brown eye pencil, mascara, a compact of light shadow and some bronzer.

"All that?" I asked, considering mutiny. Meri and Grace raised their eyebrows simultaneously. Even Cici watched with interest. I realized I was outnumbered. You know you trust your friends when you let them wield a sharp pencil to line your eyes while riding in a swaying city bus. But how could I not? Grace, Meri and I had been friends since kindergarten when we'd been in the same Daisy troop.

Meri applied the makeup with a light touch, then handed me a mirror and some lip gloss. I was stunned. For the first time, my eyes were the stand-out feature of my face. I actually looked awake, happy and...well, sort of hot.

"Better?" asked Meri.

"I suppose."

Meri scowled and was about to say more when the bus stopped abruptly, bouncing her into the back of her seat and spilling the contents of the white plastic box down the aisle. I jumped up to help retrieve the scattering makeup, chasing the mascara all the way to the back of the bus, then watched with dismay as it rolled right between the new boy's beat-up white Converse tennis shoes and disappeared under his seat. I hesitated, not sure if he'd noticed.

"Um…" I mumbled, squatting down awkwardly in front of him and pointing toward his feet. When I glanced up, he was leaning forward on his elbows and looking down at me. His tie swung crookedly back and forth between his knees, and the corners of his lips were twitching with amusement. He glanced away toward Shawn, who was ignoring him, then down at his hands, which were twirling his headphones, and then back at me. His face had a roughened, streetwise look about it, but his steel gray eyes were bright. It was his eyes that were familiar. I knew them from somewhere.

"So…what are you going to do now?" he asked, looking away again but not moving his feet.

"Um…threaten to tell everyone you stole my mascara if you don't give it back?"

"Now that wouldn't be true. I don't think that is *your* mascara," he pointed out, looking back and bouncing his heels up and down. So, he'd been watching my personal makeover session. I felt my face flush.

"*Okay*…tell everyone you stole Meri's mascara?" I said.

"Now *that* would put a dent in my reputation." He bent over to pick up the mascara. As he reached under his seat, his short white shirtsleeve pulled back to reveal the tip of a black sword tattooed on his right bicep.

I averted my eyes and masked my shocked expression before he looked up again and held out the mascara. I'd never seen a tattoo on the arm of one of my Catholic high school classmates—in fact, they were prohibited. I was about to ask him what exactly his reputation was when the bus slowed down, and I was thrown face first into his lap. He reached out instinctively and grabbed my wrists to prevent me from falling backward when the bus came to a complete stop. His touch was faintly electric, and my heartrate spiraled upward.

"Whoa…" he said, holding my wrists safely in his warm hands while I steadied myself.

"Um…sorry…" I said, flustered, and then tried to disengage myself. But he held on for a moment, his eyes searching my face before letting go. Was it recognition I saw there?

"Thanks," I said, taking the mascara. "See you around." He nodded, and then I turned to see my friends trying to muffle their explosive giggling with their hands.

"Thanks," I mouthed at them, stepping quickly back up the aisle to my seat behind Grace.

While my friends laughed, Cici whispered, "He was watching you the whole time they worked on your eyes." I glanced back over my shoulder to see if he was still watching, but he'd plugged his headphones into his ears, tipped his head back against the seat, and closed his eyes. I could swear I recognized him from somewhere, but I couldn't place him.

Grace interrupted my thoughts, asking bluntly, "So, have you talked to Jason since you pushed him in the pool?" Her blonde bob swung about her round face in time with the movement of the bus as she waited for my answer.

"No! Are you kidding?" Only Cici knew that Jason had called every day for the past week just to be told I wasn't home or I was in the shower. Cici fielded those calls. She was loyal that way.

"I heard he was just comforting Kara because her puppy died," said Meri.

"Are you still mad?" Grace asked. "Do you want us to tell him you don't want to talk to him?"

I looked out the window. "No," I answered miserably. I would have to talk to Jason sooner or later. I heard Meri's older brother Leo laughing to himself behind me and knew he thought the whole situation was funny. Worse, I knew he was right. But when I'd seen Jason holding hands with Kara, whispering in her ear, sitting with his back to me next to the pool, *fully clothed*, the urge to play "Dunk the

Bonehead" had been overwhelming. Unfortunately for me, Leo had witnessed the whole thing.

By the time the bus pulled up in front of the school, I was anxious again, and my heart was racing, but I remembered my early morning message on the radio. Just thinking about the song, "Lullaby," slowed my heartbeat back down, and I took a deep breath to keep it there. Then I stood up and took one last look behind me to see if I recognized Meri's mascara retriever. He was too busy stuffing his music player into his backpack to notice me staring. It was there, some memory of him, but it kept slipping away from me as if it didn't quite fit into the current picture. I rubbed my wrists absently, recalling the subtle, static-like feel of his touch, racking my brain for a name, but kept drawing a blank. Oh well, it would come to me. I slung my backpack over my shoulder and followed my friends off the bus.

⚡·⚡

Our high school was a squat, two-story, tan brick building built smack in the middle of a working class Cleveland suburb. Orderly rows of glass windows fanned out from the main entrance, which was cast in shadow under a large concrete overhang. The overhang was embellished with a simple copper cross within a sunburst. A sword slashed over the base of the cross, and next to it, also in copper, were the words:

> *Saint Joan of Arc High School*
> *"I place trust in God, my creator, in all things; I love him with all my heart."*
>
> —*Saint Joan of Arc*
> *1412-1431*

As I passed into the shadow that blanketed the front doors, I stopped and looked around for Cici to see if she needed help, but she'd already found her friends. I smiled, glad she was here with me.

We shared a study hall on Friday at the end of the day, and we looked forward to spending it together.

Meri and Grace waited inside and motioned impatiently for me to join them.

"Has anyone seen Finn and the guys?" Meri asked. She bounced up and down, trying to see over the wall of bustling students that surrounded her. Patrick Finnegan and Meri had been going out since the first day of freshman year, and Grace and I had adopted his friends as our own. We did almost everything with Finn, Spencer and J.C., even going out with them on and off, but fate kept interfering, and whatever couple formed always ended up just friends again. They were like brothers now, teasing us mercilessly and waiting to drive off any unsuspecting guy who showed any interest in us.

Seeing Meri look for Finn reminded me to be on the lookout for Jason. As I scanned the hall, a tall, lanky figure with red hair swooped up behind Meri and caught her up in his wiry arms, lifting her off her feet. Spencer and J.C. appeared behind him.

"Hey! Put me down!" Meri laughed. Instead, the figure buried his face in her shiny, shoulder-length hair and nibbled on her neck. "Finn! Stop! You pervert!"

Finn ignored her protests.

"A little help?" she pleaded with Spencer, who at six foot two, could still look down at her even though she was hoisted up to Finn's eye level.

"Hey now, a dude don't get between a bro and his, er…girlfriend," he said. Spencer held up his hands in a "no can do" gesture, and then crossed his arms over his chest. J.C. crossed his arms over his chest, too, and shook his head in solidarity. How nice, peer pressure at its finest. Unfortunately, the boys didn't notice the powerful figure prowling behind them.

"Mr. Finnegan! That is an entirely unacceptable public display of affection!" Finn reluctantly set Meri down on her feet, winked at us, and then turned around to face the tiny, gray-haired woman who was barking at him.

"Aw, Sister Lawrencia, I haven't seen her for days! I was just trying to let her know how much I missed her."

Sister Lawrencia waved dismissively at Finn and squinted through watery eyes at Meri. "Everything all right, Merideth?"

Meri bit back a grin. "Um…sure, Sister. Thanks."

"All right, then. Come with me, Mr. Finnegan."

Finn mouthed "See you later," to Meri and then followed the small, blue suit clad nun, who was making a beeline for the office.

"Busted!" howled J.C. after them.

"How much time you think he gets?" Spencer laughed

J.C. stood for Juan Carlos Aquila, and his deep brown eyes crinkled as he grinned. "I don't know. That was a pretty flagrant PDA."

Meri ignored them and stared after Finn, shaking her head in disbelief. "He never learns."

Spencer smiled very sweetly down at her. "That's why we keep him around, Mer. He's like a diversion for the rest of us."

Meri punched his arm.

"Hey, now, don't go physically assaulting me, or I'll have to call Sister Larry back," he complained. Meri narrowed her eyes at Spencer, who backed up a step. "Um, right…time to go," he said to J.C., and the two boys took off, almost taking out a small herd of freshman as they rounded the corner.

Grace and I dropped our stuff of at our lockers and headed to homeroom, which we shared. I wouldn't see Meri again until the end of the day. Our schedules diverged widely this year, with Grace and me taking primarily honors and science courses and Meri spending more of her time in the Art Annex.

We arrived in homeroom just as the late bell rang to find Spencer sitting in the middle row flirting with some girls I knew. Shawn Fowler sat in the back.

I slid into the seat next to Spencer. "Hey, Spence. I didn't know you were in here."

He pulled his attention away from the girls long enough to say "hi." Then the announcement bells rang.

"Welcome to the beginning of another year here at Saint Joan," droned Sister Lawrencia over the loud speaker. "Let us begin with a prayer. In the name of the Father, the Son, and the Holy Spirit…" My mind wandered as she went on and on, praying for blessings, guidance, and strength for all sorts of trials we might face this year. She finished with an appeal to God and his Angels to watch over us and a reminder that Club Day was Friday. Then the burly teacher at the front of the class addressed us.

"Okay, class. Everyone rise so I can evaluate your conformity to the dress code."

There was a collective groan from the class as chairs scraped backwards, and students shuffled to their feet. She grabbed a yardstick off her desk and moved up and down the aisles, appraising each student. I went through the standards in my head. I had my white blouse tucked in, skirt less than two inches above the knee, white knee socks pulled up over my calves—can't show off those sexy calves—and only one earring per ear…hmm, I felt my earlobes to make sure I'd taken out the extra earrings that morning. Then I glanced around at the rest of the class.

Several boys were stuffing their shirts into their pants, and a few of the girls were inching their skirts as far down over their hipbones as they dared. Despite their efforts, two girls were admonished about the shortness of their skirts. One boy's hair was too long. Those kids were lucky. They would just have to make the corrections tonight and bring forms signed by their parents tomorrow. The boy who forgot his tie, however, was sent to the office to wear whatever tie Sister Larry had requisitioned for such a situation.

When the teacher reached Shawn Fowler in the back of the class, my thoughts unexpectedly turned to the new boy I'd met on the bus, the one with the familiar eyes and the prohibited tattoo. I didn't think his short sleeves would shield him from discovery, and I shuddered to think how the administration would make him conform. They couldn't possibly require the tattoo be removed, could they? Why hadn't he thought to wear long sleeves today? I was still inexplicably lost in thought about him when the bell rang signaling the end of the period.

≈ ◦ ≈

The rest of the morning passed with no Jason sightings. Four periods down, four to go. I hoped my luck would hold. At lunch, I missed having Meri around. It was too bad our schedules didn't match up, but with Finn talking about her every second, she might as well have been there. J.C. and Grace finally told him to shut up.

I was cleaning up the remains of my lunch when my luck ran out. Jason was weaving his way toward me through the crowd in the cafeteria. Crap, I wasn't ready for this. I got up and made for the trashcan near the exit, but Jason was quicker and cut me off.

"Cate! Wait!" he said, holding up his hands to stop me.

I felt my face growing hot. A few people turned to watch and whisper.

"Look, later…okay?" I pleaded.

His ice-blue eyes flashed angrily. "No! I've been trying to talk to you all week! Why won't you talk to me? First you–"

"Just…wait, not here. Call me tonight, okay? I'll pick up."

"No. I'll drive you home." It wasn't a question. "Meet me at the front doors after school."

I nodded, and he turned and left without a backward glance. I remained in the cafeteria doorway for a moment, watching him walk away. From behind me, a girl whispered, "I heard Leo's friend say she shoved him in the pool when she caught him with Kara. Freak."

Another girl laughed and whispered back in a voice meant to carry, "If Jason were mine, he wouldn't be cheating. I know what he needs."

I hugged my books tight to my chest, resisting the urge to turn around and hurl one of them at her face. Instead, I walked away, cursing myself again for losing my temper.

As bad luck would have it, Jason and I had the next two classes together, Honors Algebra II and Computer Lab, and even though I caught him watching me a few times, he didn't say anything. I didn't know if he was respecting my wishes or was just too mad to speak.

How did I get myself into these messes? After the final bell rang, I asked Meri and Grace to make sure Cici got home okay and then walked toward the front of the building, nervous sweat prickling under my arms.

～⁂～

Jason King turned sixteen at the end of the summer and already had his license and his mom's old car. To her credit, it wasn't a minivan or a clunky SUV but a practically brand new, black Audi coupe. She gave it to him when she bought her new maroon Mercedes. Yeah. The Kings had money.

As I approached the front doors, someone shouldered past me, knocking my books out of my hands. I bent down to retrieve them, and a hand appeared to help me. I twisted to see who it was and found myself looking up into the face of the blonde boy from the bus. He didn't smile as he shoved one of my books at me. He mumbled an apology, then stood up and pushed on toward the door, pausing for only a moment to rip off a large gauze bandage taped to the top of his arm and hurl it into a trashcan by the entrance. He was gone before I could say anything. I could guess what happened. His tattoo had been discovered and the bandage was meant to cover it up. And though I didn't even know him, I felt a strong urge to run after him and make sure he was all right.

Then Jason was there to help me to my feet. "Let's go," he said.

We walked in silence to the car. He unlocked the door, and I slid onto the black leather seat, which was scorching hot from baking in the sun all day. He got in on the driver's side, unrolled all the windows and flicked the air-conditioning on high.

"Do you think it makes sense to turn on the air with the windows down?" I asked without thinking. Jason gave me a withering look. Then he put the car in drive and steered out of the parking lot as The Blackout's "Wolves," a song I happened to love, growled its way out of the Audi's high-end speakers. I waited for him to change the station. Jason didn't appreciate my darker, edgier taste in music, preferring instead his chest thumping hip hop.

Today, though, he opted for silence and switched the radio off. Then without missing a beat, he glanced sideways at me, asking, "So... what's up?" He raised his eyebrows expectantly. He wasn't giving anything away. Nice play. He'd put me on the defensive right off the bat. I should have expected that.

Jason King was smart, the smartest guy I knew, and with computers he was brilliant. We became friends while working on the same freshman service project. A few weeks after he broke up with Kara, he came over to help me load some new software on my computer. He was miserable, and being the kind and helpful person that I am, I tried to comfort him. I had always thought he was hot—blue eyes, dark hair, athletic build, knew the meaning of the word bibliophile. Jason had to be the only guy I knew who'd suggest we read *Paradise Lost* out loud to each other—which we did over the summer—for extra credit. Too bad he had that player reputation.

In the end, it didn't matter.

Comforting words turned into consoling hugs, consoling hugs turned into soothing kisses, and soothing kisses turned into never explored before, no holds barred make out sessions in his glorious, queen-sized bed and...okay Cate, you can stop thinking about that now.

Chemistry wasn't our problem.

"Cate?" Jason asked. I shook my head to clear it.

"Um, Jason, I'm really sorry about last week. It's just that when I saw you with Kara at the pool when you said you were busy, I was mad. You lied, and it really pissed me off."

"Yes. I should know better than to light up that temper of yours. Swing first and ask questions later. Isn't that your motto?"

"At least I listen to the answers...eventually," I shot back.

That was our problem. We fought. Not just over music, but over everything. Jason had opinions on top of opinions, and they were always better than mine, in his opinion, of course. I'd always thought I was pretty smart, but Jason read voraciously–philosophy, the classics, history—and he was always pulling some obscure quote out of left field to back up what he said. I couldn't compete with that, and the constant bickering was wearing me down. On top of that, I knew deep down he still had a thing for Kara. So, though the chemistry between us was hard to resist, I had planned on breaking up with him even before the whole pool fiasco. And for my own sake, I needed to do it today.

"Cate, I was just holding her hand. She was upset—"

"You can't tell me you don't still have feelings for her. You see her almost as much as you see me."

He pulled up in front of my house, put the car in park, leaned over the gear shift and dropped his voice into that self-assured throaty growl he knew I loved. "And you can't tell me you don't still have feelings for *me*."

Shit, I had to get out of the car before I did something stupid. I reached behind me, released the lock and opened the door, slid out of the car, and then slammed the door shut. "I…don't…" I said through the open window.

"So let me get this straight. You pushed me in the pool because you were jealous, even though you don't like me anymore? You've got some serious issues."

It was true. I definitely had issues. I nodded and lowered my head. Despite everything, I was angry at myself for losing my temper, and I waited for further chastisement. Perhaps flogging would come next. I looked up when it didn't come, and found him staring out the driver's side window, rubbing his forehead. In a strained voice almost too low for me to hear, he murmured, "Ahh…maybe it's for the best."

"I'm really sorry, Jason." I said, backing away from the car.

"Wait," he said. "Just…wait a sec." I leaned back in through the open passenger side window, not sure what was coming next. "Look, I should have told you I was going to meet Kara. She just sounded so desperate on the phone."

Of course, always desperate. I had to fight to keep from rolling my eyes.

"And maybe you weren't so far off the mark last week. Maybe I do still have some feelings for her." He turned to look at me. "And pushing me in the pool—Kara really feels sorry for me right now. Cate, are you sure this is what you want?"

"Yeah, Jason, it's okay."

"So…friends?" he asked.

"Friends," I agreed.

Jason reached out to put the car in reverse, smiled, and then let loose half a chuckle. "But you owe me a cell phone. Mine got a little waterlogged." I made a face, but nodded.

As he drove off, I smiled to myself, feeling warm, realizing that everything really *had* turned out all right, just like the song had promised. Yeah, okay, I was certifiable. Nonetheless, Shawn Mullins' *"Lullaby"* was officially added to my Playlist.

So…now that my Jason problem was solved, my thoughts turned to the new mystery in my life. Just who was that boy in the white Converse shoes?

Chapter 2
The Boy in the White Converse Shoes

MY BEDROOM USED to be pink. Cinderella pink. Now it was a more mature, pale yellow, and most of my princess decorations were stored away. I'd left only my Guardian Angel statue out on my dresser. I told myself my Angel didn't count as a princess. She had a job to do.

The sun reflected off the walls, creating a warm pool of light on Cici's bed. Curled up in the puddle were Lucky and Big Fat Maxell, our two cats we'd rescued as kittens from a shelter. Maxwell was white and well fed, with a princely orange spot splattered across the top of his head. Lucky was a rangy orange tabby with a rabid taste for wild chipmunk. As I plopped down on the bed to pat the two sleeping felines, Cici slipped into the room.

"I made it home alive," she said.

"I can see that," I replied. "Well done, my Padawan learner."

"You've seen Star Wars *way* too many times," she said, flopping down on her bed next to me. Then she asked with hardly a pause, "So, who was that new kid on the bus this morning?"

"Don't you want to know what happened between Jason and me?" I asked. I'd been whining about him all week.

"Oh…that. You already told me you were dumping him, and even a blind kid could tell he's still got a thing for Kara. I figured you'd get off easy."

"Well, you could have told *me* it would all end up so neatly. I was going crazy all day trying to figure out what to say to him," I shot back, annoyed by her casual attitude.

Used to my short fuse, Cici just shrugged and pressed again, "*So, who is he?*"

"I don't know who he is," I murmured, moving to my own bed and grabbing up Pigwin, my favorite stuffed animal. I fingered the little pig's hideously mismatched pink satin tutu and spiked silver collar. "But I'm positive I know him from somewhere. Something about his eyes…" I stared off through the open window at the maple tree out back. A warm feeling suffused my face. I tried to shake it off, but it was too late. My sister, unusually perceptive, had already taken note.

"I thought so!" she said. "Listen, Cate, you're just getting out of one mess—"

"What's messy about the new kid?"

"You're not going to like it."

"Just spit it out."

"You saw him hanging out with Shawn, and you obviously know Shawn's reputation."

Yeah, okay. I knew there were rumors about Shawn and drugs. "And?"

"Look, one of the girls I met today lives in the new kid's neighborhood, and she says he's living with the Gardiners as their foster child, *and* that he got kicked out of his last school."

"Oh," I said, deflated.

"You saw him smoking, right?" she tried again. She held her hands out like a scale on either side of her head. "Asthma," she said, waving her right hand. "Smoking," she said, waving her left hand. "Not such a good combination. N'est ce pas?"

She was making sense, but I had to at least find out who he was and how he knew me, and then there was the question of the tattoo, and…oh, who the hell was I kidding. I was already interested and would just have to follow the path where it led.

"I'll be careful," I said.

"You? Careful? Around a boy? Right."

"Whatever. Let's go see what Mom's making for dinner. I'm sure she's dying to pump us for details about school. If we don't give her something, she'll assume we're friendless and failing out on the first day." I hopped off the bed and was out the door before she could say anything else.

⚓

The next morning came way too early, *again,* and I put on a white blouse and gray plaid skirt, *again.* This time, though, I got up early enough for Cici to help me straighten my hair and took a little more time with my makeup. I was nervous as the bus approached Meri and Grace's stop, but the extra adrenaline coursing through my veins went to waste because the new kid wasn't on it. Instead, I had to give my friends another blow-by-blow account of my break up with Jason. Apparently, a texted version and a three-way call replay didn't suffice.

I didn't see the boy from the bus all day, and I was irritable, feeling stupid that such a small question mark could plague me so.

⚓

With the first Friday of the school year came Saint Joan's tradition of Club Day, which meant a dress-down day for anyone wearing an extracurricular club's T-shirt. Any day you didn't have to wear your uniform was a good day, and I secretly admired the way my new tight jeans and forest green WildLife & WildPlaces Club T-shirt hugged my small curves. Grace and I had started the club the year before after volunteering for two summers at a nearby wildlife hospital. Having seen firsthand the disastrous effects that carelessness and abuse have on local wildlife, and doing everything possible to save them but failing more often than not, we wanted to raise awareness.

The club tables were set up in the school cafeteria. Flanking the tables was a bank of windows, and high above them the ceiling angled up to the roof's apex, which housed the cafeteria skylights. Many of the tables were already decorated with tablecloths, helium balloons and posters.

I got to work setting up the WildLife & WildPlaces table, covering it with a dark green cloth and topping that with a cardboard tree whose branches were adorned with stuffed animals representing Ohio's native birds. I set out information I'd gathered to promote the Cleveland MetroParks and the Wildlife Rescue Hotline number. Cici eyed the stuffed animals skeptically and asked, "How many people are in your club anyway?"

"Ten, I think." In truth, since Grace and I founded the club, only six people had joined. Cici liked animals—the domestic kind that purred or wagged their tails when you pet them. Her feelings were less fuzzy for the ones that tried to bite your hand off or claw your eyes out when you tried to untangle them from barbed wire or dress their wounds. "Why don't you check out the cheer and dance team tables?" I suggested. With her many years of gymnastics, I knew she would be more interested in those activities.

"I don't know. You know what they say about cheerleaders..."

I grinned. "Sure. They're all bratty, fashion-addicted, popular girls. You should fit right in." She threw a cardinal at me, which burst into song upon impact.

"Well, it's ready," I said, after taping a poster to the front of the table. "See you at study hall this afternoon."

❦

I kept an eye out for the boy from the bus all morning, but didn't see him. At lunch, I hurried to my locker to grab the brown bag I'd packed and then rushed to the cafeteria, knowing my club table would be empty until I arrived. However, when I reached the cafeteria entrance, I saw that Finn had filled the empty seat. He was wearing his gray and yellow basketball jersey and creating some kind of aerial battle between the robin and the blue jay. J.C. was standing in front of the table picking each bird up and squeezing it to hear what it sounded like. When he turned and saw me approaching, he quickly put the little bird he was playing with back in the tree, fluffed it a little, and then stepped back from the table.

"Nice display," he offered. Finn didn't pay any attention to either of us.

I said, "Finn, you can fly away now."

"Just trying to be helpful," he said, smiling, and then, seeing I was serious, added, "Okay then, hmm, I don't think you should put the robin and the blue jay next to each other. They can't seem to get along. And, I don't like the look of the buzzard. I think he's up to no good."

"Thanks, Finn, I've got it covered," I replied coolly, holding my hands out for the unruly birds.

"Don't mention it," he said and winked. Then J.C. and Finn met up with Grace and got in line for food.

I sat down, looked at the sign-up sheet, and smiled when I saw Finn and J.C.'s names on the list. Then, I took stock of the tables on either side. A little ways down from mine, Jason was at the Computer Club table—which he was president of despite being only a sophomore—and Kara was sitting on his lap. She hadn't wasted any time. A few tables farther down, Meri's brother, Leo, was sitting at the Guitar Club table. I was surprised he had time for guitar. He seemed to spend every waking minute in the pool for swim team or at home practicing the DiMaro family's mandatory piano lessons. I let my gaze drift around the cafeteria, and there, back in the corner, was my mystery friend from the bus.

He was sitting at a table by himself with a book propped open in front of him, munching absently on a sandwich. He'd learned his lesson from Wednesday and was wearing a long-sleeved white button-down shirt with the sleeves rolled up to his elbows. His tie was straight, and his headphones were draped over his shoulder. His dark blonde hair was a little shorter, but still waved playfully a little past his ears and over his collar.

Crap! Why did I have to be busy today? I could think of a hundred reasons, excuses, to stop by his table to introduce myself and satisfy my own wicked curiosity. As I watched, a few freshman girls sat down next to him and tried to talk to him, but he only hunched down more and pulled his book in closer. When they persisted, he took a last bite of his sandwich, nodded to them, threw out his trash and then made his way to one of the club tables at the far end of the row.

He paused now and again, but didn't pick anything up until he came to Leo and the Guitar Club. He leaned over the table, looking at the flyers that were laid out, and he and Leo exchanged a few words. Leo wasn't very welcoming or friendly, but the boy nodded and took a flyer anyway. He was almost to my table when Zoe, who wrote for the school newspaper, crowded her way into my field of vision.

"Hello, customer here!" she said pushily.

I forced my eyes up to her face. "Um…sorry, what did you say?"

"I was asking for some information for the newspaper. I'm doing a story on all of the clubs in next week's edition."

"Oh, well…" I handed her a flyer just as my personal question mark reached my table.

"As I was saying…" Zoe babbled on.

He let his eyes and fingers linger on my brochures for a moment, and when he looked up from under his long lashes, his eyes were crinkled, and his lips were turned up in a slight smile.

"Hey," he whispered. My heartbeat raced a little, and I reached out and handed him a green flyer. I opened my mouth to speak.

"Cate! Are you listening to anything I'm saying?" Zoe demanded. The boy suppressed a laugh. He was standing a step behind her, and did a perfect imitation of her stance and hand motions. I laughed, and pointed to my name on the flyer and then to myself.

"I know," he mouthed from behind Zoe's back and then pointed to the time on his cell and turned to leave. As he left, I could see that the book he was reading was one by Stephen Crane, *The Red Badge of Courage*.

"What? What's funny?" asked Zoe, turning around, but he was already gone. Now he knew my name, but I didn't know his. But he *did* have my phone number. It just wasn't fair. What was I supposed to say? Come back! Tell me who you are! Not knowing is *killing me*! No, of course not. And Zoe was still peppering me with questions.

"So kids really sign up to go out and do all this…wild animal stuff?"

"Yeah, Zoe. They do. Some of us call it 'stewardship,'" I replied, letting my annoyance creep into my voice.

"Whatever," she replied and went on to the next table.

By the time I reached my study hall with Cici at the end of the day, all I could think about was the mystery boy with the tattoo. I signed in and put my forehead down on my stack of unopened books, but the pressure of unfinished homework and the race for A's was already beginning. After a few minutes, I sat up and opened my math text. Cici was sitting at the table next to me, quietly working on French homework.

The numbers on the page were just starting to make sense when the classroom door opened, and a boy with rolled up shirt sleeves and old Converse sneakers walked up to the desk and signed in. Finally, in the very last period of the week, I had a class with Tattoo Boy. When he turned around to sit down, he saw me and waved slightly, then took the only empty seat, which was on the opposite side of the room.

The suspense of finding out his name was driving me insane. Think. How was I going to get his name before the end of study hall? And then I had my answer. I got up out of my seat and approached the teacher's desk to ask for a hall pass to get a drink of water. I hesitated for a moment, looking down at the sign-in sheet, and there it was, the name I had been scouring my brain for since Wednesday.

It all clicked. I glanced his way, but his nose was already buried in his book. Then a wave of memories flooded my head, and I grabbed my hall pass and headed for the water fountain, but instead of stopping, I walked right past it into the cold-tiled privacy of the bathroom. I leaned on the sink and stared into the mirror at my reflection, whispering, "Michael Casey, I remember you."

Chapter 3
The Claddagh

My MEMORIES OF the boy with the tattoo, now locked and loaded, fired with a force unstoppable. I became lost in the beginning of another school year, eight years ago.

❧

"Welcome back from recess, class!" Sister Patricia exclaimed, clapping her hands to get our attention. "We have a special surprise for all of you today! Gather around."

My second grade classmates and I had just blown in from recess and were meandering about, trying to figure out what we were supposed to do next. Our faces were pink and our uniforms disheveled from playing out in the brisk autumn breeze blowing off Lake Erie.

As I hung up my pink denim jacket, a classmate pointed at my hair and giggled. I reached up and pulled out a few brown leaf shreds that were stuck in my frizzy curls. I pushed my glasses back up into place on my nose and then looked around the room. Standing before the blackboard was a small blonde boy in black pants and a white shirt. He was holding a pillowcase with a piece of twine tied around the top. My curiosity roused, I joined the kids on the floor and sat down.

"Now class, Michael brought his pet in to share with us, but before we begin, I need to remind you to be very quiet and very still. We don't want to scare it. Go ahead, Michael." Sister Patricia nodded her gray head toward Michael in encouragement. Michael didn't look like he needed any encouragement. He looked out at his classmates, shifting his weight from foot to foot, his eyes full of excitement.

"Well, before I take him out, you should know he can be dangerous, but I'm an expert, so don't worry," he said. Then he started untying the pillowcase.

Sister Patricia gave a little cough. *"Maybe you better first tell us again what you have in there."*

"Oh, well, his name is Red Fang," he began, continuing to untie the pillowcase and reaching into the bag. *"And he's my pet corn snake."* Then he pulled out the smallest and cutest red snake I had ever seen.

The tiny creature wasn't any thicker than a pencil or longer than a ruler. But I guess the rest of the class didn't think he was cute because all of a sudden, there was a loud shrieking sound as a few kids jumped to their feet and backed away. When Michael looked up, startled, the snake wriggled out of his hands and waved at light speed away from him across the carpeted floor.

"Nobody move!" shouted Michael. You might as well have told a waterfall not to fall, because the whole class was moving. Jumping on top of chairs. Colliding with one another. Running for the door.

"No! Don't open the door!" cried Michael. I knew what Michael was worried about. First, he was afraid someone would step on his helpless little snake and second, if it escaped out the door, he might never find it.

The snake darted behind a stack of books next to the teacher's desk, and I lunged for it, knocking over the weather calendar and the number chart, but I was too late. The little snake slithered under Sister Patricia's desk. Then Michael was at my side.

"You take the side," he said. *"I'm going under. On my three."*

I could see Sister Patricia out of the corner of my eye nodding vigorously and waving us forward with a class full of children cowering behind her protectively outstretched arms. I pressed my lips together and nodded once to show him I understood.

He put his finger to his lips and then whispered, *"One, two...three!"* On three I leapt around the desk, and he dove under it, but it was my hand that circled Fang's furiously wriggling body and then shot triumphantly up in the air to show off its prize. Blood trickled down my wrist from two microscopic puncture wounds, but I didn't care.

Michael took his snake from me and smiled, *"Thanks. I told you he was dangerous."* He held up his little friend and looked him in the eyes. *"Are you okay, Fang? Did those kids scare you? They were very scared of you! You were very ferocious! Good snake!" Then he put Fang back into the pillowcase, tied it shut, turned to the class as if nothing out of the ordinary had happened and said, "Well, that was Fang. I got him for my birthday last summer."*

There was a long beat of silence, and then a few kids clapped. One of the boys exclaimed, "Dude! That was awesome!" And then all of the boys were slapping him on the back, asking when they could come over to see his snake again.

Sister Patricia cleared her throat, "Well…thank you, Michael. Let's all get back to our seats, now. We have a lot of…" she continued on, but I wasn't paying any attention to her. I was looking at Michael and thinking, "How cool was that?"

❦

I was pulled back to the present when a girl came into the bathroom and banged open a few doors, looking for a clean stall. She uttered "Ugh!" a few times and then chose an acceptable one and disappeared.

Dazed by the movie-like clarity of the memory, I was having trouble shaking it loose. I splashed some cold water on my face and patted it dry with a paper towel, then turned to leave. The door swung open in my face, missing me by inches.

"Sorry," apologized Cici, stepping into the bathroom. "What's taking so long?"

"I know who the boy from the bus is."

"Who?"

"Michael Casey!" I said. "He was in my second grade class at Saint Paul and then…" my voice trailed off as I tried to remember what happened to him. He had been there right up until the week before First Communion, and then he'd stopped coming to school and didn't receive the sacrament with the rest of us in May. I remembered, because it struck me as odd and so sad that he missed the big day after preparing all year for it. I started explaining this to Cici, but the door bumped her from behind, and a dark-haired girl from our study hall popped her head in.

"Sister Theresa wanted me to make sure you two were all right."

"We were just on our way back," I said. Back in the classroom, I looked for Michael, but he was gone. I asked the dark-haired girl where he went.

"Called to the office a few minutes ago," she whispered. Sister Theresa cleared her throat and motioned with her eyes that we should take our seats. I gave Cici a desperate look, and then we sat down.

At that point, the numbers on the page of my math text refused to cooperate at all. I gave up and closed the book, opened a notebook and began doodling aimlessly. Of course the name Michael Casey flowed out of my pen. I circled it a few times. I chewed on the end of my pen and then tapped the name. *What happened to you? Where have you been?* I remembered that the snake incident was not the only well-meaning thing he'd done that went disastrously wrong. He was always skirting rules to make us laugh only to be bitten by unexpected consequences. But smoking? Tattoos? Getting kicked out of school? It didn't line up with the way I remembered him. He'd always been so funny, so sweet.

The only thing that matched were his eyes.

❧❧

The conversation during the bus ride home with Meri, Grace and Cici focused solely on Michael. I'd hoped he'd be on the bus, but he wasn't. Instead, my friends and I laughed about the pranks he'd pulled on Sister Patricia after she'd refused to let him bring his snake back to school. Then we guessed at the reason he'd moved away, hoping the rumor about foster care was wrong. I was completely caught up in the mystery when my sisters and I walked in the door at home.

My mom was in the kitchen, talking on the phone with an open suitcase on the table in front of her.

"The doctors say she's stable, Julia. I'm leaving now. The girls just walked in." She paused, and then said, "I know. I wish they were here, too. I'll call you when I get there, okay?" She hung up the phone and leaned over the table for a moment before looking up into our worried faces.

"Is it Mina?" Claire asked.

My mother nodded. "They just took her to the hospital in an ambulance."

Cici circled the table and put her arms around her.

"It will be okay," I offered, not knowing what else to say.

"I know, sure. It's not like we didn't see this coming." She stood up a little straighter. "Claire, I want you to order some pizza for dinner. There's money on the counter. I already called your dad, but he's at a training seminar this weekend and can't get back until Sunday afternoon."

Then she looked each of us in the eye. "I am banking on the fact that at least one of you will tell if the others step out of line. You know the house rules. No boys in the house." She looked pointedly at Claire, who rolled her eyes and shifted uncomfortably, obviously rearranging her plans in her head.

Then she looked at me. "And Claire, please make sure Catherine takes her medicine."

"Mom…" I began, but decided she didn't need to hear it today.

"Okay, well that's that. It's six hours to Bluefield. I'll take the van so you girls can have the Honda." She zipped up her suitcase and walked out the door with us following behind. She hugged each of us, got in the car, and pulled out of the driveway. The last thing we heard was, "…and don't forget to feed the cats!" And then she was gone.

"Guys, I have to get to cross country practice," Claire said. "You can order the pizza, right?"

"Oh, please," I groaned.

"Just checking, okay? I'll be home around eight. Maybe you guys could invite a few friends over to watch a movie?"

I said, "Sure."

When Claire was gone, I turned to Cici. "So let's text everyone! Party at the Forsythes!" Her eyes went wide with shock. "Just kidding. Meri's going out with Finn tonight, but I'll call Grace and see if she wants to come over and watch the *Ghost Hunters* Marathon on the Syfy channel. Do you want to call someone?"

"No, Lisa and I are going to a movie," she said. Then in a small voice, she asked, "Do you think Mina will be all right?" I knew Mina was a tough lady; she'd been cutting her own grass up until last summer.

"Yeah, she'll be okay. This is just one of those setbacks you have when you have lung problems." I knew about those setbacks, having suffered through them myself, but I pushed those thoughts away. I'd been pretty healthy since I'd started a new regimen of asthma medication, and I really didn't want to dwell on the past.

"She'll be fine, you'll see," I promised. "Now, we better order that pizza so you can eat before you go."

⁓∘⁓

After Cici left, my phone buzzed with a text message from Meri.

Meri: In Friday's bathroom. Guess whats on my finger???

Me: He did not!

Meri: lol! no stupid! its a claddagh ring!

Me: & thats not...?

Meri: Its an irish thing! U know, heart, hands, crown, like a promise ring? We started going out exactly 1 yr ago?

Me: oh congrats!

Meri: gtg. call u tomorrow!

Thinking about her ring triggered a faint memory. It tugged patiently for a moment. Then a vivid picture formed in my head, and I raced barefoot up the threadbare stairs to my room and pulled my old jewelry box off the top shelf of my closet.

It was covered in dust fluff, and the hinges were broken. I placed it carefully on the bed, lifted the lid and was surprised to see Princess Belle in her gold mesh skirt start to twirl. The first few notes of "Beauty and the Beast" began to play, teasing my ears with ghostly echoes of things long past. I felt the hair on the back of my neck prickle. Then the little princess and the music stopped.

Inside was a tangle of tarnished necklaces, a friendship bracelet, and a couple of unpaired earrings. I tossed those aside and dug a little deeper, and there, at the bottom of the pile, I found what I'd been looking for. I held it up and grinned. It was one of those fake gold rings you get from a gumball machine, and it had a blue plastic gem glued to the front. I couldn't believe I still had it. I flopped back on my bed, pulled Pigwin into my arms, and became lost in the past again.

✌🏽♔

Outside on a parking lot, wearing my pink denim jacket, I was trying to keep my plaid skirt from flipping up in the breeze. Meri was jumping rope, and I was counting for her. She stopped to look at something over my shoulder, and I turned around to see Michael standing behind me with his hands stuffed in the pockets of his windbreaker. He was looking down at the blacktop and scuffing his feet.

"Hey, Catherine. Merideth," he said.

"Hi, Michael," I said back.

"Um, Catherine, I wanted to thank you for saving Fang's life yesterday. I mean he probably would have been a snake pancake if you hadn't helped me."

I beamed with pleasure.

"Well, I brought you something to thank you, because I owe Fang's life to you and all." He stretched out his arm and opened his hand. Resting on his palm was a perfect gold ring. I picked it up and turned it over in the sunlight. It was carved into a tiny pair of gold hands holding a sparkling, heart-shaped blue stone with a dainty gold crown on top.

"Wow, Michael, it's beautiful!"

"Try it on," he suggested, grinning. I put it on one of my fingers, but it was too big, so I tried it on my thumb. It was still too big. I thought for a minute and then had an idea.

"Here, help me with this clasp." I pulled the silver chain I was wearing out from under my shirt and twisted the clasp around to the front. Michael helped me undo the clasp, and then I slid the ring onto the chain. The chain already had one ring on it, and the new ring fell down to rest against it with a little clinking sound.

"Hey, what's that ring?" he asked, reaching out and turning it around to see it better.

"I got it when I was baptized." I held the two rings up side by side. His ring outshone my scuffed silver ring in every way. My ring was a simple silver band that widened into a flat oval in front. In the middle of the oval, a script letter "C" was inscribed and on the back was a cross inside a hash-marked circle. I turned his

gold ring around and around, admiring how the facets in the sky blue stone caught the light.

"Thanks, Michael, it's really pretty," I said, feeling special.

"Well, my friends are waiting for me to play football. Maybe you can come over some time and see Fang?" His eyes brimmed with hope.

"Maybe," I said back. He nodded and then sprinted to the grassy area on the other side of the parking lot.

Later that day, I was sitting at the kitchen table, coloring in a Cinderella coloring book, twisting the gold ring back and forth on the chain, when my mom bent over to see my picture.

"Nice job, Catherine. Cinderella looks very pretty." She started to stand back up when an afternoon sunbeam caught on the facets of the ring. The reflected light danced across the table.

"Let me see that, Catherine," she said, looking more closely at Michael's ring. She looked inside. "Hope springs eternal," she read. "Honey, I think this is a very special ring. I need to have it, please."

"No! Michael gave it to me, Mommy! It was a gift!"

"I don't think Michael's mommy knew he was giving it to you. I'm sure it's very important to her, and she wouldn't want him to give it away." But I didn't understand, and I pulled it back from her.

"Please give me the ring," she said gently, but firmly. I allowed her to unclasp the chain and take it off, leaving my old silver ring alone. I picked my ring up and held it next to the gold one. "See? It's so much prettier!"

"Catherine, your ring is very special, too. Mina gave it to you with God's blessing at your baptism, and it should remind you of how much God and your family love you."

I really tried to be happy with that explanation, but a tear rolled down my cheek anyway as my mom called Michael's mother to tell her we would be right over to return it.

Michael lived in a small house in the neighborhood behind the school. My mom knocked on the door and a slender woman with reddish hair answered. She smiled when she saw me and bent down to shake my hand saying, "Thank you so much for returning my ring to me. Michael's daddy gave it to me."

Behind her I could see Michael. He looked embarrassed, so I called out, "It's okay, Michael! I understand."

He gave me a shy grin. My mom asked if I could come in to see Fang, and Michael nodded and then led me up to his room.

The next day at school, he cornered me in the coatroom.

"Hold out your hand and close your eyes," he said. He was really excited about something. So I did, and he placed something light and small on my palm. When I opened my eyes, I saw another ring, but this time I could tell it was the kind you got out of a gumball machine. I had a few just like it at home.

"I had to chop off the stone it came with, and then I glued this blue one on. My mom has lots of beads and stuff like that at home," he explained.

"Thanks! It's pretty, too." I felt special knowing he made it for me. But then I asked worriedly whether his mom knew about the blue plastic jewel. He grinned. "Sure, she helped me!"

※ ～

The almost unnaturally vivid memory faded, and I found myself grabbing at fragments of it, wanting to stay enfolded within its happy glow. I turned the little ring over on my palm, admiring it all over again. I pulled up the silver chain from around my neck and held the gumball treasure up next to my lusterless silver ring. Even the little plastic gem had more sparkle than my ring, but I was older now, and I cherished my silver ring for the love it represented.

"Michael, we have so much to talk about," I murmured. My thoughts turned again to his disappearance at the end of second grade. After I gave the Claddagh back, we became friends, and I often went over to his house to play. There was a small creek behind his home, and we spent many afternoons looking under rocks for snails that autumn and sliding on the ice in the winter. We fell into a rhythm of play that often required no talking at all, and when we did talk, we frequently finished each other's sentences. In school, we were inseparable. If I had to sit out of gym because my asthma was acting up, he always found some stupid reason to sit out with me—a hang nail, an achy foot, blurry vision—and in the classroom, I'd read with him, which he seemed to like.

After Christmas that year, Michael started missing school. When he did come, he frequently forgot things, like his lunch or homework. By late spring, I wasn't allowed over to his house anymore. Looking back, it was obvious something must have happened at home, something that eventually landed him in foster care if the rumor was true. No one ever told me why I couldn't see my friend anymore.

My thoughts were interrupted by the buzzing of my cell phone. Grace was texting that she was downstairs at the door.

"B RIGHT DWN!" I texted back and then dropped the little ring and the rest of my ancient treasures back in my jewelry box. I shoved the box onto the top shelf of my closet and bounded down the stairs to meet her.

≈∘≈

My sisters and I slept in on Saturday morning until the phone rang. Claire stumbled down the stairs to answer it. I was heading down the hall to the bathroom we shared when Claire's voice drifted up from the kitchen. She sounded upset.

"Cici," I called. "You better come downstairs." When I entered the kitchen, I heard the zip of a fly being closed and caught sight of Claire's "ex" boyfriend—the one she was forbidden to see after he ran over our mailbox one night when he was too drunk to stop—adjust his waistband and plow out the back door. My jaw dropped, but I ignored *that* situation for the moment and focused on the phone call.

"Is she upset?" Claire asked, gripping the phone tightly. She paused, and then asked, "When will you be back? Is she coming with you?"

Cici and I gave each other a worried look. There was another pause. Then Claire asked, "What can we do?" She finished by telling Mom we loved her and hung up.

"What's happened? Is Mina alright?" asked Cici.

Claire was more pale than usual. "She's okay, but she can't go home. She needs someone to take care of her."

"That's terrible!" I cried, placing my palms on the table. "She's so independent. She must be really upset."

"She is."

"Where will she go? A nursing home? She'll hate that. *Mom* will hate that!"

There was a pause, and then Claire said, "Cate, she's not going to a nursing home. After a few weeks in rehab, she's coming here."

I had to sit down in a kitchen chair and digest that. Of course, she'd come here. That was the right thing to do. My mom loved her. We loved her. She didn't belong in a nursing home far away with strangers taking care of her. Then I thought of our small house and our one full bathroom, and my mind made the next leap.

"Where will we put her?" I asked.

Claire sat down in the chair next to me. "She'll take my room, and I'll move down to the basement." I thought about that for a moment, and then my selfish side kicked in.

"Why you?"

"Cate, the basement only has one bed, and Mom thought it would be easier to move just one of us." She knew what I was thinking. I was thinking of the flat screen TV in the basement, the partial kitchen, and the half bath. I couldn't help feeling jealous. A part of me thought it wasn't fair, that this whole situation wasn't fair, but I squeezed those feelings down, knowing them to be selfish and nodded.

"Is she going to die, Claire?" whispered Cici.

I loved Mina and knew intellectually she would die someday, but realizing she was one step closer with no hope of going back was a reality I wasn't ready to face. Would she be dying here, then? I shook my head reflexively at Cici while a knot grew in the pit of my stomach.

"Hopefully, not anytime soon," Claire said. There was nothing left to say, so Cici and I went back upstairs to get dressed. Up in my room my selfish and benevolent sides warred with each other, and an undefined fear egged them both on. I needed to get a grip before Mom got back from Bluefield. I needed to go somewhere quiet and alone and just think for a while. I knew the perfect place.

Chapter 4
The Left Path

IT WAS AFTER one o'clock when I reached into my closet and grabbed the pink canvas tote Meri had made for me. On one side she'd painted a stained glass butterfly bursting from a watercolor heart. On the other, she'd written in a confident flourish, "Let Your Heart Wing It." I stuffed my music player, headphones, cell phone, and inhaler into the tote and then paused with my hand above the spotting scope that was perched on my dresser. It was heavy and bulky, and I usually only brought it on my club's wildlife hikes. I hesitated, undecided, and then dumped it into the bag with the rest of my gear. I loosely braided my blonde frizz, and put on a pair of denim Bermudas, a ribbed tank top, and my hiking boots. After lacing up the boots, I scooped up my bag and loped down the stairs.

In the kitchen, Claire had just finished lacing up her running shoes and was applying sunscreen to her face.

"Claire? Will you drop me at Lewis Woods this afternoon?" I pulled a package of trail mix and a bottle of water out of the pantry and tossed them into my bag.

"What's at Lewis Woods? More trees to hug?"

Just breathe. Nasty comebacks won't get you to Lewis Woods. I took a deep breath. "I'm going to meet some friends there to hike and do research for a club meeting." It wasn't exactly a lie. I was sure I would see some "friends," though I was thinking more of the four-legged or feathered variety, and I considered any hike to be research.

"I don't know, Cate. I don't want to be late for cross country practice."

"Please? I'll pay to fill the car with gas," I offered, dangling what I knew to be an irresistible carrot.

Claire hesitated before relenting. "*Okay*, but I can't come get you until after practice ends at five. If you want to come home before that you'll have to get a ride from one of your friends."

A choked laugh escaped my lips at the idea of one of my furry friends giving me a ride home. "No problem," I agreed.

A few minutes later, I was pumping gas while Claire happily waited in the car, texting Jones, her "ex" boyfriend.

"Does Mom know you're still going out with him?" I asked as I slid back into the car. She scowled and set her phone down in the ashtray. "So, are you sleeping with him?" I asked.

"No!" she said, but she didn't meet my eyes.

Right, I thought, but I didn't want to jeopardize my ride, so I dropped the subject and reached for the radio. Her hand beat me to it.

"Nope. Driver's choice," she said.

"C'mon, Claire! Just this once!"

She just smiled and switched it to her favorite "Top Forty" station.

I contented myself with resting my chin on my tanned forearm, which was half hanging out the open passenger side window. The hot wind filled my nose with the acrid smells of cars and asphalt and whipped my scruffy braid against my face. I narrowed my eyes against the assault.

When we pulled out of the gas station, we merged onto a street that runs through Fairview Park's commercial district. We were surrounded by strip malls and fast food restaurants, and to the uninitiated, we were stuck in the middle of suburban sprawl, but Cleveland has a secret—an escape route that can take you away from the cluttered signage, steaming blacktop and weedy lawns of the city. The congested commercial district became a residential area. Then the houses on the left fell away and were replaced by a rusted steel guardrail, which was the only barrier between the cars on the road and the one hundred foot drop down into the Rocky River Gorge. Our escape route was just ahead on the left.

Claire stopped at the next light and took the hairpin turn on to Cedar Point Road, braking hard against its steep and sudden descent. The air became heavier, and the tree adorned gorge walls rose up around us. The breeze caressing my cheek became cooler and now carried the organic scents of leaves and mud.

At the base of the hill we took a sharp right onto Lewis Road, crossed over the west fork of the Rocky River and then followed the tightly twisting curves back up the other side of the gorge. This time there was no guardrail. The car wheezed as it fought to gain altitude and prove itself worthy of the last leg of the journey. When the road leveled out, the forest opened up, spitting us back onto the threshold of civilization. To our right were a handful of homes set far back from the road, and to our left was a large fenced riding ring in the middle of a huge mown field with another spur of the forest beyond.

We pulled into a gravel parking area in front of a carved wood sign that identified the place as "Lewis Road Riding Ring," which was part of the Rocky River Reservation in the Cleveland Metroparks. The park was deserted. Claire parked the car and looked around. "Where are your friends?"

"Oh, they'll be here."

She pursed her lips and shook her wavy ponytail in a frustrated gesture. "Cate, I can't wait. I'm going to be late!"

"You don't have to wait. I'll be fine," I said.

She stared out the window and thought for a moment, chewing on her lip. "Do you have your inhaler?" she asked, resigned, but still not happy about leaving me there alone. I nodded. "Let me see it," she ordered. I dug through my pink bag, making a big production of the effort I was making.

I held up the inhaler and asked, "Happy?"

"Does it work?" was her response. Oh, for crying out loud. She didn't have to be so bossy just because our mom and dad were away. I shook it and then pressed the cylinder, releasing a white medicinal cloud into the car.

"What the...? You didn't have to do that!" she complained, waving the cloud out of her face. I smiled inwardly.

"Do you have your cell?" she asked. I rolled my eyes, but this time I dug through the bag without being asked and held up the phone.

"Tada!" I exclaimed.

She still looked doubtful. "Call me if you run into trouble. I'll be back at five unless I hear from you."

When she disappeared, I walked down the dirt path toward the woods, alone.

The sun was high overhead, turning the sky the palest blue. It beat down hot and merciless on my bare shoulders and the mostly dormant yellow grass of the field, but I wasn't concerned about my lack of sunscreen, because I would soon be under cover.

I followed the path past the fenced riding ring and bleachers and across the massive field, stopping and turning around just before it vanished into the woods to see how far I'd come. I could barely make out the sign that marked the entrance to the parking area. Turning back toward the woods, I quickened my pace, anxious to get out of the baking sun.

The path into the woods was bordered on both sides by deciduous trees and dense leafy undergrowth, but immediately beyond its entrance, the sun-dappled tangle of trees faded gently into a deeply shaded pine forest. Under foot, the crackling of dead leaves became the whisper-quiet of fallen pine needles, and from this softened forest floor, the tree trunks rose straight and parallel, mostly naked of branches, until they reached the vaulted pine ceiling high above.

I stopped there as I always did and pulled the cool pine-scented air into my nose and down into my lungs. That fragrance and the sense of sheltered solitude were some of the reasons I liked to walk in Lewis Woods. Another reason lay about a mile and half up the path.

As I began walking again, I let my thoughts drift back to the conversation I'd had with Claire that morning, to the maelstrom of emotions I needed to sort through about the changes that were coming. I began with one of my safer feelings, with the acknowledgement that I loved my grandmother deeply.

She used to visit several times a year, but since her emphysema had worsened, she could no longer make the trip alone. Instead, during the summer months my mom would drive down and fetch her back to spend a few weeks with us. Those visits were fun, but difficult. There were personality clashes and complicated TV and bathroom schedules to sort out. There was also the ever present tension between my mom and Mina over Mina's withdrawal from the Catholic Church. Both of them strong-willed, that weekly battle was unlikely to go away.

In the short term, the joy of seeing her outweighed the problems, but in the long term, I wasn't so sure. Where would my friends and I hang out? Why did Claire get the basement? Selfish thoughts like these rampaged through my head, and I hated myself for allowing it. She's sick, remember? Really sick. Maybe *dying*. No. I didn't want to think about that, and I was relieved when I came to the fork in the path and surfaced from my swamp of negativity.

Choosing the right path would take me down to the Rocky River far below. The left path would lead me out of the pine forest to the top of the ridge. There was no hesitation in my stride as I veered left toward my favorite lookout point in the Metroparks.

I forged ahead, crossing a small wooden footbridge with a handrail over a gully. Beyond the little bridge, I left the dense shade of the pine forest behind and approached the edge of the cliff, which was bordered by a narrow stand of oak trees. Several feet below the edge of the cliff, a wide ledge jutted out over the gorge. That ledge was my reward for my hot hike in.

Down on the ledge, I couldn't be seen by the casual passerby. From my bird's eye view, I could see the bridge we'd crossed when we veered onto Lewis Road, and beyond the bridge, about a half mile from where I stood, the other side of the gorge rose almost straight up over a hundred feet from the opposite bank of the river. In the valley between, several picnic areas dotted the river bank and nestled among the trees. The view, in short, was spectacular.

I picked my way down among the sharp rocks, careful not to rely on the untested roots too much for support. When I reached the ledge, I dropped down onto the bone dry dirt to sit, then retrieved my phone to check the time, but the screen remained stubbornly blank even when I mashed down on the power button.

"Guess I'm stuck here 'til five," I murmured, then tossed the dead phone back into my bag and looked around. Immediately to my left, a hollow oak tree clung precariously to the ledge. I checked to see if I recognized any of the latest lovers' initials carved there. Jason and I had carved our own initials somewhere up above last summer—a lot of good that did us. He'd been the first I'd let explore my curves, push through some of my walls, and stretch my willpower to the limit, and I wondered if I'd done the right thing by breaking up with him. I felt a painful twinge in my chest over the loss and turned my thoughts back to my grandmother's impending arrival, which made me feel even sorrier for myself. *Shit.* I shook my head briskly to clear it, and pulled out my music player.

If I had to choose between having a dead cell phone and a dead music player, the dead phone would win hands down. My music player was my security blanket. It held more than my deified playlist. It held the songs I needed to give voice to my every emotion, to lift me higher, to intensify my outrage, to drag my sorrow out of the dark and blow it away.

I naturally tended toward alternative, dark and edgy bands, which surprised most people who knew me because it contrasted sharply with my easygoing nature. Yeah, I was a girl who still loved kittens and the color pink, but I had a hidden, slightly Emo core. I loved bands like the Sick Puppies, Avenged Sevenfold, and the Offspring. I loved the angry, in–your–face truth they injected into their music. But what always hooked me the most was finding a band's one song that exposed their naked hope, their fragile, unguarded need for something to believe in. And as I ssearched for a song, I was drawn powerfully to Pierce the Veil's "Hold On Till May." In my gut, it just fit. I clicked on it, plugged my headphones in my ears and turned the music up to drown out the thoughts I was supposed to be sorting. There would be time for soul searching later.

In the meantime, I hauled out my spotting scope and pointed it at the opposite shore. The river, which usually lapped at the base of the cliff, was low, exposing a wide gray beach strewn with boulders and broken shale. On the ridge top, at least a hundred feet above the valley floor, I caught movement and adjusted the scope to refine the image. Two boys were hiking behind the split-rail fence up on the ridge. I focused on their faces, almost dropping the scope when I recognized Shawn Fowler and Michael Casey. Unbelievable. What were the odds?

Both were wearing cut-off jeans and tennis shoes. The sleeves of Michael's faded black T-shirt were ripped out, revealing his sword tattoo curving snuggly over the tanned muscles of his arm. His blonde hair, damp with sweat, was plastered to the back of his neck in dark ringlets.

You are such a voyeur, I scolded myself, but I looked anyway. My heart beat faster, and my palms got slippery as I watched him. I forgot my bad mood and smiled in spite of myself.

Then Shawn hopped the split rail fence.

"Stupid," I murmured.

Michael followed, calling out to Shawn with an angry look on his face, but Shawn continued moving toward the edge. From my viewpoint, I could see that the ridge they were standing on projected out slightly with nothing underneath. It was thin, too thin to support them both. *Shit.*

My palms were now sweating in earnest, my lips silently forming the words "move back, move *back,*" willing them across the chasm that separated us. Then Shawn stumbled.

My heart seized, and my breath locked cold in my throat as Michael reached out from behind and yanked Shawn back from the brink, but in so doing, planted his own foot closer to the edge. The ledge suddenly gave way with a shower of dirt and shale, and Michael's foot plunged through the debris into nothing. His downward momentum carried his other foot over, and he pivoted toward the face of the cliff, throwing his arms forward in a desperate bid to save himself. Shawn whirled around, dropped to his knees and grabbed hold of Michael's arms, but more of the brittle edge crumbled, and Michael's sweat slick arms slipped through his fingers. He was left holding only one of Michael's hands and he pulled on it mightily, his neck muscles corded with effort while Michael's free hand scrambled madly along the face of the cliff, searching for a handhold, his face a horrified mask of disbelief and terror.

My own hands were locked in a death grip on the scope. "Please, no," I whispered as Pierce the Veil's "Hold on Till May" shriveled to scratchy feedback in my ears.

Michael found a loose tree root and wrapped his hand around it. I could see his jaw clench tight and the muscles of his arm and shoulder bunch under his inked sword as he prepared to pull up. This time I screamed.

"NO!"

He was halfway up before the root broke loose, and his body rocketed downward. The sudden force of his descent broke Shawn's grip on his hand.

I was on my feet now, my headphones ripped from my ears, my fingers clutching the bark of the oak beside me. I dropped the scope and watched, horrified, transfixed, as Michael slid at least fifty feet down the nearly vertical cliff, his fingers digging into its crumbling face, slowing him down. Fragments of hope tore through my mind. If he could slow his fall just enough…

But I could see the bottom of the cliff. I could see that it cut in upon itself ever so slightly. He would soon have nothing to hold onto. When he plummeted past the breakpoint, I watched his hands grab desperately at thin air while his body rotated backward. He fell the last fifty feet with his back to the ground, his arms outstretched, and landed on the rocky beach below, face up, not moving.

Leaning out over the ledge, I searched in vain for some way down, some way to get to him, but there was none. The ledge I was standing on ended in a sheer rock face that dropped straight down to the flowing river below. Instead, I grabbed the scope, scrambled back up the cliff to the clearing among the oaks and stopped, my heart pounding in my chest, thoughts racing through my head.

Call someone!

Get help!

My phone is dead. Damn it! DAMN IT!

Run back to the road!

It will take a half hour to get back to the road! It's too FAR! It will be too LATE!

The isolation I'd revered had become a chain around my neck.

So, I did the only thing I could do. I turned around, lifted the scope and pointed it back across the gorge. I found Shawn at the top of the cliff, pacing madly back and forth, screaming into his cell phone, and gesturing wildly toward the base of the cliff. At least now I knew help was on the way. Thank God!

I dropped to my knees, flexing my cramping fingers a few times before swinging the scope back down the jagged face of the cliff. Debris was raining down from where it had been knocked loose followed by curling trails of brown dust. I scanned the rocky beach and found Michael about halfway between the cliff and the river, still face up, but this time I saw movement. The back of his hand rested weakly on his forehead, his teeth were clenched together, his eyes squeezed shut.

"You're not alone," I whispered. "Hang on. Help is on the way."

One of his Converse tennis shoes had been ripped off during the fall along with several of his fingernails, leaving his fingertips and toes torn and bloody. There was a nasty gash across the bottom of his chin. I watched as he tried to roll up onto his left shoulder, but fell back, a silent scream on his lips.

He opened his eyes and breathed hard a few times, his hand falling back to his forehead, smearing it with dirt. He clenched his teeth again and dropped his right arm to the ground and then swung it up and over his chest, faster this time, rolling up onto his side. Another scream left his lips, followed by a fountain of bright red blood that splashed onto the rocks and seeped into the desiccated dirt of the riverbed.

I could hear sirens in the distance. "Oh God, please," I whispered. "Hold on just a little longer."

Michael fell onto his back, coughing violently. Then he turned his eyes toward the bridge between us, curling his fingers weakly toward it, as if beckoning to the cars racing by, but they remained blissfully unaware of the tragedy unfolding less than a hundred feet away. He let his eyes drift toward the cliff I knelt on, dragging his focus up, slowly, and brought it to rest impossibly in the center of my scope. His eyes flashed angrily, and he shouted something. Then he whispered whatever he'd said over and over, the movements of his lips becoming weaker and weaker. Still, he kept his focus in the middle of my scope, as if by some miracle he could see me. I reached out my fingers without thinking, as if I could touch his face.

"Okay…it's okay," I whispered, my voice cracking. "Shh…" The muscles of his face relaxed and his eyes lost their focus, the furious spark in them dimming and then going out. The sirens were much closer now, but I knew they were too late. I lifted the strap of the spotting scope over my head and placed the instrument gently down on the dirt by my side. I didn't need to see anymore. He was gone.

Chapter 5
Waking the Dead

MICHAEL'S FALL COULD only have lasted a few seconds and his agony only a few more, but it seemed like a lifetime had passed since I'd spotted him at the top of the cliff. I felt ancient. I gradually became aware of the sharp gravel digging into my knees, and I dropped back down to a sitting position, hugging my pebble-pocked knees to my chest with my eyes tight shut.

For a few peaceful moments, no thoughts at all circulated through my head. Only a fine gray mist existed where once intelligible thoughts inhabited. It swirled in random patterns of light and dark until it resolved itself into an image of Michael's beautiful gray eyes, deep and filled with sorrow. Startled, I snapped my eyes open, and the image was immediately replaced with that of the cliff and the lovely vista beyond.

I shuddered violently. Had I really seen what I thought I'd seen? In the few moments before he died, did Michael's eyes really find mine on this wooded cliff top over a half mile away?

Back down on the bridge, an ambulance, a fire truck and several police cars had arrived, and in the washed-out glare of the afternoon sun, two paramedics stumbled down the embankment with a stretcher. The police directed traffic and held back the crowd that was gathering. I wanted to cry out to the crowd to leave Michael alone. Strangely, I didn't feel like an outsider. Instead, I felt a deep responsibility for him in my bones. I had this overwhelming need to see that his broken body was borne safely away from its dusty public deathbed.

The paramedics checked his pulse and listened to his chest. They shaded their eyes and looked toward the top of the cliff, shaking their heads. It was obvious there was no saving this one. They waved away another paramedic carrying equipment and tugged a sheet off the stretcher to cover Michael's body, pulling it up and over his face last.

The police moved in after that, and a short while later, Shawn and a pair of detectives arrived on the scene. One of the detectives went straight for the sheet, lifted it, and then paused for a beat, his shoulders slumping. He held onto the corner of the sheet for a moment, gazing at Michael's face, before letting it fall and going about his business. For the next hour, the detectives asked questions while the police took photos and scoured the scene for evidence. I stayed until Michael's body was loaded into the ambulance and the vehicle drove away.

The mid-afternoon heat was oppressive, even in the shade, and sweat beaded up around my forehead. Wishing for a breeze, I turned away from the cliff toward the forest and was rewarded with a gentle gust of wind blowing across my back. I sighed, and then headed back along the edge of the cliff and into the woods.

While crossing the footbridge, my eyes were drawn to some writing on the handrail I hadn't noticed before. Out of habit, I slowed to read it, expecting profanity or some new lover's pledge. Instead, I found a quote from an amateur philosopher. I reached out to trace the letters, written neatly with a fine point permanent marker:

"God is dead. Where art thou, Ubermensch?"

"Ubermensch," I murmured, tasting the unfamiliar word on my tongue. Another breeze, stronger than the first, rippled through the forest, lifting the hair on the back of my neck and rustling the leaves. It carried a clean pine and citrus scent, and my head filled with the thought: *The wind is changing. You'd better get back.*

By the time I reached the field, thunderheads had gathered in the west, their tops reflecting the sun and billowing up like boiling clouds of steam in the sky. Rain was definitely on the way, and my self-protective instincts kicked in, bringing with them the fervent hope that Claire would arrive soon.

She pulled up in the Honda, trailing a cloud of dust, covered in sweat, with the windows rolled down and the radio blasting some overplayed top-forties crap. As I slid into the passenger seat, I impulsively flipped to a new radio station, for the first time praying for a song to add to my Playlist, something to soothe me, something to *prove* my Playlist was real, but Claire smacked my hand away and switched it back. It didn't matter. All I'd heard was talk. Instead, I turned my head toward the open window, mouthing through trembling lips:

Are you still there, Angel?

That's when the impossibly powerful wave of emotion for the boy I hardly knew hit. It came out of nowhere, and I flared my nostrils in a feeble attempt to stem the tide of tears that flooded my eyes. My throat ached. I couldn't speak.

Claire and I sat mute, side by side for a while—which was normal for her, but uncharacteristic for me—and she noticed something was wrong.

"How was your hike? Tree hugging go well?"

"Cate?" More insistent.

"Cate…what's wrong?"

I just held my hand up. Stop. Don't go there, it said. She got quiet again, and when we pulled into the driveway, I shoved open the car door, sprinted up the stone porch steps, through the front door, and up to my room.

✍∾

When the leading edge of his power signature struck, the window pane flexed outward, groaning against the pressure. And like a wall of black smoke disturbed by an uneasy breeze, the crowd of demons parted, allowing another one of their own to enter the room.

The arriving demon flexed his long, slender white fingers and smiled at the Guardian who stood poised and ready for battle before the girl's bed. The girl had arrived just moments before, grimy tear stains marring her perfect complexion, and crawled under the covers. It was cold in the room and getting colder. He watched her pull the white quilt up and over her head.

Beside the Guardian, the sapphire eyes of the girl's bright Angel flashed. The Angel's own power signature crackled like blue lightning, warning the demon of her inborn drive to protect.

The demon ignored her. He fixed his gaze on another, a much darker Angel who hung back by the wall. "I told you I'd be back," the demon said to him. "Sorry it took so long. I didn't anticipate so much…resistance."

The glare of the dark Angel flared coal fire red. A wicked smile curled his lips. "Decimus," he hissed. "I got your brimstone barbecue all warmed up for you. Won't you join us?" Then the staff he carried burst into flames. He took a step forward, but the bright Angel held up her hand.

"Berwyn. Wait," she said sharply.

"You won't get near her again," said the Guardian. He extended the tip of his blade toward the demon's throat. "If you try, Decimus, you'll—"

"I have permission. Ask her," the demon said, his black eyes flashing pointedly at the bright Angel, who hesitated, and then lowered her shield.

"No! I promised—" The Guardian's protest was cut short by hushed words urgently spoken between the two Angels. As they argued, the Guardian's jaw tightened as he listened, and then he abruptly sat down on the bed beside the girl. His blade he left unsheathed, lying across his lap.

Eyeing the weapon warily, the demon called Decimus straightened up to his full height and walked casually over to the other side of the bed, trailing his long white fingers over the small curves of her body. "Where to start…" he murmured, "Perhaps a reminder of what she and I once shared?"

The Guardian flinched, his eyes a potent blend of faith and fury.

The demon laughed at him. "Don't worry. I told you before, this time she won't even know I'm here." Then he crawled into bed with her and disappeared.

✧

Exhausted and afraid, I was lost in a forest, looking at an endless line of pine trees that surrounded me. Night was falling fast, and I could distinguish no path to lead me out.

"Follow my voice, and I'll show you the way." The gentle whisper was familiar, and I ran toward it, just barely fighting back my fear of the dark, until I found a small brook that emptied into a deep, still pool. I knelt to drink, but my reflection took hold of my heart and squeezed it until it exploded in my chest.

I wasn't me. I was Michael.

"I need you," my reflection pleaded. My chin was scraped and my forehead was smeared with dirt. I retched up a forceful stream of slippery clotted blood into the water, obliterating the image. When the ripples stilled, I saw behind me in the crimson water, a distorted, sinuous shadow with flaming black eyes breathing a fog of icy breath down my neck.

And it was laughing.

❧❧

I sat up in bed and frantically peeled the sheets off my sweat-drenched arms. *Shit,* I thought, wiping my forehead with the back of my trembling hand. I could still feel the grime that had been there in my dream a moment ago, but my hand came away slick with nothing but sweat. *Oh, shit.*

I hadn't experienced a nightmare so vivid, so horrifying, since I was five. I shivered, remembering. During that summer's record heat wave, I'd been terrorized by almost nightly visions of similar creatures, creatures of black smoke and flame, long fingers and velvet voices. And they'd done more than just laugh.

They'd tried to make me do things.

I'd never told anyone, not even Cici, about what happened in those dreams, because I was afraid that talking about them would somehow make them more real. I was afraid I'd be labeled a freak. But that was a long time ago and those dreams were supposed to be over. I hoped witnessing Michael's death hadn't kicked off another round. I didn't think I could go through that again. God, no.

I lay back in bed, feeling sick, and looked out the window, watching the leaves of the maple tree shiver and shake as ominous clouds overtook the backyard.

Cici quietly opened the door and poked her head in. "Cate, it's thundering. You coming downstairs?"

I was still quivering, but I followed her into the hall, knowing there would be questions if I didn't. I desperately wanted to avoid that. Something deep inside me urged me to keep the secret of witnessing

Michael's death close. That it was too painful, too intimate to share with anyone. That they wouldn't understand.

Cici held a flashlight and the phone. "Just in case," she said. We slipped downstairs through the premature dark to the small sunroom at the back of the house where we always gathered to watch the storms roll in. Claire was waiting for us.

"Hey," she said.

I nodded, not yet trusting my voice, and dropped down cross-legged onto the woven rag rug that covered the gray tile floor. Claire studied me carefully, but her attention was stolen by a flash of lightning, which lit up her face and made her green eyes glimmer in the dark. I thought I was in the clear, but when the lightning faded, she turned back to me and demanded, "Cate, what are you so upset about? You wouldn't even look at me in the car today. Is it Mina? Are you worried about her, or are you just mad that *I'm* the one moving to the basement?"

Her smug accusation and the fact that she was so off base coaxed a choked laugh from my lips. I looked down at my hands and shook my head patronizingly. "Think what you want, Claire," I replied quietly, picking at the rug's pale green fringe.

Claire started to say something else, but Cici, still hovering in the doorway, interrupted her. "Leave her alone, Claire. Having Mina move in isn't going to be easy on any of us."

Claire closed her mouth and looked back out the window. Lightning split the sky again, followed by a closer rumble of thunder. The phone rang, and Claire got up to answer it.

"Forsythe residence," she said.

Pause.

"Oh my God! Who?"

Pause.

Cici asked, "What happened?"

"Someone died," Claire whispered in reply and then held up her hand to shush her.

My heart skipped a beat. My mom was the church secretary and a member of the bereavement committee, a group of women who helped plan the funeral luncheons at Saint Paul, our parish. I knew Claire wasn't stupid and would put two and two together. I stared out the windows, trying to keep a neutral expression on my face.

"Today? That's awful! Where?" Claire continued, and then after a short pause she looked at me as she replied, "My mom's not here, but she'll be back Monday. Can you call the next person on the list?" Then she said goodbye and hung up. Claire was quiet for a moment. Then she fired the question. "Cate, you saw it happen, didn't you?"

I glanced away, afraid to speak.

"What's going on?" Cici asked, looking from Claire to me. "Who died?"

Claire's eyes were still on me, taking the pulse of my mental status, as she explained, "A sophomore at Saint Joan fell off a cliff and died down in the park today."

"Who?" gasped Cici.

"A boy named Mike Casey," Claire replied. "Do you know him, Cate?"

This time I flinched, and Claire nodded quietly to herself.

Cici was on her knees next to me before I could answer. "Oh, Cate! I'm so sorry! Did you know? Oh, my God!" Cici had her arm around my shoulders as I nodded, tears spilling over again.

"I think she saw it happen," Claire said, sitting down on my other side and patting me awkwardly.

"What? How?" asked Cici.

"She was at Lewis Woods today at the time of the fall, and when she got back in the car she was really upset," Claire explained. "What did you *see*, Cate?" A huge flash of lightning lit up the whole sky, almost instantly followed by a deep resounding boom. Rain lashed at the wraparound windows of the sunroom. I leaned back against the cold brick wall and shook my head, wiping my eyes stubbornly.

"He fell. He's dead. Okay?"

"But did you see it happen?" persisted Claire.

"Please...don't..." I pleaded.

"Cate, you have to tell someone! We should let the police know. They might not have a witness—"

"Lay off, Claire. She knew him, okay? When they were little kids," Cici snapped.

"It was just an accident," I whispered.

Claire took a deep breath and then said more gently, "Look, I'm so sorry, Cate. We at least need to call Mom and Dad. They'll want to know."

"No!" I was adamant. "They don't need to know what I...that I...saw him...die."

"Cate, you have to tell them!"

"Oh, yeah, like you tell them everything? Are you going to tell them about last night's sleepover with your alcoholic ex-boyfriend?" Claire shot me a warning look, and Cici's eyes went wide, but I pressed on. "How about the fact you almost failed history? The keg parties? The infected pitchfork tattoo?"

"They found out about most of it, some of it I told them," she mumbled, on the retreat now.

"Uh huh...and how well did that go?"

"It always blows over."

"Unlike some, I don't *want* to be the hurricane that needs to blow over!" I snapped back. That stung. I could see it in her eyes. "Look, if it makes you feel better you can tell them if you think I'm losing it or something."

"What about the police?" Claire countered.

"If they don't rule it an accident, I'll come forward." I said.

"And you won't tell Mom about last night?"

I shook my head, sealing the deal just as the phone rang again. It was lying on the floor in front of me, and I snatched it up this time. "Forsythes," I answered automatically.

"Hey, Caty Bug! How are things on the home front?" It was Dad.

My jaw tightened for a second and then relaxed. "Fine, Dad. It's storming though—a good one."

"Power out?"

"No, but it's raining pretty hard. Have you heard from Mom? How's Mina?"

"She's okay, Bug, but it was a rough day. They put her on a ventilator for a while."

My stomach dropped. "But she's better now?"

"She's a fighter, Caty. Can I talk to Claire?"

"Sure," I said, reluctantly handing over the phone.

Claire listened for a few moments and then said, "Hey, tell Mom the bereavement committee called. A sophomore died in the park today—fell off a cliff." Silence, then, "No, Cate really didn't know him that well, so…"

I whispered, "Thank you" and then leaned back against the brick wall and closed my eyes while Claire finished talking to him. I listened to the pounding rain soften to a hushed drizzle, sprinkling on the roof like fine sand through an hourglass. The storm was over, the danger past, and it was late. Cici locked her wrists with mine, hauled me up off the cold floor, and we all crawled into bed. For better or worse, the person I was most likely to confide in and the person I was least likely to confide in were now partners in my grief.

✥

"It really sucks, Cate. How could something like this happen?" Meri asked on the bus Monday morning. I hadn't been able to bring myself to tell them I'd seen Michael's accident, but the news of his death had traveled fast enough.

Leo glanced over his shoulder, rolling his eyes.

Grace shot him a nasty look.

"What's your problem?" I asked him. My mood was already black. I didn't need Leo making it blacker.

Leo shrugged. "Look, I'm really sorry this happened to him, Cate. No one deserves it. It's just…" He stopped there. Leo had known me forever and could tell when my temper was rising. It was.

"Just what, Leo?"

"If you really want to know, this isn't the first time Michael's gotten himself into trouble."

"And how would you know about that, Leo? Been hanging out at the rumor mill again?"

"What's that supposed to mean?"

"Oh…nothing. It's just that it would have been *nice* if my best friend's *brother* hadn't filled the whole *school* in on an embarrassing little incident that happened at the pool with Jason last week!"

"Cate, I didn't…" he stopped, frustrated, and turned back around, saying calmly, "If you don't want people talking about your temper, you should watch it next time."

"Forget about him, Cate," Meri said. "He's just being the jerk big brother that he is." Cici and Grace nodded their agreement.

My black mood didn't improve when we got to school, and I realized I shouldn't have been so quick to discount Leo's opinion. Rumors were flying that Michael had put someone in the hospital and run away from home. They talked about the forbidden tattoo, as if none of *them* had ever considered getting one. But, by far the most disturbing assertion was that drugs were found near his body. I wondered if any of it was true. And if so, was Leo right? Was Michael just an accident waiting to happen? The suspicion squirmed in my stomach and insinuated itself into my memories of him.

Traitor, I berated myself, but I couldn't erase the damage the rumors had done.

❧ ❧

Michael's wake was held Monday evening at the Belle Grove Funeral Home, a lavishly furnished building with a pink box of tissues on every table.

Wearing a soft black sweater set and skirt, my hair smoothed back under a wide velvet headband, I walked through the archway into Michael's viewing area. Inside, I was shocked to see Zoe and the whole newspaper staff milling about, trying to look solemn and whispering to each other. They'd spent the whole day fanning the gossip flames at school, and now they'd come to see the train wreck first hand. It made me sick.

Then I saw my friends—Meri and Finn, Grace, J.C. and Spencer. Meri had told them Michael and I had been friends, and they'd come to lend support. They'd dressed up for the occasion. J.C. and Spencer had even splashed on cologne, and Finn had tidied up his hair.

"Thanks, guys," I whispered to them, and we shared hugs all around. Then my dad led my sisters and me over to the Gardiners, Michael's foster parents, to introduce us. We waited while they finished hugging a man with a Mohawk and an elaborate tattoo spreading up his neck from the collar of his dress shirt.

"I just don't understand, Ian. I thought we had gotten through to him," Mrs. Gardiner said, her voice thick with emotion. "Didn't he know how much we loved him? Maybe we should have—"

"He knew, Sue," the man interrupted in a hushed baritone. "This wasn't your fault."

Mrs. Gardiner shook her head uncertainly.

"You did your best with him," he reassured her, "which is more than I did."

"Ian, don't say that. Come see us next week. We'll talk. Okay?" she said. The man with the Mohawk nodded, his eyes damp, as he broke from her embrace and shouldered his way out into the hall. We stepped in to take his place.

"Bill, Suzanne, I'd like to introduce my daughters, Claire, Catherine and Cecilia. Catherine knew Michael when they were in second grade together at Saint Paul," my dad explained. The middle aged couple turned toward me with interest.

"I am so sorry for your loss," I offered, saying the words I'd rehearsed earlier that day in the mirror, then added impulsively, "He was such a sweet little kid…"

"Thank you so much for that," Mrs. Gardiner replied warmly. "Maybe you could stop by sometime, and we could share our memories?"

"I'd like that," I agreed, thinking that I really would.

Then Mrs. Gardiner caught me off guard by taking my hand and asking, "Would you like to see Michael, now?" I panicked. I wasn't sure if I wanted to see him, but what could I do? Snatch my hand away and run from the room? Cici sensed my uneasiness and grabbed my other hand as Mrs. Gardiner led me over to the coffin. I don't know what I was afraid I'd see, but when I stood in front of the casket and saw Michael's peaceful face, my fear was replaced with only a tender longing to turn back the clock. He looked like himself, only sleeping.

I reached out and brushed the tips of my fingers over his knuckles, not caring whether it was allowed or appropriate. They were cold and unyielding, the opposite of the warm hands that caught me when I fell into them on the bus only five days before.

Where the hell were God and His Angels when Michael fell? I sent the heated question skyward, a God-seeking bullet. Receiving no satisfactory answer, I stood up abruptly and walked out.

As soon as I reached the foyer, Cici put her arm around my waist and squeezed. "I'm so sorry, Cate," she whispered.

I squeezed her back then took a few steadying breaths and looked around. There was a mahogany table set up in the corner that held some of Michael's possessions and pictures. The first thing that caught my eye was the beat-up acoustic guitar propped up against it.

Ah…that explained his interest in the guitar club. Cici plucked at a few of the strings. "I wonder if he was any good," she murmured.

My throat was too tight to reply, so I moved along the table, stopping to study a picture of him as a small child standing between his mom and a policeman. Rugged like Michael, the officer was quite good looking except for a scar that crossed his cheek from his ear to the corner of his mouth. Michael was holding hands with both of them and grinning up at the officer who I assumed was his father.

Cici pointed to the Michael in the picture. "He was adorable," she said, a soft smile on her face.

I smiled back reflexively. "Yeah…" I said, my voice catching. I looked past the picture and grabbed the edge of the table for support, feeling dizzy. There at the end of the table was a little black velvet box, and nestled within it was Michael's mother's aquamarine Claddagh ring. The memories attached to that ring were too strong, and a lump grew in my throat. Then I was bumped from behind by someone in the crowd.

"Ah…sorry…" came the apology. Cici and I turned to see a thin boy with dark curly hair looking at me apologetically. I recognized him as a junior at Saint Joan. His intense brown eyes sought my own as he reached his hand out to introduce himself.

"I'm Luke Devlin," he said, dropping his hand when he saw the dazed expression on my face. "Did you know him well?"

"Yeah…" I murmured, my thoughts still wrapped up in the ring.

"Back in second grade," Cici added for me. "And she saw him again this past week."

A shadow passed over the boy's face. "I'm sorry," he said.

Suddenly feeling the need to distance myself from him, I took a step back and crossed my arms protectively over my chest. "You?" I asked politely.

"What?" His mind had obviously wandered elsewhere.

"Did you know him well? Michael, I mean."

"Yeah. Some…" I was about to ask how, wondering if he was just following the train wreck too, when someone touched my shoulder. I could tell from the strong scent of cologne that Spencer or J.C. had found me.

"Hey, you all right?" J.C. whispered, slinging his arms around mine and Cici's shoulders. I let him pull me in close while the boy with the curly hair disappeared into the crowd.

"Yeah. It's just hard to accept, you know?"

"No doubt," he said. "But you know Michael's in a better place, right?"

Did I? Before I could answer, the rest of my friends and family found us.

"You ready to go, Bug?" my dad asked.

I took one last look at the table of memorabilia. It was all that remained of my friend.

"Yeah," I said. "Yeah. Let's go."

❧ ❦

Around midnight, I heard the back door open and the clatter of my mom's keys hitting the kitchen counter. She was home from Bluefield. I rolled over and listened to my dad welcome her back and walk with her up the stairs.

"It's horrible, what happened to Michael," she whispered to him. "After all the trouble his family went through."

She came into my room, and sat behind me on the edge of my bed. "Catherine? Are you okay? I am so sorry about Michael. He really was a good kid."

I wanted to ask her how she knew that. Why God let things like this happen. But my lips remained stubbornly closed. I didn't want to talk about it. Not with her. Instead, I reached around behind me, placed my hand over hers and borrowed J.C.'s sentiment. "It's okay, Mom. He's probably in a better place."

She squeezed my hand back and said, "He is, Catherine. Michael is where I hope we all will be someday. Home, with God."

And as my mom disappeared into the soft darkness of the hall, I prayed that she and J.C. were right.

God, I really wanted them to be right.

Chapter 6
Cletus, the Axe-toting Freak

AFTER THE WAKE and funeral, my mom quit her job at the church and turned our dining room into a command center for directing Mina's move. Over the next few weeks, new equipment arrived almost every day: special bedding, breathing apparatus, a walker, a bedside toilet. There were disordered piles of paperwork everywhere. They were spilling out of the dining room and into the living room, while all of Claire's earthly possessions spilled down the stairs and into the basement, which was now *her* domain. Sure, she still let me watch the flat screen down there, but I had to do it surrounded by all her cross country trophies and Nike spandex. It was no longer *our* space. The whole house was in a state of flux and had moved on without me.

At school it was the opposite. My friends had thrown themselves back into their insanely busy high school routines–AP classes, sports conditioning, volunteer commitments—while I was the one who had changed. I should have cared about all that stuff too, but I didn't. I couldn't seem to care about anything. My friends noticed.

"Jesus, Cate…" Finn said, after fighting with the cafeteria windows again for my attention one day. "It's been like, almost a month since Mike died." I winced at the blunt way he dug the subject up out of the hole I'd buried it in.

"Michael," I said.

"What?" asked Finn.

"His name. It was Michael," I corrected him.

"*Okay*…look, Cate. Mer says you're not answering your phone, and you won't go out." I glanced down at my hands, which were preoccupied with tearing up my napkin into little strips. Finn looked at J.C. sideways and nodded down at the napkin. J.C. tugged the shreds out of my hands and took up tearing where I had left off. Finn rolled his eyes. "Cate, seriously, you need to go out this weekend. We'll go build a fire at the shelter down in the park and—"

"No!" I said, a little too loudly.

"Cate, so like, what, are you going to avoid the park for the rest of your life?"

"Come on, Cate. It's our favorite place," Grace chimed in.

"And we'll make *s'mores*, Cate. The kind where the marshmallows are burned all black on the outside, but soft and gooey on the inside, just like you like 'em," promised J.C. He abandoned the napkin, snatched up one of my Teddy Grahams and stuffed it in his mouth. "You know," he continued, biting the head off another pilfered bear, "the kind normal people throw into the fire?"

I had to smile at that. I knew they were right. I couldn't avoid the park forever. I didn't want to. "What night?"

"Saturday," Finn said. "My brother can drop us off. Pick you up at eight."

⁂

Saturday morning, Mom rented a car to drive down to Bluefield so she could accompany Mina back to our house in the chartered ambulance. It was just my dad and me out on the driveway to see her off. Claire had gone for an early run and Cici, who had tried out for cheerleading after all and made the squad, was attending her first practice. After my mom hugged my dad goodbye, she and I stood awkwardly facing each other.

"Thank you for understanding that I have to do this," she said. She hugged me quickly then pulled away and climbed into the car. I knew she'd feel better if she thought she had my blessing, so I set my face in what I hoped was a look of stalwart support.

"'Bye, mom!" I called and waved as she drove away.

My dad smiled down at me. "So, I think *someone* has a birthday next week—one of the big ones."

I grinned back at him.

"Oh, is it you, Caty Bug? Turning sixteen?" he teased, stroking the day-old stubble on his chin. "I think you better get some more driving practice in if you want to pass your test. How about you take your scruffy dad out for breakfast? I'll pay if you drive."

"Deal," I agreed, punching him in the arm before jogging back into the house to throw on a thick hooded sweatshirt. Even with the sunny late September sky overhead, it was a brisk morning. When I got back outside, I saw that my dad had opened the garage door and was standing next to his "baby." Not good.

"Um…Dad? Can't we just take the van? It's already in the street."

Dad's baby was gunmetal gray with mottled patches of lighter gray and pea green. He'd traded the last car he'd restored for this one—which had been towed all the way from Arizona—and spent the summer replacing parts, cutting out rusted areas, and sanding it. It had several jagged, ropy welding scars across the back and hood. Frankenstein's monster had come to live in our garage, and it looked like I was going to have to drive it.

My dad leaned on the hood and patted it lovingly, his eyes going soft. "Hon, don't you know what this car is?"

"Yeah, I think so." I was about to fire off that it was his midlife crisis on wheels, and then follow that up with "Couldn't you have purchased a nice new red Mustang like Grace's dad did when he turned fifty?" But the look of utter joy that came over his face when he thought I might actually know what was so special about his baby stopped me. Instead, I asked, "Isn't it one of those old muscle cars?"

His eyes clouded a bit as he realized I had no idea what the car's draw was.

"Climb in," he directed. "I'll try to explain on the way."

"Dad…it's a *stick!*"

"Everyone needs to know how to drive stick," he said.

"Why? Mom can't drive stick."

"My point exactly."

"*Dad...*"

"What if there's an emergency and the only car around is a stick shift? Claire couldn't drive it. It wasn't ready to drive when she was learning." My dad was certainly not blind to the sibling rivalry that smoldered under his roof, and he wasn't afraid to use it to his advantage. I shook my head, but I knew I would cave after he said that.

"Get in the car, Caty. You'll be fine. Trust me."

"Keys?" I prompted impatiently, holding my hand out.

"Oh." He dug into his pocket, pulled out the keys and tossed them to me over the hood. I caught them easily, separated out the biggest, shoved it into the lock, and tried to rotate it. It was stuck. "Sometimes you have to jiggle it, you know, find the sweet spot," he said.

"Oh, for the love of..." I groaned as I wiggled the key back and forth a few times. The lock sprang open.

It was stuffy in the car, so I grabbed the crank handle in the door and pushed it around and around until the window was rolled all the way down. Then I looked at the stick that was growing out of a ribbed rubber mound in the floor between the two front seats, waiting for my dad to tell me what to do first, but he just regarded me thoughtfully.

"In 1971," he said, "when I was around twelve, my dad bought a used Chrysler Town and Country station wagon. It was a dependable white car with a wide stripe of wood paneling down the sides." He made a face and shivered. As I sat in *his* car, I could seriously sympathize with his twelve-year-old self. My dad went on, oblivious.

"My uncle, on the other hand, who was quite a bit younger than my dad, bought a green two-door coupe with black racing stripes down the sides and across the hood. That, my friend, was a cool car. Uncle Jack took me cruising in that car on Saturday nights sometimes." Then he leaned over and whispered, "Sometimes we peeled away from traffic lights, leaving the cars next to us in the dust. I loved that car. And when I was sixteen, the girls loved that car too, especially the—"

"Ugh, Dad! Way too much information," I blurted out, throwing my hands over my ears.

"Caty, the thing is, this is the same kind of car. It's a 1971 Dodge Dart Demon. I've been looking for one like it to restore for years."

"Oh, cool," I said, feigning enthusiasm.

He wasn't buying it. "Look, let's fire it up. Maybe that will shed some light on it for you."

I looked at him blankly.

"Oh, right," he said. "Okay. First put the car in neutral." He took my right hand and placed it on the stick between our seats. "Now, push down on the pedal on your far left—that's the clutch."

I pushed it down with the toe of my tennis shoe.

"Now, shift into neutral," he said, pushing down on the ball through my hand and pulling the stick back an inch. I heard a soft "kathunk" sound and felt a popping sensation. He then slid the stick back and forth from left to right a few times. "Feel that? That's neutral," he said. Then he moved my hand and the stick through all the gears to show me where they were. "Okay. Let's get this baby on the road. Keep your right foot on the brake, your left foot on the clutch, and turn the key."

The key jangled on its key ring as I twisted it away from me. The engine turned over with a loud thrumming sound and then settled into a deep throaty growl. It definitely sounded different when I was in the driver's seat. I placed my hands in the two and ten o'clock positions on the steering wheel and felt the steady rumble of the engine through my hands and feet. It felt good.

"Okay, what next?" I asked my dad, who was nodding approvingly.

"Shift into reverse and keep your left foot on the—" I shifted into reverse and lost my focus on the clutch, releasing it. The car hopped backward, throwing me forward against the steering wheel. It made a horrible coughing sound that turned into a feeble death rattle. "Clutch," my dad finished, then said, "Okay, start her up again." When I raised my eyebrows at him, he said, "You stalled. Happens to everybody. Won't be the last time today, either." I was determined to prove him wrong. I started the car again, shifted into reverse with my foot still on the clutch and waited for the next instruction.

"Now for the tricky part. You are going to slowly let up on the clutch while you slowly depress the gas, and I mean slowly. This car has a lot of power under the hood, and we don't need to shoot out into the street without stopping to look both ways." I smiled to myself. I could handle it.

"To stop," he continued, "hit the clutch before hitting the brake if you want to avoid stalling again."

I repeated my dad's directions to myself a few times and squeezed the steering wheel firmly with both hands. Then, I pressed what I thought was lightly down on the accelerator and let up a fraction of an inch on the clutch. The car roared, and when I released the clutch, it rocketed backward out of the garage and down the driveway.

"Brake! Brake!" my dad shouted. I took my foot off the gas and stomped down on the brake and clutch at the same time. The car screeched to a stop a foot from the end of the drive and then resumed its contented throaty growl.

"Whoa…" I breathed, my cheeks flushed with excitement.

"See what I mean?" my dad asked.

I put the car back in neutral and then turned to my dad and asked, "Um…did your uncle's Demon have that much power?"

"Um, no," he admitted, chuckling softly. "I added a little something extra to this one. I shored up the chassis and installed a 426 Hemi last summer."

"What's that?" I asked.

"More power," he said, a huge grin spreading across his face.

We spent the next half hour driving around our neighborhood, and I only stalled one more time.

"Okay, I think you're ready for the highway," he said. "Let's head out to the Bob Evans in Avon Lake. I'm famished."

As we hit the entrance ramp, my breathing quickened, and my heart rate sped up. I accelerated through second and third gear and then, as the front tires hit the highway, I shifted into fourth. My back sank into the seat as we flew easily past a whole string of cars, and I had to rein in my desire to bust the speed limit.

My dad flipped on the radio and tuned it to the classic rock station. Bruce Springsteen's "Thunder Road." I couldn't have chosen a more perfect song. Feeling content, I rested my left elbow on the door, waved my hand up and down in the cold air stream blasting past us, and looked at my dad sideways, grinning. We were kindred spirits, he and I. This car was no Frankenstein's monster any more than the Millennium Falcon was a bucket of bolts.

"You like?" He grinned back.

I nodded and then teased, "So...Dad, isn't it a little like, blasphemous for a Catholic to drive a Demon?"

He laughed and said, "You know, the Demon was only manufactured for two years. Superstitions about demons were common enough that Dodge stopped making them."

"So, you don't believe in demons, devils, evil spirits or anything like that?" I asked, curious now.

"Lots of people believe in the Devil," he hedged.

"Yeah, but do you?" I asked. I took my eyes off the road for a moment to look at him. He was fidgeting.

"Well, the Church teaches that the Devil is real," he finally said, as if that settled it. It didn't.

"That still doesn't answer my question," I pointed out, now extremely curious about how he really felt.

"Hon, what I believe is this. That God is all good, all knowing, and all powerful. Why would He even leave a Devil around to mess with us when according to our beliefs, He would have the power to do away with him?" He paused and then admitted, "No, I don't believe in the Devil. I think a person's soul can have enough darkness in it to explain the evil they do, though I owe it to your mother to say she disagrees with me."

The fact that he disregarded Church teaching on the Devil surprised me, so I dug a little deeper. "So, does that mean you don't believe in Guardian Angels, either?" He gave me a half grin.

"I don't know, Bug. Pretty floaty creatures in dresses with fluffy wings? I think if God wanted an army, he could come up with something better than that." He winked then and pointed at the exit coming up. As I coasted to a stop at the end of the ramp, I thought of my Playlist.

I wondered what my dad would think about that.

⁓⁓

The sun had sunk behind the house, and cold shadow fingers were creeping across the lawn when Finn's brother, Mitch, pulled his parents' enormous SUV into the driveway. I shoved my hands deep into the pockets of my weathered fall jacket and hunched my shoulders up against the chill in the air. Cici stood next to me, a perfect fashion plate with her makeup simple but flawless, as usual.

"Do you have enough room for Cici?" I asked, as Meri pushed open the heavy door of the SUV. Cici and I were so close in age that she often joined us when we went out.

"Yeah, sure," said Meri. "Spencer and J. C. couldn't make it, so there's plenty of room." I was disappointed, but tried not to show it. Saturday nights were always more fun with those two around.

By the time we arrived at the parking area of our favorite picnic shelter, the sun had completely set behind the damp walls of the gorge. The night was deep down here in the valley and the smell of wood smoke drifted toward us over the cold, wet grass from the shelter house. I looked up to see the fireplace already glowing. My heart sank. Use of the hearth was first-come, first-served, but we rarely found anyone out here this late on a Saturday night. There were two figures walking back and forth between the fireplace and the picnic tables.

"Let's go," I said, deflated. "Maybe we can—"

"No, I think we know them. C'mon," said Grace. She grabbed my hand and tugged me out of the car. As we approached, the two figures grinned and waved. It was J.C. and Spencer.

"I thought—" I started to say, but was interrupted when they all turned toward me and shouted, "Happy Birthday, Cate!" It was then that my eyes took in the table. There was a twelve-pack of Coke and a foil pan filled with graham crackers and Hershey bars. On top, the guys had painstakingly arranged at least fifty marshmallows to form the words, "HAPPY BIRTHDAY."

"We don't do cakes," explained Spencer, giving me a gruff hug.

"Thanks, guys! But my birthday's not 'til next week."

"That's why it's called a *surprise* party," said J.C., flashing his bright white grin.

I turned to Cici. "You knew about this too, didn't you?" I accused. She smiled and looked down at her pretty new boots, nodding. J.C. took a step toward her, giving her a sly grin.

"Well, if it isn't Baby Sis, blessing us with her presence tonight," he teased. He appraised her perfect hair and outfit. "Only, your paparazzi didn't show. Too bad."

"Dude," Spencer said, "I think it's kinda nice that one of the girls decided to dress up for us." He gave Cici one of his goofy grins, and she smiled back at him.

"So, are we roasting marshmallows or what?" Finn wanted to know.

The shelter was surrounded on three sides by thick woods and up a short curving path through the trees was the bathroom. We fanned out in the woods to look for marshmallow sticks. It wasn't long before I could hear most of the group laughing back at the fireplace, but I hadn't found the right stick yet. Since I liked my marshmallows flaming, my stick had to be thick and green enough that it wouldn't burn through but also thin enough to accept a marshmallow shoved onto its tip.

As I tossed another brittle candidate back into the brush, I caught a faint whiff of men's cologne. I stood up quickly and looked around, but saw nothing. I told myself that one of the guys must have walked through here earlier, but I snatched up the stick I had just discarded, now deeming it good enough, and hurried back to the light of the fire and my friends.

Back at the shelter, Meri announced it was time to sing "Happy Birthday." I looked down at the marshmallows and asked, "What? No candles?"

"Nah…" drawled Finn, grinning, "We thought we'd just light the marshmallows on fire." And they each grabbed a marshmallow, shoved it on a stick, and thrust it into the heart of the fire. I was soon surrounded by six marshmallow torches and an exuberant but off-key rendition of "Happy Birthday." What more could a birthday girl want? "Save one for me!" I reminded them, blowing them out.

"Of course," said Grace, offering me her perfectly blackened marshmallow.

A short time later, I was licking sticky s'more crud from my fingers and watching my friends while the radio played in the background. Spencer was browning a marshmallow for Cici while the two compared strength training techniques. He was working hard to prepare for basketball try-outs, wanting badly to make the varsity team this year, and as a former gymnast, Cici had good advice to give. They were sitting close, and I checked out Spencer's expression more carefully, recognizing the eager shine in his eyes. God, he was such a flirt. He was usually harmless, but he'd better watch it this time. That was my little sister he was panting after.

Finn had straddled one of the picnic table benches near the fire and was whispering into Meri's ear as she rested her back against his chest, and J.C. had shoved three marshmallows on the end of a multi-pronged stick. He was making Grace laugh while he demonstrated the finer points of mass roast marshmallow production—or destruction—depending on your point of view.

The fire popped and hissed, its warm light lifting and pulling at the shadows in the trees that surrounded us. I felt so lucky in that moment, so balanced. Maybe things were finally returning to normal. I got to my feet and grabbed another marshmallow, wrecking the letter "B" that my friends had arranged so neatly on top of the Hershey bars.

I froze mid-swipe.

The music on the radio was warbling threateningly through the familiar opening notes of Pierce the Veil's "Hang on Till May," and a wave of nausea tossed over me. I squeezed my eyes shut. It was the song that played while I watched Michael die.

No. Don't think about him. Not tonight. Let him go. But the song's refrain called Michael to mind anyway, and when I opened my eyes again, I had the suffocating feeling I was watching my friends from far away. I felt suddenly removed.

No one noticed I was upset yet, and I wanted to keep it that way.

I backed quietly out of the shelter into the waiting arms of the woods beyond. Then my thoughts assailed me.

What's Michael to you? Why do you still care so much?

I buried my hands in my hair, and shouted back.

I don't know! I don't know!

Then, I quickly turned and headed up the trail through the trees toward the bathroom. It was colder away from the fire and the path was dark, becoming almost pitch-black as the light from the shelter lost its influence. I could see nothing of the path beneath my feet or of the forest on either side of me, and I felt ahead with my toes in case there were branches or roots strewn across the trail.

Shit. Why didn't I think to grab one of the flashlights off the table when I left? I thought about going back, but rejected the idea. *Just use the bathroom then the song will be over, and you can go back, and everything will be fine again.* I took a deep breath in through my nose and…my heart nearly stopped.

There it was again. So faint. Was I imagining it? Was it just the woods? Some late-blooming wildflowers? But even as those thoughts entered my head, I knew it wasn't. It was the subtle fragrance of men's cologne, and I wasn't imagining it.

Hugging my elbows to my chest, I looked from side to side and over my shoulder, peering into the black woods in search of the source. Visions from my childhood nightmares broke through, and my heart raced. Would the shadows grow fiery eyes next? Long fingers? Barbed tongues? I wanted to run, but I knew the moment my feet took flight, I'd fall flat on my face in the inky darkness. I took a few more steps forward and then stopped to listen again.

Nothing. And the fragrance was gone.

Big baby, I thought, and started toward the bathroom again. Thankfully, I was now bathed within its light. I felt braver, until… again, a mix of citrus and pine, a fresh clean-shaven scent, assaulted my nostrils. I spun around, but there was nothing but empty trail behind me.

Pull it together. Just breathe. I backed up and the fragrance disappeared. My head cleared slightly, and I stood there panting. Too chicken to brave the path again, I reasoned that the bathroom was my best shot at safety, and I turned toward it. The scratched and dented door was hung so it swung inward and had been propped open with a rock. I envisioned myself shoving the door open, stumbling inside and then barring it against whoever was following me.

I reached for the handle and was totally overwhelmed by the citrusy-pine scent. It stung my nostrils, burned my tongue and made my eyes water. It throbbed in my head and body, blocking out everything else.

Damn it! Think! In or out? My hand was paralyzed on the door, my eyes squeezed shut in denial of the sensory onslaught. Then the thought, *this is the part in the movie where the dumbass camper goes to explore the bump in the night alone,* flowed unbidden into my head, followed by, *must be some logical explanation, the camper says to herself—just before being disemboweled by Cletus, the Axe-toting Freak.* Upon completing that thought, I heard the bump that had heretofore been missing. Only, it was more like a barely-audible shuffling sound.

It was coming from inside the bathroom.

My heart stopped again, and I decided thinking was overrated. I opened my mouth and screamed.

The hair-raising sound that pulsed from my throat continued in waves, nonstop, until two familiar hands grabbed my shoulders and shook me. "What happened?" The two hands held me roughly at arm's length, and I opened my eyes to see J.C. looking me up and down. I threw my arms around his neck and squeezed tight.

"Thank you, God!" I cried.

His body was warm and solid beneath his thick sweatshirt. He petted me reassuringly. "*Okay...*" he said. "Now, what the hell was that all about?" I pulled away to see Grace, Finn, and Meri standing behind him, and Spencer limping up the path with Cici at his side, trying to function as a crutch.

"What happened to Spence?" I asked, stalling for time.

"Root. Path. Dark," Spencer answered, wincing with each footfall.

"Cate?" prompted Grace.

Oh, this was embarrassing. "I heard a sound," I said quietly.

"You heard a sound?" asked J.C., raising his eyebrows.

I took a deep breath and said with more force, "I heard a sound in the bathroom, and I smelled…someone."

J.C.'s eyes flicked to the door, and he reached out for the handle, but I stepped in front of him, barring his way.

"Didn't you hear what I said? There's someone in there. Can't you smell him?"

J.C. sighed. No, he didn't believe me, obviously. I looked around at the rest of my friends. They were shaking their heads at each other and shuffling their feet in the dried up autumn leaves.

Finn stepped around Meri and stood beside me. He sniffed the air near the crack in the door. "It only smells like a park bathroom." He sniffed again. "And…maybe like animal scat?"

"Scat?" asked Spencer, confused.

"You know, like an animal has been in there, and like, shit in a corner or something? I've gone out with my dad to trap and test animals for the health department, and I'm just saying, that's what it smells like to me." Finn shoved his hands in his pockets. He was right. I recognized the smell, too.

J.C. reached out for the door again, but my hand shot out to hold it in place.

"You don't smell…guy's cologne?" I asked, tentative now. I couldn't smell it anymore, but I knew I hadn't imagined it. There was someone here.

"No," said J.C. Finn shook his head in agreement.

"But I heard something," I continued lamely.

"What'd you hear, Cate?" asked Spencer, exasperated.

"A shuffling sound, like someone was dragging something around." My mind began to imagine all sorts of things that could be dragged around in a darkened park bathroom. None of them were pleasant.

"Maybe it's Big Foot," teased Spencer with a crooked grin.

"Shut up, Spence," said Meri, rolling her eyes.

"Maybe we should call the park rangers," suggested Cici.

"No!" came the immediate chorus.

Finn sighed. "They'll just drive out, find nothing—because there *is* nothing—and then make us all go home." He looked at me. "Cate, you know that's what'll happen." Yeah, I did know that, but I also knew that *this is the part in the movie where Cletus, the Axe-toting Freak, jumps out of the bathroom and bludgeons half your friends to death and then chases the rest of them screaming their asses off into the forest.* This thought entered my head as if it were the most reasonable conclusion in the world, but damned if I knew who Cletus was. I was ready to stand my ground, but I could see that J.C. would not be deterred. Testosterone and a little stubbornness went a long way.

Tell Cletus I said hi, I thought grimly. I took a few steps back and waved J.C. forward, only to detect the not unpleasant but unnatural scent of cologne again. It was layered softly over the more powerful scent of the woods surrounding us, but I felt a little better, because if it was back here by me, it wasn't in the bathroom, which was a good thing. Right? At least J.C. should be safe. I threw a suspicious glance over my shoulder, but saw nothing but trees. I looked from side to side at my friends, but they didn't appear to be picking up the scent at all. It was maddening.

J.C. put his hand on the door again.

"Maybe, you should like, grab a weapon or something?" asked Meri, clearly spooked. J.C. dropped his hand and looked at Finn, who shrugged and handed over his flashlight, which was one of those super-heavy, 18-inch long, industrial strength lights. J.C. turned it on and aimed its dusty beam through the crack in the door.

"I don't see anything," he said, angling the beam of light under the two sinks that were mounted on the wall beneath a stainless steel mirror. He pushed the door open a little and stuck his head around the corner while Finn stood behind him with his hand on his back. I changed position and stood up on my toes to try to see over their shoulders. Two yellow eyes glowed in the darkness about two feet above the floor back in the corner next to the trash can. When the flashlight beam hit them, two mangy black lips in a damp, pointed muzzle curled back, revealing knife-edged teeth that glistened with foaming saliva.

"Jesus…" Finn hissed, "Back up, J.C., very—"

He was cut off by a menacing growl. The creature flew at them, jaws snapping, spit spraying everywhere. J.C. stumbled backward and avoided falling only because Finn grabbed him under the arms and held him up. J.C. yanked on the edge of the heavy door, but it was blocked from closing by the rock wedged into the crack. Crazed yellow eyes and sharp, snarling teeth filled the gap, fighting to leverage their way out.

"Oh, shit!" cried J.C., struggling to keep the door wedged against the rock. He slammed the flashlight down through the crack onto the creature's head and it fell, senseless, back into the bathroom. He kicked the rock out of the way and wrenched the door closed; only he forgot his fingers were in the way. Belting out an ear-splitting obscenity, he pulled his fingers free and then let the door fall shut.

He cried out in pain as he staggered back from the door, cradling his hand. There was a deep purple dent across the base of his fingers, which were already beginning to swell. Blood dripped from his pinky. Bent over and bracing himself with his good hand on his knee, he shook his mangled hand. "Ahhh…damn it!" he cried.

"Let me see!" exclaimed Cici, flying to his side and reaching out for his fingers.

Finn already had his phone to his ear and was speaking urgently into it, "… rabid coyote, big son of a bitch, trapped in the bathroom." He paused and listened for a moment. "Yeah, Dad, I think J.C. was bitten, and I think he broke his friggin' hand…"

Oh, God…I wanted to pass out.

Chapter 7
The Curse of the Camels

BOTH J.C. AND Spencer ended up in the emergency room Saturday night. Spencer was released with a badly sprained ankle, but they kept J.C. to administer intravenous antibiotics. Needless to say, I couldn't sleep. If I hadn't gone all emotional over a stupid song, we wouldn't have met the stupid coyote from hell, and I wouldn't have worried all night about a freaking stalker. Shit.

But I had no time to brood about Saturday night on Sunday morning. It was the day I'd dreaded since Michael died. My mother was returning home with my grandmother from Bluefield.

When the ambulance turned onto our street, my dad grabbed his sweatshirt off a hook by the door and rushed out to meet it. He was followed by both of my sisters. I had the urge to retreat to my room and hide. How could I go out there when I had no idea what to say to her? When I was afraid of what her future held? But I made myself put on a supportive face and followed him out the door, tugging my thick wool sweater tight around me.

After the paramedics transferred Mina to a wheelchair, she looked up and gave us each a tentative smile. Her eyes were sunken in her puffy face, and her usually well-coiffed white hair had yellowed and was matted down on one side of her head. And though my mom warned us about her tracheotomy, it was still a shock to see. The plastic tubing that pierced her throat was plugged at the moment, and I wondered why it was still in place.

"I am…*breathe*…so glad to see…*breathe*…you girls…*breathe*…so beautiful…" Recognizing the breathing pattern, my stomach pitched, and then my own lungs began to itch. I knew what it felt like to ration your air between words.

Focus, I thought. *Steady.*

She reached out a frail hand and clasped Cici's fingers, revealing splotchy, reddish-purple bruises on the inside of her wrist. I stroked my own wrist with my thumb. I knew those bruises, too.

"But I'm sure…*breathe*…you're just…*breathe*…thrilled to see me…" she muttered darkly, dropping her hand. She coughed loud and long, her face flushing a deep rose red before she was finished. I fought back tears. The last time I'd seen her, she'd been kneeling in her garden with a trowel in her hand and cursing lustily about her neighbor's cat pooping in her garden.

"If I see that cat, I'll shove its tail so far up it's—"

"Mina!" I'd interrupted, and she'd looked over at me, smiling guiltily.

"I guess that's not very grandmotherly," she'd admitted. No, it wasn't. But then Mina was not your typical grandmother. She was fun, and she was fierce. And she could down three Bud Lights and still beat you in a game of Hearts.

"Who wants to be grandmotherly?" I'd asked, grinning back at her.

She had shaken her sun hat-covered head and laughed and laughed at that. "Not me, I guess. Not me."

Back on the driveway, Claire knelt down next to her. "How could you say that, Mina? We love you." But Mina just looked away.

"Come on, Mom, let's get you out of this cold." My mom grabbed the handles of the wheelchair firmly. "I can take it from here," she told the paramedics and then turned and wheeled her up the driveway. The paramedics looked surprised.

"Are you sure? We can—"

"No, I've got it," she assured them over her shoulder. My dad turned to the paramedics and thanked them. They were gone before my mom reached the front door.

After an exhausting struggle to help Mina up the stairs, she was tucked into the hospital bed in Claire's room. She patted the top of her blanket with her crooked fingers.

"Tom, hand me my...*breathe*...purse please," she said.

My dad grabbed the purse off the old plaid chair under the window. As he held it out to her, it fell open, and his expression froze. Seeing the look on his face, my mom pressed her lips together in an angry line and held her hand out.

"Mom, how could you?" she asked, pulling out a half full pack of Camel cigarettes. Cici and I exchanged shocked looks.

"I'm a grown woman...*breathe*...don't you tell me...*breathe*... what to do."

"But, you're—"

"Dying? You can...*breathe*...say it! So why the...*breathe*...hell should I give them up now?" I could see my mom's jaw tighten as they stared each other down. Mina turned her sunken hazel eyes away first, and then my mom handed me the pack, asking me to please throw them away.

I headed down the hall, but instead of going downstairs to toss the pack in the trash, I made a detour into my room. I have no idea why I did it, but I stuffed the Camels into the back of my underwear drawer, and then sagged down on my bed. My mom was right. How could Mina keep smoking when the cigarettes she was smoking were suffocating her? I shivered. I couldn't imagine a worse way to die.

I couldn't sleep that night. Not with the constant coughing and whir of machines next door. I stole down the stairs to the dining room and switched on the computer to do a little surfing to settle my mind, but after midnight, I was still restless. I needed something safe to occupy my thoughts, and my mind wandered around until it found its way to the pine forest I'd once counted among my favorite places on Earth. Then my fingers moved swiftly with a mind of their own.

UBERMENSCH

<CLICK>

Online Dictionary

<CLICK>

Main Entry: Ubermensch
Pronunciation: \ue-ber-mench\
Function: foreign term
Etymology: German

: Superman, Overman, Demigod
: Philosophical term for a new and advanced order of man

<BACKSPACE>

Wikipedia

<CLICK>

The Ubermensch (German; English; Overman, Superman) is a concept in the philosophy of Friedrich Nietzsche. Nietzsche posited the Ubermensch as a goal for humanity to set for itself in his 1883 book, *Thus Spoke Zarathustra.*

I leaned back in my chair and stretched out my arms, then interlaced my fingers behind my head.

"Ubermensch," I whispered. It was the word I'd found scrawled on the Lewis Woods footbridge the day Michael died. So, somebody hiking through the woods was looking for a demigod? A "super" man? I released the stretch and smiled grimly to myself. I wasn't the only one who was delusional.

I turned off the computer and headed upstairs, intent on going to sleep this time. But my grandmother's door was cracked open, and the light that spilled into the hall was broken by the shadow of someone moving about. I crept forward to see what was happening. My grandmother, her eyes panic bright, was choking on the phlegm in her lungs.

My mom peeled open a small sterile package, and then her hands disappeared into blue plastic gloves. When she pulled a length of plastic tubing from the packet and removed the plug from the tracheotomy hole in Mina's throat, I guessed immediately what she would do next and withdrew to my room. Then the gurgling began. It sounded like some slimy swamp thing was being sucked, kicking and screaming, out of Mina's lungs. Five seconds. Ten seconds. Fifteen seconds. Then it was over, and the peaceful hissing of her oxygen equipment refilled the night. Now I knew why the tracheotomy was still in place. She needed to have that phlegm sucked out of her lungs, or she'd die.

I felt my own lungs closing up at the thought. My next breath was tighter. A barely audible wheeze eased itself out of my lungs. I glanced at the inhaler resting on my nightstand, not wanting to use it.

Focus, I thought. *Slow your breathing down and focus.* My mom used to tell me that when I was little to keep me from panicking during an asthma attack. She'd power up my aerosol machine, rub my back and breathe with me until the attack passed.

I still did that—slowed my breathing down and focused—when I couldn't get to my inhaler right away. But it was available now. Shit. I grabbed it, used it and tossed it back, wondering how long Mina would have to live like that—feeling like she couldn't breathe, before she died.

I reached for my music player. I didn't want to know.

⁓⁓

"Try to keep it down," my mom requested early the next morning. "Mina had a rough night." Dark circles ringed my mom's coffee-charged eyes.

I wanted to say, "And how about you?" But I didn't think she'd want to talk about it. I wouldn't want to talk about it. I rolled over onto my back and realized my nose was cold. Definitely October, I thought, then shoved myself off the bed and muddled through my morning routine.

When I was ready, I bounded down the stairs and, on a hunch, veered toward the front door, opened it, and stuck my nose out. The grass was coated with thick white frost. It was days like these that reminded me why I really hated to wear a uniform. The gray plaid skirt left my lower legs exposed, and its thin fabric did nothing to keep my thighs warm. I trudged back up the steps and dug through the pile at the bottom of my closet, found a pair of old gray sweats and pulled them on under my skirt.

During breakfast, Spencer called and asked for a ride. He was on crutches, and he knew my dad worked at the auto repair shop near the school. My dad said yes, and that meant a ride in the Demon for all of us.

My dad surprised us when we went out to the garage by going to the Demon's passenger side and holding out the keys to me. The look on Claire's face was priceless when she was forced into the back seat.

"Remember the power," Dad advised.

"I *know...*" I said. I did, and I loved it.

Spencer lived in an apartment complex within walking distance of the school. His mom worked at the local Dodge dealership, and she always had the coolest cars which made me a little nervous about showing up in the half-finished Demon, but the look on Spencer's face when he hobbled out on his crutches was anything but disappointment.

"Sweet car!" he said as he folded his huge frame into the backseat next to Cici. "Hey, Cici," he said, giving her one of his lopsided grins. Definitely love struck. I shot him a warning glance over my shoulder as I pulled out of the driveway. He gave me a "what gives?" look back, and I realized he probably didn't even know he was falling for her yet.

Still early, the halls of the school were dark and deserted when my dad dropped us off. Cici headed left toward the freshman hall, while Spence and I cut through the cafeteria on the way to our lockers. Spencer's locker was down the hall and around the corner from mine, but before he left me, I grabbed his arm.

"You know she's only fourteen, Spence," I reminded him. He smiled from ear to ear, and I knew then that he was more aware of his feelings than I gave him credit for.

"Dude," he said, "she's hot, and if she's anything like you, she's nice, too."

"She's nicer than me," I said, knowing it was true.

He laughed. "Yeah, probably."

"Seriously. She's fourteen," I repeated.

He looked sideways at the French bulletin board on the wall and picked at a loose staple with his fingertip.

"Yeah, I know."

"So?"

"I'll be good," he promised. I nodded and then started hiking up my skirt to pull off the sweat pants. He laughed again, held his hands up and backed away. "I'll let you strip in private!"

"Pervert," I mumbled as he disappeared around the corner. And he just said he'd be good. I guess there's only so much a big sister can do.

I slammed my locker shut, and then I made my way through the empty halls to my homeroom, considering what, if anything, I needed to say to Cici about Spencer. I was deep in thought when I entered the partially-darkened classroom, and was completely unprepared for the wave of citrus and pine fragrance that hit me full in the face. I staggered back a few steps and looked around the room. Shawn Fowler was the only one there, and he was sitting in the teacher's chair with his feet propped up on her desk.

"Shawn?" I whispered.

"What," he said, his expression hard, as if whatever I was about to ask was none of my business. My mind reeled for a moment, processing the fact that there was nothing at all sinister in the room. No rabid coyote. No Axe-toting Freak. No invisible stalker. But it was definitely the same scent I'd smelled in the woods Saturday night, and it drew me forward. I walked the rest of the way up to the teacher's desk. Yeah, it was his cologne, and he must have sprayed it on thick that morning.

"Uh...Shawn?" He crossed his arms across his chest. "Um... what's that cologne you're wearing?"

"What the hell do you care for?" he snapped.

Then a crazy thought occurred to me. Had he been following me

Saturday night? That was insane. Why would he follow me? But I had to ask, no matter how idiotic I sounded.

"Where were you Saturday night?"

He shot up out of the chair, shoved it roughly back against the chalk tray and glared down at me. "I'll say it again. What the hell do you care for?" At that moment, there was a staccato shout from the doorway.

"Hey!" It was Spencer. He was standing in the doorway, leaning on his crutches. The crutches slowed him down as he hobbled toward me, but they added to his bulk, making him look bigger. When he slid into place behind me, Shawn retreated immediately to the other side of the teacher's desk.

"What's the problem?" he asked me, keeping his eyes on Shawn.

"Can you smell that now? Can you? That's the same cologne I smelled Saturday night just before that coyote almost bit J.C.'s hand off." Spencer and Shawn both looked at me with baffled expressions on their faces. "He might have been there, Spence!" I realized how stupid I must sound, but Spencer was my friend, and so he asked the question anyway.

"Okay. So like, is she right, Shawn?" He relaxed his stance a little.

"I don't know what the hell she's talking about!" Shawn shouted. "She's a freaking lunatic!"

"Then where were you Saturday night?" I repeated.

"I was at my aunt's house in Erie," he answered. "Okay? God!"

In my peripheral vision, I saw a shadow move across the smeary sunlit windows, and I jumped, startled.

"Shawn, you know the rules about taking the name of the Lord in vain." It was our homeroom teacher. "Report to Sister Lawrencia at once, please."

"Aw…but I was just minding my own business when—"

"No excuses, Shawn," she said. "Go."

As he left the room, I called after him, "I'll be checking on what you said, Shawn."

"You do that," he growled back.

"I will." Only I knew I couldn't. What was I going to do, ask his mom? Call his aunt? I'd probably be the one slapped with a stalking complaint.

After we took our seats, Spencer leaned over and whispered, "Are you sure that's what you smelled Saturday night?"

I nodded briskly.

"Well...he can't be the only guy who wears that cologne. Besides, why would he want to follow you around anyway?"

I had no idea.

At lunch, I found J.C. alone at our usual table. There was a huge pile of books stacked up in front of him, AP Spanish on top. He stared morosely at them as I set the six small glass jars I was carrying gingerly down on the table and took the seat across from him.

"Let me guess. Mr. Rath?" he asked, rolling his eyes.

"Water chemistry," I replied, faking a grimace. "I need to collect samples from a local body of water a couple of times over the next few months and then present my findings to the class." Most of the kids were complaining, but secretly, this was something I liked to do.

"Crap. I've got him next," he grumbled, wrinkling up his nose. "I've already got papers due in Spanish and History." He tried to scratch his forehead, but his hand was all wrapped up and splinted. I reached across the table and scratched it for him.

"I'm really sorry about your hand J.C.," I said.

"It's not that bad."

"Yeah it is. If I hadn't freaked out—"

"If you hadn't freaked out, any one of you girls could have walked into that bathroom and been torn to pieces." He paused and took a breath as if he was going to say something else, but remained quiet and looked away.

"What? What were you going to say?" J. C., like Cici, was unusually observant, and I wanted to know what was on his mind. Instead of answering right away, he hunched down in his chair, grabbed the salt shaker and started unscrewing the lid. I waited while he collected his thoughts. When he was finished, he set the silver lid carefully back on top and shoved it away from him. Then he straightened back up and looked me in the eye.

"I think someone was looking out for you Saturday night," he said. I hadn't thought about it like that. I tried to replay the events of that night again in my head, but everything had happened so fast. Could it have been Shawn? Unlikely, but I thought I'd mention it anyway.

"This morning I found out Shawn wears the same kind of cologne I smelled Saturday night."

"Cate, none of the rest of us saw or heard…or *smelled* anyone. Besides…" he stopped and leaned back in his chair, avoiding my eyes. "I didn't mean…a person." I saw where he was going, but despite all my inner feelings and fantasies on the subject, God and Angels were not something friends generally talked about in the school cafeteria. I just couldn't do it. It was too personal.

"J.C.—"

"One of you could have been killed or scarred forever. It could have been you…or Cici. *Something* was—"

"I think *you* were looking out for me Saturday night," I interrupted him. "I don't know how you held on to that door. If you'd let go…" I remembered the mouthful of fangs struggling to get out.

"Hey. I didn't want to get torn to shreds either," he reminded me.

"But…you'll be okay, right? Did the coyote have—" Finn and Grace arrived before I could finish my question and set a hot dog and fries down in front of J.C.

"Rabies?" finished Finn as he pulled up a chair and sat down. "Yup. That coyote was drowning in it. The lab tests my dad ran on its brain confirmed it. It must have been bit by something like three weeks ago and by Saturday was ready to attack anything that moved. You got your first shots in the ER right?" he asked J.C., reaching for the salt shaker.

J.C. nodded and massaged his upper arm where he must have received his injection.

"So, four more shots, bro, and you're good to go," Finn said, turning the salt shaker upside down. It dumped its entire contents onto his fries. Finn looked over at J.C., who stuffed one of his own fries in his mouth, then smiled innocently back.

"Man that sucks, Finn. Who would do that?"

"Hmm…" mumbled Finn while Grace and I busted out laughing. Finn picked up a fry, shook most of the salt off and bit it in half. We spent the rest of the lunch period helping Finn brush the salt off his fries and helping him eat them before heading back to class.

Chapter 8
The Ghost of Lewis Woods

AFTER MINA'S ARRIVAL, the sounds and smells of sickness in her room made it difficult for me to fall asleep upstairs, and I often sacked out on the sofa. Meri knew having Mina move in was hard on me and invited me to sleep over at her house the following Saturday. She'd grinned and said, "We'll have the guys over for movies and pizza, then kick them out and talk about how stupid they are all night." That sounded good to me.

On Friday, my actual birthday, my dad picked me up after school in the Demon and drove me to the BMV. I'd been waiting forever to take the driving test, but the butterflies flitting about in my stomach strongly urged me to postpone it.

"You'll be fine," my dad said, leading me into the dusty, wood-paneled lobby. There was a line of people waiting in front of the chipped white counter, and we took our place at the end of it. When it was my turn, the butterflies upped the ante and tried to crawl up my throat, but my dad was right. I did fine. I pulled in and out of parking spaces, made left and right turns, stopped and started at stop signs, merged into traffic and then conquered the cones. I passed with flying colors, and after grinning at the yellow smiley face sticker on the back of the camera, I received the most coveted prize in all of high school: my driver's license.

"Are those tears in your eyes?" I teased my dad as we walked out through the smudged glass door.

"What? These? Nah. They had dust in there from the seventies. I'm allergic to dust that old."

He didn't have to say anything. I knew he was proud. I just hoped he was proud enough to trust me with one of his most prized possessions.

❧

As soon as I walked in the door at home, I wanted to leave.

"Dad, can I take the car?" How could he say no? It *was* my birthday, and I had a perfectly legit reason for borrowing it.

"I should have seen that one coming," he said, rubbing the top of his head. "What for?"

"I have a chemistry project for school. I need to collect some water samples," I said brightly. "And I'd really like to go by myself. Please? *Please?* It *is* my birthday."

"Where are you going?" *Yes!*

"Down to the Rocky River." After Michael's death and the crazed coyote, I should have avoided the place, but it made the most sense; I knew that river best and would feel comfortable driving there. Besides, it was still light out, and I wouldn't be gone long.

"When will you be back?"

"About two hours?"

"Take your cell phone."

I hugged him with both arms, squeezed him tight and then held my hand out for the keys to the Demon.

"You want to drive *this* old man?" he asked, grinning now.

"She's a she, Dad, and yes! We have a special bond."

He tossed me the keys. "Don't be out past sunset."

I flew past him up to my room, grabbed the sample containers and stuffed them into my tote along with my inhaler, music player and cell phone, which *was* charged. I paused in the doorway, then backtracked to my underwear drawer and dug out the Camels, tossing them and a book of matches into the tote as well. Maybe it was time I did a little experiment with them, too. It suddenly occurred to me that I wanted to know what the hell was so great about them that a person would willingly turn their health to shit rather than give them up. I nodded to myself. Yeah. I'd really like to know the answer to that.

When I finally pulled out of the driveway, my dad was still rubbing his head, trying to look at ease.

"Not too late!" he called after me. "We're having birthday cake when you get back!"

But I wasn't thinking about him anymore. I had moved on. I was free.

⁂

It had rained for the last three days, and I held the sample container tightly while I dipped it into the furiously flowing river. After I screwed the lid back on and dropped it into my bag, I shook the ice-cold river water from my fingers and then stuffed them under my armpits for warmth. Check. Part one of today's experiment was accomplished.

I stood up then and surveyed the scene. The sky above was winter white and layered with steel gray cloud scraps that were being shoved relentlessly along by the higher altitude wind drafts. Down here at the bottom of the gorge the air was calm, and everything was heavy and damp and muddy. I looked for a place to sit while I thought about how to accomplish the second part of my experiment and found a large flat-topped boulder near the river's edge. I settled down on it and hoisted the pink tote onto my lap.

There in the bottom of the tote were the Camel cigarettes. I scooped out the half-empty box and examined it more closely. The camel on the front had only three tiny palm trees and two pyramids for shelter. The package proudly proclaimed that the tobacco therein was a Turkish domestic blend that had been around since 1913. How special. I turned it over and read the Surgeon General's largely-ignored warning: Quitting Smoking Now Greatly Reduces Serious Risks to Your Health. I looked up at the cold sky and choked back a laugh. I was glad someone considered suffocating to death a serious health risk.

Well, let's find out what all the hype is about. I started to pull out one of the cigarettes from within the crumpled foil lining, but paused midway and glanced over my shoulder. The road wasn't thirty feet behind me, and cars were cruising by every few minutes, their tires splashing past on the flooded pavement. I felt guilty, like I was committing some heinous crime.

What was I so worried about? I saw teens smoking almost every day. Aside from carding kids who tried to buy them, no one cared. I boldly pulled the cigarette out of the pack and held it between the knuckles of my first and second fingers like I'd seen other kids do, and started to dig for the matches and then sighed.

"Shit. I can't do this here." I looked over my shoulder again. What if someone I knew drove by? What if someone my *parents* knew drove by? It would positively kill them, that's what. I crammed the cigarette back into the pack, tossed the pack into my tote, then stood up and paced back and forth. The sound of leaves blowing in a stiff wind somewhere high above me reached my ears, and I looked up and back across the bridge toward my favorite spot in the park. The shriveled brown leaves of the oaks lining the cliff-top were rustling in the powerful wind gusts bullying their way past at the higher altitude. They were calling to me.

I would have all the privacy I needed up there. I knew I shouldn't do it, but now that I'd started this experiment, I was determined to see it through. If I didn't, it would be like coaxing a jagged splinter half way out and then leaving the remainder of the task for another day. It would jab at me painfully until I had my answers. It would bleed.

I pulled out my cell. Five-thirty. The sun wouldn't set for another hour and a half. Plenty of time. I turned back toward the car and murmured, "Let's do this thing."

The Demon rumbled an affectionate hello and pulled smoothly back out onto Cedar Point Road, surging forward at the promise of a new challenge: the steeply-climbing zigzags that would carry us up the other side of the gorge to Lewis Woods. There was no pitiful fight to the top with this car. Instead, we actually accelerated up and through the curves, shooting out of the mouth of the gorge with power to spare. I pulled into the puddle-filled gravel parking area, my heart beating fast, thinking, "I really, *really* love this car."

I hadn't been to Lewis Woods since late August, since the day

Michael died, and it was a different place. The heat, the humidity, and the bright sun-filled blue sky were gone. The parched golden grass of the field was now soggy and matted down. The summer birdsong had been replaced with the raking caws of black crows flapping by overhead. But the most striking difference of all was the foliage, which had changed from a woodsy green to a tattered blend of muddy yellow, burnt orange and brown. The transformation would have been complete if not for the pines. They remained a deep forest green and stood tall and proud in the distance, marking the entrance to the woods.

As I struck out across the field, a cold gust of wind from behind lifted my shaggy braid and beat a syncopated tempo against the corner of my mouth. The wind pushed hard against my back, slicing through my fall jacket, urging me forward and into the woods.

Dim lighting prevailed under the soaring pine rafters, like the inside of a church on any day but Sunday. All was still and quiet. I pressed on purposefully over the soft, pine-needled path, and it wasn't long before I broke through the dense shade and was looking out over the gorge at the sheer face of the cliff in the distance. I hadn't given any thought to how I would feel at that moment. I should have.

My stomach rebelled without warning, and I sank to my knees. Tears seeped into the corners of my eyes, and my nose began to run. The images of Michael's death—his body hitting the ground, the bright red blood erupting from his mouth, the anguish in his eyes—they all came back with cruel clarity, as if no time at all had passed since the accident. *God...I shouldn't have come here.*

I sat back on the chilly wet leaves and sniffed cold snot back up my nose. Then I pulled the Camels and matches out of my tote. I wanted to get this over with, get back to the warmth of the Demon and go home.

The head of the match flared brightly to life in the waning light of the day. I touched the quivering flame to the tip of the cigarette and sucked in a breath to ignite the end. It glowed deep orange, and then the tangy taste of the Turkish blend tobacco flooded my tongue. My lungs burned. I held the smoke in anyway, determined to get the most out of the experience, but began coughing almost immediately. I held the cigarette away from me with one hand and waved the remnant smoke out of my face with the other until the coughing subsided.

My fingers were shaking slightly as I tucked the end of the cigarette back between my lips and sucked in another lungful. It didn't burn as badly, and I closed my mouth this time and held in the acrid smoke for a moment before breathing it out through my nose. I watched the smoke curl away from each nostril and then suddenly felt an overwhelming urge to vomit. Crap...I was going to be sick...

"What the hell are you thinking, Genius?" came the soft ragged whisper of a disgusted voice over my shoulder. A chill wind followed the whisper and carried with it a faint citrus and pine fragrance. My heart stopped. My breathing stopped. But my head was moving. It was swiveling around to size up whatever had been stalking me. If it was Shawn, how did he find me here? What the crap did he want? And if it wasn't Shawn behind me, if it was something else—my mind froze short of letting any other images materialize.

Back within the deepening shadows of the woods, a lone figure sat. He wavered in and out of focus like the image on a TV set with poor reception. He was sitting on the wet fallen leaves, like me, with his elbows resting on his knees and his face buried in his hands. He was missing one Converse tennis shoe, and the toenails on that foot were torn and bloody.

An ear-piercing scream balled itself up in my throat, but when my mouth opened, no sound came out. I threw my energy instead into back pedaling away like a crab on the run from a death-dealing gull at the shore. I felt a searing pain in my palm as my right hand came down on the forgotten cigarette, snuffing it out. He heard my sudden movement and lifted his face from his hands, startled, and at that moment, I had no doubt. The figure was Michael, and I had gone completely and utterly out of my mind.

His eyes flew open wide, and his open hand shot out in front of him.

"Holy shit! Can you see me?" he cried. "Wait! Oh God, please wait!"

Yep, definitely crazy. Or maybe Mina's been smoking pot disguised as Camel cigarettes? Did she have cancer, too? Nobody ever tells me anything. Disconnected thoughts like these strung together frantically in my head while I scrambled backward.

Michael—for lack of a better name for my hallucination—jumped to his feet, waved both hands in my direction, shouting, "Stop! The cliff! Oh, Christ!"

I froze, then reached back with my fingertips and felt loose dirt clods and naked grass roots hanging over the edge of the cliff. A sudden updraft from the gorge blew up my back and lifted the curls at the nape of my neck; then my heart really started to pound and I thought it would explode right out of my chest. I imagined my life ending right there, right then, with a blast of my blood spurting like a geyser out over the cliff. With that macabre thought, I finally found my voice.

"No! No! No! No! You're not real," I chanted, covering my ears with my hands. All this time Michael remained very still, as if he was afraid any movement on his part would frighten me over the brink. I squeezed my eyes shut. If this was a hallucination, maybe it would just fade away in a minute.

"Please...I need to—"

"No...no...no..." I resumed chanting and dug through my tote for my music player. I was going to drown out his voice, and then I was getting the hell out of here. With trembling hands and half-closed eyes I plugged my headphones into my ears, pushed myself up onto my feet and lunged forward, but my boots couldn't gain any traction in the slippery wet leaves. I pitched forward and caught myself on my palms, which were scraped by the sharp thorny underbrush. I clenched my teeth and dug my fingers and toes deep into the cold muck like a sprinter at the starting block of a race. Then the adrenaline kicked in, and I took off at a dead run. I didn't look back.

The twilight-submerged trees whipped by in a confused rush. Good. That meant I was putting distance between me and my impending nervous breakdown. Then the song on my music player finally blasted my eardrums with sound. I didn't care what it was, as long as it was loud. I got my wish. The driving beat sent shock waves of strength through my body, and I pumped my legs harder.

Well, I took a walk around the world
To ease my troubled mind
I left my body lying somewhere
In the sands of time
But I watched the world
Float to the dark side of the moon
I feel there's nothing I can do…Yeah…

I didn't remember syncing 3 Doors Down's "Kryptonite" onto my music player. Was it talking about Michael? Was God playing D.J. again? Could my heart pump any harder? I didn't think so.

I watched the world
Float to the dark side of the moon
After all I knew it had to be
Something to do with you
I really don't mind what happens now and then,
As long as you'll be my friend at the end

My lungs were burning. The air was turning to thick sludge. I slid to a stop in the middle of the path, unable to go any farther. Bent over with my hands on my knees, I tried to catch my breath. *God? If that's You? I swear on my life that if you get me out of here with my sanity intact, I will never again go into the woods alone! I swear to you. I swear it.*

If I go crazy then will you still call me Superman?
If I'm alive and well
Will you still be there holding my hand?
I'll keep you by my side
With my super human might
Kryptonite…

The coincidence was too perfect. "If I go crazy then will you still call me Superman?" Was the Ubermensch or…or…demigod thing in the quote on the footbridge real? I yanked the headphones out of my ears, hurled them away from me and squeezed my eyes shut. I dropped the tote onto the damp forest floor and felt around blindly for my inhaler. There was no freaking way I was opening my eyes. I didn't want to know what might have caught up with me by then. When my hand finally connected with the hard plastic case of my savior, I took a deep drag, then another, and then waited for the medicine to kick in.

"Still have asthma?" murmured Michael from nearby, and then I heard him sigh. I tipped my head sideways to peer into the woods. He was leaning against a tree with his hands in his cut-off jeans' pockets and looking up at me through his long lashes. His coloring was washed out, like a retouched black and white photo, and his muted, off-kilter flickering was frightening. But the look on his face and the stance of his body were more forlorn and lost than menacing.

"Are you the Ubermensch?" I blurted out. He looked up, startled again.

"Wh…what?"

"The Ubermensch? S-s-superman?" I stuttered, backing away from him to the far side of the path and collapsing onto the forest floor. Nearly hysterical now, I covered my face with my hands and started to laugh.

"I'm going crazy…or maybe I passed out back there at the ledge…though the pot idea has merit…I must be stoned…"

"Shh…you're not crazy…*Catherine*…" he whispered, his voice now originating from a few feet to my left. He said my *name*, and I melted. I peeked out from under my ravaged palms to see him sitting quietly against a tree, now on the same side of the path as me. I hadn't heard his footfalls. I should have heard his footfalls. I shouldn't be hearing any of this…

He contemplated me with a deep sadness. A scrape slashed across his rugged jaw, and his forehead was smeared with dirt. My eyes took all of this in, but finally took refuge on the familiar sword tattoo on his arm. I had only seen the tip of it on the bus that first day of school, but now the entire tattoo was visible. A pair of unfurled wings flanked the sword, and the words "St. Michael" were inked across its hilt. It was intricate. It was beautiful.

I squeezed my eyes shut and shook my head violently. I had either lost my mind, or he was some kind of ghost. Both options sent my pulse spiraling upward. I took an explorative breath. Mostly clear. I might not be able to run, but I could still walk out of here. I pushed myself up off of the cold ground.

"Wait...*please*..." he pleaded.

My jaw twitched, but I bent down and picked up my music player from the path, brushed it off and scrolled to a new song, all the while keeping my back to the place where he had been sitting.

When I started to walk away, he shouted, "Would you stay if I told you I *was* Superman?"

I stopped, stood up straight and looked up at the fast darkening pine ceiling. His voice had translocated to a spot somewhere in front of me.

"*Are* you Superman?" My voice trembled.

There was a beat of silence and then from just a few feet in front of me, "No."

I looked up into his wavering face and saw a glint in his eyes and a grin spreading across his full lips, which almost immediately began to fade. He looked away. My breath caught in my throat. I remembered that look.

"Michael?" I whispered.

He nodded, but remained silent, a pensive look flooding his eyes. He shifted his weight from foot to foot. It was almost as if he was more afraid of what I might do next than I was of him. I reached out with tentative fingers toward the front of his black sleeveless shirt, and he stopped moving and held very still, but I lost my nerve and pulled my hand back just shy of the cloth. I looked at his tattoo again.

"Are you...are you from God?" I asked. As soon as the question left my lips, I wanted to pull it back. It sounded so childish. He screwed his brows together, confused, and then he too glanced down at his tattoo, but his eyes were as hard as flint. He tilted his head to the side, his expression dark.

"No," he said bitterly.

I backed up, chilled by his tone then realized night was falling fast, and soon I wouldn't be able to see my hand in front of my face.

"Catherine—"

"I have to go."

Why was I telling him that? Why didn't I just leave? Well, for one thing, he was standing in the middle of the path, blocking the only way out. Whether he was a hallucination or some kind of ghost, I should be able to walk through him, right? Or I could just walk around him. Yeah, that was a better idea. I took a few steps to my right, and he moved to block my path. I took a few steps to the left, and he stepped in front of me again. I swung my arms, determined to plow through him, but skidded to a stop at the last second.

"Wait! Just…I need to know if I'm dead, really dead," he said, backing up and giving me some space. I paused to consider his question, incredulous. How could he not know whether or not he was dead? How could he not know after his horrific fall? Not to mention the fact that his body, if that's what you'd call it, was not like anything I'd ever seen before and seemed to shift and flicker according to the whim of some invisible wind.

"Catherine…*please*…" His outline was becoming less distinct as the descending night robbed my eyes of their ability to see the contrast between him and his surroundings. What could I say? I opened my mouth to speak, but my emotions welled up, and my eyes began to swim. I had to clench my jaw for a moment and fight for control before I could answer.

"I watched you fall, Michael. I watched as your blood….it was…" My voice cracked, and I pointed back down the path and cried, "I was on the ledge back there! I saw it all!"

"I know. I'm sorry," he said quietly. How the hell did he know what I'd seen? Had he really seen me on the ledge as I had suspected on the day he died? I took another step backward and focused my eyes safely on the ground again while I shook my head back and forth in disbelief. It wasn't possible.

"So, I really am, like…dead?" he asked again. "I saw this movie once where they thought this guy was dead, only he wasn't, and then his spirit goes off and…and…then there was this other movie about a demon that took over someone's body and forced their spirit out." He spoke rapidly as he tried to explain why he thought there might still be hope for him. He took a few anxious steps toward me, and I took a few more steps back.

I hadn't seen those movies. This was insane. But if he really thought he might still be alive, maybe that's why he was still here? Because he didn't believe he was dead? That pretty much summed up the basic plot of a lot of ghost stories I knew. He just needed to come to terms with the truth, and then he could go to heaven and be at peace.

I took a deep breath and looked him in the eye. "You're dead, Michael," I said flatly. "I went to your wake. I touched your hand…" My voice broke again, remembering, and I lost my resolve.

He turned abruptly away from me, strode several paces up the path and then stopped, his fists clenched at his sides. "I'm such a fucking dumbass! After all these years…after I had finally found…I had to go and fuck it all up by getting myself…" He turned and glared at me. "And for what? For this?" He gestured wildly around at the forest. "What am I supposed to do now? Is this it? Here's your prize for finally *believing*: a nice forest home and an occasional conversation with a girl who thinks she's stoned? Congratulations!"

His violent outburst scared me. Maybe I just needed to give him a little emotional shove in the right direction, and he would go away.

"Didn't you see some kind of light? Aren't you supposed to follow a light?" I suggested in a very small voice.

He laughed derisively. "Oh yeah! A light! How could I be so stupid? Sure! I saw a light while I was lying at the bottom of the cliff, feeling as if a Mack truck had landed on my chest and steel spikes had been crushed through my ass." He paced back and forth like a caged tiger. "It was up on the ridge top opposite me. It was as bright as the sun! I thought, well shit, that must be the Angel of God calling me home!" He turned back to me with his eyes blazing. "But I told him to go screw himself! I had just found my home! I had done what *He* wanted! I wasn't *finished* yet!" He paused and stared off into the fading pines, breathing hard, and then cried out in anguished frustration.

The look he saw in my eyes when he finally turned back around must have betrayed the overwhelming fear that had settled into my taut body, because the fire in his eyes faded.

"I must have passed out," he went on softly, almost to himself. "I don't know for how long, but one minute I was lying on my back, feeling my body growing colder and colder while my vision faded, the next minute I was alone on the bank of the river, and my body was gone." His jaw quivered, and he clenched his teeth together. "I couldn't even see myself. I was just...*there*. You can't imagine what that felt like. I was totally...lost. I'm not stupid. I figured I was dead."

His face grew hard again, but he kept his voice steady and pointed an accusing finger down the path toward the ledge. "I've heard the stories about the light. I've seen the fucking movies. So, I willed myself to the top of the ridge where I had seen the blinding light while I died, and do you know what I found?"

I shook my head, but I knew what he was going to say.

"I found *you*. I found the light reflecting off your telescope before you shoved it into your bag and left. That's it. When you left, I was alone. No one could see me. No one could hear..." his voice cracked and he pressed his lips together in a hard line and shook his head disgustedly.

My heart broke for him. He'd needed an Angel and instead he'd found only me. "I'm sorry," I whispered.

He didn't answer.

At that moment, I realized the sun had set, and it was my turn to be lost. My eyes widened as I tried to make out the path in front of me, but all I could see was a barely discernable wall of tree trunks receding into blackness on all sides. Michael had faded into the darkness.

"I have to go," I said, stepping uncertainly forward only to stop and hold my hands out in front of me. Darkness pressed in on my eyeballs, and I shivered. With the setting of the sun, the temperature was dropping like a rock, and my fall jacket couldn't keep up with the cold that was creeping through it.

"Come on," Michael said. "Let's get you out of here before you freeze your ass off." From the sound of his voice, he was now only a few inches in front of me, and an overwhelming wave of citrus and pine curled around my face and mingled with my hair. I stepped back, afraid, stumbling over a branch in the path.

"Wh…what is that cologne you're wearing?"

"Cologne?"

"Every time you come near me I smell pine trees and oranges and…" I sniffed the air. "It smells clean."

He was silent for a moment, thinking.

"Huh," he finally said. Then he sounded amused. "I guess that just confirms I'm still wearing everything I had on when I died—the clothes, the shoes—one shoe anyway. I guess it's better than smelling moldy or rotten or—"

"But what is—"

"It's Higher," he said, and the fragrance washed over me again as he moved closer. "Shawn, that little freak, shoplifted it from the Christian Dior counter at the mall and doused me in it the morning I…" He let his voice trail off, then from farther up the path, he said, "Come on."

"I can't see you anymore," The dense cover of the pines was almost as effective as a window shade at blocking out the light. I was beginning to panic.

"Follow my voice, and I'll show you the way," he said impatiently. I had to be dreaming because that was what the voice said when I was lost in the woods in the nightmare I'd had the night he died. Only that voice had been softer, more soothing. "Walk forward," he instructed from right in front of me.

"How can you see? It's black as a freaking cave out here."

He didn't answer for a moment, and then he murmured, "I can't really *see* in the dark, I don't think. It's more like I'm part of my sur-roundings now. Like, I can feel where the trees and the edges of the path are. At night, it's kind of hard for me to know where I end and the things around me begin."

I nodded, but had no idea what he meant. Then I realized he couldn't see the nod and started to say I understood, but he interrupt-ed me.

"I can feel your face," he whispered. His faint fragrance brushed past me, and I felt heat rush to my cheeks as I blushed. "I felt that, too." I heard a muffled laugh.

"I'm glad you think this is so funny!" I blurted out. "Just start talking so I can follow your dead ass out of here." Shit, I shouldn't have said that. He didn't say anything right away, and I worried that he'd left, and I was alone in the dark.

"Are you still there?" I whispered, feeling foolish.

"What should I say?" He sounded like he was still grinning.

"Just sing or something." That would eliminate the need to keep up my end of this ludicrous conversation. Silence. When he wasn't talking, I felt vulnerable. My ears picked up the noises of small animals moving about in the woods and the wind pushing the branches along in the breeze above. I remembered the yellow eyes in the park bathroom, my childhood nightmares...

"Michael?"

"I'm thinking." I tried to wait patiently. "Remember how important song choice is," he said, teasing me with the mantra from *American Idol.*

"Oh, please," I grumbled.

"Okay, got it." I raised my eyebrows, waiting. "Patience," he said from a little farther up the path. When he began to sing his voice was quiet and hesitant, but pure.

> *"In the jungle, the mighty jungle, The Lion Sleeps Tonight*
> *In the jungle, the mighty jungle, The Lion Sleeps Tonight"*

A smile broke out on my lips, and he stopped singing and said, "Felt that, too."

"Shut up and sing!" I snapped.

"Is that supposed to make sense?" he asked, moving farther away. I didn't answer.

> *"Wim-o-weh, wim-o-weh,*
> *"Wim-o-weh, wim-o-weh"*

His voice moved farther and farther away, and I obediently followed it. I walked through the cold scents of the pine trees, damp leaves and his cologne. I think I could have followed that even if he had remained silent.

"Near the village, the peaceful village, The Lion Sleeps Tonight
Near the village, the quiet village, The Lion Sleeps Tonight"

He paused and warned, "Feel ahead with your toe to avoid that branch. Okay…um…where was I?"
"Hush my…" I filled in for him.
"Right."

"Hush my darling, don't fear my darling, the lion sleeps tonight…"

Another warm blush rose in my cheeks, and he stifled another laugh, "Maybe I'll stick to the first two verses?"
"Um, sure," I nodded, my face flushing hotter.

"In the jungle, the mighty jungle, The Lion Sleeps Tonight
In the jungle, the mighty jungle, The Lion Sleeps Tonight"

Progress was slow, and I shivered almost nonstop, but at least while listening to his voice, I forgot my fear of the dark. The cloudbank had cleared by the time I left the woods, and I could see now by the light of the gibbous moon. He stopped at the edge of the woods, the moonlight reflecting off his wavering form, and settled down on a fallen tree trunk. Out here in the open, the wind was stronger, and I hugged my arms around me for warmth.

"Um, thanks," I murmured, and backed up into the field toward the car. He clasped his hands together and kicked at a water-stained newspaper that was tangled in the tall grass in front of him. His foot had no effect on the paper or the grass, and he cursed under his breath.

"I can't go any farther," he said, sounding defeated, and then his eyebrows knitted together. "Will you come back?"

"Michael…" I didn't know how I'd feel tomorrow. My grip on the real world was slipping and that scared the hell out of me. He looked down at his folded hands.

"Whatever…" he said, his voice tight. "Do what you want."

Then he faded away into the cold, windy night.

Part Two
Michael

Chapter 9
Fight or Flight

LIKE A GHOST image that lingers after you look at something bright and then look away, it took a moment for my eyes to adjust to the fact that Michael was gone. I blinked a few times then the leftover adrenaline ripped through my veins, and I shook from head to toe.

"Oh my God," I whispered.

Without thinking, I stood up and stumbled through the tall grass over to the fallen tree trunk where I'd seen him last and looked behind it and then all around it. There was no one there, but I could still smell the woodsy clean scent of Higher.

"Oh…my…*God*…"

I dropped down onto the damp log and leaned forward on my elbows, my mind totally blown, then reached out with my toe and nudged the soggy newspaper that Michael had tried to kick free. My lips turned up slightly at the thought of him, still here in this world, and then a panic-edged breath hitched in my chest in response to the same thought.

I pulled the cold night air in through my nose, reveling in his lingering scent, but my stomach flipped as it occurred to me that it was the same fragrance I'd smelled outside the park bathroom last Saturday. Had J.C. been right about someone looking out for me? Had it been Michael? Had he been trying to warn me?

My thoughts were interrupted by the muffled buzzing of my cell phone, and I dug with cold clumsy fingers through my bag. I knew who it was, and I knew I was in for it.

"Hold on…" I called into the bag. Damn it! I knew if I didn't answer before it stopped ringing, I might as well kiss my car privileges goodbye. My hand connected with the phone, and I bobbled it to my ear, mumbling breathlessly, "Umm…sorry…lost track of time…on my way home…"

And I was. I was already jogging across the wet spongy field toward the Demon.

~~~

The demon and the Guardian watched the girl go, an icy, invisible wall between them, a forced suspension of hostilities. The demon took a step away from him, redirecting his focus from the girl to the Ghost Boy who had reappeared on the gravel path at the edge of the soggy field. With a pitifully weak power signature, the boy reached his fingertips out over the grass and then snatched them back as if he'd been burned. He took angry aim with his foot at the gravel, but thought better of it and shoved his hands deep into his frayed pockets instead. Then he lifted his eyes and watched her go, too.

The demon turned away from the Ghost Boy and back toward the girl's Guardian, his black eyes alight with amusement. "How long do you think it will take?" he asked.

But the Guardian wasn't paying attention to him. A rarity. His focus had also shifted from the girl to the Ghost Boy. It remained there…lost and far away. The demon cleared his throat, and the Guardian blinked, his eyes instantly going sharp and steely. He caught sight of the tip of a thorny, black tongue slipping back into the demon's beautiful mouth.

The demon nodded toward the girl, who was already halfway across the cold field. "How long do you think it will take me to break her?"

~~~

My mom wrapped her arms around my waist in a frantic hug when I got home, and then she stepped back, alarmed.

"You're soaking wet, and—" Her eyes, sharp as lasers, scanned me from head to toe. "What happened to your hands? Did you fall?" She paused and then added suspiciously, "What were you doing?" The eyebrows were up. I was toast.

Claire stepped around the corner and leaned against the wall. I'm sure she enjoyed watching me squirm after years of being the one in the hot seat, but she knew if she wanted to keep seeing Jones, she'd better keep her comments to herself. Cici was on the blue stairs stroking Lucky like a worry bead. His flame-colored fur stuck up haphazardly after each rub with static electricity.

Stupid...I should have at least *tried* to clean myself up before coming in the house. I looked down and surveyed the damage. My jeans from the knees down were covered in mud, my elbows and hands were a mess, and I could only imagine what my butt looked like. No, it wouldn't have mattered.

"It was slippery," I mumbled. "Just...give me a sec to clean up." What could I say? I was sitting on the edge of a cliff, smoking my dying grandmother's cigarettes when my dead friend stopped by to visit me? I don't think so.

Dad sighed. "Go. We'll deal with this later. Right now we have a birthday to celebrate."

"Well," my mom huffed, "you know your driving privileges are—"

"I *know*, Mom. I'm really, *really* sorry."

She nodded and waved to Cici. "Go help your sister get cleaned up." Relieved to be dismissed so easily, I fled up the stairs with Cici on my heels.

I went straight to the bathroom and stripped off my wet clothes, then wrapped a thick towel around me and tucked the corner in over my chest. Cici arrived with clean clothing and began rooting around under the counter for a washcloth while I filled the sink with water.

"So," she whispered, "what *really* happened to you tonight?" Avoiding her eyes, I stuck my hands under the faucet and winced as the warm water sprayed over the mud-caked cuts on my palms and wrists. Forgot about those.

"Hmm?" she asked as she hunted for a bottle of hydrogen

peroxide. Remaining silent while I collected my thoughts, I let the basin fill and gently waved my hands back and forth in the shallow pool to soften the dirt. A fine cloud of mud rose up around them, turning the water black. But as I watched, the mud tangled together like gnarled, dirt-clogged roots. They wrapped themselves around my fingers. Startled, I yanked my hands out of the water and squeezed my eyes shut. But the sink was filled with only muddy water when I reopened them.

Rattled, I took a steadying breath and then patted my hands clean with the washcloth, wincing again. There were several angry red scratches on my palms and wrists and a crusty oblong burn mark where my hand had put out the Camel.

Cici pointed to it. "What happened there?"

I grabbed the bottle of peroxide out of her hand and poured a generous stream over each palm. The scratches and burn fizzed and hissed as the solution made contact. "I don't want to talk about it," I answered brusquely. "Okay?"

"Okay, but..."

"And it's my birthday. So...I shouldn't have to talk about anything I don't want to talk about, right?" I started to wrap my palms with gauze.

"Sure." She nodded uncertainly. "See you downstairs."

༄ ༅

Eating birthday cake with my family after my surreal evening was beyond strange. Everything had taken on an aura of newness, sharp edged and overly bright. It took a herculean effort to stay focused on the table talk and smile in all the right places. But when my mom began to tell the story of how I almost died the night I was born—for like the *billionth* time—I completely zoned out, instead replaying the bits and pieces of my conversation with Michael over and over again in my head. I was glad when I could drop the charade and go to bed. I was exhausted.

≈

A pale quarter moon hung high in the jeweled night sky. I lay on the ground with cold dew from the grass seeping through the back of my fall jacket and jeans and swept my hand out to the side. My fingers broke the moonlit dewdrops on the tips of the grass, leaving a dark trail in their wake.

The world tipped crazily as I sat up and took stock of my surroundings. A few feet to my left, a deep pool reflected the moon and the stars on its glassy surface, and I could hear crickets and frogs calling to each other. If they weren't afraid of its depths, neither was I.

I rolled up onto my hands and knees and crept forward, parting the tall grass near the pond's boggy edge, sighing with relief. Only moon and stars and… Michael's face.

He tilted his scraped chin up toward me, his eyes filled with emotion.

"Will you come back?" he whispered.

My heart leapt into my throat. "No! I can't!" I cried. "I'm…"

≈

I startled awake in my own bed, murmuring, "…afraid."

The glowing numbers on the alarm clock read 5:00 a.m. I hugged my blanket closer and tried to go back to sleep, but my thoughts would not be turned from the face in the pool, from his request.

Would I go back? Would anyone in their right mind go back? Not likely. What if Michael was followed by legions of less benevolent spirits? Spirits like that thing that laughed at me in the nightmare I'd had the day Michael died. Spirits like the ones that stalked my sleep when I was little. A cold sweat broke out on my forehead, and without thinking I bolted out of bed and made for the safety of the light in the hall. Yeah. Sixteen years old, and I was still running from nightmares.

Clinking sounds drifted up from the kitchen. My mind flashed a warning: Mom. Avoid at all costs. But a remembered comment led me down the stairs instead. It was cold, and I grabbed the afghan from the back of the sofa, wrapped it around my shoulders and wandered into the kitchen.

She was standing at the sink in her robe. On the counter, a few pieces of medical equipment were laid out on a paper towel to dry. As I moved closer, she was startled, then seeing it was only me, raised a sudsy hand out of the basin and wiped her flushed forehead with her wrist.

"This is a surprise," she said, opening the drain to let the sudsy water out. She didn't bring up the car, so I guessed that lecture was scheduled for later.

"Couldn't sleep."

"Want to talk about it?" She pulled out the telescoping sprayer to rinse out the sink.

I fidgeted. "Um…I wanted to know what you meant when you said something about trouble in Michael's family…you know, the night before Michael's funeral."

She finished rinsing out the sink and stared at her reflection in the dark window. "Do you want some tea?" she asked.

She knew I didn't like the bitter tea that she liked, and seeing the look on my face, she reassured me, "I have some vanilla chai that we can sprinkle with cinnamon sugar." That sounded okay, so I sat down in a chair, pulled my bare feet up off the cold tile floor and tucked them under me to keep them warm.

"Michael…" she murmured as she rummaged around in the cupboard. "I'll never forget the look on your face when I asked you about that ring. It was like you had just found out you were Cinderella and were headed off to the castle to live." She filled two mugs with water and popped them into the microwave. "I knew as soon as I saw it that it was real gold and aquamarine."

I smiled involuntarily at the memory.

"It *was* beautiful," she acknowledged. "But it obviously wasn't Michael's to give away." The microwave beeped, and she took out the mugs and dunked the tea bags. She placed one in front of me and held up her hand. "Now, wait a few minutes. Then we'll add the milk and sugar."

I leaned down and let the hot, sweet steam warm my cold nose.

"When you went upstairs with Michael that day, Janine—that was his mom's name—and I visited for a while. She was incredibly grateful to us for returning the ring. You see, Michael's dad, Aidan, gave her that ring when Michael was born. They'd tried to have a child for years and lost four babies to miscarriages before he came along." She got up to get the milk and cinnamon sugar, added them to the tea, then instructed with an expectant smile, "Taste."

I took a sip. It was good, *really* good.

"Thanks, Mom."

She nodded her approval. "Michael was their miracle baby. But a few months after you gave the ring back, Michael's father died, and his mom—she just couldn't cope. You'd think Michael would have given her reason enough to—" Her eyes clouded over, and she took a sip of her tea and then glanced away. I didn't remember anyone telling me his father had died.

"What happened to his mom?" I prompted quietly.

"Drugs," she said, just one word and no more. Then the little bell that my mom had placed next to Mina's bed rang, meaning she was having trouble breathing and needed to be suctioned.

My mom jumped up from the table, but before she went upstairs, she said, "I'm so sorry about what happened to him. He deserved better."

෨෪

My dad woke me up Saturday morning by throwing open the curtains above the sofa and letting the bright October sun beat its way through my eyelids. Then he cheerfully offered me a deal. My car privileges were suspended for a month, but I could subtract a week for each car I washed. Three cars. Three weeks. That meant I was only grounded from the car for one week. I could have done worse.

By two o'clock, I was finished and had passed inspection. The worst part had been cleaning out everything from under the seats and figuring out what to do with it all. On the positive side, I'd had several uninterrupted hours to think about what had happened the night before and decide what I wanted to do next.

For starters, I decided there was no way I could talk to anyone about seeing Michael's ghost without incurring some serious head shrinking. Plus, until I could drive again, I couldn't go back to the woods even if I wanted to without someone coming with me, which was definitely out of the question. In the meantime, I planned to keep busy and hope that I could forget about Michael, that I could convince myself it had all been a bad dream.

⚜

Meri grabbed my bags as soon as I stepped into her foyer on Saturday night and started to paw through them, intent on playing her favorite game: dress up Cate. I kicked off my shoes, and let my eyes wander around the house.

The two-story foyer was immaculate. There were no dust bunnies in the corners or piles of shoes on the stairs. In the great room to my left, the baby grand piano that Meri and Leo practiced on for hours every day was polished, and there were faint lines on the plush ivory carpet confirming it had been vacuumed recently. The house smelled good too, like lemon furniture polish and lavender candles. The fragrance blend was a welcome change from the ascetic scent of disinfectant that had pervaded our house in the last week.

When Meri finished rumpling half my wardrobe, she looked up at me and pouted. "I told you to bring something cute to wear."

"My T-shirts are cute," I countered. "It's only the guys coming over."

She stuck out her bottom lip. I had to remind myself that it was more about the process of getting dressed up than actually showing it off that made Meri's day.

"You can do my hair and face, and I'll even wear some of your jewelry if you want," I promised, trying to appease her.

"'Kay," she smiled.

⚜

Grace and the guys showed up after that, and we settled in for a night of pizza and movies. Spencer was still on crutches and was planning to start physical therapy the next week, hoping he'd be ready for the upcoming basketball season. He asked me discreetly if I thought Cici might want to work out with him. He wanted me to talk to her. I rolled my eyes.

"That's low, Spence. Pulling the injured card," I peppered his face with popcorn. He managed to catch one of the kernels in his mouth before giving me his puppy dog "please" face. I shook my head.

Around midnight, Mrs. DiMaro came downstairs and booted the guys out, forcing us to watch an extended version of the "Meri and Finn Goodbye Kiss."

"You guys are sick," groaned Grace, but I couldn't help but be a little jealous. I had never kissed anyone like that. Sure, there had been Jason, and he'd been a good kisser, but no way had he loved me—not like Finn loved Meri anyway.

"Come on," I prodded, dragging Meri away from Finn and shoving her toward the basement. "Let's get our stuff set up for bed." As we clomped down the stairs with our blankets and pillows in tow, I was happy my plan was working. I hadn't thought of Michael all evening and as long as we kept talking, I could continue to stay in my happy place. I really wanted to stay in my happy place.

♒

I was on my hands and knees staring hard into the deep, moonlit pool with my hair hanging loosely like dripping seaweed around my face. Something was gripping the back of my neck, preventing me from moving. It wanted me to see what was in the water.

My neck was stiff, my throat burned, and I felt tremendous pressure behind my eyes and forehead like I'd been there for a while. But that was nothing compared to the vice-like clamp that gripped my gut when I saw Michael's face. No longer peaceful, his eyes were filled with sharp, armor-piercing terror. Billowing up from the bottom of the pool underneath him was a dark inky cloud, and tendrils of thick knobby roots were forming and wrapping around his legs and torso. As the black cloud gradually spread outward and upward, Michael's eyes grew wider.

"No!" he shouted. "Please, Catherine! Come back!" He reached for me,

his bubbled words floating to the surface, and then he was yanked down by the roots into the blackness. Swallowed whole.

"*No! Oh God, Michael! I'll come back! Please!*"

※※

Then someone was shaking me, and I snapped my eyes open to find myself tangled up in my sleeping bag, covered in sweat with two pairs of eyes staring worriedly back at me from the amber darkness of Meri's basement.

"Cate! We've been trying to wake you for the last five minutes!"

"I need to go back," I told them. My throat hurt like hell. My eyes drifted closed again. "I'll come back."

"What's she talking about?"

"Must have been a bad dream."

Their words held no meaning for me. All I wanted was the soft blanket of sleep that descended. As it settled into place, a voice whispered, *shh…I'm so sorry…just rest now…*

※※

The next morning, it felt as if the whole world had shifted, and my fear for my own sanity—my own safety—suddenly paled next to my fear for Michael. The dream had been too vivid to ignore, and the fact that my neck still ached, my throat still burned, and my eyes were bloodshot—as if I actually *had* been upside down—only made me believe the dream more. Something was trying to tell me that Michael was in trouble. I needed to go back to Lewis Woods. I needed to go back today. The need was so overwhelming that I could hardly think of anything else.

"I have to go," I announced as my friends were sitting down for breakfast. Mrs. DiMaro, who had just served up a platter of blueberry pancakes and fruit in her sunlit kitchen, looked annoyed by my lack of appreciation.

"Why? What's the matter?" Meri wanted to know. I glanced toward the door, anxious to leave. She pointed to the breakfast on the table. "Don't you want to—"

"No," I answered shortly and then reached for the excuse I never thought I'd use. "I…um…forgot to bring my inhaler and…" It was perfect. I faked a cough into my hand then looked at Leo, who had just filled a plate.

"Can you take me home, Leo?" He looked down at his food and then at me, exasperated, but he set the plate down and motioned toward the door.

It was cooler than the day before, but the sun was still shining. As the station wagon rolled down the driveway, Leo asked, "You okay?"

I nodded and then stared out the passenger side window. The last person I wanted to talk to about any of this was Leo.

"*Okay*," he said, and left it at that.

Only music sounded in the car the rest of the way home, a song called "Mirrors" by a local band named House of Cards, which was odd. I'd never heard any of their stuff played on the radio before.

❧❧

My dad and sisters had gone to Mass without me, and I peeked in through the crack in Mina's bedroom door to check on her. Her chest jerked up and down erratically as she struggled for air, even in her sleep. Her coloring was gray. In the room next to hers, my mom was passed out diagonally across her king-size bed, exhausted from another long night.

I briefly admired her strength and stamina, but for the first time I wondered if my mom had chosen the right path. Keeping Mina alive took all of her time and energy, leaving little room for anyone or anything else. There were nice places nearby where Mina would be well taken care of, and I couldn't understand why my mom had taken this massive burden onto her shoulders alone.

Back down in the kitchen, I paced back and forth, absorbed by my own problem. I knew I couldn't ask my mom or dad or Claire to drive me to the woods; they wouldn't want me hiking alone. I could have asked Leo, but I figured I'd already used up my goodwill allotment from him for the day. Think. I needed someone who could drive. Someone who didn't mind going outside the rules and keeping secrets. Only one name came to mind, and I would have to swallow my pride to call him.

Jason.

Shit. I hated the thought of going to him for help. It was the same thing I had despised Kara for last summer, but I couldn't think of anyone else.

My stomach growled pitifully, and I grabbed a strawberry Pop Tart out of the kitchen cupboard and shoved it in the toaster. Then I pulled out my cell. Despite being in some classes together, Jason and I had hardly talked since the first day of school, and I was nervous about calling him. Then I realized how ridiculous I was being. Here I was, planning to head into the woods alone in search of a *ghost*, and I was afraid to call an ordinary guy I had known let's just say *pretty well* last summer. Stupid. I punched his number into my cell.

"Hey, Cate. What's up?" he said. I smiled at his usual greeting. The Pop Tart bounced out of the toaster, and I pulled it out and tossed it onto the table before it could burn my fingers.

"Just wondered how you were doing."

"Fine..." said Jason. I knew he knew there was more. I imagined his eyes narrowing with interest while he tried to puzzle out what I really wanted and why. He was smart, but I knew my motive was safely locked behind closed doors that read: "Thoughts of the seriously insane only." He wouldn't guess I fit into that category.

"And Kara?"

"She's great!" He paused and then laughed. "I actually might have to thank you for pushing me in the pool. She's very...*attentive*, now."

I rolled my eyes. I was sure she was.

"Um...Jason? Can I have a ride somewhere this afternoon?"

"That depends."

Crap. "On what?"

"Did you get my new cell yet?"

Oh right. "Still working on it...the funding that is."

"Well…" he paused, and I held my breath. "If you *are* working on it, then I guess I can give you a ride. Pick you up in fifteen minutes?

"Sounds great."

I tested the Pop Tart with the tip of my finger before picking it up, took a bite and raced quietly upstairs to get changed. I threw on a pair of old but respectable jeans, a long-sleeved shirt, a sweater, and then ran a comb through my silky straight hair. Meri had done a great job on it.

I packed my tote with the usual necessities and then started back down the stairs only to pull up short when it occurred to me that I might need one more thing. I didn't know why it was important, but I raced back up to my room, dug it out of its hiding place and shoved it in my pocket. Then I dashed off a note to Mom and Dad, telling them I was going for a drive with Jason, laced up my hiking boots, grabbed my coat and headed out into the cool fall sunshine.

⚬❧

When Jason turned off the Audi's engine in the parking lot of Lewis Woods, he surveyed the muddy autumn field and the forest beyond. "So…you want me to just take off now? As soon as you get out of the car?"

I nodded, not wanting to give anything else away.

"And this is because you want to do some reflecting for one of your club projects?" His eyes lingered on my face, and then he absently pulled down the sun visor mirror to check his dark hair, which was always freshly cut and perfect. He ran his fingers through the front to muss it up. I had forgotten how much I'd liked to do that for him.

"Right," I confirmed.

"And you didn't ask your parents or your sister because…?"

"I missed you?" Even as a partial truth, I knew that wouldn't fly.

"Nice try," he said with a touch of sarcasm.

"Look, Jason, my parents…well…they wouldn't think it was such a good idea for me to be off hiking through the woods alone. You know my parents," I reminded him. "They worry."

Both of Jason's parents were successful plastic surgeons, and he and his sister spent most of their time on their own. It had always amused him when my mom gave me the third degree every time we went anywhere together.

He rolled his eyes and smiled. "Yes. I remember. So I guess I'm springing you from the Big House, then?" I smiled back, relieved.

"Something like that. Can you be back in two hours?"

He leaned in. "Sure." Last summer, this would have been the point where we kissed—for a while—but instead, I ignored the electricity that was building in the air between us. I turned my face away first and reached for the door handle to let myself out.

"Um…okay. Thanks," I said.

"Cate?" he called after me. "You know you can call me if you ever need anything. I meant what I said. We're still friends."

"I know, Jason. Same."

As he drove off, I turned and faced the forest, mulling over the fact that my parents had no idea where I was. A small voice inside my head chastised me for lying to them. *You should call them*, it urged. *At least tell them where you are.*

You're stalling, I shot back.

I knew it. I was stalling. Everything visible in the landscape before me—the field, the autumn leaves, the white fence around the riding ring—they were all painted bright by the glorious October sun, everything but the pines. They were the only dark point on the horizon, and that's where I was headed. I was scared. I won't deny it. But I knew Michael needed me, and I ordered my feet to move.

Chapter 10
Something to Wrap Your Head Around

As I walked into the mouth of the forest, I studied every shadow and breathed in deep, but I detected only the cool scents of pine trees and autumn air. I don't know what I expected. That Michael would immediately emerge out of thin air and welcome me back?

Doubting my sanity, I moved deeper into the woods. Then I remembered my promise to God during my last visit, that if I made it out the woods alive with my sanity intact, I would never venture into them alone again. I smiled ruefully as it occurred to me that breaking a promise to God was probably not the best way to begin a ghost hunt.

"Sorry…" I whispered, letting my gaze drift from tree to tree—and then I smelled it: Higher. It was faint, but unmistakable. He was here.

My heart sped up, and the adrenaline rush that followed poured an emotion into my veins somewhere between sheer terror and pure ecstasy, not unlike the feeling you get as you crest the first hill of the Millennium Force at Cedar Point Amusement Park.

"I know you're here," I whispered, and then I waited and listened. Nothing.

I walked farther down the path, and the scent seemed to follow me, still faint, but intoxicating. When I reached the fork in the path where the pine forest ended, I looked down the autumn leaf-covered trail that descended to the river and then up toward the overlook, unsure which way to go.

"Michael…" I whispered. His name tickled the roof of my mouth.

Nothing.

Crap, how do you call a ghost anyway? What could I possibly offer to entice him to show himself to me?

I took the path up and out of the pines, and the wind picked up as I approached the clearing above the gorge overlook. The view was bright and clear under the turquoise October sky, but the wind had blown away the ethereal fragrance I had grown accustomed to over the last mile. I felt a stab of fear in the pit of my stomach.

"Please don't go," I whispered.

Nothing.

"Stay. *Please*," I said louder.

Nothing.

Then I shouted, "I'm here to help you, you stupid dumbass!" My voice echoed over the brink and back like a boomerang.

Nothing.

I dug into my pocket, letting my fist close around the small object I'd felt compelled to bring. I knew why now. I stretched out my arm in front of me and opened my hand to reveal the golden plastic ring with its blue bead sparkling on my palm.

"You still owe me!" I shouted into the wind.

Nothing.

"You still owe me," I whispered.

"I can't believe you hung on to that…*Catherine*…" His voice was a sigh that disappeared into the wind as he whispered my name. A shiver ran down my spine. I let my eyes fall closed and lifted my chin to answer. Then the stillness was broken by the sound of a couple of elderly hikers coming up the path.

They shot me curious, anxious looks as they rounded the corner obviously having heard my shouting. I eyed the hikers impatiently and then leaned casually against a tree and stared at them, unabashed, sending thoughts such as "Get the hell out of here," in their direction. They stopped briefly at the overlook, glancing frequently back over their shoulders at me. Then, growing uncomfortable under my unwavering gaze, hurried back down the path in the direction they had come.

I knew Michael was here, and my heart pounded like mad at the thought of seeing him, talking with him, but we needed to be somewhere more private, somewhere I could speak freely without looking like a raving lunatic. Having no idea whether or not he would listen to me, I turned my head to the side and whispered conspiratorially, "Follow me." Then I turned my back on the overlook, stepped off the path, and headed deep into the forest.

When I reached a tiny clearing surrounded by tightly packed trees, I dropped down onto a moss-covered log to wait. The midafternoon sunlight penetrating the canopy reflected off the bronze, pine-needled floor, casting everything it touched in sepia tones.

I spent the first few minutes craning my neck from side to side, hoping to catch a glimpse of him the instant he materialized—*if* he materialized. After waiting for a while, my heartbeat slowed, and I looped the little ring onto my pinky finger and spun it around, watching the scattered points of light it threw move in an arc across the woodland floor. I don't know how long the ring entertained me before I realized I was no longer alone.

I lifted my eyes slowly and found him sitting cross-legged on the forest floor with his back against one of the larger pine trees just a few feet in front of me. My heart ached as my gaze trickled down over the cuts and bruises his otherworldly body bore from his fall. He was still wearing his cut-offs, still missing one shoe, and he was studying me unselfconsciously, as if he didn't realize I could see him yet. His wide-set eyes were luminous and deep, like the churning wake of a ship on a north Atlantic morning. When our eyes finally locked, he looked startled, and then a look of profound relief flooded his features.

"I didn't know if you would show yourself to me again," I whispered, afraid that if I spoke too loudly, I might scare him back into the afternoon breeze.

He shook his head slightly, his eyes clouding over. "I wasn't sure if I would make it back," he murmured, and then he looked away, his jaw tensing. His coloring was brighter today in the afternoon light, but he flickered gently against the forest backdrop. He was at once entirely alien and entirely human.

"I don't understand," I said.

He knitted his brows together. "I…um, how to explain it…" He ran his hands through his hair, which still looked uncomfortably damp with the sweat his body had pumped out on that hot summer day he died. "I…" He paused again, looking down at his hands. "Remember how I told you that it's sometimes hard for me to tell where I end and the things around me begin?" He paused, waiting for me to consider that.

I nodded.

"It's getting harder," he said, looking me worriedly in the eyes. "It's like I'm losing myself—like I'm disappearing."

An electric current sliced through my heart as I thought of last night's nightmare. I saw him being dragged under…

"Into darkness?" I prompted, scared of what his response would be. He looked up, surprised, and then leaned forward and gestured with his hands as he answered.

"Yeah…it's like, I watched you come into the forest, but I couldn't stay focused on you." He paused and shook his head, frustrated. "But then I saw you smile, and I felt more…pulled together somehow, more like me. But it wasn't until you held up the ring—that stupid little ring—that I felt entirely here. It was like it gave me something to wrap my head around, to pull me back." His gray eyes were intense as he struggled to help me understand.

"Back from where?"

"I don't know. Nowhere…nothing…" His eyes darkened with fear and confusion. "If you hadn't come back—"

"But I did," I pointed out. A rustling sound caused us both to glance into the woods to see the tail of a chipmunk disappearing into the hollowed-out stump of a tree.

He rubbed his temples with his fingers, thinking. Then his eyes lit up with amusement. "Why'd you come back anyway? I didn't think you believed I was real. I thought you thought you were stoned."

"Yeah, well…those weren't my cigarettes, and when I saw

you Friday, I thought maybe someone had spiked them with pot or something." I stopped there, not wanting to tell him about the nightmare that had warned me to come back. I didn't want to add to his fears. Instead I just said, "You *really* scared the crap out of me."

He pulled his knees up and wrapped his arms around them. The light faded from his eyes. "Do I look that…different?"

I didn't want him to feel worse, but there was no point in denying the obvious. "Pretty much. Yeah," I said. "You sort of, um…waver at the edges a little, and your coloring is kind of…off."

He held his scraped arms up in front of him and turned them over and back. "I don't look faded or wavery to me," he murmured, examining them from every angle. He dropped his arms and raised his eyebrows, his eyes and thoughts refocusing on me. "And what the hell were you doing smoking, Genius? I thought *you* were supposed to be the smart one, smarter than me, anyway." His voice scolded, but his eyes teased. I looked away self-consciously. I didn't want to talk about dying grandmothers either, so I moved off the log and sat closer to him, holding up the gumball ring between us.

"So…you remember?" I asked. His eyes lit up at the sight of it.

"How could I forget? When all those other kids ran screaming to the back of the classroom, you dove after Fang. You sent Sister Patricia's piles of graded spelling papers flying, you know, just like flying all over the place." He waved his hands around his head to illustrate. "You saved him. I had to give you *something.*" Then an incorrigible grin spread across his face. "Though, my mom was pretty pissed at me."

He reached under his shirt and pulled up a washed out gold chain. Threaded onto the delicate chain was the beautiful, though faded, Claddagh ring. But how could that be, when I had seen the little ring safe in a velvet box on the table at his wake? But then I remembered I'd seen him too, in a box that day, and I realized the Claddagh was a ghost, like him.

He fingered the ring carefully and then let it drop back down on top of his shirt, saying, "I always knew it was special to her, but my mom never told me why. And when she died—" He looked away again and then abruptly stood up and turned his back to me.

I was shocked to find out he didn't know that the ring was a celebration of *him*, so I pushed myself up off the prickly ground and stood quietly behind his shoulder.

"Michael…"

He shook his head and shifted his weight from foot to foot, refusing to turn around. The fingers of his left hand were clasped tightly over his sword and Angel wing tattoo, exposing only thin bands of it. His knuckles were white.

"Michael…" I called again, more softly. "Yesterday morning I asked my mom what she knew about you. She told me your parents wanted you so much, that they waited years for you and had almost given up hope that they would ever have a kid. Then, when you were born your dad gave that ring to your mom, because you were his *miracle*."

He reached out his index finger and traced a deep blackened crack in the nearest tree that had been gouged out by a lightning strike. I could smell the scent of the damp bark mingling with the clean fragrance of Higher.

"Hope springs eternal," he murmured, reciting the inscription on the ring from memory. His jaw flexed again, and he added bitterly, "Some miracle." He let his hand drop to his side.

I walked around in front of him and waited until he met my eyes.

"You *are* a miracle," I said. If I believed what our faith taught us, we were all miracles, and I searched my head for proof, then I remembered the malevolent yellow eyes that threatened me last Saturday. "Take last week, for example. If you hadn't been there, I would have been coyote chow or a chew toy at least."

"How did you know?" He leaned back against the tree he'd been studying, bringing his face level with mine.

"Pine trees and oranges," I reminded him. "And clean. I smell it every time you're near me."

"I guess I have Shawn to thank for that," he laughed half-heartedly, bouncing his back against the tree.

"So…what happened? How did you know about the coyote?" I asked.

His face took on a more animated expression, "When I first died, I hid out on the ledge up here, and I sat there without moving for days. I guess I was like in shock or something, and then one night this coyote came right up in front of my face and sniffed me, like she knew I was there. I was so relieved that *something* had noticed me that I started following her around. It was awful before that." He looked down at his feet, bouncing his back restlessly against the tree for a moment before going on. "With her around, I didn't feel so lonely. She seemed to sense my presence and even curled up next to me sometimes."

His eyes darkened. "One night she chased after this bat that couldn't get off the ground, and she got bit. Then when she started to act sick, I felt bad because I couldn't do shit for her. I didn't want her to die, and I didn't want anyone to get hurt." He stepped away from the tree and paced back and forth, agitated.

"That night in the park, I saw her nose her way into the bathroom. See, earlier that day some idiot clean freak mom was like, 'Oh my god, it smells like crap in here,' and then she propped the door open to air it out. Stupid…I figured the coyote was looking for a place to die, so I settled down nearby in the woods to wait her out. Then you and your stupid friends showed up—"

"Hey!"

"Well why the hell didn't they notice when you left to go to the bathroom, huh?" he growled. "Though I did think the whole tiki torch marshmallow thing was kind of cool. I…" His expression turned suddenly thoughtful.

"What?" I backed up and leaned against the lightning strike tree he'd just vacated, enthralled to hear about that night from his point of view.

"Um…" he stopped pacing and gave me a shy grin. "It was kind of like I was invited to your birthday party. Happy Birthday, by the way." I grinned back at him, and it almost seemed normal, almost ordinary, like we were just two friends hanging out on a Sunday afternoon, trying to stay out of trouble.

"Thanks," I said.

"Anyway, when you headed up the path to the bathroom I was like freaking out about what would happen to you if you walked in. The coyote was pretty fucked up by then. I tried shouting at you, but you couldn't hear me, though you did seem to notice something—" He stopped talking and searched my face for confirmation, his eyes filled with curiosity.

"I already told you, I smell Higher every time you're nearby, and it scared the crap out of me. I thought someone was following me," I shuddered, remembering how scared I'd been.

"*I* was following you, Genius," he teased.

"Yeah…well…I know that now, but last Saturday I almost ran *into* the bathroom to get away from whoever it was and then—"

"I sort of tried to block the door," Michael interrupted, "and we…um…overlapped…"

My eyes went wide with shock as I remembered how his scent had resonated through my whole body, blocking out everything else. It almost burned.

"We *overlapped?*"

"Well…it worked didn't it? You didn't go in, right?"

"Michael," I said slowly, "do you have any idea what that felt like?"

He scratched behind his ear, embarrassed. "Yeah…um…it was kind of weird for me too."

"*That's* the understatement of the year. But, I hadn't quite made up my mind to stay out of the bathroom until…" I stopped, trying to remember. Then it came flooding back.

"I had the strangest thought…" I murmured. "I thought, *this is the part in the movie where the dumbass camper*, me in this case, *is attacked by Cletus the Axe-toting Freak*—only I had no idea who the hell Cletus was, and…" I went on for another minute before realizing he'd stopped listening. When I looked up, I saw real terror in his eyes.

Then he started to fade.

"What?" I said quietly.

"H-h-how did you…?" He took a step back. He was fading fast.

"It's *okay*," I reassured him. "See? I'm fine." I could see almost all of the detail in the bark of the tree behind him right through his chest.

"Michael! What's wrong?" I called, but it was like he couldn't hear me. After a few minutes, his coloring started to come back, and he nodded quietly. I wondered what I'd said that scared him so—and he *was* scared, terrified of something—but I let the subject drop. He had enough to worry about.

"Hey," I said. "When did you first figure out who I was that first week of school?"

His eyes regained their focus, and then I think he actually blushed.

"What?" I said.

"Um...okay. Like I was hoping I would see you that morning, the first day of school that is, and that you hadn't moved away. And I was pretty sure it was you when I walked past you on the bus. Your hair *is* kind of signature."

I rolled my eyes, "Thanks."

"Though...it's all limp and flat today. Did you use one of those iron thingies on it?"

"It's called a flat iron," I corrected. I couldn't help grinning.

"Whatever, I like your hair better the other way."

"So you knew for sure it was me when you first saw me on the bus?"

"Um...no. Your friends called you Cate, and I remembered you as Catherine," he admitted. I loved the way he said my name, all drawn out and familiar, like my mom said it, only way less annoyingly.

"What convinced you?"

He blushed again and cleared his throat. "Um, when you fell into my lap, I..."

"You what?"

"Um...snuck a peek down your—"

"You're a pervert! I'm hanging out with a pervert ghost!"

"Wait! No! *Listen!* I was looking for your *ring*, stupid!"

I felt around inside my shirt and pulled out my silver chain. He moved in closer to see my ring, the one that was engraved with the letter "C."

"That one," he said simply, pointing.

Suddenly, I was way too warm. After all these years, he still remembered. It could have been so different. Should have been. But now he was dead and...suddenly dizzy, I bent over with my hands on my knees, overwhelmed by my emotions. He dropped into a crouch beside me.

"Whoa...Catherine..." his voice came at me through a long dark tunnel. "...*Catherine*..." A tear dripped off the tip of my nose and splashed down into the pine needles. Michael lay down with his back on the ground so he could look up into my face.

"Hey..." he said quietly.

"Why did this have to happen to you?" I whispered.

He rolled his head to the side, his brows pulling together as he thought about it. Then he looked back up into my face. "I don't know." Then he reached a battered hand up as if he intended to wipe my tears away, but at that moment another teardrop rolled off my lashes and fell right through his fingers, as if they weren't even there. We both watched as the tear continued its journey downward through his arm and then splashed untouched onto the ground.

Startled, my breath caught in my throat. How had I forgotten so easily what his death really meant? That he wasn't *really* here. That he was trapped somewhere—other. I saw his jaw tense, and the fingers that he'd opened for me tightened back up into a fist.

"No more tears," he said. "None."

I squeezed my eyes shut and wiped them carelessly with the back of my hands. When I opened them again, he was gone. I stood up and whirled around.

"Michael?" I cried out to the empty forest.

His fragrance washed over me, and I stopped spinning.

"I won't come back unless you promise me," he warned. His hard-edged voice seemed to come from everywhere.

I shook my head. "I can't! You deserve—"

"No more tears. Promise me."

"Why?"

He reappeared several yards away. "Catherine..." he pleaded.

"Can't you understand? I've already caused enough..." He stopped and looked away. "I'd rather be nothing than—"

"Don't say that!" I cried, remembering him being swallowed whole in my dream, tangled up in thorny roots. That's not what was supposed to happen. That's why I came back. "You can't say that. You have to try to stay focused until we figure out how to get you...um... wherever you're supposed to be."

He laughed derisively. "What? Like Heaven? Hell? Do you really want to roll the dice and see where I end up? I haven't exactly been an Angel since second grade."

I remembered the rumors that spread like a cancer through the school. The rumors about drugs, and fights and running away. Surely they'd been exaggerated. Rumors always were. But did I really know anything about him? Anything at all? I tried to think of a way to reassure him. I did know one thing, something I had seen with my own eyes, and I dragged it out as proof that he'd done something good while he was still alive. "Maybe not an Angel, but I know Shawn would be dead if it weren't for you. I saw you pull him back from the edge of the cliff."

"Maybe not one of my brighter moves," he mumbled.

"God had to have seen!"

"How can you really be so sure He exists anyway?" he shot back angrily. "I haven't seen any evidence, and you'd think being *dead* might grant me a few perks like that."

"He does," I said quietly, but how could I possibly prove it when I wasn't always sure myself?

"No more tears," he said flatly.

"*Okay...*"

"Promise."

"Fine...I *promise*," I said, and he nodded, satisfied.

Just then we both turned at the sound of someone calling my name. Jason. Shit. I dug my phone out of my bag and checked the time. I wasn't late.

"Who's that?" Michael wanted to know. He came closer and stood next to me.

"Long story."

He raised his eyebrows.

"My ex-boyfriend, *okay?* He brought me here today."

"Didn't you just turn sixteen and get your license?"

I flashed a guilty grin. "Grounded from the car."

"In the first week? What'd you do?" he smiled, amused.

"First day actually. *Someone* kept me out past sunset last Friday."

"Oh…" His smile faded a little, but his eyes still gleamed.

"I get my car privileges back next weekend." Then I looked him hard in the eyes. "I'll be back. Sunday. You *be* here," I ordered. His smile faded a little more.

I dug the little plastic ring back out of my pocket and threaded it onto a tiny branch of the tree with the blackened lightning crack running from top to bottom. "Here. Wrap your head around that." I heard Jason calling me again. "I have to go."

He nodded, watching me as I backed out of the woods. I didn't want to take my eyes off him either.

"Be here. You're not meant to be nothing," I said.

He rolled his eyes, but nodded again, and I turned around and headed toward the path. When I glanced back over my shoulder, he was gone.

I found Jason in the small stand of oaks above the cliff. He was wearing his heavy basketball jacket half-zipped up over a ribbed crewneck sweater. His jeans had strategically placed rips near his knees and crotch. He smiled at me, and for the first time I noticed he was unusually tan for October in Cleveland.

"Hey, Cate," he said.

"Why'd you come back so early?" I asked, trying to look calm, but I was having serious trouble stepping back into the real world. I walked away from him toward the overlook to give my expression a chance to normalize.

"It's been a while since—" He stopped mid-sentence as he followed me. "What happened, Cate? You're covered in pine needles."

"Just…um… meditating, you know…"

He caught up with me and took in the look on my face. "Are you okay?"

"Uh huh," I nodded briskly. "Hey! Let's go see our initials." I sped away from him along the cliff top trail, stopping in front of a gnarled oak tree that was clinging to the edge. The letters JK & CF were scored into its bark. Beyond it, a breathtaking view of the valley opened up.

"Okay, what's going on?" he asked when he caught up with me again. He hated it when he didn't understand something. I kept my eyes on the cliff in the distance and tried to keep my breathing steady.

"Nothing."

He wrapped his fingers around my shoulders and turned me around. "Cate…look at me. Damn. You're shaking."

I reluctantly let the pressure of his fingers lift my chin, and he studied my face for a moment, his ice blue eyes filling with concern.

"You're eyes are bloodshot…" He hesitated and then asked, "What did you and your friends do last night?"

So that's what he thought? That we'd been drinking or smoking pot? "Jason, you *know* I'm not into that stuff. We were just up really late." I turned back toward the cliff. *Breathe normally.*

"People change," he murmured. Then he came up close behind me, and I could feel the warmth of his cheek radiating against mine as he looked out at the valley from over my shoulder. He was quiet for a while, and then he swept his hand out over the gorge, whispering:

"The world was before them, where to choose
Their place of rest, and providence their guide:
They hand in hand with wandering step and slow,
Through Eden took their solitary way."

They were the last words of Milton's epic poem, *Paradise Lost*, the book we'd read together at Huntington Beach last summer. At the end of the book, God banished Adam and Eve from the Garden of Eden for eating the forbidden fruit of the tree of knowledge.

"I thought you hated that book," I commented, taking a small step away from him. The memories of those warm summer days spent so close to him on the sand were picking up heat.

"Yeah, sure," he recalled, "You can't expect me to take seriously a book that tells the story of how an Archangel, *Saint Michael* no less, battled Satan and threw him out of heaven just so Satan could come back and ruin the lives of Adam and Eve. But it does raise the interesting question: *If* God were to exist, would it really be fair for Him to forbid Adam and Eve to seek knowledge and understanding? What could be wrong with that? *Maybe* Satan actually did them a favor. Maybe people need to stop looking to a conveniently absent God to solve all their problems."

I rolled my eyes in response. Even though Jason's parents had sent him to Catholic school for the past nine years, the ideas of God and Devil had yet to make much of an impression on him. Good thing he wasn't dead, too. But I had to hand it to him, only Jason could figure out a way to root for the Devil, the lowest of underdogs.

He was quiet a moment, then pointed to our initials and laughed softly, "Do you remember what we did after I carved that?" He took a step closer, his lips now just inches from mine, and reached up with his finger and looped a stray strand of my hair back over my ear. "I love your hair like this, so smooth…"

"*Please* tell me you didn't date a guy who goes to a tanning salon." The sarcasm and the sweet fragrance hit me at the same time. I jumped and spun around.

Jason reached out and grabbed my elbow, pulling me away from the edge. "What?" he asked, his gaze darting around to see what had startled me.

"Oh shit…sorry. That's the second time I almost scared you off the cliff this weekend," Michael chastised himself, though he was grinning. "He can't see me, can he?" I looked back at Jason to see him still scanning the forest, oblivious. I obviously couldn't answer Michael's question. In fact, I really couldn't even *look* at him without appearing completely insane. So I closed my eyes instead and counted to ten. When I opened them, Michael was circling Jason, looking him up and down.

"This is way too cool…" he murmured.

"Are you sure you're all right, Cate?" Jason asked again.

"Yeah…I just…um…stayed up too late, like I said…" I rubbed my temples viciously.

"So who dumped who?" Michael wanted to know, coming to a stop in front of Jason's right shoulder. Michael was a few inches shorter. "By the way he was looking at you, I'd guess it was *you* who dumped *him*. Am I right?" His eyes shone bright with humor. It was clear this was making his day.

"We should probably go, then," Jason suggested. I nodded mutely, and Jason turned his back to me and started up the trail. Michael folded his arms over his chest and glanced in his direction.

"Basketball jock. Designer labels. He sounded kinda smart, too. I'll give him props for that. But…I don't like him; he likes your hair all flat," he concluded. Then he wondered, "How much can he bench?"

I opened my eyes wide at Michael and motioned with my head that he should go away. "Are you crazy?" I whispered. I was close to losing it. How the hell was I supposed to balance two different… dimensions…at the same time?

"Yeah, probably. Being dead sort of pushes you over the edge," he replied. Then he gave me an impish grin and a pleading look. "C'mon Catherine…I never have visitors that can actually see and talk to me."

A smile stole across my face. "I'll see you next week," I whispered, but even as I said it, I saw worry creep back into his eyes, and I wondered how I would last a whole week away from him, not sure if he was safe. Would he still be here after seven days adrift with no one to talk to? Or would he fade away into inky nothingness? The thought sent a ripple of fear down my spine. The nightmare had made it clear that I was supposed to help him, but I had no idea how. Maybe if I knew what really happened that day on the cliff last August, maybe if I knew what he'd been through during the years he was gone, maybe *then* I could help him overcome whatever trapped him here. But with no faith in God, where would he go once he was free?

"Are you coming, Cate?" Jason called. He'd just noticed I wasn't behind him and had turned back around.

"Coming. Yeah. Sure." I jogged to catch up, glancing over my shoulder one last time to see Michael leaning against a tree studying his tattoo. His faith in God had been strong at one point. The tattoo proved that. I just needed to help him find it again.

Chapter 11
The Hit Man

WHEN SPENCER HOBBLED toward the Demon on his crutches the next morning, struggling to hold onto his backpack and a newspaper at the same time, Cici hopped out of the car to help him. While her back was to me, he gave me a lopsided grin and a peace sign.

"Determined little shit…" I mumbled as I narrowed my eyes and peace signed him back.

"Hi, Cate," he said when they reached the car. "Cici just offered to come to the gym after school to help me with my physical therapy exercises."

"Isn't she sweet," I said, smiling back and gunning the engine. My dad looked at me sideways and raised his eyebrows. He'd decided mercifully that my grounding from the car didn't apply when he was in the car with me. I ran my hands over the slender steering wheel, feeling the car's powerful vibrations through my fingertips. That's right, baby, you go right ahead and growl for mama.

Once on the road, Spencer cleared his throat and unfolded the newspaper. "Um…hey, so did you see today's paper, Cate?"

Out of the corner of my eye, I saw my dad shoot him a pained look. "Now's not a good time, Spencer," he said.

"You didn't tell her, Mr. Forsythe? All the kids at school are going to be talking about it," he pointed out, thrusting the paper up into my dad's lap.

"Tell me what?" I asked, trying to see the paper and keep the car in my lane at the same time.

"Spencer…" my dad groaned.

"Um, Mr. Forsythe? Wouldn't you rather her know *before* she gets to school?"

"Know what?" The car swerved slightly.

"Pull over, Caty. NOW." My dad wasn't messing around. "We'll switch, and you can read it for yourself."

I let the car coast to a stop near the curb and then reached out and snatched the paper off his lap. My hand fumbled with the driver's side door latch while my eyes took in the headline of the Metro section:

Drugs Involved in Tragic Death of Local Teen

I looked back at Spencer, and he ran his fingers though his shaggy hair uncomfortably.

"I'm sorry, Cate. But I thought you'd rather hear it from…" I tuned him out and got out of the car. Traffic was blasting by a few feet to my left, buffeting the paper and making it impossible to read. My dad led me back around to the passenger side and made me get in. Then I dug hungrily into the article while my stomach flipped its contents up into my throat. I could hear Spencer whispering to Cici and Claire in the backseat, filling them in.

Drugs Involved in Tragic Death of Local Teen

According to the coroner's report released yesterday, no drugs were found in the body of Michael Casey, a student of Saint Joan of Arc Catholic High School, who fell to his death from a cliff last August.

"Thank you, God," I whispered. Michael hadn't been on drugs when he died after all.

However, police have now confirmed that a half-

empty bottle of Ritalin was found near the victim. The medication was prescribed to a former foster child of Bill and Suzanne Gardiner of 342 Snowdrop Way, who were Casey's foster parents at the time of his death.

Shawn Fowler, also a student of Saint Joan of Arc Catholic High School, who was hiking with Casey when he fell, stated that Casey had taken the pills from the Gardiner's medicine cabinet and brought them to the park intending to share them with him. Fowler said, "Michael got really angry when I refused. Then we went for a hike, and he got too close to the edge and slipped."

"That little lying sack of…" I murmured.

The Gardiners have refused to comment.

Detective Lucas McCready said, "Some students are turning to prescription drugs to get high because they think they're safer than street drugs, which is a dangerous assumption."

This was not the first time Casey, who was no stranger to the juvenile court system, was found with drugs. Last winter, he was charged with misdemeanor possession of marijuana on the grounds of Fairview High School, his former school of record, and was placed on probation. He subsequently was charged with felonious assault after pushing a young man through a plate glass window during a fight.

The coroner has ruled Casey's death an accident. He was only fifteen at the time of his death.

My mouth flooded with hot, salty saliva, and I clamped my teeth together to keep from throwing up.

"I'm so sorry, Cate," consoled Cici from behind me. Something cold and solid tapped me on the shoulder, and I turned to see an open bottle of Gatorade in Spencer's extended hand. I took it gratefully.

So the rumors were true. Michael had warned me, but I hadn't believed him. I hadn't wanted to believe him. Had he really tried to get Shawn to use Ritalin with him?

As we unfolded ourselves out of the car in front of the school, Claire tugged on my arm and whispered, "At least you're off the hook now."

I looked back at her, puzzled.

"Your promise?" she reminded me. "The police ruled the fall an accident. You're off the hook. Did you think I forgot?"

Right. I wouldn't have to relive Michael's death for the police. Justice had been served. Or had it? I watched as she walked away from me and disappeared into the shadow that blanketed the school's front doors.

Grace and Meri were waiting for me in the school foyer. The news travelled fast.

"I'm sorry the rumors were true," consoled Grace.

"He probably had a tough life," Meri said. They were trying to make me feel better, but I was having a hard time focusing on anything but sifting through the jumbled mess that was becoming Michael's past.

"Cate...that was the first bell." Grace tilted her head sideways in front of me, trying to coax me out of my stupor.

"Huh? Oh." I followed her wordlessly to my locker, realizing for the first time that other kids were staring at me and whispering. Fingers were tapping on phones up and down the hall. A tall girl I didn't even know held up her cell and took my picture.

"What the...?" I blinked a few times, confused.

"They all know you two were friends," Grace murmured as we reached our lockers. In the month and a half since the accident, word had gotten around that Michael and I had known each other. They were now looking at me with new eyes, probably wondering if I was involved in whatever Michael had been involved in. The mystery and drama was the perfect breeding ground for more rumors.

Meri glared back at them.

"And she knows a few hitmen, too," she informed the onlookers, slamming her locker shut. Most of them got suddenly busy with their own lockers, and I had to smile at Meri's feistiness. She was so tiny, but it never stopped her from speaking her mind.

"Thanks," I said.

"No biggie," she said and squeezed my arm before heading off to class.

⋙⋘

A few hours later, I was standing in the entrance to the cafeteria with my tray balanced on my hands, listening to the overwhelming din of the students echo off the walls. The noise was too much, and I veered to the right and pushed open a pair of glass doors that led out into a small courtyard between the cafeteria and the school's north wing of classrooms. There were a few stone benches planted next to a circular, flagstone path that surrounded a small garden which was well past its summer prime. In the center of the garden was a life-sized bronze statue of Saint Joan of Arc.

Most images of Saint Joan show her standing upright with her armor gleaming and her sword upraised, but this statue was different. It was weathered with the green patina of age, and instead of standing she was kneeling; instead of grasping a sword, her hands were clasped in prayer, and her eyes, full of anguish, were lifted upward to God, the true source of her strength. I liked the statue because it showed her vulnerability, and it reminded me that faith didn't always come easily, even to the best of us. And I liked the courtyard because it was usually empty on cold days. But *surprise*, today it was occupied.

Shawn was standing on the path, surrounded by three large brutish boys who were taking turns shoving him back and forth between them. The largest, a football player named Lance, who could often be found anywhere a fight broke out in the school, was taunting him. "You holding out on us, punk? You a big tough guy? You want *me* to fall off a cliff?"

I might have been pissed off at Shawn, but how could anyone torment him about the accident?

"We know you're like, dumb and all, but you should have shared the smart pills," Lance sneered.

"Hey!" I blurted out. All three of them looked in my direction, and Lance let loose a wicked grin and sauntered toward me. Shawn looked down at the ground and then toward the safety of the double doors that led out of the courtyard into the north wing. The two other boys blocked his exit. I gripped the tray I was holding tighter.

"Maybe you know where we could score some pills. Weren't you like his girlfriend or something?" The words slid out of Lance's mouth like oily fumes, and my eyes narrowed as I realized he was talking about Michael.

"Shut the hell up," I shot back. He took a step closer and cocked his big, fat, bleached blonde head to the side, cracking his neck.

"Did you hear that? Sounds like she doesn't want to share her source either," he said, looking over his shoulder. He turned back toward me and poked me hard in the shoulder with his index finger. I stumbled backward a few steps. My tray tilted precariously.

"See," he said very quietly. "You'd fall easy, too." My blood rushed to my temples. Then I heard the glass door from the cafeteria open behind me.

"So...Lance," I heard a boy's voice say. "Did you lose your way outta here? I mean, like I know the path is circular, but..."

Lance immediately stepped away from me. "Just sizing up your competition," he said, his chin jutting out defiantly.

"She doesn't know anything, Lance," the voice assured him smoothly. "So you can like, go find someone else's ass to play with."

Lance looked back at me and hissed, "Stay away from cliffs," and then left through the north wing doors.

Shawn started to walk past me in the opposite direction when the voice behind me said, "Wait." Shawn waited.

I turned to see who had managed to disperse the bullies and

found the tall, thin boy with the dark curly hair and brown eyes I'd met briefly at Michael's wake. He was standing on the flagstone path, his arms relaxed at his sides, wearing a thick charcoal gray sweatshirt over his white collared shirt. He didn't seem big enough to scare off Lance. What was his name? Lou...? Lewis...?

"Call me later, Shawn," he said.

Shawn started back toward the door, but I had a few questions for him first.

"Wait," I tried, but Shawn kept walking.

"Shawn," the boy said, glancing over his shoulder, and Shawn pulled up again and circled back around, avoiding my eyes. At the moment, I didn't care who the boy standing next to me was. I was going to take advantage of whatever influence he had over Shawn, and I didn't waste time getting to the point.

"Why did you lie about who slipped at the top of the cliff? If it hadn't been for Michael, it would have been *you* who fell," I accused. I heard the boy next to me whistle sharply through his teeth.

"How the hell would you know that?" Shawn spat. "Everyone knows Michael was a pothead and—"

"You're lying!" I burst out. Even after everything I had read in the paper, everything the kids were saying at school, I still couldn't believe it. "Who really brought the drugs to the park?"

"He did, you stupid little—"

"Okay, you can go now, Shawn," said the dark-haired boy, his tone dismissive. Shawn clamped his mouth shut and stalked back into the cafeteria.

"He's lying," I murmured.

"Yeah...probably. But you won't get him to admit it," the boy next to me said. I glanced at him, startled. He actually believed me, believed Michael was innocent.

"Luke Devlin," he said.

"What?"

"I'm Luke Devlin," he repeated. "I met you at Mike's wake?" He shifted his weight to his left foot and tilted his head, studying me.

"Right," I replied. "I'm—"

"Yeah, I know who you are. Look, if I were you, I'd stay outta Lance's way from now on. He's just pissed off about…some stuff. And I wouldn't worry about Shawn. He's like, at the bottom of the food chain. Do you get what I'm saying?" His brown eyes glittered darkly as he imparted this warning.

"Yeah…sure," I stammered, not getting what he was saying at all. As Luke left, I thought about what Lance had said. That he was sizing up Luke's competition. Was Luke dealing drugs in the school, then? Stuff like Ritalin? And even if he was, how had he gotten Lance to back off?

Maybe I knew a hitman after all.

Chapter 12
Coincidence

MY DAD FINALLY handed over the keys as promised after Mass on Sunday, but not to the Demon.

"You still have to earn *that* privilege back," he said. I groaned as I slid behind the wheel of the van. It was like driving a massive white refrigerator on wheels, and it seemed to get larger and heavier as I approached the steeper grades of the park.

I told my mom and dad I was going to take more samples from the river and then head over to Jai Ho, a local tea and coffee shops to study. By the time I pulled into the Lewis Woods parking area, I already had the water sample stowed in the dashboard cup holder. My hands were shaking as I turned off the car. I was praying that Michael was still here. If he wasn't, I would never know what happened to him, and I didn't think I could live with that.

I struck out across the cold, desolate field, patting my back pocket where I had stuffed the article from last Monday's paper. I hoped I wouldn't need to show it to him to get him to tell me what happened last August on the cliff. I was worried about his reaction. How do you ask someone if they are a pot-smoking, pill-popping juvenile delinquent prone to violent outbursts without making them upset? The obvious answer was: you didn't. But I knew we needed to talk about it before he had any hope of moving on. He probably had mountains of unresolved feelings to deal with. My many years of watching the Syfy channel and reading supernatural fiction told me that. Sure, laugh, but that's all I had.

I saw him as soon as I reached the thicket of long dead wildflowers, and my heart leapt with relief. He was sitting on the hollowed out log at the edge of the woods, bouncing his heels up and down with the excess energy he never seemed to run out of. He jumped to his feet when he saw me, grinning.

"Now there's the hair I remember!" he called as I approached. I smiled back. I'd tied it up in a ponytail but had left it frizzy curly for him. It was the least I could do.

"Turn around so I can see the back," he ordered, twirling his downward pointing index finger around in a circle.

"Um...okay..." I said and spun around while he laughed to himself.

"What?" I demanded to know, trying to run my fingers through the back to smooth it out.

"Those little tiny curls in the back around your hairline. They're still there," he said. "I used to want to yank on those so bad when I sat behind you in class."

"Well, then I guess I'm lucky you can't do that now," I teased back and watched as a faint shadow crossed his face. "I'm sorry, I..."

The shadow was gone as quickly as it had come, but so was the smile. "No, it's fine. Whatever."

But I knew it wasn't. "I was worried about you," I admitted. "That you might not be here today." The pale sunlight seemed to penetrate the outer layers of his subtly-flickering skin, but he looked steadier, more solid than last week.

"Yeah...well...I've been practicing staying focused. I can pull myself together and stay visible a lot longer now." He pulled his fingers into a fist to illustrate. "And when I do let go and disappear..." He opened his fist and spread his fingers apart. "I don't feel so lost and mixed in with everything else. I still feel like me...mostly."

"Can you still feel the edges of things around you?" I wondered, fascinated.

"Sure. Temperature, texture, shape. Everything. It's actually kind of cool...especially if there's something warm or soft nearby." His eyes gleamed, and a teasing grin spread across his lips. My face warmed as I remembered the blush he'd detected in the dark last week.

He laughed. "I'm just *kidding*," he assured me. He looked down at his hands and flexed his fingers. "I respect your...um...personal space."

I cleared my throat self-consciously. "So...you're not worried about losing yourself in darkness anymore?"

"No...but..." and there was that little shadow again, haunting the corners of his eyes. "I just have to be careful..."

"Careful of what?" I prompted, worried.

"Sometimes I think it would be easier to just let go completely," he said, becoming uncharacteristically still. I watched, alarmed, as his eyes became unfocused and distant.

"Well...don't," I said.

Fatigue and self-doubt replaced the emptiness in his eyes. "I won't. That stupid little gumball ring you hung on the lightning strike tree? It helps me remember why I want to stay."

He was struggling, and I had the sense that he couldn't hold out against the dark nothingness forever. We needed to get started trying to figure out why he was stuck here. But before I could work up the courage to ask the uncomfortable questions, his eyes brightened with excitement.

"Hey, Catherine," he said, grinning again. "I want to show you something."

Then he vanished.

I whirled around a few times until I heard his voice from inside the woods, farther up the shady path. "Meet me at that little wooden footbridge near the overlook."

"Why don't you walk with me?" I said, not moving my feet.

He appeared suddenly at my side, and I jumped. "It's still hard for me to move long distances while I'm visible. I can't seem to stay focused long enough, you know? First I'm here, and then I'm a few inches from here, and then...it's *really* exhausting."

"You should practice, then," I suggested. "Improve your focus and strength, right? Don't you think?"

He disappeared again. "Just meet me at the bridge."

I rolled my eyes, and waited stubbornly.

"Please?" he whispered from the cold air near my left ear. "... *Catherine...?*" he breathed into my right ear, and I rubbed it reflexively with my shoulder in reaction to the soft, unexpected sound. I shoved my hands deep into my jacket pockets, resigned, and walked down the familiar path alone. Who could resist that?

Like last Sunday, the clean scent of Higher followed me, and I knew he wasn't far away. He was watching from somewhere nearby, and the thought produced a small quiver in my chest. When I arrived at the footbridge, he was sitting up on the handrail and studying me expectantly. He looked enormously pleased with himself.

"What do you see?" he asked, running his ragged fingertip over the top of the railing. I walked onto the bridge, my feet crackling through dry, fallen leaves, to look closer. There were a few glittering hot pink hearts painted with nail polish on the handrail next to a carving of a crown, and an empty beetle carcass hung from an old spider web. Then I saw the phrase that so intrigued me on the day he died:

"God is dead. Where art thou, Ubermensch?"

Is that what he meant? I pointed to it.

"A+, Genius," he said, hopping off the railing and leaning back against it. "Isn't that what you called me that first night you saw me?"

I nodded.

A triumphant look lit up his whole face. Then he asked, "So... why'd you call me that? What's it mean?"

What was I supposed to say? I think God speaks to me through the radio? That I thought He was trying to send me a message about a "superman?" I wasn't ready to acknowledge that yet, not out loud anyway. Admitting I could see and talk to ghosts was bad enough.

"How do you do that?" I asked instead.

His curiosity was replaced by confusion. "Do what?"

"You know, *lean* against things? Stand on the ground? I would think you'd fall right through."

He scratched the back of his head. "Hmm...I don't really lean against stuff, because...well...I can't. It only looks that way to you because I hold myself *close* to stuff. It anchors me so I don't...like... drift, you know? I don't like drifting." He looked up to see if I was following.

I nodded, and he went on.

"So...nothing really feels solid to me, except...um...me," he ran his fingers through his damp hair, which parted for them as they passed, "and the stuff I'm wearing." He pulled up the gold Claddagh and twisted it on the chain, then let it drop back down under his black sleeveless shirt.

"Everything else..." He let his fingertips fall through the splintered wood railing of the bridge. "It doesn't exactly hurt when I pass through things...it just feels...strange." He looked up to see my reaction. I was mesmerized. Emboldened, he went on.

"So like, I really don't need to be standing on anything at all." He held his hands out away from his body and levitated about eighteen inches above the ground. I took a step back startled, and he dropped abruptly. "Sorry...I guess that's a little weird."

"Umm...yeah. Wow."

"Yeah...I know," he agreed, brushing his hands together nonchalantly and then "leaning" back against the railing. "So, why uberwhatzit?"

"Uber*mensch*," I corrected. I would have thought with all that energy, he would be more easily distracted.

"Whatever." His bright eyes were still on me, waiting, curious.

I inhaled deeply. "The day you died, when I left, I noticed this quote on the bridge: 'Where art thou, Ubermensch?' It stuck with me for some reason, and I looked the word up a few weeks later. It's German. It means *overman* or *superman*. I guess after that, I associated the word with you."

"So...you thought *I* was superman?" he asked, his lips turning up a little at the corners.

"Yes…no…" I sighed, embarrassed. "Look, it's not important."

"It's important to me. Seriously." He tried to rearrange his face into a more solemn expression, failing miserably. The twinkle just wouldn't quit.

"How do you even remember what I said that night? It's all so confused in my head now."

"I remember everything you said to me that night, Catherine," he replied, genuinely serious this time. He caught my eyes with his and held them. "It was like the first time anyone had talked to me in six *fucking* weeks. And it was you. I *knew* you." I looked away. "You were the only thing about this whole damn town that was familiar, that felt like home."

"I'm sorry I refused to talk to you."

"Well, shit, can't imagine why you did that." Sarcastic, then he laughed. "I mean, you only saw me fall off a cliff and bite the dust, like for real, a few weeks before."

I looked down at the bridge railing and patted it absently with my palms. "Yeah…I know, but—"

"Okay. So I get that you think of me when you think of superman or uberwhozit, which is very cool, by the way…" I sighed. He was still teasing me. "But what made you think of it *that* night?"

This was the part I didn't want to talk about, but it was obvious we'd never get on the subject of his fall if I didn't give him *some* explanation. "Um…okay. While I was trying to run away from you, this song came on my music player. 'Kryptonite.' Do you know it?"

He shook his head.

"One of the lines goes 'If I go crazy then will you still call me Superman?' It made me think of this quote on the bridge." I looked up again. He furrowed his brows, trying to understand.

"Look…you need to listen to the whole song," I said. I dug my music player out and scrolled to the song. Then I held up the headphones between us and put one earpiece into my ear and nodded for him to listen to the other. He moved in closer.

"Now before you listen, you need to understand that I knew it was you from the first second I saw you that night, only I thought I was hallucinating, you know? The spiked cigarette theory? Maybe post-traumatic stress disorder? This song is what made me believe you were real. Okay?"

He nodded. Then I pushed play.

As the first verse played, he started to roll his eyes, but then the crease between his brows deepened. During the second verse, he looked back at me curiously, starting to get the connection. By the end of the refrain, a distant look appeared in his eyes, and I knew he was turning the lyrics over in his mind.

I shut the song off after that and waited while he stared off into the woods for a few minutes, thinking.

"It was like the song was talking directly to me about you. You know, telling me it really *was* you," I said finally. "So—"

"It's just a song," he countered brusquely. "A coincidence."

"I don't believe in coincidences," I murmured. "I think maybe…" But I lost my nerve to say what I was going to say, and hugged my arms in close to my chest, avoiding his eyes. Underneath all of my doubts and fears, I believed this song, like all the others, was God's way of trying to tell me something. I also knew that tomorrow, or perhaps even later today, I would wonder how I could be so delusional, so why say it out loud.

He zeroed in on my conclusion anyway. "Come on, Catherine," he said, shaking his head. "So you're saying that what, like someone, like maybe *God* or something, played that song for you?" His voice was dripping with condescension, but his eyes told another story. He was paying attention.

"Hey! You asked!" I shot back, getting in his face.

He took a step back, surprised by my temper.

"All I know is that I was scared out of my mind that night, and all I wanted to do was get the hell out of these woods, but that song got my attention, and I stopped! I *stayed!* Isn't that what you wanted that night? For me to stay? I think maybe God was trying to tell me that." There it was. My cards were on the table. My blue eyes flashed stubbornly as I steeled myself for his reaction. I wasn't disappointed.

"Maybe your God just likes to fuck with your head," he mumbled.

"Nice," I said. "If it wasn't God, then maybe it was you?"

"Me?"

"Yeah," I said. I was skeptical, but the idea had a certain appeal. Maybe God wasn't the only one who could reach me through music. "If you listen to the words of the song, it's almost like it could have been you trying to tell me something that night." I paused and pondered that while his mouth dropped open, startled by the idea.

"Can you do that?" I wondered aloud. "You know, focus your thoughts somewhere? Like you focus the rest of you?"

"Catherine, you're insane."

Right. I knew there was a reason I didn't talk about this stuff. Then, we both turned suddenly at the sound of some hikers coming up the path.

"Let's go," I whispered, motioning toward the overlook.

"Why?"

"Because I don't want to be standing here talking to myself when they walk by. I may be insane, but I'm not stupid."

He laughed, but he vanished anyway, murmuring, "Lead the way."

I rolled my eyes. "You really need to work on that walking thing."

"Would you walk to California if you could fly?"

"California my...we're only going a quarter mile," I complained. I could hear the sound of his breathing mingled with the sound of crunching leaves beneath my feet, and his sweet citrus and pine fragrance wrapped comfortingly around me like a warm cloak. He was very close.

"You're keeping your distance, right?" I narrowed my eyes at the surrounding forest. He just laughed.

When I reached the edge of the cliff, I lowered myself down onto the ledge where I was the day he fell. It was colder there, and the wind was stronger, but it was less likely that we would be interrupted. With each wind gust, a shower of leaves spiraled off the trees that lined the ridge tops on either side of the gorge. Brown. Orange. Yellow. Red. Most of them eventually found their way into the rushing river that flowed past in the valley below and then disappeared around the bend.

It felt good to be sitting there again, knowing he would soon be sitting beside me. I watched his ethereal body take shape, gradually gathering and filling in to reveal him sitting next to me with his chin resting on his knees, which were drawn up in front of him. The thumb of his left hand rubbed up and down over his tattoo while his dark lashes and gray eyes moved subtly as they took in the view of the opposing cliff in the distance.

"Anyway..." I began after a while, reluctantly disturbing his peaceful profile, "Now that I know you're *not* Superman, and you're actually just a ghost who somehow got himself stuck—"

"So I've gone from Superman to being a shit-for-brains ghost?" He turned toward me with his lips turned up in a sarcastic grin. "You really know how to build a guy's confidence."

I ignored his comment. "I think I'm supposed to work on getting you...*unstuck*."

"I already told you. I don't think I want to know where I'm assigned to go next."

"But you believe there is a next?"

"Not really." He stuck his chin out stubbornly, his eyes steely. "No."

"For me, then? Can't we at least explore the possibility?"

"What do you want me to do, Catherine?" he said. "There's no light or whatever. Nada. Zippo. Okay? Just me, floating around in this ether crap, bored out of my fucking skull." His shoulders slumped. "Who do you think you are anyway? Jennifer Love Hewitt or that creepy little kid that sees dead people?"

"News flash. I do see dead people."

He gave me a pained look.

"Look. Think about it, you have to be appearing to me for a reason. We need to figure out what it is. The way I see it, you're either haunting me because you hate me, you're trying to save me from something, you need my help to deal with something from your past, or you don't know you're dead."

He shot me an angry glance. "Well, you can cross the last one off. Being dead is one thing I'm sure of. It sucks."

"Okay," I nodded encouragingly. He looked sourly back out over the valley.

"I might hate you," he went on in a teasing tone. "I don't know. We haven't spent much time together yet." He glanced over at me to see my reaction to that, and I rewarded his efforts by rolling my eyes. "Okay, okay. I'm not an evil spirit that's come back to destroy you or whatever." He waved his hands in the air magnanimously.

"That's good to know."

His eyes brightened a little as he went on to the next possibility. "So…maybe I'm just trying to save you from a life of extreme suburban boredom?"

"Succeeding, but I don't think that's a compelling enough reason to dodge the grave—which brings us to the third and only option left."

He rolled his eyes again and stuck his scraped chin back out. "This is stupid, Catherine. Nothing I did mattered when I was alive, why would it matter now that I'm dead?"

"I think we need to start with what *really* happened on the cliff last August." I held my breath, waiting for his temper to flare again.

He bristled sharply. "I fucked up."

I braced myself for worse. "Very descriptive."

"How about, I'm an asshole. I fucked up. I fell off a freaking cliff. I died."

"Okay, we're making progress."

A flicker of a smile crossed his lips, and then his eyes darkened again. "What do you want from me?" he whined. "You're so damn bossy."

I smiled at that. I was bossy. I was also undeterred. "Tell me what happened *before* you were up on the cliff."

"I was born. I was an asshole…"

I closed my eyes and took a deep calming breath. I wasn't going to get anywhere this way, so I reluctantly dug the newspaper clipping out of my back pocket and smoothed it out on the dirt between us. He slouched closer to me, and I watched as his eyes scanned the article, too curious not to read it. He sat quietly for a while staring at the paper, and after a few minutes passed I looked up to see his reaction. He sighed roughly, and banged his forehead on his knees a few times.

"Can't you just read it to me?" he asked, his face still buried in his knees. I picked up the crumpled paper with the tips of my fingers and then stared at him questioningly until he looked back at me, an expression of pure misery on his face.

"I have dyslexia," he said.

Chapter 13
Diary of a Cliff Dive

MY STOMACH ROLLED. "When did you find out?"

"What?"

"That you have dyslexia."

Michael scowled. "Last winter. The Gardiners had them test me at Fairview. It took *hours*."

"So all this time—"

"Yeah…stupid, lazy, goof-off, troublemaker. I've heard it all." His jaw tightened for a moment, and then he laughed harshly as if to prove it didn't bother him.

"I'm so sorry," I said. My voice caught in my throat.

His eyes flashed. "You promised."

I nodded quickly, blinking hard to stave off any wetness that might be gathering. Then it suddenly dawned on me why he was so excited when he found the word Ubermensch.

"Then how did you—"

"Recognize that uberwhatza word?" He smiled grimly. "When you have absolutely nothing to do 24 /7 you find ways to keep yourself occupied. I've read, or at least tried to read, every word on every tree in this whole place."

"Ah," I said. I looked down at the newspaper clipping and cleared my throat. "You're not going to like this."

"Yeah, I figured that." He scowled again. Then, I began to read.

Drugs Involved in Tragic Death of Local Teen

According to the coroner's report released yesterday, no drugs were found in the body of Michael Casey, a student of Saint Joan of Arc Catholic High School, who fell to his death from a cliff last August.

However, police have now confirmed that a half-empty bottle of Ritalin was found near the victim. The medication was prescribed to a former foster child of Bill and Suzanne Gardiner of 342 Snowdrop Way, who were Casey's foster parents at the time of his death.

He leaned back against the cold face of the cliff and groaned. "Bill and Sue must be so pissed at me."

I looked up, surprised. "No. They're not. You should have seen them at your wake and funeral. They were totally sad. They loved you so—"

He groaned again. "I'm such a shit. They were so nice to me and look what I—"

"Michael," I interrupted, "they don't blame you. They blame *themselves.*"

"Do you think that makes me feel any better?" His eyes blazed angrily. "How could I be so stupid?"

I tried to think of something to say to soothe him, but no words came.

"Just..." He nodded at the paper with eyes that were overflowing with self-loathing and motioned impatiently for me to keep reading.

Shawn Fowler...

"God, I *hate* that kid..."

I looked up, but he waved his hand for me to go on.

...also a student of Saint Joan of Arc Catholic High School, who was hiking with Casey when he

fell, stated that Casey had taken the pills from the Gardiner's medicine cabinet and brought them to the park intending to share them with him. Fowler said, "Michael got really angry when I refused. Then, we went for a hike, and he got too close to the edge and slipped."

I looked up again, waiting for him to protest Shawn's blatant lie about Michael being the one who strayed too close to the edge. He just looked defeated and moved his index finger around in a circle to tell me to keep reading.

The Gardiners have refused to comment.

Detective Lucas McCready said, "Some students are turning to prescription drugs to get high because they think they're safer than street drugs, which is a dangerous assumption."

This was not the first time Casey, who was no stranger to the juvenile court system, was found with drugs. Last winter, he was charged with misdemeanor possession of marijuana...

Out of the corner of my eye, I caught him studying my face carefully, his jaw locked tight, but I plowed on, pretending his past didn't shock me.

...on the grounds of Fairview High School, his former school of record, and was placed on probation. He subsequently was charged with felonious assault after pushing a young man through a plate glass window during a fight.

The coroner has ruled Casey's death an accident. He was only fifteen at the time of his death.

He laughed bitterly. "They just *had* to put it all in there. The juvenile delinquent. The bad seed. He finally made his last mistake. I'm sure the talk around school has been interesting this week."

"You could say that," I admitted.

He was quiet, just staring down at the base of the cliff where he'd taken his last breath, and I left him alone with his thoughts for a while. Then it was time to ask the burning question. The one I was afraid to hear the answer to. I cleared my throat.

"Um…so, how much of it's true, the article, I mean?" I asked.

"I don't know. I guess it sums my life up pretty well. Classic Screw Up." He regarded me accusingly, his eyes narrowed to slits. "I never said I was fucking innocent. What does it matter? Why do you even bother to visit the dead stoner? Why don't you run back and join all your perfect friends in your perfect little lives, so you can all be perfect together?" He looked away, his jaw tight, his eyes flint hard.

"Because…" I stammered, not surprised but still stung by the ferocity of his response. "Because I don't think you can judge a person by knowing only their worst moments."

"Trust me. That's not all of them."

"The article can't all be true," I practically pleaded. He raised his eyebrows at me like he thought I was so naïve. But I knew there had to be more to the story.

"The pot?"

He raised his hand and made an exaggerated checkmark in the air above the cliff. "Check," he said.

"The assault?"

"Check."

I shook my head in sorrow. What had happened to him? He continued on in monotone, firing off his sins rapidly, one after another.

"Smoking? Check. Drinking? Check. Pills? Check. Stealing? Check. Hooking up?" He paused and looked up at me and then lowered his long lashes and looked away. "Check."

Oh God, he was only fifteen…

"What about the Ritalin?" I whispered.

He just shook his head disgustedly.

"Not everyone believes you're the one who brought the Ritalin to the park," I tried.

He closed his eyes and tipped his head back against the cliff. His mouth clamped tightly shut.

"If *you* won't talk to me about what really happened on the cliff, I know other people who will."

"Go ahead," he said quietly. "I really don't care what anyone thinks."

"I could talk to Shawn."

"Shawn won't tell you anything."

I cast about looking for something to leverage against him, to pry him open. "Luke Devlin thinks you're innocent."

That name got his attention, and he snapped his head up. "How do you know Devlin?"

"He was at your wake, and then I ran into him in the courtyard at school. He broke up a shoving match between Shawn and Lance and—"

Michael vanished and then reappeared instantly a few inches in front of my face, his eyes wild and dark. He was leaning forward on his fingertips, his toes only partially on the edge of the cliff, and for a split second I was worried he might fall again.

"Promise me you'll stay away from Devlin," he spat.

I gasped, and pressed myself back against the cliff, feeling as if I'd had the wind knocked out of me. He rocked back on his heels, which *were* over the edge, and ran a hand through his hair. He flickered violently.

"Oh shit...I'm sorry...I..." He glanced down at the frothy river and the jagged boulders one hundred feet below him and then back up to my face, which was probably as pale as his was at the moment. "Sorry, shit..." Then he leapt back over to where he'd been sitting a few seconds before. My heart pounded in my chest.

"Catherine, I—"

"Who's Luke Devlin?"

"No one you want or need to know."

"Look, I'll make you a deal," I said, thinking I'd finally found my way in. "I'll stay away from Luke if you tell me who he is and what happened last August. I really, *really* think it's important."

He snorted and looked away.

"I can call him right now. He gave me his number." Which of course he *hadn't*, but I started to pull out my phone anyway. Michael glared at the phone, his eyes in turmoil, and when I started to dial, he threw his nearly translucent hand out in front of me.

"Just...wait..." He rested his head back against the cliff. Then he said softly, "Just...promise me you'll stay away from both Shawn *and* Devlin and that you'll stay...*clean*."

It took me a moment to realize what he was asking me. Then I almost laughed. "What. You think I'm going to hit up Luke or Shawn for a fix?" Right. That sounded like me.

"And you think you're too perfect? Too good? You think you're *immune*?" he asked derisively. "It's always the smart ones."

"Fine! Whatever," I shot back, but he nodded, accepting my coerced agreement to his conditions.

The cuts and bruises, still fresh on his rugged chin and arms, seemed to stand out more starkly against his pale skin as he faced me and set his jaw. "Fine. Go ahead, then. What do you want to know?"

This wasn't the way I had wanted to start this discussion, but I'd take what I could get. "Was Luke your dealer?"

"Was. Before."

"Before what?"

His breathing quickened, but he didn't answer.

"Before what?" I persisted.

"Just *before*, okay? Before I decided I didn't want to be a stoner anymore."

"Why?"

"It doesn't matter," he said. "The reason doesn't exist anymore."

I was startled to see him starting to fade again, so I backed off that question. "So, is that how Luke knows you're innocent? Because you weren't buying anymore?"

"Devlin knew I quit." He paused, then laughed darkly. "Yeah... he knew I quit alright. I quit just about everything: pot, pills, drinking, skipping school—everything except smoking. I was still working on that when…"

"When you fell?" I prompted gently.

"Yeah…"

"So…if you quit, where did the Ritalin come from?"

He shifted his weight uncomfortably and looked up at the sky, as if trying to decide whether or not he would stick to our bargain. "I guess it doesn't really matter anymore," he mumbled, and then he ran his fingers back and forth through his hair so it stood up wildly over the top of his head.

"Shawn lives behind the Gardiners," he began, "and when I first moved in with them last fall, Shawn and I used to smoke pot together in the cement drain pipe at the park down the street. After I *quit*, I would just smoke while he got high." He looked up anxiously to see the expression on my face, which I fought to keep neutral. Then, the story just poured out of him, effortless, like air flowing out of hole in a tire, releasing pressure.

"So I transfer to Saint Joan, right? And when I met with them last August, they told me I was way behind in reading and writing. Big surprise. So, they're like, "Oh, we have all kinds of programs for *that*, Mr. and Mrs. Gardiner."" He did a perfect Sister Larry high-pitched phlegmy accent, and I bit back a grin as I imagined how that meeting must have gone. He ignored me and kept talking. He was on a roll.

"So, I'm really trying, you know? I even got that book that you'll be reading later this year, um, *The Red*…?" He looked up and scratched the back of his head.

"*The Red Badge of Courage*," I filled in for him.

He snapped his fingers. "Right. Anyway, from the way she said *programs*, I knew that could mean only one thing—more work for me." He smiled ruefully. "I knew I *needed* it, but I didn't *want* it. Then, I made Big Mistake Number One. I complained to Shawn about how dumb *I* was and how stupid *they* were, and he said, 'Can't you take drugs to help with that?' And I reminded him that I'd quit all that stuff. The next morning we went down in the park, supposedly just to hang out. It was so damn hot outside, but I just had to get out of the house—"

"I know the feeling," I interrupted, and he looked up at me impatiently. "Sorry."

"Shawn drove over to pick me up, and after he splattered me with Higher, he must have seen the Ritalin in Bill and Sue's medicine cabinet. Shawn has a bad habit of helping himself in other people's medicine cabinets. When he saw the Ritalin, he probably figured he'd hit the jackpot. It's sorta like speed or cocaine-light for us non-ADD types. He brought it that day for himself, but he *said* it would help me. Right. Sure." He clenched his fist as he remembered.

"We were sitting in the front seat of his car in the Nature Center's parking lot, burning up in the heat, and I was so mad when he showed me the bottle. I was trying to figure out how to get the pills back in the Gardiner's cabinet without them knowing when he said, 'So, like are you gonna take it or what?' And I told him, 'No, you stupid dumbass.' Shawn just smiled and said, 'Well, then I guess there's more for me.'"

Michael paused and shook his head in disbelief. "He's such a fucking idiot! I should have taken the pills from him right then. I mean, I weigh at least thirty pounds more than he does, it would have been easy. Right? But I just sat there and watched as he pulled out a couple of tablets. He said, 'The guy I talked to told me I should take two if I wanted to clear my head and study better.' He dropped five in a plastic baggie and set it on the dashboard, and then he pounded them into powder with the flat side of his pocketknife. I told Shawn, 'Whatever. But I'm not taking any.'" Michael rolled his eyes, remembering. "So he opened the bag and said, 'I know,' and then he gave me this stupid grin. Then he dumped most of the powder onto his tongue, and I was like, 'What the fuck, Shawn? You're gonna waste yourself,' and he's like, 'That's the plan.' Then he pressed his nose to the inside of the bag and snorted the rest."

"Wait. Shawn took all of them? All five?" I interrupted, incredulous.

"Yeah. He's *really* stupid." Michael shook his head again, disgusted, and then went on. "At that point, I was just worried that I was going to have to drive the fucking car home. I never even got my temps and never had any practice. 'Just wait,' Shawn said. Then he leaned his head back on the seat to wait for the buzz to kick in. 'How long?' I asked him, and he said, 'The guy I talked to said about thirty minutes.' And I'm like, 'The same guy who told you to take only two? How the hell does he know?' But Shawn just said, 'Dude. He knows. Like, he knows everything.'"

"Do you think he was talking about Luke?" I asked.

"Maybe, but I haven't known Devlin to deal in pharms." He thought about that for a moment. "I don't know."

His eyes narrowed again as he searched for the thread of his story and when he found it he groaned. "I was really pissed so I got out of the car, slammed the door, and went through the Nature Center to the deck out back that looks out onto the river. I thought about leaving him there. I could have walked home. It would have taken a while, but I could have done it. I thought about calling Sue and Bill, but I didn't want to get in trouble, so I just stood there and stared at the water. It was running so low and the sun was reflecting off these long slow ripples. It calmed me down, and I thought maybe I would just go back out to the car and sit with him, you know? Make sure he didn't do anything stupid." The soft laughter that followed that statement had a dark, serrated edge to it. It could have cut through steel.

"Big Mistake Number Two," Michael said. "Shawn was already out of the car, and as soon as he saw me, he started talking a mile a minute. He wanted to go check out the cliff. He wanted to race me up to the top. He was talking to moms and kids who were on their way down and telling them his plans, and I thought, 'Oh shit, here we go.' I looked back in the car to see if I could grab the bottle and at least keep him from taking any more, but he just grinned at me and patted his front pocket.

"I said, 'Come on Shawn, give me the pills. Let's just get back in the car and wait for you to come back down. You can have your buzz, and I'll just take a nap or something.' But he wouldn't listen. He didn't want to *waste* his buzz sitting in the car, and he started up the trail to the top. I followed him. Big Mistake Number Three."

He paused there and tensed his jaw again. "I'm so *stupid!* I should have dragged his ass back into the car. What was I thinking?"

"You were—" He looked at me with eyes that smoldered. "Okay…shutting up now," I said, and he dropped his gaze and sighed.

"Look, Catherine, this is just really hard."

I had no idea how to make it easier, so I just nodded while Michael pushed on.

"So Shawn, when he finally got to the top, he was like, 'This is so awesome! Do you see this?' He couldn't get enough of the view, couldn't get close enough, and when he hopped the fence, I didn't even think. I just knew I had to get him away from the edge." Michael's eyes filled with fear. His chest heaved.

"Then the whole fucking cliff just disappeared under my foot, and I thought I was done right then!" He paused and slowed his breathing down. "I thought I was going to make it, you know? When I grabbed onto that root…"

"And I knew you wouldn't," I murmured.

His anguished eyes found mine and searched them, reaching through the shadows that I knew were still there whenever I thought about his death. His expression softened as he finally realized how I must have felt that day, watching him die. We both looked away, the intimacy of the moment too much for words. We just sat there, wordlessly, side by side, watching the world go by below us, hoping that maybe it would move on to a new scene soon. Something different. Something better. It didn't. It still sucked. The whole thing just sucked.

After a while, I looked back over at him. He had his face buried in his knees again and was rocking back and forth. I reached out my hand, wanting to comfort him. He must have sensed my tentative fingers, even with his eyes closed, because he flinched away.

"I don't care about all the things you did," I whispered. He lifted his chin and rested it on his knees, his eyes expressionless, lost in thought. I studied his quiet profile, thinking through all of the things he'd told me, and realized there was one thing that didn't add up.

"Michael…" I called his name softly. He blinked his way back from wherever he had retreated and bounced his back restlessly on the face of the cliff behind him. "There's one thing that's bothering me.

If Shawn had the pills in his pocket, how did they end up next to you at the base of the cliff?"

He cocked his head to the side and thought about that for a moment. "That son of a bitch. Shawn must have tossed them over the cliff after I fell. It shouldn't surprise me. He wouldn't have wanted to get caught with them. I was as good as dead, and they came from my house so who would know the difference?"

I thought about Shawn, looking over the edge of the cliff at the broken body of his friend far below and then deliberately tossing the pills down on top of him, ridding himself of the evidence that he was the one responsible. "It's not fair—"

"Catherine—"

"Everyone thinks you screwed up again, and you didn't. I'll kick his ass!"

The corners of Michael's lips twitched upward at my suggestion.

"Why do you think that's so funny? Don't you see? Maybe that's what I'm supposed to do for you. Maybe I'm supposed to clear your name."

"Who the fuck cares about my name?" His words bit. Hard. Then he said in a voice I could barely hear, "There aren't any Casey's left anyway."

"I care. You should. I could talk to Luke. He seemed to know—"

"For Christ's sake, Catherine! You promised me you'd stay away from him if I spilled my guts to you. I did. If I can't trust you…I swear to God, I'll…"

His chest was heaving harder than it had when he had talked about his fall from the cliff, and I wondered what could be worse. I'd seen him start to fade or look away when he was upset, but his strong emotions didn't repel him from me this time, and his eyes held onto mine like a powerful vise, refusing to let go. I was easily overpowered.

"Okay, Michael. Okay." I surrendered, "I'll stay away from Luke. I promise. You can trust me."

He finally tore his gaze away and looked down at his hands. "He's dangerous, Catherine. He fucks up people's lives. You have no idea—"

"It's just not fair," I said again. "You should hear what people are saying." It wasn't right. Justice hadn't been served at all.

"Like I said. Who cares? It's not like it really messes up my lifetime GPA," he pointed out sarcastically. "So maybe I would have gotten a C+ for the last three months of my life. I still get an F for the first fifteen and a half years. That's F for—"

"Enough with the F-words already!"

A grin spread over his lips. "What. You think maybe I cuss too much?"

"Maybe a little."

He tried to stifle a laugh. "You just said ass, and I've heard you say shit about a dozen times."

I could feel my face coloring. "The F-word is different."

He tried to look contrite, but it was a no go. Instead he just said, "So…maybe you shouldn't keep bringing up shit I don't want to talk about?"

"Maybe," I murmured, but I knew I wouldn't stop pushing him, not until we'd figured out why he was still here. I looked out over the gorge and saw that the sun was about to set behind the cliff in the distance. I glanced over at Michael reluctantly. It was time to leave. "I have to go. You know, parents, car, homework…"

He rolled his eyes and stood up. "Yeah. You do have all that. But you'll be back?" The look in his eyes was a mixture of forced tolerance, worry, and hopefulness. In other words, I was all he had. If he wanted to talk to someone, it was me or nobody.

"I'll come back later this week, maybe even tomorrow if I can get the car." I lifted my eyes up toward the clearing among the oaks above us and then glanced back to say goodbye, but he was gone.

"Why do you do that to me?" I whined.

"Dramatic effect…" he murmured from somewhere nearby, and then I heard muffled laughter.

"Stupid ghost."

Chapter 14
The Ghost, the Witch and the Jack-o'-lantern

LUKE DEVLIN. I'D promised Michael I'd stay away from him, and I intended to keep that promise, but that didn't stop me from watching him, and when I did, I found him discretely massaging every part of the student body. He regularly met with kids from every social caste in every grade level, and I was shocked that I hadn't realized he dealt drugs before. But if he was so dangerous, why had he stepped in to help when Lance threatened me? And what did he know that convinced him that Michael was clean when he died? Keeping my promise was driving me crazy. I wanted answers to those questions.

On the flip side, I did make it back to the woods to see Michael the next day, and aside from the days I volunteered at the wildlife hospital with Grace, I saw him almost every day for the next few weeks. I told my mom I was going to Jai Ho to study. She couldn't leave Mina alone, so she didn't need the van, and she could see how much I wanted to get out of the house. She didn't ask me why I felt that way, and I didn't ask her why she was practically killing herself to take care of her mother alone, but it was becoming increasingly obvious that she didn't want that choice to burden the rest of us. It was *her* sacrifice. That meant whenever I wanted to go anywhere, I pretty much got the green light without the third degree.

Mother's guilt is a wonderful thing.

As for me, I didn't feel too guilty. My parents only asked where I was going, not whether or not I was going to *stay* there. I got my homework done, kept my grades up, and ran any errands my mom asked me to. And I *did* study at Jai Ho for a while each day, but then I'd grab a steaming cup of chai and head out to the frigid woods to be with Michael.

Michael was mostly glad to see me, but he was careful to steer our conversations stubbornly away from his past. He refused to buy into my argument that exploring his past might free him from his forest prison. Instead, he spent his time with me laughing about the latest gossip at Saint Joan, following animal tracks to their burrows—which he was really good at—and telling me stories about what stupid hikers did in the woods when they thought they were alone. But his brave front didn't fool me. A faraway look was growing in his eyes, and I was impatient to draw him back out, to find out more, to help him go *home*.

By the end of October, my friends noticed my absence. I covered by claiming I was swamped with homework, which satisfied them most of the time because they were swamped too. I rarely invited them over because…well, there was no place to hang out at my house, and I always had some reason on the tip of my tongue for not going out. I don't know why, but I couldn't seem to make the leap back and forth between my friends and Michael, so I chose the latter. Michael needed me.

But Cici—we shared a room. I couldn't avoid her, and she knew *something* was up.

The weekend before Halloween, she came home from a hayride that J.C. had organized for the Social Action Club with four pumpkins she'd bought to boost the club's donation to charity.

"Only four?" I teased as she kicked off her mud-caked flats and shrugged out of her cropped jacket.

"Well…not many people showed up, and J.C. was kind of disappointed." The accusation was subtle, but unmistakable.

"Oh…" I said.

She covered the kitchen table with old newspapers and set the pumpkins on top. "Which one do you want?" she asked, pulling out a few sharp knives, big spoons and my mom's huge all-purpose, metal bowl. She just assumed I wanted to help carve them. I hadn't even thought about Halloween.

I reached out with my fingertips to touch the pumpkins' cold, lumpy surfaces. Which one? I looked them over more carefully than a sixteen-year-old probably should have, and then chose the smallest. It was about the size of a cantaloupe, and I knew as I picked it up and moved it down to my father's end of the table, that it was destined for something special this year.

"So…" Cici said casually, picking up a knife, "What's new?"

"Just studying," I said, serving up school again as my excuse for not being around.

"So that's all you do at Jai Ho every day? Study?"

"Yeah…"

"Oh. It just seems like you're spending a lot of time doing homework—for you that is."

I avoided her eyes, picked up a knife, and stabbed it into the top of my pumpkin. "Yeah, well, sophomore classes are harder than freshmen classes," I said. *Shit.* I hated lying to her, *hated* it. Maybe I *should* talk to her about Michael. Tell her *something*. But my thoughts warned against it.

She'll think you're crazy. She'll tell. You can't help Michael if you're locked away in some insane asylum.

She broke into my thoughts. "It's some new boy, isn't it?" Her eyes were all lit up, begging to be let in on the secret. "Someone you don't want me to know about."

I choked on a laugh. "No!" I cried. "Just me and some tea and a whole lot of homework."

"*Fine*," Cici said, her eyes raking over me suspiciously. "But you're going to the movies with me and J.C. this weekend. Okay? That new zombie one? J.C. wants to see it, and Finn and Spence are too busy with basketball."

"Maybe," I hedged, but I knew if I wanted her off my back, I'd have to spend more time with her.

Yes. You have to be more careful.

Claire and my dad swept into the kitchen to help. It wasn't long before the big metal bowl was full of pumpkin slime, and our masterpieces were finished. My dad's had slanted eyes and a mouth that was wide open and moaning. Cici had carved a bat face complete with pointy fangs, and Claire's had cat eyes with vertical slits for pupils. Mine was traditional: triangle eyes, a triangle nose and a huge gaping grin with a few buck teeth. You couldn't go wrong with the classic.

"Come on! Let's take them upstairs to show Mina!" suggested Claire, grinning. I hesitated. I hadn't really been in to see her since she'd moved in at the beginning of the month, but the wave formed by my sisters and dad carried me up the stairs and down the hall, where I let myself get hung up in the doorway for the hundredth time. I didn't want to go in. It was cold in there, damp and somehow dangerous.

My mom, who'd just finished giving Mina a breathing treatment, smiled as Claire held out her pumpkin for Mina to see. Mina's pale lips turned up in her pink puffy face. I was envious of the easy relationship Claire had with her. The smell of unwashed sickness in the room, the rattle of her breath, the red splotches on her thin arms, none of it seemed to bother Claire in the least.

I remained snagged in the doorway until a small point of light appeared on Mina's face. She shielded her eyes with her dry crooked fingers. The sun had come out from behind the clouds and filled her room with warm golden light. It was reflecting off something into her eyes.

The light drew me in, and as I moved toward her bed, I watched the little spot of sunlight move off her face and down onto her chest. I looked around to see what was caught in the late afternoon sunbeam. It was my silver ring. It had somehow worked its way out from under my shirt, its usual hiding place, and for a moment it gleamed as if it were brand new, free of scratches, and polished until it shone like the sun itself.

Mina reached out with her fingers to touch it with joy in her eyes, but the joy was short-lived. It was replaced by a hardness I didn't understand. Her brows knitted together, and she turned her face toward the wall.

"I'm tired," she said. The warm sunlight disappeared as the sun dipped back behind the clouds, and the temperature of the room felt like it dropped ten degrees. I looked down to see that my ring had reverted back to its usual appearance, dull, scuffed, and unremarkable. Claire glanced up at my mom uncertainly, who motioned with her head that we should leave and let Mina have her rest.

For that brief moment when the sun appeared, I'd suddenly had an overwhelming urge to talk with my grandmother, spend time with her and reminisce about better days, but now I was left feeling cold and uneasy, shut out. The feeling followed me into my bed that night and teased up forgotten memories.

⚍

"Fear," said the Demon, his shiny black eyes softening with the awe he always felt when his methods produced the desired effect. "It makes even the strongest among them turn their backs on those they profess to love." He looked up from the girl into the eyes of her Guardian.

The Guardian's eyes flared bright silver. His lips curled back. "Not always," he retorted.

"True," the Demon conceded. "But we're still just priming. Fear is a good primer. Watch and learn."

The Guardian's jaw flexed, and he returned his protective gaze to the girl. Her skin glistened. She was beginning to sweat.

⚍

It was dark, and I was lost and alone in my parents' cavernous, king-sized bed. I was eleven again. I had the flu. I was scrawny and weak and shivering with fever. I hadn't seen my friends in weeks, and I had hundreds of homework projects due that I hadn't even begun. I'd fallen headfirst out of my life, and I was still falling.

Blink.

I was choking. I grabbed a tissue and coughed up a thick green scab of phlegm from deep within my clogged lungs. With trembling hands, I added the tissue to the other hundred in the big metal bowl that sat next to me on the bed.

Blink.

There were shadows moving about at the foot of the bed. I tried to point them out to Claire, who was sitting with me. My mom floated in carrying the big metal bowl, which was now filled with ice and water. She dipped a washcloth in and wiped my burning forehead.

Blink.

I inhaled, but froze mid-breath. A knife stabbed me in the back, and I gasped. Another thrust. Another arrested breath. I panicked. I could either suffocate or be stabbed to death. My lungs made the decision for me and inflated. I doubled over. Mom! I think I'm dying.

Blink.

The fluorescent lights of the hospital waiting room stung my eyes. The hard molded plastic chair cut into my back and legs. I leaned my head back against the hard, tiled wall and closed my eyes, waiting. I waited forever.

Blink.

I was wheeled down a hall into a dark room where I climbed onto a thin mattress. I took shallow breaths. I didn't want to disturb the knife. I was afraid it would cut deeper. She has pneumonia. Give her oxygen. Give her penicillin. Give her Tylenol. Tylenol? Were they freaking kidding me? Where was my Morphine?

Blink.

It was after midnight, and the knife was gone. I was clammy. Cold. The vampire was here again. There were tiny red needle marks all over the inside of my elbow. Blood draws.

"Arterial Blood Gas," the vampire whispered in the dark. I nodded.

He paused as he held up the needle. "It will sting a little more than the others."

I nodded again.

He felt my wrist, found a bulging artery and slid the hypodermic home. The knife was back. It was lodged in the artery in my wrist. He pulled it out and a deep purple bruise ballooned up. It spread and faded to red, an ugly red splotch on the inside of my wrist. He pressed down on the bruise firmly with a cotton ball, and it throbbed. It throbbed. It throbbed.

I don't want to be sick anymore! I want to be sixteen again! God, please wake me up!

The room began to darken and blur. I was underwater, looking up through the surface, drowning in the deep pool of my nightmares. My naked feet were cold, and I looked down and saw dark inky roots ascending. I strained my foggy vision back toward the surface. Michael was looking down at me from the beautiful citrus and pine scented air above. He plunged his hand into the water toward me, obliterating my view of his face. I couldn't reach it. I couldn't reach it. I couldn't...

Blink.

There were dark shapes around the foot of the bed.

They laughed at me in the deep, still pool.

They wanted me to drown.

Where was the music?

There should have been music.

⁊ ⁊

I woke up with a start in my own bed and thrust my moon-washed forearms up above the blankets and inspected them. They were smooth and milky white, but I rubbed my wrists, knowing they had not always been so. Like Mina's, my wrists had once been punctured too. I knew what it felt like to have setbacks—the kind you have when you have lung problems. But I was strong now, not weak, not like her.

Rolling over, I grabbed my music player off the nightstand and shoved the headphones in my ears.

Don't think, don't think, don't think...

I scrolled to the top of my Playlist, frantically searching for the missing music, "It's Only Life." It was the first song I'd heard that made me wonder, what if?

What if someone was watching over me?

Were they still?

Tears are forming in your eyes
A storm is warning in the skies
The end of the world it seems
You bend down and fall on your knees
Well get back on your feet...yeah...

Don't look away, don't run away
Baby its only life
Don't lose your faith, don't run away,
It's only life…

❧❧

The next morning, I shuffled out into the cold, dark hallway and glanced back over my shoulder into my grandmother's room. She was propped up on pillows with oxygen tubes in place under her nose. She was watching me. Our eyes locked and held before I broke the connection and headed down the stairs to the kitchen. I'd visit her later.

There's plenty of time.
My mom will take care of her.
Sure. She's good at that.
She's got everything under control.
Yes. Of course she does.

❧❧

It was sixty-five degrees, which was unseasonably mild for a Halloween night in Cleveland, but the warm wind tearing across the moonlit field swore to holy hell it would unleash a bitter cold front on all of us tomorrow. The weathermen were even calling for snow.

The stupid wind kept knocking my velvet witch's hat off, and I finally stopped trying to keep it on my head, letting it hang instead by its black satin strap across my back. As I trudged across the field, it bounced up and down against my shoulder blades, happy to remind me it was the winner of our little battle of wills. My hair had won, too. I'd left it loose under the hat, and now—without the hat or a hair tie to keep it in check—it was free to attack me from any direction it chose.

I was coming straight from passing out candy in costume at Meri's house and was still wearing my short black dress and green fishnet stockings, though I *had* switched out my peep toe pumps for my aging hiking boots. I was excited. I had a surprise for Michael. One that I hoped would bring back happier memories. One that I hoped would draw him away from the dark nothingness that ceaselessly called to him.

I should have been afraid as I stood in the gaping mouth of the woods a few minutes later, alone, with a pitifully small flashlight in my hand, but my heart thrilled with nothing but anticipation. The magic that was Michael always affected me the same way. I paused in the forest vestibule to savor the feeling and the smell of the woods. Nestled in among the pines and sheltered from the wind, the air was so warm and muggy it smelled as if someone had brewed a cup of pine needle tea.

"Michael," I whispered.

Strange, he almost always met me at the start of the trail before stubbornly disappearing to meet up with me later back at the cliff or the lightning tree.

"Michael?"

Nothing. Not even a whisper of his signature clean and woodsy scent. I started to walk down the trail alone when I heard a soft exhalation above me and then...

"Boo," Michael said solemnly, appearing suddenly out of the heavy air in front of me.

I should have expected it, but my heart stopped anyway and I cried, "Shit! Michael you scared the crap out of me!" He grinned devilishly, laced his fingers behind his head and rocked back and forth on the balls of his feet. His eyes twinkled with delight. Halloween seemed to agree with him.

"Isn't that my job on Halloween?" he wanted to know. "I am a freaking ghost after all."

"You're a pain in the..." I grumbled, but I couldn't help grinning. He was so pleased with himself. "How did you get that close without me smelling you?" I asked, leaning in to inhale a nose-full of his clean citrus scent. It helped to chase back the shadows.

"Ah..." He looked embarrassed by my affection for the way he smelled, but tried to hold still. "That was easy. I just stayed above and downwind of you."

"Above?" The fact that he could do that still freaked me out a little.

"Sure," he said, as if it was no big thing. Then he appraised me from head to toe and shook his head back and forth a few times, laughing. "What're you supposed to be? A witch?"

I nodded.

"Hmm, I like the boots with the fishnet. Very fashion forward of you."

"Ha ha. I didn't think my high-heeled pumps would fare too well out here in the middle of the woods."

"No, probably not." His eyes drifted away from me to the peaceful empty forest, and he became still and quiet. With the twinkle absent from his eyes, he looked tired. Exhausted. The darkness was calling him, even now, even with me standing right in front of him. How could I compete with the solace it offered? I cleared my throat, and he blinked hard and refocused his eyes. He looked me up and down again, zeroing in on my butterfly bag.

"So, what's in there?" It bulged suspiciously and the strap dug in to my shoulder.

"A surprise."

His eyes regained some of their light, and he studied the bag with growing interest. He took a step toward me.

"No, you have to wait," I instructed, laughing. I put my arm out so he'd have to walk through it to get to the bag, and he grinned at me wickedly. I definitely had his attention now.

"You know I could go right through that." He took another step toward me.

"Yes, but you don't *like* to do that." My heart rate spiked as he stepped closer still. He was pale, and he was flickering, and his eyes were deep gray craters on the edge of the flashlight's cone of light. He looked almost...frightening. "Besides, the bag is closed. Even if you—"

He raised his eyebrows, and I realized he could pass his face right through the bag if he wanted to, and I snatched it behind my back. He disappeared and materialized instantly behind me.

"Cheater!" I squeaked, turning swiftly around. My breath momentarily failed me. *Calm down stupid, its only Michael.*

"Okay, okay," he surrendered, relaxing his stance, and I exhaled softly. His eyes lingered on my hair for a moment, and then he added, "Um…I'll meet you back by the lightning tree. It's really windy along the cliff top, and I don't think you'd survive the beating your hair would give you." Then he disappeared again.

"Thanks," I said sarcastically. But with him gone, the shadows closed back in. "You're still here, though…right?" I whispered cautiously.

A wave of his scent washed over me, and he laughed.

"Yeah, Catherine, I'll stay nearby." And he did. His fragrance followed me all the way back to the lightning tree deep in the woods.

❦

As I settled down on a waterproof stadium cushion, I aimed the light around the tiny clearing until I found Michael leaning casually against our tree. I glanced up above his head at the little plastic ring I'd looped onto one of its branches, and he followed my gaze and grinned.

"I scared off a raccoon last week that was intent on stealing that thing, the little thief." I was about to ask him how many of the animals could see him, but he rubbed his hands together impatiently and squatted down in front of me. "So…what've you got in the bag?"

I dragged it up onto my lap, reached in and pulled out a book of matches, and he groaned. I looked up, alarmed. "What?"

"Catherine," he groaned again. "Don't be a dumbass. Didn't you learn your lesson last time?"

"What last time?" I asked, reaching into the bag again and lifting out my perfect little jack-o'-lantern. "What are you talking about, Michael?"

When I looked back up at him, he was grinning. Then he looked off to the side and into the woods, sighing as if in relief. "I thought…" He laughed softly. "I thought for some stupid reason you brought a pack of cigarettes."

"You thought that was the surprise?"

He nodded sheepishly.

"Crap, Michael. Do you like this one better?"

"It's awesome." He sank down in front of me and watched me pull the top off and light the little candle I'd placed inside. I fit the lid back on and then gently set the glowing jack-o'-lantern on the ground between us. It cast wavy triangles of light onto the forest floor and a warm earthy glow upon his otherworldly skin.

"Happy Halloween!" I said.

His eyes crinkled up at the corners. He stared quietly at it for a while, deep in thought, but slowly, his brows knitted themselves together, and he suddenly threw up his hands in frustration.

"I'm sorry I thought...I just..." He cleared his throat, flustered. "You have everything going for you...two great parents...you're smart..." He paused and then glanced away self-consciously. "You're freaking adorable..."

My heart thrilled at that, but when he looked back, he was upset. "I couldn't understand that first night why you wanted to screw that up, by smoking, that is. You know it was stupid, right? I was glad when it looked like you were about to hurl..." he went on and on as if he were scolding a small child, which was how he was making me feel, which was stupid, because he was actually younger than me. Why did he have a monopoly on rebellion? Why did I have to be perfect?

"You never did tell me why," he pressed. I knew him well enough now to know that I wouldn't be able to distract him again, but the reason he sought was stuck in my throat.

Where did he get off asking me for it anyway? He was no bastion of—

"Catherine, you're smart enough to know the consequences..." He shook his head again, and that's when my reason tore itself free and threw itself violently into his hypocritical face.

"You don't think I know the damn consequences?" I snapped hotly. "I see them playing out every day at home! In my *perfect* world. It sucks to watch...to hear someone dying in the room next to yours, and it sucks worse to know they did it to themselves. I wanted to know if it was worth it! I wanted to know if—"

He was startled by my furious counter attack, and he fumbled his words. "Wh...what are you—"

"My grandmother is dying," I said sharply, and then I stared him down. There. The splinter was out.

Oh Christ...

I wasn't prepared to face the mangled mess it left behind. I didn't want to deal with that part, so I clamped my mouth shut and looked away. He was silent for a moment, just breathing. Then he sighed himself into the glowing candlelight and reappeared within my new field of vision. He was nearly invisible within my shadow.

"Catherine..." he whispered.

I wrapped my arms around my legs, and buried my face in my knees.

Tell him...

No.

Let go...

No!

You don't have to be alone in this. He really—

"NO!" I lifted my eyes and set my jaw. He was startled again. The small amount of candlelight that made its way around me reflected temptingly in his darkened eyes.

"*Catherine...*" he whispered again, and though I could still see the faint outline of his face a few feet in front of me, the sound of his voice came from just above my left ear, and I closed my eyes and leaned into it. How did he do that?

"How long does she have?" he asked quietly. He was trying to draw me out. His voice was hypnotic.

I shook my head, but my thoughts broke my rules. They let themselves out. Just like my reason. Only they just wanted to be understood.

"I don't know...months...weeks. No one tells me anything. I guess I don't ask. I don't want to know," I murmured and then looked up into his face. Yeah. I wanted someone to understand.

"She's suffocating, Michael." I pulled out my inhaler and held it up for him to see. "I know what that feels like, and it scares me." I looked down at it with growing resentment, my muscles tensing all the way up my back, in my throat, in my jaw, and I cocked my arm back to wing the damn thing into the shadows that surrounded us.

"Don't!" His voice was an anxious bullet that knocked my arm down. "What if you *need* it?"

I let my hand drop back into my lap and twirled the little case in my fingers. I was too much of a baby to do what I really wanted to do, which was to chuck it all—the meds, the inhalers, the doctor appointments—just to see what would happen, to see if I could survive without them. And at that moment, I finally realized what I was afraid of.

"I don't want to die like...her..." My voice caught, and I breathed hard to smooth it out.

"You won't..." he started to reassure me. I was used to that. People worrying about me then telling me everything would be alright. It was annoying. Extremely. I just rolled my eyes and stuffed the offending object back into my pocket.

"Right," I said, scowling.

"Catherine...I'm sorry."

"It's fine." I turned my head away and gazed back into the eyes of the jack-o'-lantern. I'd cut out his eyes and made him smile. I felt my jaw tense and focused on relaxing it. "Can we please talk about something else now?"

In my peripheral vision, I saw his shape slowly fill in to the left of the jack-o'-lantern, and I shifted my gaze slightly to take in his expression. He was studying me carefully, and for a minute, he didn't say anything. Then he looked down at his feet.

"Um...I really miss my left Converse," he said, and then he wiggled the mangled naked toes of his left foot. "It was my favorite."

He glanced up anxiously into my face from under his long lashes to see if he'd said the right thing. He had, and I almost laughed. Almost. I'd forgotten that he knew what it felt like to desperately not want to talk about something. I escaped with him to the new topic.

"So…is that the only thing you miss?"

He thought for a minute. "I miss my favorite jeans. They were light blue, like totally broken in, and they had this little frayed hole above the right knee." He gestured with his hand to show me where. "A real hole, not one of those pansy holes made by the manufacturer."

I felt the tension easing out of my shoulders. "Go on."

"Um…" He closed his eyes for a minute and then said, "Bruce Springsteen." He lifted his hands to an imaginary guitar and started to play as he hummed the opening notes of "Thunder Road."

"I love that song! It was playing on the car stereo when my dad let me take his car out on the highway for the first time!"

He paused in his playing and asked, "What kind of car?"

"A 1971 Dodge Demon."

"So…you drive a Demon, and you talk to ghosts dressed as a witch. That's freaking awesome!" he laughed and picked his air guitar back up. "That's the song I would've picked if I'd learned to drive." Then he looked off into the forest, still strumming, and added, "It was my dad's favorite. He liked to play that when me and my mom and him went out for a drive. He would sing it to her, horribly…" He paused, cleared his throat and went back to concentrating on his playing.

"So you must have inherited your voice from your mom then?"

"Among other things," he murmured. He didn't look up from his playing, so I let it go.

"So, we have your tennis shoe, your jeans, Bruce Springsteen, anything else?"

He bobbed his damp blonde head up and down a few times as he played and then lifted his fingers up.

"My fingernails," he said matter-of-factly. "They feel weird, weirder than the rest of me, like…really numb…" He brought them up near his face to study the ragged nail beds. They still looked raw and incredibly painful.

"Do they hurt?" I nodded to his fingers.

He shook his head, and a wry smile crossed his lips. "Nah… it's like I spent the morning with a special effects artist. The cuts and scrapes feel like they're painted or glued on, mostly numb to the touch."

He looked up at me, and I inched closer, reaching out tentatively with my fingers.

"Can I?" He pulled his hands away, but glanced up cautiously into my face and then held them back out palms and forearms up, fingers curled over, steady and waiting for my touch. I lifted my hand over the place where his fingernails should have been, then took a quiet, anxious breath before gently touching the tips of his fingers. He shivered but kept his hands and arms still. I felt nothing solid, but a fuzzy sensation travelled up my arm, like a pulse of heavy static electricity without the shock. I yanked my hand back, startled, and looked up into his face. He gave me a strange look.

He said, "See? No pain, but...shit. That felt weird."

I rubbed my forearm absently. "Have you touched anyone else since you became a ghost? Does it always feel like that?"

He laughed out loud. "What. Do you think I've been cheating on you, Genius?"

My cheeks burned. "I was just—"

"Relax." He lifted his chin and laughed again. Then he looked away self-consciously. "Yeah, I did a little experimenting right after I—" My eyes went wide.

Seeing the look on my face, he hurriedly added, "Chaste experimenting, strictly G-rated, and no, it only feels that way with you, with anyone else it feels...um...strange, but not nearly as intense. And no one but you ever noticed I was there. I don't know why."

I inched closer still to get a better look at the lacerations that laced his forearms, but my attention was drawn to older, completely healed wounds beneath them. Small, pale and shiny raised circular scars. There were three of them on his left arm. I had one to match them on my palm. My cigarette burn. I held up my palm next to his arm for comparison.

He saw what I was looking at and pulled his arms quickly away and tucked them in close to his body.

"What happened to your—" But I didn't have to finish the question. He'd been burned, too. Either he'd done it to himself or he'd been abused. My stomach rolled completely over.

"Oh, Michael…"

"You promised!" he snapped, and I dropped my hands and concentrated on keeping my eyes dry.

My cell rang, and I blinked. Then, Michael was gone. I cut my eyes from the empty space in front of me to the face of my cell.

10:00 p.m. My dad's phone. He was probably wondering when I was coming home. I ignored the call and looked around for Michael. He had reappeared and was observing me pensively from a distance.

"You should go," he murmured. "You shouldn't be out here this late alone." He faded slightly for a moment and then cocked his head to the side as if he were listening for something.

"I'm not alone."

"Yeah. You are. There's nothing I could do if anyone…you know…"

I had never thought about that, and I gathered up my stuff. When I was ready to go, I walked over to him and glanced up into his ghostly, pale face.

His jaw twitched, and he nodded stiffly. There was tension between us. I'd uncovered part of his secret, and he was keeping the rest of it locked up tight. He didn't trust me enough to share it. I'd find out though. If my mom couldn't or wouldn't tell me what happened to him when he was little, I'd find out another way. I'd find out who was responsible for burning him and, God forbid, anything else that had happened to him. I'd make sure they paid, and then we'd deal with the pain that was left behind together.

Maybe then he could go home.

Chapter 15
The Death of an Innocent

THE HISTORIC KING home was perched on a cliff overlooking Lake Erie in Bay Village. It was over a hundred years old and built almost entirely out of weathered local limestone. The home, which had been in Mrs. King's family since it was built, was meticulously landscaped in the front and bordered on three sides by a high wrought iron fence. The back was largely overgrown. Rose bushes overran the brick patio, and tangled vines crawled all over a wrought iron gazebo. The only explanation was that Jason's mother, Dr. Natalia King, liked the seclusion the dripping foliage provided for her family.

I'd struck out with my own mom earlier that day. It was November first, All Saints Day, which is a holy day on which Catholics are obligated to attend Mass. As usual, she had fought with Mina over receiving Communion, which Mina continued to refuse, just like she had ever since her son was denied a Catholic funeral after he committed suicide. But that happened years ago, before I was born. The Church didn't treat suicides that way anymore, but that didn't matter to Mina. She was still angry, and it was likely she would stay that way. I could hardly blame her. I think I would have felt the same way.

But my mom was troubled deeply over Mina's separation from the church, and by the time I came home from school, she was in no mood to talk about anything. She waved me away when I approached her about Michael's childhood and then disappeared into her room and locked the door.

So here I was, in the middle of Plan B. After draining my savings account, I waited on the King's front steps with a new cell phone while the wind buffeted me from all sides. It was bitter cold, and the heavy gray clouds that hung low in the sky were supposed to pelt us with ice later. The Halloween wind the night before hadn't been bluffing.

Evelyn, Jason's thirteen-year-old sister met me at the door. She was dark-haired and tall, like Jason, and she was just beginning to show her curves. She smiled when she opened the door. Evelyn had always liked me—unlike her mother, who'd never thought I was good enough for her son. I was too "middle class." Except for the one time she walked in on us in his room, Jason and I spent our time together when his mom wasn't around. Embarrassing doesn't even begin to describe that moment. She'd only had to give Jason a look before he was showing me out the door, but that look in her eyes still haunted me.

"Hi, Cate," Evelyn greeted me. "Does Jason know you're—"

"Hey, Cate!" Jason called from the top of the marble staircase in the two-story foyer. Then he fired his gaze down on his little sister. "Did you finish your homework, mud face?"

She rolled her eyes before she nodded.

"Then you'll find some sushi in the refrigerator. I picked some up on my way home from school." Evelyn's face lit up, and she took off toward the kitchen. Sushi was her favorite food. Jason leaned over the iron railing and called down to me, "Come on up!"

I kicked off my shoes and headed up the cold stairs, passing the oil paintings of his grandparents on my way. The house was huge, but in a carved-up, mazelike way, and when only Jason and Evelyn were home, which was most of the time, it seemed as if the rooms and hallways went on endlessly, losing themselves in hidden corners. There were six bedrooms and four bathrooms upstairs. Jason's room was all the way down at the end of the hall at the back of the house. He waited at the top of the stairs until I reached him and then stepped aside so I could go ahead of him, brushing his hand lightly across my back. Manners were paramount in the King household.

His queen-sized bed was next to a huge, wood-framed window that looked out over the cliff at Lake Erie. If I could have had any room in the world, this would have been it. From his bed, you could see the sailboats, the freighters, and the summer storms whipping the waters up into chaos, and it seemed like it stormed almost every time I was here last summer. But today, the entire view was shades of gray: dark gray choppy water, lighter gray clouds, and lighter still, the rocky concrete break wall that stretched far out into the lake. Even the crumbling stone fence that separated his backyard from the fifty-foot drop down to the small beach below was gray.

Jason grabbed an armful of textbooks off his bed and dumped them on his desk on top of a pile of binders that were thick with dog-eared notepaper. He shoved a black suit down toward the foot of his bed. I saw the Armani label before it rolled up on itself.

"Sorry, I've got three tests tomorrow and a paper due in Latin, and I'm supposed to do this benefit thing with my mother tonight."

"I can come back," I said.

"No. It's fine. Just let me..." He pulled his suede comforter up over his wrinkled sheets, propped a few pillows up against his ornately carved mahogany headboard and settled down against them, facing me, his light blue eyes, as always, curious and attentive.

"So...what's up?" he said. He never changed. Now that the mess was hidden away, he seemed perfectly relaxed in bare feet, a pair of faded black sweats and a white T-shirt. I was on edge. It felt strange to be in his room after the way we'd been last summer. On top of that, I could feel all of the muscles in my back tensing as I thought how best to phrase the question I needed to ask him. I decided to start with restitution.

"Well, I finally got your new phone," I said, holding out a white bag.

He grinned and said, "Cate...I was just teasing. I already bought a new phone." I looked around his room at all the state-of-the-art computer equipment and upscale vintage furniture and felt kind of stupid. Of course his parents would have bought him a phone. They could afford it.

"What did they get you?" I asked, setting the bag down on the floor, and sitting down on the edge of the bed.

"They? No. My parents believe in making Evelyn and me work for what we get." He held up a brand new cell phone and waved it back and forth.

"Then, how did you—" I started to ask, and he grinned, spreading his hands out and gesturing around his room.

"You're looking at a highly successful online entrepreneur." I looked around and finally noticed all of the little boxes that were stacked up everywhere. I plucked one of the boxes out of its pile and saw that the return address was from Doctor Jackson King, M.D., Jason's father. I raised my eyebrows, and he just shrugged and said, "People trust a doctor more than a sixteen-year-old kid. My dad knows. He doesn't care."

"So what are you selling?"

He took the package out of my hands. "I started with old baseball cards and traded my way up to small electronics," Jason said, placing the box on his bookshelf next to what I knew to be one of his prized possessions, the World War II era knife he'd inherited from his grandfather. Then he came back and sat next to me on the edge of the bed. "So, really Cate, what do you need?"

Not knowing where to begin, I turned around, pulled my feet up onto the bed and sat with crossed legs looking out at the water. It was getting darker.

"Damn, Cate," he said, crawling over behind me. "You're so tense. What's the matter?" He sat up on his knees and massaged my neck and shoulders. I closed my eyes and relaxed into it. His hands were strong and his fingers, perceptive. He quickly found the knot that had taken up residence above my right shoulder blade and focused his efforts there. He worked his thumbs over and back rhythmically to loosen it up. I started to feel warm and found myself suddenly wishing for more…but shit, this was awkward.

I turned halfway toward him, which disengaged his hands, and then pulled my knees up under my chin and wrapped my arms around them protectively.

"How's Kara?" I asked pointedly. As in, hey, Jason, remember you have a girlfriend? As in, hey, Cate, remember you dumped him? He sat back with his feet tucked under him, his brows furrowed.

"Her parents split up, and she moved back to Indianapolis with her mom last week. I thought you knew that." He looked out the window. The wind was picking up, and the vines hanging off the gazebo were swaying. I should have known. The whole school was probably talking about it—but then I'd pretty much removed myself from the social scene lately.

"Are you guys going to try to—"

"We broke up, Cate," he answered abruptly. "She wanted it that way. A clean break, she said." Well, that sucked. The last time they broke up, he was a mess. I reached out my hand and touched his knee. "I'm sorry, Jason."

His contemplative eyes took on a wicked gleam, and a slight smile turned up one corner of his lips. He slid his left hand under my outstretched arm and the other under my knees and pulled me up onto his lap.

"How sorry?" he whispered into my neck, caressing the hollow with his nose and circling my bare ankle under the damp edge of my jeans with the tips of his thumb and forefinger. The warmth I had felt before sank down deep into my thighs where it began a slow burn.

"Ummm..." was all I could manage. He worked his lips upward under my chin, kissing me softly as he forced my neck up into full extension.

"Um...Jason...?"

He pulled his face back a few inches and appraised me with glittering, ice blue eyes. "I'm free," he pointed out.

"Didn't we already try this once?" I protested without much conviction.

He lifted his chin thoughtfully and said, "Ever try? Ever fail? No matter. Try Again. Fail again. Fail better." Then he lifted my calves up with his right arm and tilted me back onto the bed.

"I agree with Samuel Becket," he murmured deep in his throat as he positioned himself over me. His hands sunk into the mattress on either side of my head. Despite his player reputation, he'd always been gentle and patient with me, respecting my limits, and so he paused there, waiting for my signal.

The storm suddenly broke loose on the thin span of glass separating us from the elements. Slushy ice drops smacked hard against his window, and the view of the lake disappeared. The shingles on the roof rattled as a blast of wind exploded over the top of the house. I thought of Michael trapped out in the storm.

"I can't do this," I said, feeling inexplicably panicked, and pushed myself up off the bed. I walked over to his bookshelves, pulled out *Paradise Lost* and held it up. On the cover was a picture of the Archangel Michael with a fiery sword poised in mid-air above a chained dark devil.

"Don't you remember that we argue about everything?" I reminded him.

He got up and grabbed the book roughly out of my hands. "Maybe I get a little intense in my opinions sometimes."

"A little?"

"Okay, maybe more than a little. But that doesn't mean I didn't like talking to you about this stuff. You're smart, Cate. You helped me redefine my views."

"So I've created a convert?"

"Hardly…" He rolled his eyes and shoved the book back onto the shelf. "Cate, you came over for a reason. What is it?" He was annoyed with me. Again. But I reminded myself that this was for Michael, not me. I took a deep breath and sat back down on the bed.

"I need you to do something for me, Jason." I tried to keep my voice even. "I need you to find out what happened to Michael. Why he was put in foster care and what happened to him after that."

Jason's expression didn't change…much. "Do you mean your friend who fell off the cliff last August?"

His name is…was Michael Casey. Father, Aidan. Mother, Janine. I need you to…um…hack or whatever it is you do into wherever you need to hack, to find out."

"Why?"

"Jason...he was a really good friend of mine, and I've heard rumors..."

"What kind of rumors?"

"Rumors that he was abused," I said. "I just need to know the truth."

"Is that what's been bothering you since we broke up? Michael's death? I thought maybe it had something to do with you and me."

I looked away and nodded. My throat felt tight. My face felt hot. My eyes filled. Shit, this was supposed to be a fact-finding mission, not a freaking therapy session.

"He was my friend, Jason," I squeezed out. "I can't sleep...I can't..."

He sat back down on the bed, wrapped his longs arms around me and rested his chin on top of my head, all trace of his earlier irritation gone. "Sh...Cate, you're a wreck. Do you want something to calm you down? Help you sleep? My mother has some valium..."

I pulled away and looked up into his face. He was serious and that startled me.

"Just hold on." He got up and disappeared down the hall. I was worried he would come back with a bottle of pills. Instead, to my relief, he came back with a whole roll of toilet paper.

"Sorry, I never have tissues in here." I took the roll gratefully, and he pulled his leather desk chair over so he could sit facing me. He leaned forward with his elbows on his knees and waited for me to clear out my nose.

"Look, Cate, if I do this for you, you have to promise me you'll let it go after that. This is the stuff that can really screw with your head, all the 'what ifs' and 'if onlys.' Michael's dead. Nothing you do now is going to bring him back." He brushed my chin with his fingers and then pushed my long, wavy hair back over my shoulders. "Okay?"

"So you'll do it?" I asked, suddenly hopeful.

He gave me a wry smile and then grabbed a yellow legal pad off his desk. "Tell me everything you know about him."

≈≈

During the weeks I waited to hear from Jason, Michael retreated farther and farther emotionally from me. It was almost like he knew I was getting closer to whatever memories were haunting him. We spent less time talking and more time sitting quietly together on the edge of the cliff. The leaves fell away and the snow began to fly. The bare-naked sycamores along the riverbank spread their white, rippled claws upward and outward from the base of the cliff, and ice formed on the water, thin skins that formed and disintegrated over and over.

It was during Thanksgiving break that Jason finally called and asked me to meet him at Jai Ho. He had some information for me. When I pulled up in the Demon, he was already there waiting for me in his Audi. The sky was spitting snow crystals at us, but nothing was sticking to the ground yet. He gave my parka a strange look.

Since my mom quit her job, I hadn't been able to bring myself to tell her my winter jacket was too small. I knew they were expensive, so I'd poked around in the basement and resurrected one of my dad's old coats. It was ridiculously huge on me, but with a few sweaters underneath it was toasty warm. It was perfect for long walks in the snowy woods with Michael. I raised my eyebrows at Jason and pointedly fluffed up the fur around my hood. We couldn't all be the lord of an online fiefdom.

I slammed the Demon's heavy door just as he came up behind me.

"Aren't you going to lock it?" he asked, seeing the lock button still popped up.

I shook my head. "If I lock it, I'll never get back in," I shrugged and then turned and headed into the coffee shop.

Jai Ho was a little hole in the wall in the same small shopping strip as the 7-Eleven on my bus route. In contrast to the national chains' upscale, warm and cheerful feel, Jai Ho's décor was cluttered and utilitarian. There were no plushy booths, only tables and chairs with stainless steel legs spread out between the smudged white walls. The serving counter was piled high with coffee, tea and Indian food staples.

Jason unzipped his dark leather jacket as he stepped up to the counter. "Hey, Ravi. Namaste. A double espresso, please." Then he looked down at me. "What would you like, Cate?"

"I don't need you to pay for me," I grumbled. He rolled his eyes, I rolled mine back, and Ravi smiled. I let him buy me a vanilla chai. What I needed was a job, but right now I didn't have time for one.

We sat down at a table in the corner. Jason shrugged off his jacket and tugged the sleeves of his gray Saint Joan hoodie down to his wrists. He pulled a manila folder out of his backpack and laid it on the table in front of me.

"I've been busy with basketball, so I haven't been able to crack his entire file yet, but I found this information on a criminal case against his first foster parents, Tilda and Bryce Johnson."

I reached across the sticky table for the folder, but he placed his hand down flat on top of it.

"Cate...there are some graphic photos in here. I want you to know that they're not of Michael before you open it."

Not of Michael? He searched my eyes to make sure I understood. I nodded, then he flipped open the folder.

The first photo was of a young child, maybe five of six, laid out on a steel table. Steel table? I leaned forward to examine it. My eyes zeroed in on the cigarette burns, only these hadn't healed yet. There were three on his chest, dark red and crusty. The child had bruises too, on his face and on his upper arms where it looked like someone had squeezed him too hard. His skin was doughy white, except for his lips and fingertips, which were bluish.

I sat abruptly back in my chair, feeling sick, and stared at Jason.

"The kid was murdered, Cate. By the Johnsons."

"What was his name?" I whispered.

"Stephen Angeles."

I started to shake my head, and then I bent quickly back over the photograph and found the date. Michael would have been around eleven.

"Was Michael there when—"

Jason was already nodding before I finished my question, and I blinked a few times. Habit when I was talking about Michael's past.

Keep the eyes dry at all costs. Jason easily interpreted the gesture and started to pull the file back toward him, but I shook my head vehemently, and he let go. I started flipping through the rest of the papers. There were several photos of the child from different angles, including one of the back of his small, blood-caked head. There was also paperwork on when he arrived at the Johnsons', which wasn't too long before his death. The trial ended abruptly when the Johnsons pled guilty to second degree murder in exchange for a more lenient sentence. There was no paperwork on Michael.

"Is that it?"

"Isn't that enough, Cate?" he asked. "Doesn't that answer your questions? It's obvious that Michael must have been abused, too. That must be why he turned to drugs and—"

"He was clean when he died!" The words erupted from my throat like lava from a volcano, and the people at the table across the room from us turned to see what was going on.

"Sh...what are you talking about? Everybody knows—"

"He was clean," I whispered forcefully. "I know it. Luke Devlin knows."

"Cate, listen to yourself! We talked about this. You can't change who Michael was just because you don't want to believe it. If anyone had reason to be on drugs, it was Michael. He probably needed them just to forget—"

"Forget what? This murder? What else?"

Jason usually had incredible control over his impulses and emotions. He'd demonstrated that time and again during our summer romps in his bed, but he flinched subtly.

"You have more, don't you?" I accused. I could see it in his eyes. He knew more about what had happened to Michael than he was telling. He just didn't want to upset me. "What else do you have? Let me see it."

He pressed his lips together unhappily, but reluctantly dug one more photo and another plea agreement out of his coat pocket. I glanced at the plea agreement first. Seven years. They'd pled guilty to child neglect in Michael's case in exchange for a sentence of just seven years added to the murder sentence. I tossed the plea agreement aside, disgusted, and pulled the photo across the table. I didn't understand what I was looking at. It was a photo of a wooden trap door in a dirty concrete floor, closed and bolted shut. I looked up at him questioningly. Jason pointed at the photo.

"That's where the police found him."

"Found who? Found Michael?" I looked back at the picture, at the trapdoor, and a low moan escaped my lips. "In there?"

Jason nodded.

Oh shit…

⁂

The snow was up to my ankles by the time I hiked into the woods that afternoon, and it was still coming down in heavy white clumps. The huge flakes somehow made it through the dense pine rafters and into the shadowy gray interior of the forest, clothing the ground in damp white wool. White. Cool gray. Deep green. I missed them all. My eyes kept coating the soothing colors with Michael's hot blood. In my mind's eye, it spilled bright red from his mouth onto the newborn snow, steaming as it melted its way down to the ground. My emotions had reached the boiling point. They had gone from rich, black sorrow to riotous rage. What else had the Johnsons done to him?

And Jason—when he'd refused to give me more details about the abuse Michael suffered, I'd stormed out of the coffee shop. He'd begged me to stay and calm down and looked worried when I left. I suppose I should have been grateful for the information he did give me. I'd have to call him later and apologize—

"What's wrong, Catherine?" Michael was speaking before he fully materialized. His eyes were screwed up with concern. "Is your grandmother okay?" Since the night I exploded about her illness, he never failed to ask about her, and I never failed to shut him down, subject closed.

"She's fine," I said vaguely, then asked, "Why would you—"

"You just seem…stressed," he said, shifting his weight restlessly. "You're usually pretty happy when you walk into the woods."

My simmering rage made my voice shaky, and I took a deep breath to steady it. "Not here, Michael." I wanted to be safely cocooned in our lightning tree clearing before I told him why I was upset. He was going to be pissed that I dug into his past again.

"Okay." Where I failed at patience, he excelled. He would wait forever for me to be ready to talk about something I didn't want to talk about. "Then, I have a surprise for you. Ask me where you should meet me today." He relaxed and grinned.

"What?"

"Go on. Ask me. Where should I..." he prompted, rolling his hand around in a circle in front of him.

"Okay...where should I meet you?" I asked uncertainly.

He smiled. "Why don't I just walk *with* you?" he said. "I've been practicing."

"I'd like that..." I murmured, still buried eyebrow deep in dark emotions.

"I thought you'd be happy," he said as he fell into step next to me. He sounded disappointed.

"I am. I just..." I looked sideways at him and saw a drop of sweat drip down his arm. It slid over the tattoo on the rounded muscle of his bicep and then followed the muscle's contour back toward the crook of his elbow before disappearing on the inside of his forearm. Another drop ran down the back of his neck, which was glistening with sweat. He looked hotter than hell.

"Crap, Michael. Aren't you cold?" I don't know why I never thought to ask before. With his one bare foot, sleeveless shirt and cutoffs, the poor kid was half-naked.

"I wish. It still feels like it's over ninety freaking degrees to me, just like on the day I died. And when I concentrate, like I'm doing right now, I get even hotter."

"Oh. You don't have to—"

"Hey, there's practically squat I get to do for you. You come out here and entertain my sorry ass no matter what the weather is..."

I started to shake my head. I wasn't going to be entertaining him today.

"…don't ruin it by being all, you know, self-sacrificing, Catherine."
He rolled his eyes and then looked ahead again. He was concentrating
hard. For me. Why did I have to be the one to dredge up his past? I
started to get angry again, and I felt my forehead tense up. He glanced
over at me, quiet concern evident on his face, but didn't ask.

We lapsed into an uneasy silence after that, both of us checking
the other out every now and again, until we reached the lightning tree
clearing. It was still snowing, but it was a heavy wet snow, good snowball
packing snow, and the temperature felt more like forty degrees than
freezing. I started to get warm under all my layers and unzipped my
parka, revealing the heavy cable knit wool sweater I had on underneath.

"So there *is* a girl under there," he teased. I glanced up at him and
then looked away. The horrific knowledge I carried in my head was
screaming so loudly to get out that I was shocked Michael couldn't
already hear it. But he was tense. He could sense something. He was
already bristling.

"What, Catherine…"

A small rush of anxiety coursed through my body. The kind you
feel before you're about to confess something horrible you did. God,
was I doing the right thing by making him face his past, or was I just
torturing him?

"What?" He moved to where he could see my face again. I forced
my eyes to meet his. If I was going to shatter his day, the least I could
do was look him in the eye when I did it. My jaw slid forward slightly
as I braced for his reaction.

"Michael…I know about Stephen," I said quietly.

He didn't move for a second, not a muscle. Then he clenched his
jaw and blew a harsh breath out through his nose. Then he vanished.
Shit.

"Screw you, Catherine!" His voice boomed off the trees louder
than any human voice I'd ever heard, and I threw my hands up over
my ears for protection. Usually I could home in on which direction his
voice was coming from, but this time it came at me from all sides, as if
he were everywhere at once.

"What gives you the fu…freaking right to shove my nose back

in shit like that? Huh? Just because you're some stupid girl I used to know doesn't give you the right to get inside my head and...and..."

"Hey!" I shouted back as I spun around, trying to locate him. "For your *information*, I didn't even *want* to come back after you chased me that first night through the woods!" Did he really think I'd chosen to help him all on my own? Just for fun? It was the nightmares that made me come back. It was time he knew that. "But...but...you were in these dreams I had and..." I couldn't finish the thought. He'd just ridicule me again like he did with the song, call me insane—

"And what?" His voice coalesced into one location, and he reappeared abruptly in front of me. I jumped.

"Don't do that!" I shouted breathlessly.

"What dreams?" he demanded to know. He was standing less than a foot in front of me, his hair soaked with sweat, his intense gray eyes compelling mine to meet his.

I took a deep breath and spat it out. "I have the right to dig into your past, because in my dreams you begged me to help you."

He moved closer until his face was only inches above mine, and his expression had taken on a sense of urgency. "When? How?"

"The night you died and the two nights after I saw you the first time in the woods. I saw your reflection in a dark pool of water... and...and in the last dream you were drowning! You asked me to come back! You said you *needed* me."

I didn't think his eyes could get any more intense, but they did— and with his face so close to mine, I could almost feel them searing the uppermost layers of my skin. I plunged on.

"In the third dream, something held me above the water and forced me to watch you drown in darkness. I woke up with a sore throat, a stiff neck and bloodshot eyes as if...as if it had really happened. As if the dream was *real!* That's how I knew you were disappearing! That's how I knew you were in trouble. *That's* why I came back!"

He backed away from me with a stunned look on his face, then turned his back to me and shook his head slowly. "It's not possible," he whispered.

"Yeah! It is! Don't you see? It's like I've been telling you all along, something or someone wants me to help you and…" I bit my lip as my confidence abandoned me. Hot acid rolled up the back of my throat. "Helping you confront your past is the only thing I know to do, except from what I found out today, I don't know if you're strong enough."

He clenched and relaxed his fists a few times, then turned around to stare at me with eyes that were fiercely determined. Then he slowly crossed his arms in front of his chest, grabbed the sides of his black shirt, and in one fluid motion, pulled it up and over his head.

"I'm strong enough, Catherine."

Chapter 16
Cherish

MY JAW DROPPED open as several things competed for my attention at once. Michael wasn't tall, but he was perfectly proportioned. His sturdy muscled shoulders and upper arms flowed into powerfully developed chest muscles. Beneath them, faint indentations ran down the center and sides of his stomach, hinting at a solid six pack underneath. It was obvious he'd worked hard before he died to stay in shape, to stay strong. But the strength had come too late to prevent the cigarette burns that covered his chest. He must have been too little.

At least fifteen pale round scars were etched permanently on his chest, and the anger that filled my throat burned hot. Red hot. I remembered my mouth and snapped it shut, and then I strode up to him, my eyes blazing.

"How could they do that to you? The bastards!" I reached out my fingers without thinking, intent on tracing the evidence of the abuse the Johnsons had inflicted. If I could touch the scars, maybe I could do something to—

"Don't..." he whispered, and I looked up into his face to find his eyes closed and his jaw tight. He shook his head once, then relaxed his jaw, opened his eyes and searched for mine. There was pain there, but there was also something missing: the steel bars were gone.

"Why are you willing to show me this now?" My voice was hushed and unsure. I didn't understand. I hadn't had to do anything at all. No begging. No pleading. He'd torn his lock apart and opened the cage that hid his pain-filled childhood memories all on his own. Now, he was inviting me in. I dropped my eyes down to his chest and allowed them to linger over each burn, each point of torture, and I wondered how he had endured it.

"Because I know now that you're not just being a freaking pest. I believe you when you say you were led here. I trust you now because…" His voice caught, and he cleared his throat, suddenly lost in his explanation. I lifted my eyes back up, and he glanced away into the snowy woods.

"The night after I died I felt so damn lost…" Raw and uncensored emotion spilled into his voice as he went on. "I called out to you…I'm sorry. I'm so sorry! God! What have I dragged you into?" He buried his fingers in his wild damp hair.

I didn't understand. "Michael, what are you—"

"In my *dreams*, Catherine. I called out to you in my dreams. I had the same dreams as you on the same nights, the pool, the drowning, everything. And…" He tilted his head to the side, his narrowed eyes filling with awe. "You must have heard me."

I was suddenly cold. The wet chill stole its way right through the front of my sweater.

"I didn't…know you…dreamed," I stammered.

"Catherine," he sighed. "Zip up that puffy thing you call a coat."

I rubbed my arms briskly with my palms. "What? Why?"

"Because…you look cold…"

My teeth chattered, and I zipped the parka back up. He broke eye contact and backed away from me a few steps toward the tree with the lightning burn, the tree that held our childhood ring. He caressed it with his hand then tightened his fingers into a fist and punched through it saying, "How is this possible? How can I be affecting you when you're not even here? When you should be home safe in your own bed? How do you know things about me that I never told anyone?"

"I don't know."

"It beats the shit out of me too." He held his thumb and index finger up about a millimeter apart. "But I know I was this close to fading out for good when I had those dreams." He whistled sharply through his teeth and then plowed on.

"In that first dream? When you…when you coughed up all that blood, I thought you were dying."

I hadn't wanted to share that grizzly detail.

"And that thing that was behind you?" he asked, his voice teetering on the edge of full-blown panic. "What the hell was *that*? Did *I* put that in your head?"

My blood chilled. He'd seen everything. Was it all real, then? My scalp tingled, and I felt panic rising in my own chest that was hell bent on matching his. I forced it down. No. Michael was the one in danger here. *He* was the one who was lost.

"And in the last dream? That was the worst. I called for you. I was desperate! But when you came, you were struggling. You were screaming my *name*! And someone *was* holding you above the water, like this…" He reached around behind his head and grabbed the back of his neck with his hand.

My heart leapt into my throat. "Who?"

He shook his head and sweat droplets flew off his hair. "I don't know! I couldn't *see*! The water was rippling too much!" He shook his head again in frustration and then leaned back against the tree and closed his eyes to block it all out.

When I walked over to stand in front of him, he snapped them back open and asked anxiously, "And now you're telling me you could actually feel the effects of that when you woke up? Like for *real*?"

"Michael…"

"Christ! With dreams like that, I can't believe you came back at all."

But I'd had dreams like that before. The nightmares I'd had when I was little. They were nightmares so real they chipped away at my sanity even when I was tucked in between my parents in their bed. But I didn't need to be afraid of them anymore. They were over. Isn't that what the voice in the light promised me?

I tried to shake myself back into the present, but I became lost, a small child trapped in her nightmare memories—black, shadowy figures peering with gold-fire eyes over the edge of the bed, beautiful faces tempting me to—

"Catherine…" His voice and fragrance funneled inward and grabbed hold of me. A fog was lifting…

"Wh-what?"

"You kind of zoned out there for a minute," he said quietly, pausing to study my face, and I tried to erase the blank look I knew I was giving him. I didn't want to talk about those nightmares. They had nothing to do with what was going on now. They'd happened over ten years ago, before I'd even met Michael.

With him leaning against the tree, his eyes were level with mine, and they were filled with worry. "Look what I'm doing to you." His jaw twitched, and then he leaned in toward my face and whispered, "What if something happens to you?" His woodsy clean scent drifted into the space between us, and without the bars, his oceanic eyes were bottomless. My heart beat faster, and I felt as if I were falling…

Michael pulled his face back abruptly, and I cleared my throat, unzipped my coat and let it drip off my shoulders. "Um…h-how can you be so sure it's you sending me the dreams?"

"Who else would it be?"

I looked up pointedly, and there was the derisive laughter I expected every time I mentioned God to him. He shook his head back and forth patronizingly. I guess I knew that wasn't going to fly.

"It's going to be okay," I insisted.

"How do you know?"

"The dreams led me back to you, didn't they?"

He smiled grimly. "Maybe that's all part of my evil plan," he mumbled only half-jokingly. "Maybe we've been focusing on the wrong reason I'm still here. Hell, I don't have any idea what I'm capable of. I'm a freaking…freak of nature! Maybe I really am like, some nasty demon intent on, you know…" He pointed at me and then slashed his index finger half-heartedly across his throat.

"Don't be stupid," I said.

"Maybe you should leave now while you still can and never come back," he suggested morosely.

"Yeah, sure. And have you haunt me in my dreams for the rest of my life?"

"God!" He threw his hands up in the air and cried, "Don't say that! What if I actually did that?" He was starting to lose it again. His form was fading.

"Michael..." I soothed. "You should know by now I could never leave you here alone. Never."

"I don't see why not..."

"Seriously, I'm way too much of the stalker type."

He looked down at his feet and bounced his back against the tree, but his outline stabilized. Then he looked back up at me through his lashes, still visibly shaken.

"Um, Catherine...it's not just the dreams. There's something else you knew that no one, and I mean no one, else knows."

My scalp prickled. "What do you mean?"

He sighed and waved over at the mossy fallen log in the small clearing. "You'd better sit down. This is going to take a while," he said. "I want to start at the beginning. I want you to know everything. You need to know what you've gotten yourself into."

I raised my eyebrows, but he clamped his mouth shut and shooed me away again, so I turned and scooped the heavy snow off the log and sat down. Michael joined me, sitting lightly on top of the snow's surface across from me, still holding his black T-shirt twisted up in his hands. The temperature had dropped a little and the heavy snow flakes became gentle flurries that flew sleepily through his lithe, muscular body with no resistance at all. My eyes kept trying to follow the trajectory of each flake and predict where it would fly out on the other side of him. It was distracting, and I had to concentrate to stay focused on his face.

As he settled himself down, he absently stroked his tattoo. The small sword yielded under the rhythmic pressure of his thumb, undulating up and down like a sine wave. Then he ran his fingers through his hair and wrapped his arms around his splayed knees. He began with a question.

"Did you know my dad was a police officer?"

I nodded. "There was a picture of you looking up at him in his uniform at your wake."

"That was the only picture I had of him. I thought that was so cool, you know? That he was a policeman." He paused, and his jaw tensed briefly. "That winter of second grade? My dad was shot and killed during a police raid. I don't know the specifics. No one would ever tell me. I don't even know if they caught the asshole that did it."

"That's awful" I cried. "You still don't know what happened?" He shook his head and held up his hand to ward off more questions. Then he grasped his knees again and rocked restlessly back and forth.

"So my mom? She got sick after that, or at least I thought she was sick. She was in bed a lot and was taking all these pills and injecting herself." He moved his thumb down to his forearm, lightly trailing it up and down from the inside of his elbow to his wrist. My stomach dropped. My mom told me drugs were involved, but...

"Heroin?" I asked. He nodded. Crap. That was hardcore.

"Yeah." He looked away and blew out softly through his mouth. "So she was mainlining almost daily, only I didn't know what that was back then. I started doing for myself, you know? Trying to catch the school bus on time, eating a lot of peanut butter sandwiches, making her peanut butter sandwiches, but she never ate them. I'd find them when I got home from school all crusty and dried out on the plate I'd left next to her bed. Sometimes she'd be up by then, almost normal, and ask about my day. Other times she'd just be gone."

"Why didn't you tell anyone?" My stomach churned to think of him so small and alone.

"Who, Catherine? What was I going to tell them? I was completely clueless." He shook his head in frustration. "People knew, though. The neighbors started pulling their curtains closed when my mom's new 'friends' came and went. Sister Patricia came by once. And someone must have called Social Services because they showed up a few times. But my mom was good at hiding her habit. Better than others I've seen. Looking back, I think maybe nobody wanted to hassle the widow of an officer killed in the line of duty."

I started to get angry again. "If someone knew, why didn't they do something? They just looked the other way? Passed you off like a freaking baton?"

"Pretty much," he said and shrugged, but his eyes held mine for a moment. "By May my mom was really hitting it hard. One afternoon I came home from school, and I couldn't wake her up. She was still breathing, but..." He dropped his eyes and focused on his fingers. "One of the neighbors came over to drop something off. She's the one who called the squad. She drove me to the hospital and waited with me until Social Services got there and then she left." He paused and looked up from his fingers. "She told me everything would be alright."

"And she never bothered to make sure?"

He looked away.

My pulse pounded. "Who was it? They should know what—"

"It was a long time ago. I can't really remember. Look, it's not the point of—"

"But Michael, you said you'd tell me—"

"I'm dead. Got it? Game over. It doesn't matter anymore. Drop it." His eyes were darkening, deepening, and his voice was rising. The sound of it wound around me eerily for several long seconds after he closed his mouth, and the hair on my arms stood up. I glanced away, unnerved. "Just...listen," he said grimly. "You need to hear this next part, because it concerns you."

I looked back sharply, my mind stumbling ahead, trying to figure out what he could be talking about. He took a deep breath and picked up the pieces of his story.

"Late that night the lady from Social Services took me to this old house. The Johnsons' house. It must have been over a hundred years old. The Johnsons were all like, 'Oh isn't he so cute!' and 'You're gonna like it here!' Even at the age of eight I'm thinking, 'Right. Sure.' The first time I saw Mr. Johnson? I thought of the Joker, you know? Like from *Batman*? He smiled at me, but there was something like totally not right about his eyes. They didn't smile with the rest of him."

His jaw twitched, and he shook his head as if he were trying to shake a memory loose.

"I just wanted to go home, you know? But they put me to bed in this room all by myself. When I woke up in the middle of the night, I had to take a leak, and I didn't even know where the bathroom was. Stupid whack jobs. Like that's the first thing you show a foster kid: where the freaking bathroom is." He rolled his eyes and then leaned in and spoke more quietly.

"I had to go bad enough that I finally got up, and as I walked down the hall, I heard this moaning sound coming through a doorway that was cracked open. I couldn't help it. I peeked." He shook his head disgustedly. "And so I'm standing there, right? I'm wondering if someone's sick when this pimply-faced excuse for a human teenager climbs off his foster sister and sticks his head out through the crack in the door."

Michael raised the pitch of his voice and added some manic gravel to it. "'Hey, stupid,' he said to me. 'I wanna show you somethin'.'" Then Michael leaned back and threw up his hands in front of him, as if he were warding off the teen all over again. "I was like, 'No way,' and I tried to bolt, but he grabbed me by the arm and dragged me down the hall, down the stairs and out onto this dirty back porch. The concrete was all uneven and cracked." Michael paused and then scratched at the back of his neck anxiously.

"I just can't understand it, Catherine. How you knew about this." He glanced away, then back. "See. There was this beat up wooden door in the floor and—"

"I've seen that door! Jason showed me a picture of it. I couldn't believe it!"

"Jason? Isn't that your tanning bed-hopping boyfriend? Did he use his super techno smarts to help you stalk my past?"

I looked away guiltily. "Ex," I said.

"You don't think maybe he's trying to impress you? Just a little?"

"No," I said defensively. "We're over."

"Uh huh. Well, he might have shown you a picture of the trapdoor, but that's not what I meant about you knowing things you shouldn't know. That foster kid told me something that night that you won't find in any freaking cyber file." His eyes became cloudy and distant, and he nodded a few times. "Yeah. I'll bet that teen thought he was so funny, scaring the crap out of a little kid..." Michael's face went slack for a moment, and then he made a face as if he'd smelled something bad. He lowered his voice more.

"The kid unbolted the door and pulled it open, and this nasty, only-something-dead kind of smell poured out of the dark hole. Then he said, 'You know who lives down there, kid? The Johnson's first foster kid, only he's all growed up now. They keep him locked up down there because he murdered their second foster kid with an axe. Yeah.' And then he belched this laugh right in my face and shoved me down the crumbling concrete steps and slammed the door shut. All I could see were piles of dirt as tall as me and spider webs before the door closed. 'Do you see him, stupid? He sleeps back in the corner with his axe, Cletus the Axe-toting Freak! Do you see him, you stupid ass kid? Do you see him?'" As Michael's voice faded he watched my face carefully, waiting for the reaction he knew would come.

I was momentarily paralyzed by the wave of shock that slammed into my chest, and I was finding it hard to breathe. How the hell did his most terrifying childhood memory flash through my mind on the night the coyote attacked? Without that "Cletus the Axe-toting Freak" memory, I would have charged into the bathroom and been torn to pieces. It probably saved my life. No. It did save my life. I was stunned. I was lightheaded—

"Breathe, Catherine," Michael said suddenly from the air next to my ear, and I sucked in a deep shaky breath. "How did you know about that, Catherine? How could you possibly know? I never forgot that night, and I never told anyone. Telling would have made it—"

"Real," I whispered.

"Yeah."

"Shit."

"Yeah."

We were both quiet for a few minutes until a flock of crows landed in the trees above us and stirred up our silence with their raspy calls. The chaotic rustle of flapping feathers drew my eyes upward, and I watched them force their way up through the tops of the pines on their shiny black wings. I gripped the edges of the deeply-grooved log I was sitting on with my fingers. The world had shifted, and I was dizzy.

"I just don't get it," he mumbled anxiously and then looked at me curiously. "Can you read my mind? Did you read that thought in my head? Did you pull the dreams out of my head?"

I shook my head in confusion. "No…I don't think so…it's got to be you. You're the supernatural…whatever." I waved my hands in his direction. He started to shake his head. I raised my eyebrows, and he sighed again.

"Shit. I don't know…maybe. Maybe you were right about me putting thoughts in your head. Like that song, 'Kryptonite.' I have to admit, that song pretty much said everything I was thinking when I first saw you that night." He dipped both of his hands into the snow and then pulled them back out without knocking a single icy flake out of place. Then he asked suddenly, "What am I thinking right now?" He furrowed his brows in deep concentration, and I stifled a laugh.

"What? I'm serious," he said, but then the corners of his full lips turned up, too. He mashed his lips back together and said, "No. Seriously." Then he closed his flickering eyelids and rubbed his thumb and forefinger across his forehead. I cleared my throat, closed my eyes and tried to concentrate, too.

"Okay," I said. "You're thinking this is all so stupid."

He looked annoyed and said, "Yeah…but you could have guessed that."

I fought back another grin. It was true. He wasn't that hard to read when he was fired up.

"Try again," he said, closing his eyes and placing his fingers on his temples. I laughed outright.

"Catherine!"

"Okay…" I closed my eyes again and waited to be inspired. I didn't see anything except the back of my eyelids for a few minutes. Then a picture of Stephen, the murdered boy, flashed in front of me, and my stomach soured. My eyes flew open, and I found Michael staring at me, waiting with a pensive look on his face.

"What did you see?"

"I…" I shook my head and bit my lip.

"What. Did. You. See?" he asked again, enunciating each word slowly. And I wondered again why I had to be the one to poke and probe his wounds.

"I saw Stephen."

"Wrong." He dropped his chin and rubbed his hand over his face. "But then…Stephen's never that far from my mind."

"I'm so sorry, Michael."

He looked up with eyes full of anguish. "I froze, Catherine, when it all started. He was just a little kid, and I ditched him when he needed me. The Johnsons…" His voice was swallowed up by his grief.

"Michael, they tortured you! You were only eleven. The cigarette burns—"

"If it had only been cigarette burns, I would have at least tried to beat the shit out of Mr. Johnson when he went after Stephen. The cigarettes were nothing," he said bitterly. He looked down at his forearm and pointed to the top burn.

"This was my first. I got it for biting that foster kid when he finally let me out of that hole in the floor." A choked, dark laugh erupted from his throat. "Yeah, but it was worth it. He thought twice about bothering me after that."

"And the rest?" What could those awful people have faulted him for?

"Talking back, breaking things, running away. Mostly running away. They were ticks on the government's ass. What can I say? They drew their foster care paycheck every month and did their best to ignore us or make us miserable, depending on the day." He glanced down at all the burns on his chest. "I guess I'm a slow learner. They realized eventually that they needed a bigger stick to threaten me with."

My tongue felt thick in my mouth. "I don't understand."

He sighed and opened his mouth, but let it fall closed helplessly, soundlessly. Then he shook his head and tried again, with the same result. When he finally regained vocal traction, he said, "Catherine, there are other ways to burn."

He stood up slowly and motioned with his chin for me to do the same. Then he turned to expose his naked back to me. Misshapen black and blue bruises from his fall marred his upper back, and there was a ragged laceration over his right shoulder. I took a step toward him and looked more closely, and he dropped his chin and sighed softly. Underneath the destruction his fall had caused, there were three ugly maroon scars running diagonally all the way across his back. They cut him from his right hip bone to the tip of his left shoulder blade. The end of each thick scar was curved and sharpened to a point.

And the snow kept falling through him, as if he wasn't even there, as if he'd never mattered at all. My throat ached. I wanted to soothe his ruined back with a handful of soft icy snow, to clean and bandage his wounds, to help him heal, but he was trapped somewhere beyond my reach.

"Bastards. What did they—"

He looked back over his shoulder at me. "Fireplace poker," he spat. "Three strikes and I finally heeled for them. Like a stupid fucking dog…sorry, Catherine. And when Mr. Johnson was done with Stephen, he found me cowering in my room with my tail between my legs and locked me in the cellar. I was eleven years old, and you'd think I'd be over my fear of the dark by then, but all I could think about was a nut job with an axe waiting in the corner for me to fall asleep. Two days, Catherine. I was scared shitless for two days before the police showed up and found me in that hellhole. And when I crawled out of that hole, I told myself, never again. Never ever again. No one else would ever die on my watch. I'd be ready the next time." His whole body flexed hard then, from his fists to the cords of muscle in his neck. He stared off into the woods, nodding silently.

Next time. It was then that I realized how deep his wounds went, down to the core of his being. He'd spent the next four years of his life trying to numb the pain, forever looking over his shoulder, always on defense, trusting no one. Jason was right. Michael had plenty to forget.

"He was evil, Michael. A sick bastard. Not everyone is like that."

"Maybe. But you never know, do you? People can turn on you over the stupidest things." He sighed and paced away, then back and pointed at me. "You have to be ready, Catherine. So I did whatever I could to get stronger. I ran and did push-ups, pull-ups—whatever I could think of. I kept waiting for the day I'd reach six feet. My dad was over six feet tall, so I figured I had a good chance." He paused and tilted his head to the side, thinking. "I wonder if I would've been six feet tall if I'd lived longer." He looked down at me as if he wanted my opinion, but didn't wait for me to answer.

"Wherever I went, I was always on the lookout for a weapon I could use to protect myself. I tried carrying a knife for a while, but for some reason I tended to get searched frequently. Can't imagine why." He gave me a cynical grin. "I guess my reputation sort of preceded me. But…" He paused and looked me in the eye for dramatic effect. "It paid off. Like in a big way." Then he started pacing again, his feet leaving no trace at all in the snow, his hands gesturing animatedly in front of him to help him explain.

"See, there was always something nearby that might be handy in a fight. A trash can lid, a sharp pencil, a flower pot." The corners of my lips inched up at the thought of him wielding a deadly pot of pink petunias, and he turned and said, "Hey, don't laugh. You'd be surprised what you can do with a flower pot. And I had plenty of practice. I went through several foster families, and none of them lived in the best neighborhoods.

"So, I ended up in this Roberta lady's house when I was twelve. She lived in one of those dumpy duplexes on the near East side, and she had a collection of the most awesome weapons right on her living room wall above her orange plaid sofa." When he looked at me this time, a slight grin played at the corners of his lips. "Take a guess," he said.

He had me there. I had no idea. I'd seen people hang medieval swords and shotguns on their walls, but I couldn't see someone like that being approved for foster care. I shook my head.

"A wild guess?"

"Trophies?"

"Not bad," he nodded approvingly. "But no. She had a whole collection of cast iron frying pans. She was freaking nutso about them!

I mean, like who the hell collects frying pans? She oiled them and blogged about them and cooked us sausage and eggs in them. They had these Indian heads on the back, and she said they were made a long time ago in Wapawhateverville, Ohio. Very valuable." He grinned dangerously and then went on.

"I couldn't give a flying um...well, you know...why they were valuable to people like her, but for kids like me, they had one purpose only. Weapons Grade Food Utensil. Those suckers were *heavy*. The biggest pan was over sixteen inches across, and when I pulled it off the wall one day to test it out, it was a good thing I used two hands because it weighed more than a freaking bowling ball. I put it back. Rejected. I couldn't have swung it with any kind of speed or accuracy. But the Number Five, now that was perfect. It was about eight inches across, light enough to wield without breaking my wrists but heavy enough to do some serious damage." He swung his arms in a quick arc in front of him to demonstrate and his muscles rippled across his body in time with the movement. His body was a finely tuned machine.

"Did you ever—"

"*Oh* yeah," he said. "Her boyfriend was a freaking redwood and a total dickwad. I had a three year old foster sister. Cherish. She was adorable. She had thick reddish hair like my mother's, but it was curly, like yours." He let his eyes linger on my hair for a moment. The strength of his gaze made me blush, and he smiled, and then glanced away.

"She tripped over her Little People house one day and started to cry, and I don't know why, but she wouldn't stop. Roberta couldn't console her, and her whack-job boyfriend was on the phone. He said, 'Shut that little bitch up, Bertie!' And I was like, *Oh shit, here we go.* I eyed my favorite pan. When Cherish kept bawling, he slammed the phone down and grabbed her out of Roberta's hands. I grabbed the Number Five.

"When he started to shake her, I shoved him in the back. 'Hey! Treespawn!' I said. 'Pick on someone your own freakish size!' He threw her down hard on the sofa and started to turn on me. 'What. Like—'" was all he spewed out of his mouth before I had the Number

Five slamming into his big, ugly face. When he started to fall, I was like, *shit, please don't fall on top of Cherish*, but he didn't. He broke the glass coffee table into a billion pieces and was out cold."

I was breathing fast and staring at Michael in amazement. He took a deep breath and slowed his speech down. "So I sat down on the sofa, shaking like a leaf, major adrenaline overload, and I picked up Cherish and balanced her on one knee and the Number Five on the other, and said, 'Call an ambulance, Roberta. I just broke his effin' jaw.'

"Cherish stopped crying then and started tracing the Indian head carving on the bottom of the pan with her tiny fingers, and I kissed her on the top of her head. I told her I'd protect her. So when Roberta got off the phone and tried to take her from me, I waved her off with the pan. I told her she didn't deserve to have little kids when she kept dickwads like her boyfriend around. She called me a psychopath. 'Whatever,' I said. I held onto Cherish tight until the police got there and then handed her off to them. They took one look at the fallen redwood on the coffee table and arrested me."

"With handcuffs and everything?"

"Yeah, Genius," he said sarcastically. "That's usually what people mean when they say 'arrested.'"

"But you saved her!" I protested.

He rolled his eyes. "Cherish couldn't tell them what happened, and Roberta was...um...less than helpful. Who were they going to believe? I'd already been in trouble for fighting in the neighborhood and ditching school. I just wish I knew what happened to that little girl."

I couldn't say that Cherish was probably alright, because there was no way I could know that. Not after what he'd told me that day. For all I knew she was six feet underground too, and that thought made me sick. So instead I asked, "So what happened to you?"

"I had some dumbass lawyer tell me to plead it out, so I copped to some assault-type charge and was sentenced to probation and six months community service."

"That's totally not fair!"

"It was just picking up trash and painting fences. It really wasn't so bad…" he said, kicking distractedly at the snow with his toe.

"So what went wrong next?" I was fuming. How could one kid have the whole world's ration of bad luck dumped on him?

He stopped kicking his foot, but didn't look up from the snow for a long beat. When he finally raised his eyes, he said, "My mom got custody of me."

I was shocked. I'd assumed his mom was dead by then. "Was that—"

"Good?" he finished for me. "Depends on what you'd call good."

"What's *your* definition of good?" I asked, afraid to hear his answer. I backed up slowly, sat back down on the log, and patted the spot beside me. He eyed the log nervously and shifted uneasily on the balls of his feet. What was it he didn't want to tell me? I already knew that he'd experimented with drugs.

"No more secrets, right?" I reminded him quietly. "We're mind-melded, remember?" A pained look flooded his eyes in response, and he crossed his arms over his bare chest, debating something within himself. Then he turned and flopped down next to me on the log and leaned forward on his elbows. He looked down at his balled up black T-shirt, which he was twisting and untwisting around his ragged fingers.

I waited him out for a while and when he didn't say anything, I said, "Michael, you already told me you had some problems with drugs."

He tipped his head in my direction, a look of utter disbelief filling his eyes. "Are you freaking kidding me? *Some* problems? Is that what you heard me say? You weren't *listening*." He looked back down at his T-shirt and shook his head patronizingly. "It's not me that's avoiding my past. It's you."

"Michael…"

He sat up and turned toward me, his jaw set and his eyes forthright. "I'm a drug addict, Catherine," he said flatly.

"You're not a…" I stopped when I saw the stone sober look in his eyes. "Yeah, but you changed."

"Just because I *stopped* using, doesn't mean I didn't want to. That I don't *still* want to."

That revelation shocked me. Still? Even now? Jason's words rolled through my head: If anyone had reason to be on drugs, it was Michael.

"But Michael, after the stuff you went through? Anyone would have—"

"No, Catherine. You're still not listening! You've got some crazy idea in your head that I was just a victim. Always the victim. Poor Michael, none of the stuff he did was his fault. But you're wrong!" He started to fade and flicker in waves. His eyes were narrowed and filled with savage self-hatred.

"After I finished my probation? I didn't just lose my halo. I tore it off my head, blowtorched it and then threw it under a bus. Understand?" He leaned toward me, his eyes challenging me to face facts. He was right. I didn't want to face them. I didn't want to hear them.

"Michael…" I groaned.

"Just shut up and LISTEN! You need to know who you're mixed up with, who has access to your mind!" He leaned back and ran his hand through his wild damp hair and then slowed his speech down and lowered his voice.

"My mom petitioned for custody after I pled out on the assault charge. She'd cleaned herself up and was working two jobs to pay the rent on a crappy one-bedroom apartment for us over here on the west side. She was never home. At the time, I would have defined that as good. It meant I could do what I wanted when I wanted. That's when I met my good friend, Devlin." A dark squall hijacked his eyes at the mention of Luke's name, which came out as a deep-throated hiss.

"Yeah, Devlin. He was only a freshman at Saint Joan, and he was already dealing. He needed help. I gave it to him. Did you hear that? Are you listening now? I helped your favorite drug dealer. Got that? And no one held a gun to my head either. No one forced me. It was *my* choice. My stupid…" His jaw twitched, and he had to take a moment to steady his voice.

I was miserable watching him struggle through his confession. "Michael, you don't have to—"

He raised his eyebrows over hard-edged eyes and pointed sharply at me. "No more secrets, remember? *Your* rules. Not mine." He paused and leaned back over his hands.

"So...I made contacts and deliveries for him in the neighborhood while he handled the school, and for that he hooked me up with pot for free. Sometimes we even shared a bottle of Captain Morgan or a line of coke or whatever else he happened to have on hand.

"Once he got a whole bottle of Oxy in trade, and he gave me a handful just because we were friends. A handful! Do you know how many Oxycodone pills are in a freaking handful? I was damn lucky I didn't have a regular source for those, because they would have taken me down hard. I mean it, Catherine. For the first few weeks after I finished them off? All I could think about was the incredible high they packed." His gaze drifted away from me to the forest, and then his eyes lost focus as he remembered, as he craved. I could see it now, and my heart ached for him. He blinked a few times to get back on track.

"See, for me, it was all about pain relief. Shit, I figured I was *entitled* to a little pain relief by then, and I was willing to do almost anything to get it. Stealing. Dealing. Girls. It didn't matter to me." He paused then and buried his face in his hands. "Christ! Why was I so stupid?"

"But you changed," I soothed.

"I should have changed sooner! Maybe then I could have—"

"What, Michael?" I prompted softly. "Could have what?"

He looked away.

"No more secrets," I whispered to the back of his head. He turned his gaze back on me, his gray eyes filled with deep regret and heart rending loss.

"I was placed with the Gardiners, because my mom started shooting up again when I was a freshman at Fairview, and you know what, Catherine? I didn't even care! I was too busy feeding my own drug habit." He ground each word out bitterly. "Maybe I could have helped her. Maybe I could have saved her. Maybe she wouldn't have overdosed and died—"

"You're not responsible for your mother's death."

He rolled his eyes, and then said under his breath, "You have no idea, no idea at all."

He pushed himself roughly up off the log and walked a little way into the forest. He was quiet for a long time, his arms folded across his chest, his scarred back bared for me to see. It was snowing harder, and his subtly wavering form blended softly with the heavy curtain of silent flakes that fell around and through him. I waited for a while, and then I stepped quietly into the woods and stood next to him. His eyes were closed, and his chin was lifted. He was listening.

"The darkness, the quiet, it still calls to you, doesn't it?" I whispered. He remained still for another minute and then looked sideways at me, his eyes full of fatigue.

"I'm tired, Catherine. I'm tired of *thinking*. I'm tired of *feeling*. And with the dreams, the thoughts…maybe it would be better if—"

"Don't say it!" No way, I thought. "You're meant for something more. There's got to be a reason you're still here! You didn't fight your way through your whole life just to fade away!" A tiny black hole was born in my chest in that moment. It started sucking the breath out of my lungs.

"But Catherine…don't you see now how screwed up my head is? How much crap is locked up inside it? I hate that any part of my mind has touched yours! I might as well be some evil spirit who—"

"Would you just stop with the whole evil spirit thing?" I interrupted harshly, adding more softly, "My mind isn't so perfect, either."

"Christ!" he cried. "I don't understand any of this! Maybe if I knew *how* I was connecting with you! Maybe if I knew *why*…"

It was then that I remembered the last dream, the one where I'd been in the hospital. I still wasn't convinced it was Michael sending me the dreams, but *he* believed it, and that scared the crap out of him. I thought knowing about the fourth dream, the one in which he tried to save me, might reassure him that he wasn't all bad.

"You were in another dream I had before Halloween. Did you know that?"

The startled look on his face told me he didn't.

"In the dream I was sick. Really, really sick. I had pneumonia like when I was eleven, and suddenly my hospital room was submerged underwater, and I was drowning. I was trapped in the same pool as the other dreams, only this time it was *you* who tried to pull *me* out. Don't you see? I don't think they're just nightmares, Michael. I think the dreams are someone's way of telling us that we need each other. That I—"

He snorted derisively. "What could you possibly need me for? There's nothing I can do for you. Ever since I saw you leave with your telescope, I've been stuck in these woods." He threw his hands up in the air, exasperated. "Where do you get this stuff anyway?"

"Syfy Channel," I deadpanned. Well, it was sort of true.

"Shit, Catherine. You're impossible," he sighed, but a reluctant smile fought the corners of his lips, and then a small crease deepened between his brows. He took a step closer, his scarred chest hot and steaming in a dimension far beyond my own, and reached out unexpectedly to brush his ripped fingertips through the outer layers of my hair. A soft muffled rush of electricity caressed my scalp wherever they traveled.

"You have these tiny perfect snowflakes caught in your curls," he murmured.

I turned my face into his open hand, my heart racing as his static tingled through my cheek, forehead and chin. His signature fragrance saturated the nerve endings in my nose, and I opened my mouth to breathe him in deeper, but he pulled his hand abruptly back and cleared his throat.

"Um…you should go. It's getting late," he said, yanking his shirt back on over his head and stuffing his arms through the sleeve holes.

"Right…" I blinked a few times and then checked the time on my phone. It was after five and the sun would set soon. There was never enough time.

As usual, he started to disappear without even saying goodbye, but before he was gone, a thought occurred to me, and I called out impulsively, "I'll find out, Michael!"

He was almost completely transparent, but he paused and asked, "Find out what?"

"What happened to Cherish," I said. Maybe that would give him something else to hold onto. Maybe it would give him another reason to stay.

His image strengthened slightly.

"Ex tech-stalker boyfriend?"

I nodded.

His eyes filled with hope, just a little, and he returned my nod wordlessly. Then he was gone.

I felt empowered. After all these months, I'd finally found something I could actually do for him, and as soon as I reached the deeper snow of the field, I was yanking off my snow-stiffened mittens and digging my cell phone out of my pocket. I needed to apologize to Jason, and then I had two favors to ask. He'd forgive me. He always did.

Chapter 17
Every Part of Me

IT WAS THE second Sunday of Advent, the season Catholics all over the world prepare for the coming of Christmas. My mother loved going to Mass during Advent, but she would miss it again today to care for Mina, and as my dad, my sisters and I left for church, I marveled again at the sacrifices she was willing to make for her.

Another warm front had blown through the north shore—at least warm for Cleveland in December. It was in the upper forties and had rained for the past few days and except for a few sooty piles clinging to the curbs, the snow was mostly gone. Soggy brown leaves flattened themselves against the driveway, and a dreary overcast sky pressed down upon us.

Inside the church, it was different. It was warm and peaceful and quietly alive. Just inside the entrance, we paused to look at the miniature stable that was set in a pile of fragrant straw. Mary and Joseph, a shepherd and his sheep, a cow and a donkey, and a few of God's faithful Angels were all gathered inside to wait for the birth of Christ. Baby Jesus, of course, was still M.I.A.

The Mass itself was subdued, and the altar was adorned simply with a few evergreen sprays and loops of purple ribbon. Two of the purple candles were lit in the Frasier fir Advent wreath, which was set on a stand to the right of the altar. The remaining pink and purple candles would be lit during the next two Sunday Masses.

No, we weren't celebrating Christmas yet. That would have to wait until Christmas Eve. The transformation that took place every year between the fourth Sunday of Advent and Christmas Eve was pure magic. There would be full-sized, live Christmas trees with red bows and thousands of tiny white lights flanking the altar and dozens of gloriously full poinsettias arranged down in front. The whole church would smell like a joyful pine forest and melting candle wax. I imagined the ladies from the church spent all night making the change happen.

For now, though, we were waiting. My faith wavered depending upon the events of any given day, but the deeply-held beliefs and traditions of Advent lifted it up and strengthened it. It was hard *not* to believe in God this time of year. As I sat through the quiet Mass, my heart ached for Michael who couldn't be there with me to experience the warmth and hope that the season of Advent brings.

He'd stayed. And he was waiting, too—waiting for word on his beloved little Cherish. She would be five now and in kindergarten if she'd been able to escape Michael's fate.

It would be a gross understatement to say Michael had no Christmas spirit. The Sunday before, when I mentioned to him that Advent had begun, and it was only a few more weeks 'til Christmas, he scowled and then disappeared for a while, refusing to come out until I promised to keep my "merry freaking Christmas" thoughts to my seriously delusional self. He didn't believe in God, and he wasn't going to be forced to celebrate a stupid holiday in His honor just because… blah…blah…blah…

But I wasn't going to give up that easily, and he knew that, so he told me not to bother coming back on any more Sundays until after Christmas. He said, "I'll be too busy celebrating my own personal holidays by thinking deep, dark nasty demon-type thoughts that only *I* can understand."

If only I could bring a little bit of the Advent season to him. He was already surrounded by evergreens. All I needed were the candles, and I knew just where to find them.

When we got home from church, I ran up the stairs toward my room, but was brought up short by the sound of my grandmother arguing heatedly with a man in her room. There was no place to go in the house to keep from eavesdropping, so I didn't bother to try.

"I'm so sorry Philomina, but that was over twenty years ago. We don't do things that way any—"

"Get out...*breathe*...of my room...*breathe*...you sniveling twat!"

"I can understand your anger, but you need to let go of the hate in your—"

"Robbie was my...*breathe*... son. If you think...*breathe*...I will ever—" Her words were interrupted by explosive coughs, and I peeked through the crack in the door. *Here we go again,* I thought.

"I think I'd better go," said the man, who I recognized now as Father Rocci, Saint Paul's middle-aged parish priest. "She has free-will Anne. She needs to make her own choices. I can't keep intruding on her like this. If she wants to see me, she'll call."

"Out!" my grandmother choked.

Father Rocci gave Mina a genuine smile and said, "I will be praying for you, Philomina." He pushed his way out the door but stopped when he saw me standing in the hall.

"So you won't come back to see her?" I asked him.

"Not unless I'm invited. I have to respect her wishes," he said gently and started to leave again but turned around and added, "By the way, Catherine, I never did tell you personally how sorry I was about the death of your friend, Michael."

"Did you know him, Father? Did you know his parents?"

His brown eyes grew sad, and he nodded. "Yes. It's terrible what happened to them. Just keep praying for him, Catherine. Michael was a troubled soul."

I know, I thought, intending to do a lot more than pray for him. He needed more than prayers. Even I was smart enough to know that. He needed me, no matter how ineffective or faith-weary I turned out to be. He had no one else.

I ducked into my room to continue my search for candles, getting down on my hands and knees to pull my memory box out from under my bed. It was crumpled at the corners and covered in dust fluff. I pulled off the torn lid and sorted through its internal treasures—my grade school yearbooks, a pair of size 3T Cinderella shoes, a crystal wand, my First Communion veil.

I found what I was looking for nestled within the veil's pearly crown: the Advent wreath I'd made in preschool. It was made from four cups of a cardboard egg carton. Each cup was filled with green clay, and stuck in each lump of clay was a candle, three purple and one pink. A piece of green tinsel garland was wrapped around the candles to hide the clay and make it pretty.

I held it up and looked it over. Well, pretty it wasn't, but it was small and portable. It would do the job, I decided, so I stuffed it into my now fairly ratty pink bag. If I couldn't bring Michael to our church's Advent celebration, I'd bring the Advent celebration to him, whether he liked it or not.

I checked to make sure I still had matches and dressed for the cold, wet weather. Hiking boots, wool socks, old jeans, long-sleeved shirt, sweater and fall jacket. It was too warm for the marshmallow. Before heading downstairs, I rolled up a bandana and tamed my hair with it.

"Mom! I'm going to Jai Ho to study!" I called from the foyer. "Dad, can I take the Demon?" I don't know when it happened, but lying to my parents had become second nature to me. I felt a twinge of regret over that fact, but I didn't know how it could be helped.

"Sure!" called my dad.

"Wait!" hollered my mom.

I stopped, annoyed. She came around the corner with that "sorry, but too bad" look on her face. "Catherine, I need you to get your flu shot this afternoon. Your pediatrician's office—"

"But Mom! I have tests this week." Another lie.

She ignored my protest and went on in a louder voice, "Your pediatrician's office is having a flu shot clinic this afternoon and—"

"Can't I get the shot next week?"

Mom paused and looked up at the ceiling. "With your asthma, you're a high risk patient," she said, making a strong effort to keep her voice even.

"But Mom…"

"Catherine! It's important! Do it today, or there *will* be consequences. Do you understand?" Her voice was hard-edged, her eyebrows were raised, and her teeth were starting to clench together. Bad combination. Time to cut my losses and run.

"*Okay…*" I agreed, then turned on my heel and was out the door before she could call after me the automatic and obligatory, "I love you."

I tried to pull open the Demon door, but it was locked. Shit. It took me several minutes to find the "sweet spot" that allowed the key to turn. Shit. Shit. Shit. I guess it would be safe to say I was in a bad mood now.

When I pulled into my pediatrician's parking lot, I noticed way more cars than usual. Doctor Fontana's office was on the first floor, and I knew it well. It would be impossible to list the number of times I visited over the last sixteen years with allergies, colds, asthma. I was what they called "a frequent flyer."

There were at least twenty-five people waiting in chairs and a few kids sitting on the floor. I approached the receptionist's window, and she didn't even look up.

"Flu shot?" she asked and then waved toward the sign-in sheet. I didn't bother to nod. I looked at the sheet and my heart sank when I saw the long list of names already on it.

I leaned over the counter and asked, "How long?"

"At least an hour, probably more."

I hesitated. There was a flyer on the glass window that said they were having another flu shot clinic on Wednesday. I'd been healthy for so long. Damn it. I took my medications. I brought my inhaler with me everywhere. I saw the doctor, like, all the time! I did everything they asked me to do. I didn't need a flu shot today. I didn't *want* a flu shot today. I wanted to see Michael.

"I'll come back Wednesday," I whispered over the counter.

*You should stay…*whispered a voice from deep within. I knew in my heart the voice was right, but I left, and it felt good.

I wasn't sure, but I didn't think Michael would really refuse to talk to me just because it was a Sunday in Advent. I shouldn't have worried.

Advent was the last thing on his mind when I entered the woods that day.

"Come with me!" he cried, urging me forward. "I need your help!" He'd already turned and jogged off the path into the woods to the left before I could ask why. It was gloomy in the forest, and my feet kept slipping on the wet pine needles while I tried to keep up with him. He was moving fast and flickering in and out of focus as he struggled to remain visible so I could follow him. It was a good thing he'd been practicing. As it was, I could only track him for a few seconds at a time before he disappeared and reappeared several feet or yards ahead of where he'd been a moment before.

He pulled up abruptly not far from the edge of the cliff and motioned quietly with his finger for me to follow him. When I saw what he was leading me toward, I froze with my heart in my throat.

Two yellow eyes set above a mottled gray muzzle raked sharply over me. The coyote was lying on its side, but as soon as it saw me, it lurched to its feet, stretched its black lips back over its glistening fangs and growled deep in its throat. I started to back away with images of another set of murderous teeth rolling sickeningly through my head.

"Wait," Michael said calmly. I froze again, and he walked over to the canine, knelt down, and placed his hands on either side of its pointed snout. He looked it in the eye for a moment, then looked back over his shoulder at me and said, "He's hurt."

He shifted a little to the side so I could see. I had been so preoccupied with the coyote's mouthful of teeth, that I'd missed the arrow protruding from his chest. He stopped growling and whimpered a few times piteously, and I could see that he was having trouble standing.

"Can you help him?" Michael's pleaded.

I took a step closer, and the coyote jerked its head up, training his eyes on my face.

"Can't you take him to that wildlife hospital you always talk about?"

I dropped my gaze to the ground and bit my lip, then looked back at Michael. He had complete faith in me.

"Michael, they'll euthanize him. They're not allowed to rescue coyotes. It's state law."

"Why the hell not?"

"They're considered a nuisance species."

"But they're beautiful." He ran his fingertips across the coyote's back, and his fingers became lost in thick gray fur. He *was* beautiful, but...

"Yeah. And they also eat Rover and Fluffy and farmers' chickens. And they *bite* people. Remember?"

Michael turned his wrath on me then. He stood up, his hands clenched into fists at his side. "So you're just going to let him die? Whose side are you on anyway?"

I eyed the coyote warily, and he eyed me.

"Maybe I can…" I took another step forward, and the coyote steadied his stance and growled again. He was posturing, showing me he wasn't weak, lest I forget. Michael knelt back down and whispered soothing words in his ear, and the coyote dropped his muzzle and sat down on his haunches.

"Do you think he'll bite me if I try to—"

"No, he trusts me," Michael murmured. He was holding his hand out flat, palm down, and passing it back and forth through the coyote's right ear. That was easy for Michael to say. He was safe wherever he was, which was far away from here. Plus there was the fact that he was already *dead*.

I crouched down low and moved slowly toward him, and while the coyote's gaze never left my face, he remained docile. When I was close enough to touch him, I reached my hand out in a closed fist, and the coyote sniffed it with his wet nose, then looked at Michael and whimpered again. My heartbeat started to slow.

"See? You're fine," said Michael reassuringly. "So, can you help him?"

Feeling somewhat safe for the moment, which was probably the stupidest assumption I'd ever made in my life, I looked at his wound. The end of the arrow, with its neon fletching, protruded about three inches from his chest near his right shoulder, and the bolt disappeared in a pool of matted fur and sticky blood. It was angled up and outward toward the coyote's side, and it looked to me like it passed through his shoulder muscle, missing his vital organs. But with only three inches exposed, how deep was it buried? The arrows I'd seen at the wildlife hospital were almost as long as my arm.

"Do you have any idea how long this arrow is?" I asked.

Michael, who was crouched down on the other side of the coyote, held his hands up about eight inches apart. I was surprised. That was pretty short.

"What did they use to shoot him? Did you see it happen?"

"Yeah." He drew his eyebrows angrily together. "It was a couple of stupid teenagers. They were using this thing that looked like a handgun with a bow stuck to the top of it, and they were shooting wildly at anything that moved. But the balls-free bastards ran when he charged them." He turned back to the coyote and whispered, "Didn't they boy? Yeah. You showed them."

If the arrow really was that short, maybe I could pull it out. At least that was something. I fingered the fletching and thought about that. "Do you know what kind of tip the arrow has?"

"Like, what kinds are there?" Michael was back to running his palm through the coyote's pointy ears.

"Was it blunt, like the kind hunters use for target practice or was it razor-tipped?"

He stopped playing with the coyote's ears and thought for a moment. Then he pressed the tips of his fingers together in a tent shape, held them up for me to see and said, "Razor. Three blades stuck together, like this. I found another one in the mud after they left."

Shit. There was no way I could pull it out without tearing the coyote's shoulder muscle to shreds.

"I'll have to push it through," I said. Michael clamped his lips together in a grim line and nodded. He whispered more soothing words into the coyote's shaggy velvet ear.

I reached out tentatively and pressed my fingers to the edges of the wound, confirming the arrow's trajectory. Warm, viscous blood oozed out from between my fingertips. The coyote whimpered again, but held still.

I grabbed my bag and pulled out the mini first aid kit I began bringing after my first disastrous meeting with Michael, the one that resulted in my scratched up wrists and palms. I still had scars from that. I retrieved the tube of antibiotic ointment, unscrewed the cap, dropped the cap on the ground and stuck the tube between my teeth. I'd have to push the arrow out fast, no wimpy half-hearted attempt, and then be ready to apply the ointment before...well, I just hoped that wouldn't be the moment he decided to take my face off. I eyed him nervously, feeling his hot, moist breath pant against my cheek.

"Ready?" I asked, my mouth full. Michael nodded confidently. Right. Okay. I placed my right hand flat against the coyote's side, near where I thought the tip would emerge, and grabbed the tail end with my left hand.

"On my three," I said, taking a deep breath. I heard Michael murmuring softly again.

"One...two...three..." I counted and then pushed hard and fast and felt the tip ripping its way through muscle. But just as the tip bared its razor-sharp head out the other side, the coyote floundered against me.

"No!" I cried. I almost had it! The coyote bucked again, and I stupidly wrapped my right hand around the arrowhead, yanking with all my might, and as the coyote hurled himself past me, I pulled the arrow free.

"Ahh!" I cried, dropping the arrow. I jumped to my feet and shook my hand up and down, flinging drops of my blood onto the carpet of pine needles. "Shit!"

The tri-blade tip had sliced a deep cut across my palm, and I pulled my hand in to examine it. An icy sting burned all the way through it, and my fingers throbbed.

"Catherine! Oh shit!" Michael cried, springing to his feet.

"It's not bad," I said. *But it might need stitches*, I thought. I held it out for him to see.

The copious amount of blood didn't faze him. He touched the edges of my palm with the tips of his fingers, and I felt the familiar soft static course up through my wrist, but I was expecting it and kept my hand still. He looked into my face and studied it for a moment and then said, "Catherine, I'm sorry…"

"Oh…it's fine!" I said forcefully, trying not to let my eyes well up and pondered how I was going to stop the blood that was quickly pooling between the gaping flaps of skin. I picked up the tube of antibiotic cream and squeezed some onto my hand, and then I yanked the wide bandana out of my hair and wrapped it a couple of times around my palm. I tied it off and pulled it tight with the fingers of my left hand and my teeth. I held out my hand and flexed it a few times. *That should hold it for a while anyway,* I thought.

When I looked up, Michael was grinning at me. "Did I ever tell you that you're amazing?" he asked.

"Hmm… " I replied and then shook my head. "No, I don't think I've ever heard that phrase come out of your mouth in reference to me. Maybe seriously delusional or…dumbass or um, *insane*…and then there was freaking pest…"

"Okay! Stop! I get it! I can be a real dick sometimes," he laughed.

"Sometimes?"

He rolled his eyes. "Whatever…" he said, still grinning. Then he nodded in the direction the coyote had run off and said, "Thanks. I owe you. I don't think I could have stood losing another one."

"Oh? So you owe me now?" Maybe I could use that. He was immediately wary.

"Um…maybe? Depends?" he replied cautiously, rubbing the back of his damp blonde head.

"Oh, relax!" I said, watching him fidget. "What I want is really simple." I grabbed up my bag and pulled out the little Advent wreath for him to see.

"*Catherine…*" he whined.

"You let me light the jack-o'-lantern," I pointed out.

"Halloween's another one of my personal holidays."

"Michael…"

He rolled his eyes, shifted all his weight to his right foot and tilted his head to the side. "Go ahead. Light the stupid thing," he said.

I pulled out the matches and triumphantly lit two of the purple candles. Then I crossed myself and prayed: *May Christ our Savior bring His light into the darkness of our world...um...Michael's world...as he waits for His coming. Amen.*

I looked up to find him staring intently into the flames.

"Now, doesn't that kindle your Christmas spirit?" I wanted to know.

"No," he growled, but not too deeply, and that was progress. *Baby steps...*

Then it started to drizzle.

I felt a few drops on my cheeks first and then on my hair. Then they began to color the little cardboard egg carton with dark polka dots. It wasn't long before the first flame fizzled and the second one sputtered and went out.

"Crap," I said.

Michael laughed then, hard and long.

I glared at him.

"I'm sorry...I just can't help it..." He doubled over laughing, tears streaming down his cheeks. I stuffed the little wreath back in my bag and swung it through his ungrateful self and then tossed it into the woods.

"You win! I give up! Have your little nasty demon pity party!" I pouted and walked away from him across the path to the edge of the cliff. Mist was rising from the icy river below and rain was dripping from the bare branches above. Everything was gray. I was getting wet and decided I'd stay drier under the pines, so I started to turn back and—

"Michael!" I cried. He had soundlessly taken up position just a few inches behind my left shoulder.

"Sorry," he said, looking out over the gorge. Then he suppressed another grin. "And sorry about laughing back there...it's just...um... you're so flipping adorable when you're trying to convert me." Then he glanced down self-consciously at his feet. When he looked back up, his eyes were serious, and he ran his fingers back and forth through his hair, which I'd come to learn he did when he needed to say something he was afraid to say. I braced for whatever it was.

I was blindsided anyway.

"And thanks for everything, for putting up with me." His jaw flexed as he struggled to maintain eye contact. "I should have said it before. I should have said it the first time you came back after I chased you halfway through the woods, I should have said it when you came back after the hundredth time I cussed you out."

He looked down at my injured hand, which I was holding protectively close to my chest, and he stroked the edge of the makeshift bandage with the tips of his tingling fingers. The fine vibrations overrode the pain, and I held my hand out closer to his chest in an unconscious bid for more relief. He read the gesture and sandwiched my hand between both of his.

"Better?" he asked softly.

I nodded and then pleaded, "Michael, you don't have to say—"

"Catherine…" he cut me off, and then went on in a voice that was soaked with emotion, "all you've ever done is try to help me, and I've been such an ass and…"

"*Tried* to help," I corrected. "Today was the first—" But he raised his voice over mine and kept on talking, "…and thank you for coming back tomorrow, even after I practically force-fed you to a coyote today, because I know you will, because that's what you do. You come back for me over and over again." His throat filled with husky gravel. "No one's ever done that for me before."

"I don't know any other way to be," I murmured. "You're my best friend. It's like you always have been." I glanced away and dropped my hand down through his palms to my side. It immediately began to throb again, and I held it back out to him. He wrapped his otherworldly hands back around it and turned to watch the mist piling up in the gorge. It rolled over and over upon itself, higher and higher, until it finally cut off our view of the opposing cliff in the distance. It seemed like such a long time ago, the day he fell.

We stood there for a while, and then he cleared his throat. "Um…

Catherine, there's something else you can do for me today." His brows were knitted worriedly together, but he kept his eyes focused on the thickening mist. Now *I* was the one who was wary, but it didn't matter. I'd do anything for him. Anything.

"Whatever it is, Michael—"

He held one of his hands up to stop me. "Just hear me out before you start making promises." I closed my mouth and waited.

"See, I've been thinking about the connection you and me have, you know? Especially, how you knew about that whole Cletus the Axe-toting Freak thing. I keep going over and over it in my head, and I keep coming back to the same thing." He stopped and glanced uneasily down at our hands and then back up through his lashes.

"I want to test an idea I have about how you knew." He paused.

"Okay…"

"Um…do you remember what happened to us when you had that thought?"

I thought back. I had just reached the bathroom door and placed my hand on the handle when I was overwhelmed by his scent and…

"We overlapped?"

He nodded and waited for his request to sink in.

"You want to…overlap…with me…again?" I stammered. That seemed simple enough. We'd just…and then…

Seeing my flustered expression he let go of my palm and backed quickly away, waving his hands in the air in front of him. "Just forget it. It was stupid." He folded his arms over his chest and avoided my eyes. "It was—"

"No, Michael," I said, closing the distance between us again. He was right. That had to be it! Maybe he transferred the thought when our *minds* overlapped. The idea had promise. "I think we should try it," I said.

He met my eyes uncertainly. "I just…" his voice stalled out, and his jaw twitched. "I just want to understand what I am…what's happening to me. You don't know how hard it is, not knowing…"

"So let's try it. What have we got to lose?" I walked back under the pine trees to get out of the worst of the drizzling rain, and swung my arms back and forth restlessly. "So…how should we do this?" I asked.

He rolled his eyes. "Catherine, you don't have to pretend for me."

"Okay. So I'm a little…apprehensive."

He rolled his eyes again and waffled. "I don't know. Maybe…"

I raised my eyebrows at him, and he sighed. "Okay, then. I was thinking you probably shouldn't be standing in case you um…you know, pass out or whatever."

Right. I retrieved my bag from the woods, pulled out my stadium cushion and sat down on top of it with my legs crossed. He plunked down on the ground across from me. A shiver bubbled through my chest from both the cold and anticipation.

"And…" he went on, "I was thinking that I'd try to read your mind, too, you know, if that's okay with you."

"I…yeah…sure…" I pulled in a nervous breath and held my palms up facing him. He reached out his palms and brought them together with mine. That part we had down. They began to tingle again, and we were just barely touching, and though I couldn't exactly remember the sensation I'd felt when we'd overlapped last time, I knew it had been at least a hundred times more intense than that. But I was ready. So I thought. "Now what?"

"Then, I guess we…" he fumbled over his words, but I understood. We both leaned forward, but we were too far apart sitting like that, and it was way too awkward. "Shit. This is stupid. I don't think I can…"

"I think maybe we should kneel," I suggested, tucking my feet under me and kneeling up. He sighed and then flashed to an identical position facing me. The top of my head only came up to his chin.

"You're so…small…" he breathed doubtfully into my forehead. We were close enough now, that I could feel gentle static radiating from every inch of him. My heart fluttered, and he gave me a worried look.

"Catherine, are you—"

"Just shut up," I said, and then took a deep breath. "To boldly go where no man has gone before," I murmured as I held my palms up on either side of me again. He grinned and placed his palms against mine.

"Syfy Channel?" he asked, his lips turning up. I spread my fingers apart in a traditional Vulcan greeting, and he allowed his fingers to follow mine.

"Live long and prosper," I said solemnly.

"It's a little late for that, don't you think?" he teased, still grinning. "God, you're such a freaking geek." His grin faded a little, and then he cleared his throat and asked, "Are you ready?"

I nodded, keeping my eyes focused on his.

He leaned forward then, and I was falling into his deep slate-gray eyes again, but this time he was asking me to. He wanted me to. But I pulled back abruptly, suddenly self-conscious.

"Will you feel…everything? Like, you know…all the edges of me?" I blushed deeply. He was experienced and…well…ripped, and…um…his lips were like…amazing…and I was suddenly afraid I wouldn't measure up. Like it mattered…like he ever thought of me in that way anyway…like, he was dead, right?

He pulled back and studied me for a long moment.

Then his eyes softened, and his outline began to blur. His voice drifted away from him and sifted into the misty rain. "No more secrets," he murmured. He rested his weightless forehead against mine, and I longed to feel his breath on my face.

"Don't you know deep down…*Catherine*…" My name whispered past me and then curled silkily back around my ears. "I feel you every time you set foot in this forest, every part of you."

I gasped. Cool air rushed in to soothe my overheated lungs. He dropped his eyes guiltily, and his voice caressed the tiny curls at my hairline.

"Don't be mad…*Catherine*. I never could control it. I didn't tell you because I thought you'd never come back. It's just…what I am, now. I'm a part of this place and everything in it. And…" He lifted his soft gray eyes. "*You're beautiful.*"

Then he pulled his voice back, uncertainty clouding his features, waiting for rejection. "Are you still ready?"

I nodded without breathing.

"Then listen closely," he whispered.

He leaned forward again, and as his lips brushed past mine, my whole face vibrated with his hot static, and my nose became saturated with the intoxicating scent of Higher Dior. I closed my eyes as he pressed farther, and I opened my mouth to taste him, and he was sweet and salty. I breathed him deep into my lungs, feeling my whole body resonate with the essence of him. A trillion tiny pins and needles massaged my skin and the feeling only intensified as he settled deeper. My eyes burned. My nose stung. My lungs seized. My whole body rang out like a tuning fork. And then, just when I thought I would pass out, I opened my eyes and saw...light. It was warm, and it was pure, and it was completely unexpected, and it suddenly didn't matter that my consciousness was collapsing. I wanted to stay in his light forever.

Then he was ripping himself away from me, and I was gasping for air. I leaned forward on my hands while my body settled itself down. When I finally looked up, he was sitting a little ways away from me, with his elbows resting on his knees and his head cradled in his hands. I crawled the few feet that separated us, utterly spent, and knelt beside him.

"So...since the very beginning, you've felt...every part of me?"

He nodded without looking up. "It's just way more intense and detailed when we touch," he mumbled into his knees.

I was quiet for a while, and he asked, "Do you hate me?"

"No," I whispered, "I was just thinking that it's not fair that you can feel all of me, and all I feel when I touch you is static."

I reached out with the fingers of my wrapped hand to trace the angel wings of his tattoo. He looked up and covered my hand with his and the searing pain in my palm disappeared under a new wave of fuzzy vibrations. His eyes beamed earnestly.

"I can feel your heart rate and breathing slow and each muscle in your back and neck relax when I touch your hand. Can you feel it?" He trailed his fingertips back and forth across the bandana. "That's how I knew I could take your pain away." Then he grinned and said, "Usually your heartbeat speeds up when I get too close. I never could decide whether or not that was a good thing."

"It's a good thing," I assured him, grinning self-consciously back.

"Mmmm. I'll have to remember that. So…what did you hear?"

"What did I–"

"When we overlapped, Genius. Or did you forget?"

"I didn't—"

"Catherine, you totally forgot, didn't you?"

"Hey! You might have been dealing with heartbeats and… whatever, but my whole body was ringing and buzzing like the rim of a wine glass you'd just run your finger over. And it was sort of hard to breathe."

He shook his head back and forth. "I can't believe you! So you heard nothing?"

"Um…no."

Then my cell phone rang. I dug it out of my bag and looked at the screen. It was Jason. He'd have to wait. A while. Like, forever, as far as I was concerned. I never wanted this moment to end. I tossed the phone back in my bag.

"Can you at least tell me what *you* were thinking?" Michael wondered hopefully.

"Um…I have no idea…nothing? Maybe?"

My cell rang again. I rolled my eyes and dug it out of the bag again. It was my dad.

"I've got to get this," I said. I switched the phone to my left hand and held my injured hand out to him. He grinned and wrapped it up again in his left hand.

"Hey, Dad," I said. Michael began to trail the index finger of his free hand up and down the inside of my forearm, right through my jacket and sweater. I shivered. Maybe this wasn't so unfair after all.

"Hey, Bug. Just checking in. Are you still at Jai Ho?" he asked.

"Mm hmm," I mumbled. "I don't know when I'll be—"

"You need to come home. Now." An edge had crept into his voice. I sat up straight, and Michael's hand froze.

"Is everything alright?" I asked.

"Cate. Come home. We need to talk."

I looped the straps of my bag over my shoulder and stood up.

"Okay, okay. I'll be home in a half hour. I need to finish something."

"I'll see you when you get here," he said and hung up.

Another call flashed. It was Jason again.

"Why did you lie to your dad?" Michael asked, standing up.

"You heard that?"

"Um…my hearing's pretty good, too," he admitted.

"My parents wouldn't want me out here alone. They'd just worry and—"

"Catherine…so no one knows where you've been coming every day?"

I shook my head. I guess I figured Michael knew that.

"What if something happened?" he worried.

"Come on. They're waiting for me." I didn't want to talk about it. I'd deal with my parents in my own way. The steady rain had finally made its way through the sheltering pine boughs above us. My hair stuck to my cheeks in wet waves.

"You shouldn't lie to your parents," he grumbled, and I raised my eyebrows.

"Yeah…well. Look where it got me," he pointed out. We walked in silence for a while through the misty rain, and then I remembered he hadn't told me the message he'd tried to send me.

"So what *were* you trying to tell me, when we…you know…"

He grinned but shook his head. "Nope, I'll keep trying. It's a good message. Short. Simple. And you'd never guess it."

"Come on!" I pleaded. We were almost to the forest entrance, and I'd have to wait until tomorrow to continue my interrogation if I couldn't pry it out of him today.

"Nope. I—" My cell phone rang again, and I pulled it out. It was Jason. Again.

"I'd better get this, too," I said.

"Hey, Jason."

"Hey, Cate. What's up? Why didn't you answer your phone?"

I glanced at Michael. "I was kinda in the middle of something."

Michael stifled a laugh.

"Listen, Cate." Jason sounded upset. "I just wanted to warn you that your dad might call. I was at Jai Ho looking for you, and when I didn't see you and you didn't answer your cell, I called your house and—"

Oh shit.

"You didn't, Jason."

"Well, how was I supposed to know you were lying to your parents?" he shot back, defending himself.

"What did you tell him?"

"Just that you weren't there."

Crap. I was busted.

"They know," I mouthed to Michael.

"Got that," he said back. It wasn't going to be pleasant when I got home.

"Why did you want to talk to me in the first place?" I asked Jason.

"I wanted to tell you that Cherish was adopted."

"Yes!" Michael cried, bending his elbow and pulling his fist in. I smiled. Michael was happy and nothing else mattered to me.

"I don't know where she is yet exactly," continued Jason. "Her records are sealed. But I think I'll be able to find out."

"Thanks, Jason! You're awesome! I forgive you for getting me in trouble."

"Well, I need to go," he said brusquely.

"Wait. What about the other thing?"

He was quiet.

"Jason?"

"Cate…let's get together and—"

"Who was it, Jason?"

Michael stiffened.

"Cate…please don't—"

"If you don't tell me now, Jason, I'll just come over and bug you until you do. Then I'll be in worse trouble."

Michael stopped and faced me, his face ashen.

Jason sighed heavily and said, "The name on all of the Social Service complaint reports in Michael's case was Anne Forsythe.

Part Three
The Snare

Chapter 18
The Amateur Healer

"CATE? ARE YOU still there?"

"My mom?" I whispered, and then something snapped within me. It blasted apart all the reasons for all the love and all the respect I'd ever had for her, and without them I had no weapon to use against the fiery black tempest that fought to take their place.

"Cate?"

"Catherine, don't…" Michael's eyes were wide with alarm.

"My *mom* is the one who dumped Michael into foster care and never looked back?" My voice was tight, and it was rising steadily.

"How do you know she never looked back?" Jason asked reasonably. My blood rushed with deadly rhythm through my ears. My vision dimmed under an explosive red glare.

"He's fucking dead, isn't he?"

Michael winced as if I'd slapped him across the face.

"Cate…where are you? Let me come and get you, and we can talk."

"I've got to go." My voice was hoarse, deflated. I hung up the phone and slammed it into my bag. When I looked up, Michael was standing between me and the only way out of the forest. So, here we were again.

He stretched his hand out in front of him.

"Wait," he said.

"Get out of my way, Michael."

"You need to think before you—"

"I have thought about this," I said. "I've thought about this since the day you fell, since I saw your body slam into the ground, since I watched your life drain out of your…" My voice caught in my aching throat. "How could she do that? How could she just abandon you like that? You were my friend—"

"Catherine—"

"She's going to know what happened to you! She's going to know every ounce of pain you ever suffered! I'll make sure of that!"

"Catherine…" he moaned. "Please, don't! How could your mom have known?"

God, I felt sick. "How can you stand to look at me?" I cried. "After what she did to you? How?"

He took a step toward me and turned his palm upward, reaching for me. "I haven't wanted to look at anyone else since that day I saw you on the bus. Even then I knew—"

"Knew what? That I was the daughter of the woman who left you to rot?" I cried. "Why didn't you tell me?"

"Give me your hand." He spoke softly, taking another cautious step toward me.

"Why the hell didn't you tell me?" I cried again, backing away.

He dropped his hand and fixed his grief-stricken eyes on me.

"Because I didn't want anyone else's life turned to shit because of me!"

"She can handle it! She handles everything! She's a freaking *machine!*" I shot back. "Now, get out of my way."

He folded his arms across his chest and shook his head.

Well, I wasn't afraid of him anymore, and I took a deep breath and plowed right through him. God, he felt so good, and I almost turned around, almost. Instead, I stormed out of the forest through the break in the trees.

"What about you?" he shouted after me. I spun around a few feet beyond the entrance. It was pouring now, and I was soaked to the skin. I shivered violently. "What will it do to you if you make her suffer? If you shove her face in this?" He tore his shirt off over his head, exposing all of his scars to the gray light of day, and then he paced back and forth helplessly just inside the forest boundary. He was trapped.

"I don't care what happens to me!" I shouted back.

His lips curled angrily back from his teeth, and he stabbed his finger at me, "I never should have told you any of it! I should have kept my stupid mouth shut! I thought you wanted to help me, but you were just looking for someone to blame!"

"Well I found her, didn't I? And she's going to pay!" I turned and stalked toward the Demon that was waiting for me.

"Catherine! Please!" His voice was like sorrowful thunder. It shook the forest, but it couldn't follow me. It was trapped, too. I was on my own, now.

⤨

The ride home was precarious at best and almost fatal at worst. I could barely see through the driving rain, and the bone deep pain in my right hand made it just about useless on the gear shift. At the bottom of the hill, the car kicked up a huge wave of rainwater and hydroplaned sideways, almost careening off the road and into the river.

When the Demon finally slid to a stop, I flicked on the radio and was rewarded with the tortured war cries of "Point of No Return," a Starset battle anthem. The music was a match made in hell for my mood. Perfect.

Jason's Audi was parked on the street in front of my house when I pulled into the driveway. He opened his car door. I knew he'd come to stop me from taking on my mother in the state I was in, and him I couldn't walk through, so I threw open my door and ran for the house, my feet squishing water out through the laces of my boots with each footfall. I reached the door just as he caught up with me.

"Go home, Jason!" I spat under my breath. He was soaked from his short run from the street. Water trickled down his face from the spiky wisps of his hair above his forehead and beaded up on his leather jacket. He shook his head and stuck his arm in the doorway before it closed.

"I'm responsible for this," he muttered, as he slid uninvited into the house behind me. "I thought your dad might need some backup when you got home."

I scowled at him.

The house was funeral home quiet. My mom and dad were sitting on the couch waiting for me; I walked in as far as the foyer and stopped. My boots released a lake of water, and rivers were rushing down my jeans to join it. Next to me, Jason wiped his wet arm across his face in a futile effort to dry it. Claire was on the stairs, waiting for the fireworks to start, and Cici was nowhere to be found.

My heart pounded away in my chest, and I wondered if Jason could hear it, standing so close to me. I was sure he could hear the hitch in my chest that accompanied each of my runaway breaths. On the upside, I could barely feel the pain in my hand, which I'd tucked into my pocket to avoid more questions. I glanced down at my blood-free left hand, which thankfully, I'd had the presence of mind to wipe off.

My mom jumped to her feet. "She's freezing, Tom, let her change and—"

My dad pulled her back down onto the sofa. "It can wait, Anne. Jason, I think you better go home. This is family—"

"What, are you afraid he'll hear the family's dirty secrets?" I lifted my chin defiantly. "If he leaves, I leave with him!"

I could feel Jason's hand on my back. "Great. Let's go," he whispered into the dripping mass of my wet hair. Yeah, I bet he'd like that about now. He knew what was coming.

My mom was on her feet again, with my dad immediately up and flanking her.

"Don't you dare talk to your father that way!" she shouted. "Now, where have you been?"

Should I lie to them again? Half lie? Tell the truth? I couldn't decide. They were all bad options, so instead I just looked away. What were they so mad about anyway? It was one time! One time they'd caught me in a lie!

"Your father went up to Jai Ho and talked to that Raver."

Oh shit.

"Ravi," Jason corrected reflexively.

My dad glared at him, and Jason pressed his lips together, but didn't drop his ice blue gaze.

"He said you come in almost every day," my mom accused, "and study for about a half hour, get something to drink and then leave. That's hours a day almost every day that we've had no idea where—"

"You're spying on me now?" I shrieked.

"We wouldn't have needed to spy on you if you had been honest in—"

"I can't believe this!" I shouted. "I get practically straight A's! I don't ask you for money! I'm not out doing drugs or drinking or piercing the odd body part or... or..." I shot dagger eyes at my sister. It wasn't fair! I did everything I was supposed to do!

"At least we know where your sister is and what she's doing!" my mom shouted back. "We might argue, but at least we talk!"

"You do?" Hard laughter erupted from my throat. "Yeah?"

Should I drop the bomb?

Oh yes... definitely drop it...

Yeah! They needed a little perspective!

"Did you know she's having sex with the boyfriend you forbid her to see? Mr. Mailbox Buster? Right here in this house? Did you know that, Mom? You're so damn busy—"

"Is that true, Claire?" My dad's face had gone gray as mortar. "What the hell—"

Claire narrowed her eyes at me and whispered, "You're such a bitch." She disappeared up the stairs then, so I answered for her.

"Yeah, Dad! It's true!" I shouted sarcastically. "You don't even know what the hell is going on in your own home!"

My mom crossed the distance between us in seconds and slapped me across the face. I heard Jason's sharp intake of breath next to me. He grabbed me above both elbows just as my right hand was coming up to retaliate.

"I told you once. Do not talk to your father that way! I can't believe this disrespect—"

"You have no right to judge me!" I said.

"I'm your mother! I have every right—"

"No! You don't! Not after what you did to Michael!"

She blinked. She had no idea I knew, and I couldn't wait to tell her that I did.

"I know you knew his mother was a heroin addict, and that she left him alone most of the time to fend for himself! And what did you do? Made a few phone calls? Let the county deal with it? He was only eight! Did you know he spent day after day thinking his mommy was sick and that he needed to take care of her? Did you know he watched her shooting up and crashing down over and over?"

My mother's anger turned to shock and then her shock turned to shame. That's what I wanted to see, but it wasn't enough. Not nearly enough.

Yes…make her suffer…like Michael suffered…

"So then you dumped him at the hospital into the loveless lap of Social Services? Do you know what happened to him after that? Do you have any *fucking* idea?"

"Catherine…I…"

"They burned him, *Mom*. With cigarettes, *Mom*. And when he didn't bend for them, they branded him with a fireplace poker. Not once. Not twice. Three fucking times! Did you know that? Did you ever bother to find out what happened to him? My friend? My best friend?"

"That's enough, Cate!" my dad shouted.

"There were drugs in that house…" my mom said. "And then they moved him to a bad neighborhood on the other side of town. It wasn't safe—"

"No shit, it wasn't safe! A boy was murdered right in front of him!"

"Do you think one day goes by that I don't regret all of it?" my mom said. "That I'm not sick inside about what happened to him? After he moved in with the Gardiners, I heard about the murder and—"

And then it was suddenly all clear to me. The timing of her finding out about Michael's abuse. Her determination to stop at nothing to care for Mina. Why she wouldn't get the help she needed, that we all needed.

"You can take care of your mother for the next hundred years," I said coldly, "But it will never make up for you leaving Michael to die."

Her shoulders sagged, and all of the fire went out of her eyes. There. I'd cut her to the bone, but I didn't want to stay to watch her bleed.

"I can't stay here anymore," I whispered, suddenly very tired. I turned to Jason, and he reached behind him for the door handle, but my dad was in my face in a flash.

"I forbid you to leave this house!" he shouted. And then he growled at Jason, "You take her from my home, and I'll have the police all over you in seconds." Jason looked at me, and I shook my head. I knew my dad's threat was empty, but I'd watched my sister storm out on my parents, and I'd seen what it had done to them. I'd watched them worry that she would never come back or if she did, it would be in a body bag. It was something I'd swore I would never do no matter how upset I was.

Jason let go of the door handle, and then Claire was at the top of the stairs. "Mom! Something's wrong with Mina!" My mother's eyes darted between me and the stairs. "You need to come now!"

My mom turned and ran up the steps with my dad right behind her. I started after them but slipped in the puddle and almost went down.

Jason grabbed my arm, asking, "Towels?"

I nodded toward the pantry in the kitchen, and he left me leaning against the wall in the hallway while I listened to the drama unfolding upstairs.

"Go call 9-1-1!"

"What's wrong with her?"

"She's burning up! I don't know…"

Retching sounds and stifled moans cascaded down the stairs, and then Jason was back, chucking half his pile of towels at my chest. We bent down and began wiping the slippery floor dry, speeding up our efforts as the wailing of sirens got closer and closer.

My dad shoved open the front door, and the two paramedics raced up the stairs with a stretcher spanned between them. They spoke in calm rapid whispers, my mom's taut voice interrupting with questions and information. Then I heard the springs of Mina's bed releasing and the zip of straps being tightened as they prepared her for transport.

She was ashy gray when they carried her down the stairs, and she was curled up in a fetal position, writhing in pain.

I turned away. I couldn't watch. It was all wrong, all wrong...

When the front door swung open, I looked back to see my mom hurrying out the door behind the last paramedic and my dad and sister grabbing their coats off the hooks in the hallway. I started to follow them out the door, but my dad braced his hand on my shoulder and said, "I don't think that's a good idea, Bug." My eyes smarted at the use of my nickname. "Dry off. We'll call you." Then they were gone.

I turned and headed toward the kitchen, I don't know what for, but stopped when the extreme heaviness of my feet reminded me I still had my waterlogged boots on. I bent down to untie them, but my right hand wouldn't cooperate. Blood had soaked through the bandage, and my palm was pulsing with searing waves of pain again. *Why couldn't Michael be here to...*

My throat tightened up at the thought of him, and I rested my forehead on my wet bended knee.

Then someone was bending down in front of me, unlacing my boots.

"Step out," Jason said. He pulled the bindings loose around my ankle, and I pulled my soaking wet foot out of the boot.

"What did you do to your hand?" he asked. His eyes were downcast. He was loosening up the laces of my other boot.

"I..." Well, what the hell was I supposed to tell him? Michael, who was supposed to be *dead*, asked me to save a coyote that, by the way, *he could talk to?* I started to laugh hysterically and couldn't stop, and then my eyes were swimming.

Did I ever tell you that you're amazing?

Jason grabbed my wrist, pulled his grandfather's knife out of his pocket, flicked it open and slit the bandana off my hand. The cut extended all the way across my palm and blood was still oozing into the deep crevice. I stopped laughing, and he looked up into my face.

"You need stitches," he said flatly.

"No," I said.

"Cate," he sighed. "With the amount of flexion and extension your hand does, that cut will just keep opening back up over and over."

I shook my head. "There's no way I'm going to the E.R. Not with my whole family there hating me." The blood started to overflow the edges of the wound and drip down my wrist. Jason rubbed his forehead.

"Why can't you learn to think before you go off like that?" He stuffed the knife back into his pocket and pulled off my other boot, then hauled me up by my left hand and walked me into the kitchen. My jeans were cold, wet and uncomfortably stiff, and my hair was plastered all over my neck and face. Water dripped down my back under my sweater, and I shivered.

"She deserved it," I whispered, ashamed that I still felt that way with Mina so sick, but my hatred wouldn't go quietly. It festered. It was at home in my heart. Jason stuck my hand under the faucet, turned on the water and started rinsing off the blood and grime.

"Shit!" I cried.

"Why didn't you tell me your grandmother was living with you?"

Because I've been avoiding that fact myself, I thought, but didn't say it out loud. Instead I just said, "She's dying."

He looked up from the water pouring out of the faucet with genuine concern in his eyes. "I'm sorry, Cate. Does she have cancer?" he asked, grabbing the role of paper towels on the counter. He pulled off half a dozen, folded them over on themselves and then pressed them down on my hand.

I sucked in a breath through clenched teeth. "Emphysema," I spat and then breathed out slowly through my mouth.

He glanced up, and I could tell by the knowing look in his eyes that I didn't have to explain it to him. Then he picked up the paper towels and examined the wound, poking his fingers at the loose flaps of skin, then pressed the paper towels back down.

"Ahhh! Shit!" I hissed.

"Cate. You need stitches," he said again, exasperated.

"No! I can't face them again tonight! Just…wrap it up tight. There are bandages and tape upstairs in the hall closet."

He rubbed his forehead again, then went upstairs. I heard him searching roughly through the hall closet, and then he came back down with some gauze and first aid tape. He wrapped them tightly around my hand.

"Go get into some dry clothes," he said, leaning over the table and looking me in the eye. "I'm going back to my house to get some supplies. I'll be back in twenty." Then he was gone, too.

By the time he got back, I had changed into a dry T-shirt and pair of sweats, and I was sitting in the kitchen with my chin resting on the table and my injured hand stretched out in front of me. Jason came in without knocking and set his backpack down on the table. I felt the kathunk it made vibrate through my chin. I didn't look up.

He pulled out a bottle of sterile saline, a sealed sterile packet of… something, a syringe…

Syringe?

I jerked my chin up off the table. "You're going to give me a shot?"

He looked up from the supplies and fixed his no-nonsense eyes on me. "You need stitches, Cate, and we can do it with or without anesthetic. Now, if it were me—"

"*You're* going to stitch me up?"

"Or I can take you to the E.R." He stood there, waiting. Crap. This was the worst day of my life.

"Cate," he sighed. "My dad is a plastic surgeon. What do you think he and I do for fun?"

"Do I want to know?"

"I'll give you a relevant example. Once, he gave me a box of suture kits, showed me how to use them, and then let me go at it on a stack of split Styrofoam cups. And when I sliced my leg open? He showed me how to anesthetize it and then let me stitch myself up." He pulled his pant leg up and showed me a scar on his shin. "So, which is it going to be?"

I thought for a moment and then stretched my palm out to him. I didn't really care whether he could do it or not, but it seemed better than showing up at the hospital unwanted.

He asked me for a bowl. I dragged out my mom's huge silver bowl from under the sink and put it on the table. He cut the temporary bandages off my hand and rinsed the wound above the bowl with the sterile saline. He washed his hands and swabbed both sides of the wound and the top of the Lidocaine vial with alcohol, and then started to peel open the packet containing the sterile syringe, but stopped and looked up.

"Before I do this, I need to know what you cut yourself with," he said. I shook my head and looked away. Insane. That was me, and I didn't need the whole world to know it.

"Look," he said. "I'm not going to tell anyone if you…uh…did this to yourself. But I'm not stitching you up until I know. You might need a tetanus shot, Cate."

"What?" What did he mean? Did this to myself? And then I understood. "No!" I said defensively. "It was an accident!" He raised his eyebrows, and I rolled my eyes. The thought of telling him made me queasy, but I'd rather him know than everyone else, so I nodded reluctantly to my pink butterfly bag that lay in a sopping wet heap by the front door. He picked it up, dropped it on the kitchen table and started to dig through it.

"Careful!" I said. He slowed down his movements, and then his eyes went wide as he gingerly pulled the arrow out. It was covered in blood from its tri-blade tip to its neon fletching.

"What the…" The look he gave me was equal parts shock, worry and unbridled disgust. "So you disappear for several hours every day and somehow manage to lacerate your hand with an arrow that looks like it's been through…something that was alive…at least at one point?"

"I pulled it out of a coyote," I said matter-of-factly.

He shook his head, bewildered, as he dropped the arrow in the trash. Then he came back to the table and sat down next to me.

"Cate…what's going on with you?" His voice was strained. "It's like you've disappeared into some world where no one can follow you. You're obsessed with Michael. I *told* you…" His voice trailed off when he noticed my eyes glaze over. My thoughts had returned to the cool forest. He had no idea how close to the truth he was, and I blinked a few times and then looked away. He sighed and started to open the syringe, but stopped again.

"Did you say coyote? Didn't your friend J.C. get bitten by a rabid coyote a few months ago?" My heart skipped a beat as I grasped where he was going.

I nodded.

"Damn," he muttered under his breath. "Where's your computer?"

I started to get up to show him.

"Just point," he instructed, frustrated again. "You're already sterile." I pointed to the dining room adjacent to the kitchen, and he disappeared around the corner.

"This coyote didn't have rabies," I called anxiously after him.

"That you know," he muttered back.

After several long minutes, he called, "How old is this computer?"

"Old," I answered. It was slow. Grandpa-merging-onto-the-freeway slow. And I was sure his computer at home worked at warp speed.

When he finally came back in the kitchen, he said, "The rabies virus is only present in saliva and brain tissue. Did it bite you?"

I shook my head.

"Then you should be safe. Unless…you didn't pull the arrow out of its head, did you?"

"His chest," I whispered.

He nodded and washed his hands again, sat down next to me and finished opening the syringe. He set the vial in front of him on the table and punctured the top expertly with the needle, flipped it upside down and drew up the anesthetic, and then he paused with the needle poised above the wound and asked, "Are you ready?"

Then listen closely...

I started to feel dizzy. I missed Michael so much. How could I have left him the way I did? Maybe I could go back to the woods tonight...

"Cate? Are you still with me? Do you need to put your head down?"

I shook my head, the corners of my eyes going damp, and looked away. "Go ahead..." I whispered, biting my lip hard.

I felt a few sharp stings as he injected the anesthetic in several places on either side of the laceration, and then I heard him peel open the suture kit. Glancing back, I saw several curved needles with thread already attached and a pair of forceps and clamp. He mounted the first needle, and I looked away again. I felt him probe each side of the wound to make sure it was numb, and then he carefully tugged the needle through my skin and tied it off to execute the first stitch.

"So..." he said quietly. "How did you know all that stuff about Michael?" I glanced back to see his brow furrowed in deep concentration as he threaded the needle through my skin for the second stitch. I was fascinated with his progress and nauseated at the same time.

"Um...I found someone who knew him when he was in foster care."

His hands paused for a second before he whipped them around to tie off the second stitch. He nodded to himself and then looked up at me.

"I probably should have just told you myself what I knew," he said, and I nodded. He should have, but I understood why he didn't. He was quiet after that, executing what looked to me later like eight perfect stitches. When he was finished, he covered the stitches with a square of gauze and then wrapped first aid tape snuggly several times around my hand. I lifted my hand up off the table and flexed it a few times, impressed. With my hand attended to, the storm of emotions clouding my mind abated some, and the sting of embarrassment rushed in to take up the slack.

"Jason…I'm sorry about dragging you into our family hurricane."

"You weren't that bad."

I raised my eyebrows.

"Well…let's just be glad there wasn't a pool around." He smiled grimly.

"Thanks," I said sarcastically.

"Don't mention it," he said, his smile turning overly sweet, and then he gathered up all the waste and threw it in the trash. "Honestly, I think my family would benefit from a Cat Four or Five hurricane. We never talk about anything…unpleasant." He pulled out a couple of pill bottles and set them on the table.

"Now, something for infection, something for pain, and something to help you sleep…" The Amoxicillin and the Motrin I could do, but I eyed the bottle of Valium like I thought it would bite.

"Jason…I can't. I don't need anything to help me sleep." He filled a glass with water and sat down across from me with his arms folded and relaxed on the table.

"Cate. Look. Truth time. You were a basket case not…" He looked down at his phone, "ninety minutes ago, and you have no idea how strung out you look right now. If you don't believe me, go look in the mirror."

I didn't need to look in the mirror. I knew he was right. I was still shaking on the inside with anger and shame and bone-deep longing for Michael. I hesitated. The thought of forcing my body into a deep dreamless, sleep was appealing.

Don't do it…

"No," I said. "I can't." I'd promised Michael I would stay clean and taking Valium that wasn't prescribed to me would be breaking that promise. Somehow, I was sure that he would see it that way.

"Fine," he said. "I thought you might say that."

He pulled out an over-the-counter box of antihistamine capsules. I knew two of those usually knocked me out within an hour or so. I nodded. That I could do.

"Great! Finally!" he said. He dropped one Amoxicillin, two Motrin and three antihistamine capsules in my hand. I tossed one of the antihistamines back to him, and he sighed. I downed them all with one swallow. I was an expert pill-taker. I could take six or seven at a time back in the days when my asthma was worse.

He took me by the hand and led me out to the sofa in the living room, sat down and pulled me down next to him, wrapping his long arms around me. He felt right, comfortable, and I leaned back against his chest. But when I closed my eyes, I was immediately confronted with an image of Michael, eyes brimming with worry, pacing back and forth just inside the tree line, waiting for me to come back.

I sat back up, swung my feet around onto the floor, and leaned forward on my elbows, my good hand buried in my hair. I felt like I couldn't breathe. Michael would worry about me all night. How could I have done that to him? What if he left? He wouldn't...

Jason sat up next to me and put his arm around my back. "What happened to you tonight?" he murmured into my hair. I just shook my head and pulled my elbows in closer.

"Look, Cate. I'm trying to understand, but I just don't get it. What is it with you and Michael? Why can't you let it go?"

I wanted to answer him, needed to answer him, and I tried to order my emotions into rational thoughts, thoughts that I could explain. "All these years...we could have watched out for him. We could have kept him safe and gotten him help with school. We could have had him over, like on Christmas or his birthday or the freaking Fourth of July! We could have been there for him! He'd be alive today..." *And sitting here next to me instead of you,* I thought in the deep ocean of my mind. "But he's not. My mom stole that from me," I went on darkly, and I felt Jason stiffen. "I don't think I can ever forgive her for that." It was like a cloud of dark ink had poured itself into my soul. I was drowning in it.

Then the phone rang. I grabbed it off the table, relieved to have something else to concentrate on.

"Hey, Bug," my dad said.

"How's Mina?" I asked him.

"She's in surgery. Her bowel ruptured, and she's full of infection. It's a side effect of being on the prednisone for so long."

"Is she going to make it?"

"The doc's not sure."

I sank back against the back of the sofa and covered my eyes with my hand.

Shh…Just breathe…

"Listen, Caty. Cici is sleeping over at Lisa's, and we'll be here pretty late. Are you alright on your own?" I looked over at Jason and decided I'd done enough lying for one day.

"I'm not alone, Dad. Jason's still here."

There was a long pause on the other end of the line and then my dad growled, "Let me talk to him."

I rolled my eyes and handed the phone over. "My dad wants to talk to you."

"Yes, Mr. Forsythe?" Jason was one of those guys who felt perfectly at ease around parents. He nodded and said yes a few more times and then one of course not before hanging up the phone. He looked sideways at it and fought down a grin.

"What did he say?"

"He told me I wasn't allowed in your bedroom, and then he said that, in fact, I wasn't allowed in any of the bedrooms, and that I was to keep all of my clothes on and not take any of yours off."

"He did not!"

Jason stifled a laugh and then forced his face back into a serious expression. He made the adjustment easily. "Okay, okay. He told me to remember you were his daughter, and that he was glad I was here if it made you feel better." Then he grabbed me by the hand and pulled me back against his chest. He did make me feel better. Whenever I was close to him, touching him, my emotions seemed to settle down.

Jason reached out to wrap his arms around me again, but just before his arms closed protectively around my waist, I noticed two tiny red bruises on the inside of his elbow. He'd had blood drawn recently, and I felt a stab of worry. Was he sick? I was too exhausted to ask.

It was the middle of the night when I was gently shaken awake by my father.

"Time to go, chief," my dad said to Jason. We both sat up and stretched.

"I'm going to walk him out," I said, grabbing my dad's old coat off its hook and plugging my arms into the big puffy sleeves.

It had stopped raining and the moon was out. Everything was slick and shiny, and it felt rudely cold after having been curled up against Jason's chest. Jason opened his car door, leaned back against it and pulled me into a bear hug, sliding his arms inside my coat and around my back.

"Thanks, Jason," I murmured into his chest. Jason tucked two fingers under my chin and lifted my face.

"I still care about you, Caty," he reminded me, borrowing my father's nickname for me, and then he leaned down and kissed me with urgent tenderness. His lips were like warm wet velvet, and they were softly familiar. They tugged at my thoughts, attempting to lead them back to a simpler summer. I wished I could surrender and follow, but the sizzling chemistry that existed between us last summer had faded.

I pulled away and looked up into his confused eyes. "Jason...I love someone else." I knew in my soul it was true. My heart beat faster just by saying the words out loud.

Jason pulled back and stood up tall. He was smart. The smartest guy I knew. And his eyes flashed blue fire for a second and then filled with pity.

"I can't compete with a ghost," he said. And then he slid behind the wheel of his black Audi and left.

Chapter 19
The Messenger

AFTER JASON LEFT, I crawled up the stairs and into bed, eventually finding my way back to sleep, back to the dark pool in the woods that Michael and I shared in our dreams.

≈≈≈

Our moonlit pool was surrounded by snow and wrapped in a thick layer of ice. With my bare hand, I scraped the snow off its surface and punched my fist through the ice into the painfully cold black water beneath. I couldn't find Michael's reflection. He was gone, and it was deathly quiet. Only the quiet whoosh of my frosty breath disturbed the night. Then I felt static building up behind me. My scalp prickled a sickening warning as I twisted around to see.

Michael was standing over me, leaning forward, unsteady on his feet. He wasn't pale and flickering. He was flesh and bone and...dying. Blood ran down his chin and dripped from his fingertips.

"Look what your mother's done to me," he moaned then fell to his knees and vomited a fountain of hot arterial blood at my feet. It soaked into the snow, turning pink at the edges.

"Michael!" I cried, reaching for him, but out of the corner of my eye, I caught the lightning flash of a flaming sword slicing toward him.

"Stop!" I screamed, too late. He was rent in two from the left side of his neck down to a point below his right arm, and both halves exploded into massive clouds of brilliant white sparks. The fiery hot concussion knocked me backward onto the

ice. I caught a glimpse of the stars above me before the ice cracked, and I plunged beneath the fiendishly cold surface.

As I was sucked down into the deep, someone whispered, "He lies."

～≈

I startled awake in my empty room, gasping, "Who lies?" No one answered, and I collapsed back onto my pillow and curled up on my side.

"I'm sorry, Michael. If I'd known what happened to you, maybe I could have protected you," I whispered. Tears gathered in my eyes, and with Michael not there to witness them, I let them fall.

～≈

The Guardian couldn't see through the exploding silver flames, but he found the demon's throat among them, grabbed it, and slammed him up against the wall, sustaining a first degree breach burn in the process. Despite the power drain, he squeezed harder snarling, "You lie!"

Six demon blades were drawn and pointed at the back of the Guardian's neck before their Master hit the wall. The demon could have retaliated. He had the right of first reprisal. But why change tactics in the middle of a war when the ones he was using were working so well? Instead, he glanced at the girl who lay moaning softly on the bed, her Bright Angel beside her.

"She's not holding up under the pressure as well as you thought she would, is she?" he mused.

"She'll make it," the Guardian spat.

"Are you sure?"

"She'll make it…" the Guardian repeated, but more to himself this time. A firm, leather-clad hand gripped his shoulder.

"Let him go," the Dark Angel urged quietly, but the Guardian wasn't ready yet.

～≈

The next morning I woke up to find Cici sitting on the edge of my bed, ready for school, her eyes flashing angrily.

"You lied to me!" she accused.

I blinked the fog of sleep away and grabbed my glasses, which were sitting on the nightstand between our beds.

"What?"

"I told you I thought you were too smart to have that much homework all the time. You said you were going to Jai Ho to study, but then you'd come home and study until after midnight sometimes. I *knew* you were lying."

"Cici…" I groaned as I swung my feet over the side of the bed and onto the floor.

"Are you going to tell me or not?" she asked. I stretched, and she eyed my bandaged palm. I clenched my hand into a fist, wincing as the stitches tugged painfully.

"Tell you what?" I snapped.

"Where you've been going…" She was distracted by the bandage wrapped around my hand. I was glad it was wrapped up securely. No one needed to know how bad the cut was.

"No," I said, standing up and heading for the bathroom.

She followed me. "Come on, Cate! You know you can tell me anything! What's going on?"

Feeling trapped, I walked into the bathroom and shut the door in her face. The door creaked as she leaned against it. "I saw the pine needles stuck to your bag," she whispered. I froze. "Who is he, and where have you guys been meeting?"

I had no sane response to her questions, so I said nothing. What was I *supposed to* say? Tell me! Somebody please tell me!

"Fine! Don't talk to me! See if I care!" she finally said, and then stomped down the stairs.

I'm sorry Cici, I just can't.

I got ready for school, swallowing one of the Amoxicillin that Jason had given me along with a couple of Motrin. Upon arriving downstairs, I learned I was on house arrest with no parole date in sight.

No surprise there, but hearing my dad say it, sunk my heart down into the pit of my stomach, where it huddled like a lump of melting ice.

How was I going to make it through Christmas without contacting Michael? How could I leave him alone in the woods for that long? Feeling suddenly sick, I shoved my bowl of cereal away, sloshing milk all over the table, and fled to the stairs where I sat with my arms crossed tightly over my stomach until my dad was ready to leave. I followed him into the garage and slid into the passenger seat of the Demon. We were alone in the car. Dad had banished my sisters to the bus so he and I could "talk." He wasted no time getting started.

"I know it's been hard on you having Mina move in, but how could you lie to me like that? Over and over?" The sound of the Demon's engine responding to my father's hands only made me feel that much more powerless. I looked out the window. He could talk. I wasn't.

He tried again. "We're *worried*. We don't know *what* to think. You need to let us in." Let him in where? They'd never understand. They'd never believe me. No one would believe me.

Then his voice took on a harder edge. "You know you really hurt your mother with your accusations yesterday. She feels terrible."

"Good," I growled under my breath, and then I closed my eyes and rested my forehead against the window for the remainder of the ride to school.

❧❧

On my way to my locker I passed Jason in the hall, but he only glanced my way, pity still filling his eyes. He looked exhausted. Neither of us had gotten much sleep the night before. He was pale with shadowy circles under his eyes, and his dark hair was mussed way beyond fashionable. I wanted to grab him by the arm, ask him if he was okay. I wanted to thank him again. He'd done more for me than anyone could ever expect from an ex-boyfriend.

But I left him alone. I'd already hurt him enough.

At my locker, Meri, Grace, and Spencer were all waiting, looking at me as if someone died.

"Cici called Spencer," Grace explained when she saw that I was confused by all the attention. I opened my locker and started shoving things around.

"Whatever..." I mumbled into the metallic cave. It was my word of choice for the day. It required no emotional or cerebral input.

"We're sorry about your grandmother..." Meri said. She grabbed the door of my locker when I tried to slam it shut. "...and about your mom." There was true compassion in her eyes. I knew my friends cared, but—

"Your mom probably didn't even know," she went on, and I felt my empty stomach turn sour. I tugged on the door until she let go. Then I slammed it shut.

See? They don't understand...no one understands.

"Look, *Mer*, you don't know what you're talking about," I retorted in a sharper voice than I intended. Her eyes crumpled and then narrowed nastily.

"Well...maybe if you talked to me once in a while, I would!" she said and stormed away toward the Art Annex. I watched her go, wondering if I should chase after her to explain or apologize, but I didn't have the energy or the will.

Grace and Spencer fell into formation next to me as I headed for homeroom.

"Dude, so...like, you want to talk about it?" asked Spencer, swerving to get out of the way of a crowd of students barreling past from the opposite direction. I shook my head and ducked into our homeroom, taking a seat in the back. They took the seats next to and in front of me. I rolled my eyes and opened a book to bury my nose in.

Shawn Fowler, smelling of stale cigarettes and powdered donuts, rolled in right before the teacher called the class to order and took the seat next to mine. He ignored me or studied me threateningly by turns through the entire class. What was it with people refusing to leave me alone, today?

I coasted through my next three classes, barely present, and was desperately relieved when my lunch period began. I went to my locker and grabbed my coat and the peanut butter sandwich I'd packed, and headed to the one place in the school I knew no one would be on a dismal day like today.

The flagstone courtyard was cold and empty. All of the dead flowers had been mown down and the bushes had been cut back to their stumps. It was snowing lightly and there was a speckled dusting of flakes on the ground.

"Hey, Saint Joan," I said to myself and to her, I guess. Maybe she was listening. "Do you mind a little company?" I settled down on one of the benches near the saint's statue, wrapped my scarf another time around my neck and tucked my chin down under it. Then I took a bite of my sandwich, which I chewed and swallowed with effort.

"How did you do it?" I impulsively asked the long dead saint, but my voice was strained. "How did you not go freaking out of your mind when it was only you hearing the voices of God's Angels and Saints?" A layer of sparkling snow was accumulating on the statue's mottled green head like a halo. I stood up and walked over to stand in front of her, my throat constricting. I took another bite of my sandwich, but it wouldn't go down.

"Shit," I mumbled with my mouth full. "I don't know what the hell to do, now! I need to get a message to him, and I don't know how!" I looked up at the sky helplessly.

"Can you pray for me, Joan? Ask God to send me some kind of a sign?" My nose was beginning to run. I forced the bite of sandwich down my throat only to have my stomach turn over when it hit bottom. "Crap. I can't eat this." I shook my head disgustedly and turned around, looking for a trash can.

"Hey," said J.C. quietly. He was standing just inside the courtyard with his hands in his coat pockets and his glossy black hair tucked warmly under a navy blue Cleveland Indians hat.

"You're not an easy chica to find," he said, eyeing me and then the statue. "I can come back if you're not finished with your...uh... conversation."

My heart heaved itself into my throat. "Ahh...how much of that did you hear?"

"Hmm..." He came over to stand next to me in front of Saint

Joan and clasped his hands behind his back. "Enough to tell you that you probably shouldn't go cussing at a saint if you want her help."

"Crap," I said.

"That's a better word choice, but…" he teased, fighting back a grin.

I rolled my eyes. I wasn't in the mood. "What the hell do you want, anyway?"

He cleared his throat and took an infinitesimal step away from me. "Um…okay. Finn wanted me to tell you that Meri told him that she's pissed at you. He also wanted me to tell you that Meri has turned his life into that of a forty-year-old virgin." He glanced up at the saint and back-pedaled. "Only between you and me and Saint Joan, they're nowhere near close to doing it anyway, and he wants you to make up with her. I think that's it."

I really needed to talk to Meri. "Tell Finn to get in line. My dad's pissed. My mom's beyond pissed. Cici's…"

"Cici's just mad you won't tell her what's been bothering you. She's mad at your mom, too," he said.

"When did you and Cici become best friends?" I'd missed more than I thought.

"We've been…texting…" he said evasively. Great. They'd been talking about me. The two most observant people I knew.

"So what's the message?" he asked. He reached out and peeled a slimy brown leaf off Saint Joan's arm. "Maybe I can take it."

I blinked. I blinked again. Then the hair stood up on the back of my arms under my coat. I looked at the statue of Saint Joan and then up at the sky again, only not so helplessly this time. Had she prayed for me? Had God answered her prayer? Of all my friends J.C. was probably the least likely to drag me kicking and screaming to an insane asylum if he knew what was really going on in my head. After all, he was the one who suggested someone was looking out for me the night the coyote attacked.

But I couldn't tell him everything.

"What?" he asked, contemplating me seriously with his liquid brown eyes.

"Look. J.C., you believe in God, right?" I asked, laying some groundwork. You would think the answer to that is a given at a Catholic school. It isn't.

"Yeah," he said and shrugged his shoulders and looked away. "Sure."

"And you believe that our souls live on after we die, right?"

"Sure. Yeah," he nodded. "What does that have to do with your message?"

I took a deep breath. My heart thumped faster.

"I've been talking to Michael, J.C." I paused, and when he didn't flinch, plowed on. "It...um...makes me feel better about his death."

J.C. thought about that and then backed up to sit down on one of the benches, motioning with his head for me to join him. "I don't think that's weird, Cate. I check in with mi abuelo all the time. He died a few years ago." I raised my eyebrows, not understanding. "My grandfather. We were tight, you know what I'm saying?"

I nodded.

"So you have a message for Michael? Why can't you just tell him yourself?" He was quick. I closed my eyes and dove in.

"I talk to him in Lewis Woods. A lot. I feel...closest to him there." I pried my eyes open to take in his expression. He still wasn't laughing so I went on. "That's why I'm grounded," I groaned. "I've been going there, like almost every day, and I told my parents I was going somewhere else. They want to know where only..."

"Why can't you just tell them?"

"Are you kidding? I can't believe I'm telling you, and that you're still sitting here listening. There's no way I can tell them." Then I was suddenly worried. "Look, no one knows, J.C., no one. You can't tell anyone. It's just that...I'm grounded, now. Totally. Like, for I don't know how long, and...I need someone to take my place in Lewis Woods until I can go back. Maybe I could write a letter—"

He was shaking his head.

"I thought you said I wasn't weird." My cheeks were burning again. I felt so stupid.

"Maybe not weird for you, but weird for me. I didn't even know the guy."

"It doesn't matter," I said, talking fast. "All you need to do is read the letter and—"

"Read it? Can't I just leave it for him somewhere? People do that, right? Leave letters or flowers or stuffed bears—"

"He has...um...had dyslexia," I said looking down at my shoes and biting my lip.

He laughed, predictably. I stuck out my chin, and he stopped laughing. "Okay. Okay...if it will make you feel better to keep up the...um...ritual..." He gathered his dark brows together over his eyes. "You get me a letter, and I'll go take it into the woods and read it, but if I ever find out you told anyone, I'll kick your butt."

We walked back into the noisy cafeteria, and it felt as if some of the weight had been lifted off my shoulders. I can do this. Michael and I can make it through this, I thought. I threw a backward glance over my shoulder at Saint Joan as the door closed behind us.

"Thank you," I whispered.

Now, the only problem was what to write.

I stayed up late composing the letter and tucked it into the vent of J.C.'s locker on Tuesday morning. He'd gotten his license at the end of November, but he couldn't take the letter until Thursday because he had to share the car with his two older sisters. I was unbelievably difficult to live with during those two days.

Mina lingered in intensive care, and my mother spent almost twenty-four hours a day at the hospital, coming home only to shower and change. As it was, the few times our paths crossed, my temper seethed and her guilt overflowed. Fire and gasoline. We managed to avoid a full-out conflagration. Barely. It helped that I wasn't speaking to her.

Thursday after dinner, my dad insisted we all go to Saint Joan's home varsity basketball game. Cici was cheering, and he said we needed to show our support. Of course, he came along to babysit me. He'd lost all faith in me.

While Cici changed, we bought some popcorn and climbed up to the top of the bleachers to sit with the Finnegans. Maeve Finnegan, the youngest at only six, sidled up next to me and stuck her hand in my bag of popcorn. She'd inherited the clan's trademark red hair and green eyes, and had Finn's sense of humor, poor thing.

Finn made the team but was riding the bench for now. Jason was starting guard. He was tall, and he was good. I'd watched him play before, but he looked sicker today than he had on Monday. Tired. Pale. He lacked his usual quickness. His head obviously wasn't in the game, and he turned the ball over several times in the first half.

I looked around for the Kings. They were sitting near the top of the bleachers to our left, and Jason's dad, in a pair of pressed black chinos and a buttoned up golf shirt, was watching the game with rapt attention. Each time Jason fouled his dad's jaw tightened, and he shook his head in disappointment.

Cici was at home among the cheerleaders, just as I knew she would be. She was the smallest, but she bounced with enthusiasm through the routines and stunts, looking incredible in her gray and white Warrior tank and short pleated skirt. Between cheers, she laughed with her new friends and put up with Spencer's flirting…which was almost nonstop. He was shameless. He'd only made the JV team and was disappointed, but he sat behind the Varsity team's bench during every game to absorb and learn as much as he could. Meri sat with him.

As the halftime buzzer rang, the Warriors had the game tied up, and Jason was fouled. He stepped to the free throw line for the go-ahead points.

"Come on, Jason," I whispered, but he missed both shots, and he lifted his head to glance up at his father. I turned around and saw Dr. King grimace. Jason dropped his chin and followed the rest of the team back to the locker room. What was wrong with him? I was just thinking about trying to sneak in a word to him when I felt a tap on my shoulder.

"I need to talk to you." It was J.C., and he was pale too. His lips were pressed together in a thin line, and he motioned with his head that I should follow him. The look in his eyes said it was urgent. I glanced over at my dad. I was grounded and wasn't supposed to be talking to my friends, but he was busy talking to Mr. Finnegan, so I slipped off the bleacher and chased after J.C. He moved rapidly toward one of the exits and then led me to a table in the far corner of the cafeteria.

"What's wrong? Did you take the letter?" I asked, worried he'd chickened out.

"You didn't tell me everything, did you?" he accused in a hushed voice. His eyes were shiny with a mixture of emotions that were impossible to read.

"What do you mean?"

He reached into his backpack, pulled out a smallish white box and set it down carefully on the table. When I read the words on the box I almost fainted.

J.C. nodded to himself. He could see the answer to his question in my eyes.

"Okay..." he whispered, nodding again. "*Okay...*"

The words on the box, printed in black and silver lettering, were "Higher Dior."

J.C. yanked out a chair, sat down across from me and leaned across the table.

"Cate, is that what you smelled the night the coyote attacked? It was him, right?"

I nodded, then reached out with the fingers of my good hand and wrapped them around the box. It was solid and real, and it smelled like...Michael. I closed my eyes and breathed in deep. Tension I didn't even know I had released from my neck and shoulders.

High-pitched laughter erupted from a group of kids at a table on the other side of the cafeteria, and we both jumped and glanced their way, suddenly worried about eavesdroppers.

"This is, like, totally wacked," J.C. whispered across the table. He rubbed the thick black stubble on his chin with the back of his left hand.

"Michael was wearing it the day he died…this cologne," I explained in a halting voice. J.C. was nodding again. How far had his mind stretched to absorb all of this? What exactly happened in the woods today? "Where did you notice it?" I asked cautiously. He hunched down in his chair and concentrated on his fingers.

"At first it was like, really faint. I thought I was imagining it, but as I got closer to the cliff where you told me to read the letter? The scent got much stronger." He looked up, both shock and awe evident in his eyes.

"And when I started to read, the scent circled me and then settled next to me. I mean, I could tell exactly where it was coming from! It was like, right there!" He pointed to the chair immediately to his right to illustrate.

"Did you see anything? Hear anything?"

"No! Do you?" His eyes opened wider. I looked down at my hands.

"You should have warned me!" He looked away and then mumbled, "I mean, I wasn't scared or anything, but it would have been nice to know."

"But did you read the whole letter?" I asked, hoping he had. Michael needed to hear it. He had to know I was coming back. That I was okay after my stupid temper tantrum.

"Yeah. Then, I swear he followed me back out of the woods, but the scent stopped where that path goes into the forest."

One side of my lips curled up as I remembered *my* first encounter. "Did you run?" I asked.

"Hell no!" he said, looking from side to side. "But like, I went straight to the mall after that and smelled at least a hundred different colognes before I found this one."

I opened the box and set the bottle on the table. It was a silver and white rectangular bottle, with the words "Higher Dior" written in raised white-on-white lettering. It was pale and shimmery, like Michael himself.

"Can I keep this?" I asked, trailing my index finger across the top. I could almost feel it tingle.

J.C. nodded, studying the expression on my face. "So…is he, like, some kind of ghost or what?"

I opened my mouth to answer, but Cici bounded up, tossing her noisy pompoms on the table. J.C. raised his eyebrows in an exaggerated fashion, and I shook my head. No, she didn't know.

"Hey, guys!" she said. "Halftime's over. We're taking a break."

J.C. checked out the back of her skirt with interest and said, "Isn't that skirt a little short for you, baby sis?"

"No!" she shot back. She flipped it up in his face and said, "See? Spankies!" Then she flopped down next to him, and her face fell a little.

"What am I going to do about Spencer?" she groaned, for once oblivious to the charged atmosphere surrounding her.

"What about him?" I asked, playing dumb. J.C. and Cici both looked at me as if I were blind.

"He wants to go out, and I just don't like him that way. I mean he's a great friend, but…"

"Do you want me to talk to him?" I asked. He was *my* friend.

"No," she groaned. "Maybe he'll give up." I didn't think that was likely, but I nodded and patted her on the shoulder from across the table.

"So…" she went on, changing the subject. "What are you guys talking about?" Her antenna was back up. She was still trying to get to the bottom of my disappearances.

J.C. covered, saying, "I was just looking for volunteers to come help out at the soup kitchen on Sundays. I'm heading up the committee for the youth group."

"What time?" she asked.

"Well…we leave around six in the morning," he said apologetically, already expecting rejection.

"No way," I groaned. That was way too early.

"I'll come!" offered Cici, adding, "Some of us *like* to get up early." Her tone was sarcastic. Her eyes were on me. Then she reached out and grabbed up the bottle of Higher, asking, "Whose is this?"

"Mine," said J.C. quickly. "I got tired of Axe."

"Me too. Too many guys wear it." She sprayed it on her arm and smelled it.

"Nice," she said and then looked from J.C. to me curiously.

"What?" I asked, trying to keep my face straight.

"That's what you smell like, Cate. When you come home from…" She made quote marks in the air with her fingers. "…Jai Ho."

The straight expression on my face crumbled, and I stood up abruptly and went to the bathroom. J.C. could deal with that one.

Chapter 20
The Gift

"ARE YOU SURE you'll be okay?" J.C. wanted to know as he pulled into the parking area in front of the woods. It was Christmas Eve morning. Mina had returned home the day before, and my dad had been too distracted with helping to coordinate her care to resist my tireless pleas to be allowed to Christmas shop with J.C.

It was the perfect cover story. J.C. picked me up early, and we swung by the mall, where I bought a few gift cards, but the gift that mattered most to me was already tucked into my dingy pink bag. It was something for Michael, something I knew he would love.

J.C. looked at me doubtfully as I opened the passenger door and exposed my face to the wintry air. The sky was blue and the sun was out. It was reflecting so brightly off the massive snowy field that my hand shot up automatically to protect my eyes from the light.

"I'm good," I said and shut the passenger door firmly. Through the window, I could see curiosity overflowing in J.C.'s eyes. Though we now talked about Michael frequently, he didn't know I could actually see and hear Michael, but I was sure he suspected. I think he was content just to be part of the mystery. I waved and mouthed my thanks as he drove away. I had my phone, and I'd call him when I was ready to go.

Fatigue weighed down my black snow boots as they crunched over the icy path. My throat was achy and congested, and my nose was stuffy. With all of the stress at home and my worries for Michael, sleep had fled from me night after night, and the cumulative effect of that was beginning to take its toll. I didn't care.

I had given a second letter to J.C. to deliver for me, which had promised Michael I would come on Christmas Eve morning, and there was no place in the world I would rather be. But fear tempered the excitement I felt about seeing him again. Fear that he would still be angry with me for storming out on him, fear that I wouldn't know what to say when I saw him, and fear that he wouldn't trust me anymore. Fear seemed to color everything in my world lately. It had settled in my heart like a cold claw, pricking it sharply when I least expected it, causing my heart to race and my lungs to stumble.

By the time I approached the entrance to the forest, the bright sun had made me so hot and sweaty in my oversized coat that I unzipped it to try to cool off.

He was waiting for me at the very edge of his boundary.

His hands were stuffed deep in his frayed cut-off jeans' pockets, and his pensive gaze flicked between his feet and my face. He was pale, and he wavered in and out of focus rapidly, like he was anxious, too. He backed slowly away from his invisible boundary line to give me room to cross and stand in front of him, and the moment my toe crossed the border, his expression changed, and his eyes filled up with worry.

"You're warm, and your breathing's all scratchy."

I shrugged out of the coat, but the chill ate its way right through my wool sweater, so I put the coat back on. Then I was hot again.

"It's warmer out there in the sun than it looks," I said, avoiding his eyes. I was suddenly overcome with shame for the way I had left him the last time we saw each other. My heart was pounding, and I felt unsteady on my feet. "And I'm…just tired…"

"What is it?" he asked, taking a step closer, my awkwardness having freed him of his own anxiety. He trailed the backs of his tingling fingertips across my cheek, and his worry deepened.

"I'm fine," I said, looking up.

"You're not." He searched my eyes. He could feel everything within me, my heart thumping wildly, my muscles tensing, my tears priming. I'd forgotten. I was a quivering mess beneath the surface, and I wanted to bolt back across the boundary line to hide it from him. But it was too late for that. There was no point now.

"I missed you..." Tears wet down my lashes. I couldn't help it. To hell with all of our stupid rules! "I'm sorry I wasn't here for you! I'm sorry I flipped out and ruined everything! I'm sorry—"

"Do you honestly think I never had a melt-down like that?" he broke in, his eyebrows knitting together above sober eyes.

I thought about that. Yeah, I could imagine him flipping out way worse, actually. I heaved a sigh that stuttered a few times as it eased out of my lungs.

Then he leaned forward, glancing self-consciously sideways at the trees to his right, and whispered in a hushed rush, "I missed you, too."

Before I could process that, he'd turned around and started walking away, though his voice stayed with me and echoed softly in my left ear. I heaved another bumpy sigh.

"The view from the cliff's awesome today," he called over his shoulder. "You coming?"

So that was that. He'd already forgiven me. I nodded and fell into step next to him, moving my feet fast to keep up. I cleared my throat and coughed a few times, and he slowed down, almost effortlessly remaining visible and at my side.

Though I couldn't smell the blissful scent of the pines through my stuffed up nose, the evergreen forest was comfortingly familiar, blessedly shady and unearthly quiet. New-fallen snow has a way of magnifying silence that soothes raw nerves and enlivens the soul. Everything outside of the forest and the two of us seemed far away, but Michael wasn't willing to leave it that way.

"So..." Michael rubbed his fingers anxiously through his hair. "You and your mom?"

"We'll be...fine..." I mumbled, and he rolled his eyes.

"Catherine, you're talking to the ultimate lie detector," he said. "And besides, J.C. told me you and your mom haven't spoken since—"

"He talks to you?" I was incredulous. "I mean, besides the letters?"

"Yeah. And by the way," he pointed out with a touch of sarcasm, "having dyslexia doesn't mean I can't read at all."

I felt my face flush. "I'm sorry. I just—"

"I know, I know. I just thought you should know."

"What else did he say?"

He opened his mouth, and then shook his head and stuffed his hands in his pockets.

"I don't think I should talk about it," he said.

I was confused. "Why not?"

"Look, Catherine. He has some serious shit on his mind, and he thinks I have some direct line to God or something, you know? What he said is, like, confidential or whatever."

"How often does he—"

"He's been out here maybe five or six times."

That blew me away. "What do you do?" I asked.

"He talks, and I just sit with him and listen, you know?"

"He knows you're there," I said. "I mean, he *knows*."

"I know! It really freaked me out at first, but I got kinda used to the company."

"Have you tried…touching…"

"No! He's a guy!" Michael cried, then, "Okay…maybe once or twice."

"And?"

Michael rolled his eyes and then softened them for me. "You're still the only one I make the earth move for." He looked sideways at me and grinned meaningfully. I blushed again, and he looked down at his feet.

"So…do you want me to give him a message or some advice… for his…um… issues?"

"No! How the hell would I know what to tell him? I screwed my own life up enough, and I'm busy working on yours," he growled.

"Michael…"

"How's your mom, then?" He was intent on proving his point, but I knew I would definitely lose that debate, so I kept quiet.

"I thought so," he murmured. We'd reached the little footbridge, and he stopped in the middle of it and whirled around to face me.

"I never asked you to avenge my death, Catherine."

"Then what *am* I supposed to do for you?" I looked down at the trampled snow at my feet, feeling useless. I'd tried to help him face his past, and I'd made sure the people responsible for the destruction of his life were paying, but he was still just as stuck here as he was the first day I'd met him in the woods.

He bent over and tilted his head so he could look up into my face.

"Forgive her," he said softly, urgently. "Tell her you're sorry. Tell her—"

"I can't do that!"

He stood up abruptly and looked away, his jaw flexing in frustration. "I knew this would—"

"I had another dream, Michael."

He swung his head back around, alert and on guard.

"You came to me at the edge of the pool. Only you were alive again…barely. You said my *mom* did this to you." I gestured with my hands toward his ghostly body.

He shook his head. "No…"

"And then you…and then you…" I couldn't describe how I'd felt when he'd collapsed, bleeding and dying, before me, and I sagged back against the bridge's handrail. It had all been so real, like it had been within my power to touch him, to save him. My throat ached more…

"Whoa…hey…" he soothed.

"I think you blame her, too, deep down," I whispered. "You tried to say more, but—"

"No! I wouldn't have said that! I don't blame her! Just because you dreamed it, doesn't make it true!" But his eyes were conflicted. He wasn't sure of anything. "Catherine, you have to forgive her."

I shook my head and turned away from him. I heard him sigh behind me, but he didn't press me. He knew I wasn't there yet, and he was willing to accept me where I was. I looked down at the quote on the bridge. Someone had crossed out the word "dead" and scrawled "alive" next to it. Now it read:

God is ~~dead~~. Alive Where art thou Ubermensch?

"J.C.," he said, distracted. "That kid's a true believer."

I looked up questioningly, but he just motioned for me to keep following him.

～⊃ ⊂～

He was right. The view from the cliff was beautiful. Azure sky. Crisp, clear sunshine. Everything below us—the trees, the park benches, the boulders—they all wore mounded caps of snow. Rippled ice clung to the edges of the river, reflecting the sunlight brilliantly. Someone had even decorated the bridge railings with evergreen garland and red bows.

I picked my way down to the ledge and rested my back and head against the cold damp cliff. My head was starting to ache along with my throat. I really needed to get some sleep.

Michael looked at me worriedly. "You do feel warm today."

I swiveled my head to the right and said, "It's this stupid coat." But I was too tired to take it off.

He reached out and touched his fingertips to my bandaged hand, and it filled with soothing vibrations. I turned it palm up and held it out to him, and he traced the crease of my palm with his thumb.

"Stitches?" he asked.

I nodded.

"Let me see," he instructed, twirling his index finger around above the bandage. I unwrapped my hand, and he counted the stitches.

"They did a nice job. So...what the hell did you tell the doctor?" he wondered, the corners of his lips turning up.

"I didn't go to the doctor. That was the night I had the blowout with my mom and they took Mina to the hospital. Jason was there." I shuddered, remembering how awful it had been. "He sort of..."

"Sort of what?"

"Um...he uh...kept me from...taking a swing at my mom." Michael laced his fingers above his head and blew out sharply through his mouth. Stupid...I shouldn't have told him that. "And then he stitched me up," I went on matter-of-factly, trying to change the subject.

"*Jason* stitched you up?" He was flabbergasted. I guess it didn't seem that strange to me anymore.

I nodded.

"When is he taking them out?" he wanted to know.

"We're sort of not speaking to each other either."

Michael shook his head in exasperation. "And why is that?"

I was quiet, and my heartbeat sped up. He waited.

"I can't give him what he wants," I murmured softly and turned my gaze out over the cliff.

"And what is that?"

I looked down at my feet. "Just leave it alone, okay?"

"Okay. Fine. Whatever. But Catherine...you have to have the stitches taken out, or they'll, like, get infected. Believe me. I've gotten enough stitches to know."

"I thought they would just, you know, dissolve or something," I said, looking down at the eight perfect little knots.

"No. These won't," he said, his brows pulling together. "Wrap it back up and keep it clean." He looked out over the cliff while I bound my hand back up. When I was finished, he dropped his chin slightly and shook his head a few times. He was worried about a lot of things today.

"And your grandmother?" he wondered softly, his gray eyes still focused on the gorge.

"...will be dead in a few months. She's back home. It's..." My voice caught, and I felt the now familiar pressure of tears behind my eyes.

He turned to face me. "It's what?"

"Just...hard..."

He nodded and looked down at his hands, murmuring under his breath, "You shouldn't be fighting with your mom right now."

I shot him a stubborn, "stay out of it" look. I didn't want to talk about it. He was quiet for a while. Then he pointed across me to the deep hollow at the base of the wind-ravaged oak tree that was keeping us company on the ledge.

"J.C. left your letters here for me," he said quietly. "Will you read them to me? The whole guy voice and Hispanic accent thing didn't quite do it for me." Despite my black mood, I had to suppress a laugh as I imagined what that must have sounded like, and then I found the letters in a clear plastic bag, anchored by a rock just inside the tree. They were ragged and a little damp, but still legible. I looked up at Michael, and he inched closer to me and nodded. I cleared my throat.

❧❧

Michael,

What to say...I'm grounded. I guess you figured that. I screwed up. I didn't think far enough ahead of my temper to realize it would keep me away from you. I'm such a stupid idiot. Needless to say, things really suck at home right now. I wish I could move into the woods with you. Maybe I could get a tent? My grandmother is in the hospital, and they're not sure if she'll make it. My mom's never here, which is probably a good thing. Michael, listen to me, I'll come back for you. I come back in my mind every day. 100 times a day. Please wait for me. Don't give up hope. I know God has a plan for you. We just don't know what it is yet. I'll be there as soon as I can.

Love, Catherine

P.S. Don't worry about me. I'm okay.

I looked up to see Michael's reaction. He was grinning softly to himself.

"A tent?" he asked, raising his eyebrows.

"I was pretty desperate," I admitted.

"Mmm..." he said and then nodded toward the next one. I looked down at it and swallowed hard. The ache in my throat flared. It had been longer since I'd seen him when I wrote the second letter, and my emotions had poured themselves unfiltered onto the page. I was suddenly self-conscious.

Dear Michael,

I am amazed and confused that J.C. senses your presence in the woods. But I won't complain. Knowing you're still there and waiting for me makes everything else bearable. He gave me a bottle of Higher Dior. I keep it in my sock drawer. It smells like you. Cici says that's how I smell whenever I came home from "Jai Ho." She seems to sense your presence, too, then. I guess a little bit of you rubs off on me whenever we're together. The doctors say my grandmother will be coming home soon...coming home to die. But they say her death is still a ways off. Several months maybe. I don't want to be here when it happens.

It's only six days until Christmas, and when I light my Advent candles this Sunday, I will pray for you. There is light in you. It's there, and it's burning bright.

I'll come on Christmas Eve, even if I have to snow shoe or hire a reindeer. Wait for me. <u>Please</u> wait for me. I don't think I can live without you.
Love, Catherine

I stuffed the letters back in the bag, shoved them back under the rock inside the tree hollow where he could see them, and then wrapped my arms around my knees. I looked away from him, my cheeks flaming, my ears roaring with the sound of my own mortification. Had I really ended my letter like that?

I didn't know he'd moved until he was crouched down in front of me, up on his toes, pale and wavering against the blue sky backdrop. His heels were hanging over the edge of the snow packed cliff, but I wasn't afraid for him. I knew what he was.

"Did I ever tell you that you're amazing?" he asked, his voice winding around me like soft gauze. I looked back into his eyes and nodded but didn't say anything, because inside I was trembling. He reached out hesitantly and trailed his feather-light fingertips through the small curls that framed my forehead and then down across my face.

Gentle static followed them through my cheekbones.

"Your cheeks are so cold," he murmured. He let his tingle tipped fingers travel lightly down the side of my neck and then sunk them down through the thick layers of my coat and sweater where they followed the contour of my collarbone out to the tip of my shoulder, leaving a trail of goose bumps behind.

"Warmer..." he murmured, a small crease forming between his brows. And I *was* warmer. I flushed hot from head to toe, and his lips turned up slightly. He let his fingertips roll over the edge of my shoulder and travel down the outside of my arm, which was still tightly wrapped around my knees, and then down past my wrist. I extended my index finger to give his fingertips something to kick off. They made the leap from my fingertip to the base of my calf and then he worked them upward through my jeans toward the tender back of my knee where they drifted back and forth. He leaned in closer.

"Very...*very*...*warm*..." he observed, and I had to close my eyes against the rush of heat that flooded my veins. This was insane. If I was amazing, then he was unbelievable, a ghost in my world, touching me. I wanted to reach out and touch him back. I wanted to follow the sweat slick contours of his arms and chest, the strong line of his jaw, the intricate architecture of his hands, but that wasn't possible, and it wasn't fair.

"Michael, I—"

"Shh..." he said, ending his fingertip odyssey on my lips where they explored the curves and valleys they found there. I opened my eyes to find his waiting for me, and they were filled with longing.

I knew how Meri felt then, when Finn touched her. I knew Michael loved me, too.

"Hot," I whispered simply.

"Freaking freezing," he responded, grinning, still tracing the bow of my lips with his fingers.

"Hot," I insisted and released my grip on my knees and leaned forward between them with my hands on my icy boots. He tipped his body in toward me and anchored his free hand against the cliff behind my head, then tilted his head to the side and met me half way, brushing his weightless lips against mine. My entire face tingled under waves of hot static, and I closed my eyes and pressed forward to respond, wanting those full lips crushing mine, but there was nothing to respond against, and I started to fall...

"Catherine!" he cried, and I jerked my head back reflexively, startled.

"Christ! Don't forget about the cliff!" His chest heaved, and he rubbed the back of his neck viciously with his right hand. And then he was gone. Shit. He'd pissed himself off again.

I waited, and when he didn't show back up, I climbed up to the clearing above the cliff and found him sitting with his back against a tree, hugging his knees to his chest, contemplating his mangled bare toes with intense interest. I sank down next to him and tilted my head over in front of his face.

"I love you, Michael," I whispered.

"Love what? Love *this?*" he growled, thrusting out his arms and hands to display the angry lacerations and raw fingernails that my mind had blocked out recently. I didn't see them anymore. I just saw Michael.

"Yes," I soothed and reached out with my fingertips to brush them across his unearthly torn skin.

He pulled his arms away.

"There *is* light in you. I saw it when we overlapped. When I opened my eyes—"

He looked over at me plaintively. "Where the hell does your faith come from anyway? Where does J.C.'s? You with your *church* and your *prayers* and your stupid candles. How can you be so sure with so much...shit in the world?" He turned away from me, whispering, "So many empty promises."

I looked helplessly up at the slivers of sky that peeked through the pines, resigned to the fact that our winter heat wave was over. He needed something else from me now. He needed my faith, but I feared mine wasn't strong enough. I wondered for the hundredth time why this task had fallen to me.

"Church? My parents? I don't know," I stammered. "I have my doubts, too."

Tell him about the music!

I bit my frozen lower lip.

"No!" He pointed at me angrily. "You're holding out on me! I can feel it." I forgot who I was talking to.

"You'll laugh," I said, sticking my chin out.

"I won't," he said, equally defensive. Crap. He would laugh. He'd laughed before. But even as I protested, I knew I'd tell him. I couldn't keep anything hidden from him.

"Music," I said.

"Music?" He looked disappointed. "You mean like church music?"

"No…" I groaned. It really sounded stupid when I thought about saying it out loud. He waited.

"I have a Playlist. Okay?" I took a deep breath and then went on bravely. "I think of it as God's Playlist. It's a list of songs I've heard when I felt like I just couldn't take anymore, songs that played when I needed to hear them the most, as if they were played just for me. Most of the time they remind me that God's there, somewhere, keeping an eye on me. They're like…a lifeline."

I looked over at him to find a blank look on his face. At least he wasn't laughing. He looked sideways for a second, thinking about what I'd said, and then he said, "Like 'Kryptonite?' I thought we agreed that was me. That song and the dreams and—"

"No. *You* agreed. *I* still think 'Kryptonite' and the dreams were God's way of telling me He wanted me to help you, or He wanted me to know that *you* wanted me to help you. But *you* wouldn't buy into that, remember?"

Michael thought about that for a moment. Then he fired back, "What about my axe-toting freak memory then?"

"I don't know where that one came from," I mumbled, still confused by that.

"Aha!" Michael cried. "See! It *was* me! Your friendly neighborhood evil…"

I glowered at him, and his eyes started to roll, but he caught himself.

"*Okay*, then," he said, trying to keep his voice and lips steady. "Besides 'Kryptonite,' how many songs on *God's* Playlist?"

"Ten or twelve. I've lost count." I let my eyes go steely, and he turned his face away for a second and then looked back, still completely serious. I had to give him props for trying anyway.

"And they would be?"

Which should I start with? Which one was I willing to share? I decided on a lighter one.

"Okay…um…on the first day of school I was worried because I wanted to break up with Jason. Only I'd pushed him in the pool for—"

"You pushed him in the pool? He's like, twice as big as you!"

"He didn't see me coming," I mumbled. Then Michael did laugh.

"I told you, you'd laugh! Forget it!" I crossed my arms over my chest.

He held his hand up. "Hey! Not fair! I didn't laugh at your *Playlist*, I laughed at the thought of you pushing Jason in the pool. What'd he do?"

"He was holding hands with Kara," I huffed.

"Okay…" he said, obviously amused by my flare of temper. He straightened his face with effort and said, "Finish your story then."

"*Anyway*…everyone was talking about me, and I was really upset about it, and this song came on the radio, and one of the lines said everything would be alright."

"And that's it?"

"*No*…everything *did* turn out alright," I explained. "Jason didn't really care that I wanted to break up, and only a few stupid idiots were still talking about me."

"So that's your proof that God exists?"

"It's not proof. It's…reinforcement. And that's only one example."

"I think I need to hear another one," he grumbled, resting his chin on his knees, obviously not impressed.

I contemplated the snow at the edge of the cliff while I thought about it. My memories got more personal from there, and they would be harder to talk about.

"Do you remember when I told you I had pneumonia when I was eleven?" I began, and he nodded half-heartedly.

"It started as the flu, and I missed like, a month of school. I was so lonely. I missed my friends and my homework was piling up. I felt like everyone had forgotten me, and then just when I started to feel better the flu turned into pneumonia, and I ended up in the hospital. I was really sick, coughing up nasty brown crusty crap that choked my lungs and feeling like someone was stabbing me every time I took a breath."

He looked up from his knees and started paying attention.

"They were sticking needles in my veins it seemed like every hour, testing for this and that. Then there was the arterial blood gas test. They take that from your artery, and it hurts like hell. It left purple bruises all over my..." I looked down at my wrist.

He reached over with his fingertips and brushed the phantom pain away. "I'm sorry Catherine...I didn't mean to—"

"But that wasn't the worst of it!" I went on in a rush. "The worst was feeling like a total weakling. Like I had no strength at all. I couldn't even make it from my bed to the bathroom, and here my older sister was running 5 K's, and my baby sister was flipping over balance beams backwards and my friends were having sleepovers without me and going to the mall...and I couldn't even walk to the stupid bathroom..." I shook my head, the emotions crashing and breaking over me all over again. Why did I have to be such a baby? "I know it sounds stupid. I mean I wasn't going to die or anything. But at the time I already felt dead, like there was no way I could fight my way back again. I was so tired, and I wanted to give up and—"

"Catherine, no..."

I nodded.

"It was the middle of the night, and I was lonely and scared and I pulled out my music player from the drawer next to the hospital bed. I heard a song that I'd never heard before. One I'd never downloaded. A song called "It's Only Life." It said not to lose my faith...not to run away...almost like it knew what I was thinking.

I looked up to see a burgeoning desire to believe in Michael's eyes, but he was fighting it. My throat constricted with emotion. I wanted badly to believe, too.

"And so...I just lay there in the bed, feeling like shit, looking up at the ceiling tiles, crying like a baby. It was like someone knew what I was thinking and was sitting right next to me, singing that song just for me."

Michael was quiet for a minute and then he asked, "So...who do you think is picking the songs?" That question made me squirm, but I thought of Saint Joan and shoved my theory out there anyway. Something told me he *needed* to hear it.

"I think maybe I have an Angel...or something," I mumbled.

"An Angel," he said, clipping the sarcastic edge from his voice at the last moment.

"Look. I had something happen to me when I was five that..." I shook my head and clamped my mouth shut. No, I was delusional, obviously.

"You can't start to tell me something like that and then stop," he protested. "I promise I won't laugh."

I gave him the evil eye. Sure.

"Five year olds aren't reliable witnesses," I pointed out stoically. Only my parents knew about the nightmares, but I'd never told anyone about the voice in the light that ended them. And yet again, it was like something was whispering deep inside me that he needed to know. It told me it was time to share my darkest secret and flickering hope, that I'd been saving them for this moment. And so I began. "When I was five," I said, wrapping my arms around my knees and focusing on the snowy trees at the edge of the cliff. "I went through this stage where I had horrible nightmares every night."

"Like after I died?"

"Worse. They went on for weeks." I closed my eyes, and chilling images rose up in my head. I snapped my eyes back open, gasping involuntarily, and locked them on Michael's, anxiously trying to anchor myself in the present. It was so long ago, and yet I was still afraid to go back there.

"What?" he asked, alarmed by the spike in my heart rate.

"There were these black shadowy creatures. Their eyes were like flames. They surrounded my bed every night, and without even touching me, they pressed me down to keep me there. I couldn't move. Michael...they told me I was beautiful...that I was perfect...that I was more special than all the others..."

I looked away, biting my lip, wishing I could end the memory there.

"That doesn't sound so bad," he said quietly.

But I wasn't finished.

"They told me the 'others' didn't deserve to live," I whispered, unable to look him in the eye. "They made me watch kids being tortured, murdered...with fire...with stones...and knives. They laid them all out on the side of a road, burned and maimed, like some sort of sacrifice. Then one night they put the knife in my hand and told me it was my turn to—"

"You had dreams like that when you were five?" he interrupted, incredulous. "What the hell did your parents let you watch on TV?"

"That's just it! I'd never seen anything like it! I don't know where the dreams came from, and I was starting to lose my mind, Michael. I mean, I was having a hard time figuring out what was real and what wasn't." I looked down at my palms and then buried my hands deep in my coat pockets.

"One night, I was lying in my parents' bed with my mom and dad sound asleep on either side of me, and I was *still* scared. I saw the creatures even when I was awake, even with my eyes open, and they were creeping up onto the bed. The mattress bumped and swayed under their weight...and I just cried out in my mind, God please help me! Make them go away!"

Every inch of Michael was listening now.

"And I was suddenly surrounded by warm blinding light, and someone pulled me up onto their lap and wrapped their arms around me. And I felt a love pour into my soul that couldn't be contained. I felt safe, like nothing could touch me. He told me I didn't need to worry about the shadow creatures anymore, because he'd make sure they didn't come back."

I looked up at Michael, still filled with awe after so many years.

"You mean you *dreamed* someone picked you up," he clarified, his skepticism trumping my hope.

"Maybe…I don't know. Sometimes I think it was God or an Angel, sometimes I think I just imagined it or dreamed it, but that was the last nightmare I had for a long time."

The story was true. All of it. I could still see that light, how it penetrated right through my closed eyelids, and I closed my eyes to bask in its remembered glow. I forgot Michael was there. When I finally opened my eyes again, I was startled to see him staring back at me.

He shook his head back and forth. "No…Catherine…" he faltered. And then his lips curled back and his voice dug in harshly. "Do you really think there's a God out there that can answer your call for help? Really?"

He definitely wasn't laughing.

"Coincidences happen, you know? You think they mean something, but they don't. You fall far enough? You can make yourself see…" His voice failed him again, and he clenched his jaw and looked away. Then he buried his face in his knees.

His total disbelief was a slap in the face. I knew he didn't mean to hurt me, but it stung anyway. I probably would have felt the same way if our roles had been reversed, but the memory I'd shared was too personal to let his rejection just roll off my back. Instead, it clung to me like a heavy, wet towel on a cold, windy day at the beach.

We sat side-by-side in silence for a while. I started to feel the cold through my coat. It was relentless. And the achiness I'd felt before was spreading, intensifying. My skin protested sorely as it shivered against the scratchy wool of my sweater, and I realized Michael was right. I was sick. I had a fever. He'd sensed it, but it wasn't high enough yet to alarm him, and I was glad. I'd tuck myself into him and continue to share what little faith I had. It was Christmas Eve after all. I couldn't give up. But how could I reach him?

Far below us, an old beat-up station wagon with a naked Christmas tree lashed to its roof lumbered over the bridge. Kind of late to be getting their tree, I thought, and then I remembered my gift for him. I wasn't as excited about giving it to him anymore, but it was a place to start.

"I have a present for you," I said. He refused to look up.

"Close your eyes," I instructed.

"They are closed. I'm thinking," he mumbled into his knees. He could be glum if he wanted to. It was Christmas Eve, and he was getting his gift. I pulled out my music player and scrolled to the song I'd downloaded for him and held up one of the ear pieces near his ear.

"Now listen," I said.

First we heard a few sleigh bells.

Then a layer of piano and an ample side of sax.

And then Springsteen's rough-rocking voice belting out "Merry Christmas Baby."

It didn't exactly fit our mood, but it *was* Bruce Springsteen, Michael's favorite songwriter, and I hoped Michael would appreciate the thought anyway. I'd downloaded a bunch of songs for him to listen to. He looked up from his lonely hiding place, tilted his head to the side and gave me a reluctant half-smile. It was perfect.

We listened to half a dozen Springsteen songs, all the classics and a few from off the radio's well-beaten path. It seemed to cheer him up for a while. He bounced his heels in time with the music and mouthed some of the words silently to himself. When "Thunder Road" came on, he leaned his head back against the tree, pulled out the Claddagh from under his shirt and twisted it back and forth on the chain with his eyes closed. Then his mood went south again.

"What's wrong?" I asked. What *wasn't* wrong?

He shook his head, and I waited.

"Look...I'm sorry..." he said with feeling. "I shouldn't have said what I said before. Just believe whatever you want to believe if it makes you feel better. I just can't."

I watched helplessly from my place by his side as he struggled valiantly with some unseen enemy. He was so lost. And yet, he hadn't always been.

"Michael..." I pleaded. "Help me understand why. Explain it to me. What about your tattoo?"

Glancing down at his inked sword, Michael winced and then, instead of answering my question, he let his gaze drift out into the quiet woods, humming the opening notes to Springsteen's "Thunder Road" and murmured, "My mom loved that song, too."

He met my eyes, then glanced quickly away again. "She could really sing, you know? I got that talent from her," he informed me and then added darkly, "along with our special talent for falling into any addictive hole we happened to walk by. I was in one of those holes when Shawn called to tell me he'd heard they'd found my mom's body behind a dumpster on the near west side."

I sucked a sharp breath into my lungs. Michael wavered out of focus uneasily and lowered his lashes. Shit. How deep would this hole go?

"Yeah, Catherine, I was stoned when I found out my mom was dead. Totally wasted. Isn't that sick?" He kept his eyes on the frayed laces of his shoe. "And then it was all downhill from there. And when I crashed into the bottom? *That's* when I finally looked up." He aimed his eyes upward as I often did when I was too self-conscious to use the word "God." Only he didn't keep his eyes there. He looked back down at his tattoo and winced again. Then he gathered up his voice, and we began our journey down into the pit.

Chapter 21
The Tattoo

"So...even through the pot haze," he began, balancing his elbows on his knees, "I felt my gut, like fill with ice when I hung up the phone. I remember wishing I was buzzing on something stronger. Way stronger. In fact, I was wishing I was passed out somewhere, completely oblivious." His forehead scrunched up, and he sighed again.

"But...I wasn't. And I got it in my head that I needed to go and see if what Shawn said was true. I hadn't seen my mom since I'd moved in with the Gardiners, but I'd heard she was evicted and living on the streets. If she was dead, I wanted to see her. It didn't matter that I was stoned off my ass and that everything I looked at kept pulsing and shifting to the right."

"Michael, I'm so sorry..."

He flicked his eyes impatiently in my direction and then looked back out at his hands. "Yeah...well...that was my life." He paused and then plunged back in to his dialogue, faster, like he wanted to be done with it.

"I caught the bus and got to the scene about a half hour later. The cops were still crawling all over the place, and an ambulance and a few cruisers were parked nearby. All I could see from behind the crime tape was a mound under a white sheet halfway hidden behind an overflowing dumpster. It was one of those record hot days last May, and the trash reeked. There were flies everywhere, landing on my sweaty arms, landing on the sheet. I wanted to puke. I wanted to leave. But I couldn't. She was my mom, you know?"

He looked over at me again, and I nodded, trying to fathom how he must have felt, but it was impossible.

"Anyway…um…since my brain had checked out a few hours earlier, I thought it would be a good idea to just duck under the crime tape and head straight for her body, which is what I *did*. I ran into the chest of this crabby, middle-aged detective before I realized it wasn't such a good plan."

Michael looked away and rolled his eyes at himself, embarrassed by his own stupidity. "So the detective said, 'Hey kid! Where do you think you're going? Get back behind the tape!' At that point, my brain finally checked back in, and I mumbled something like, 'I…uh…knew the victim…' I avoided the detective's eyes for obvious reasons and focused on his buttons, which were sliding down the front of his dress shirt. Then I was thinking, *oh shit, I hope he doesn't realize I'm totally lit up.* Lucky for me, he had other things on his mind.

"The detective looked around at the crowd stuck behind the tape and smiled real big at all of them. Then he was like all sarcastic, 'Well that's very interesting, kid, because *we* don't know who the victim is and…um…none of the schmucks we interviewed over *there* know who the victim is. Now, how is it that you think *you* know who the victim is?'

"So I said, 'Look! Can I just see her? I got a call,' and he was like, '*Right.*' He looked over at the crowd again, and then he grabbed me by the arm and pulled me over to the lumpy sheet. I heard the words heroin overdose and half-starved being kicked around. 'Let's see what ya got, kid,' he said. Then he nodded at one of the crime scene techs to pull the sheet up.

"And there she was, Catherine, friggin' dead. Just like I always knew she would be, except knowing and seeing are two different things, and I had just enough time to turn away from her and the cop before my lunch burned its way up my throat and fired itself out of my mouth and nose.

"She was a mess. Pasty skin, cracked lips, bony thin." Michael wrung his hands as he talked, as he tried to face the memory of his mother lying like so much rotten garbage next to the overheated dumpster. "Her arm was thrown up over her head and it was covered with pus-filled track marks. There was dried spit covering her chin and...and..."

"Michael, you don't have to..." The memory was crushing him. He took a deep breath and blew it out through his mouth. Then his eyes flashed with anger, disgust.

"I'd never done heroin, Catherine! I mean, I'd kind of prided myself on the fact that I'd drawn the line there, you know? Like I was somehow better than she was, because I stayed away from the hard stuff? I'd watched her shoot up, but I could never understand why she did it. Why she'd chosen the rush of heroin flooding her veins over me!"

My throat constricted painfully for him. "She was sick..." I offered lamely, but he gave me a look that said, 'yeah, right,' before going on.

"So I just stood there gagging, and then I wiped my mouth with the back of my hand and asked the detective if she was wearing a ring. A gold Claddagh."

Michael glanced up at me meaningfully while his fingers absently sought comfort from the Claddagh's outline resting safely beneath his black sleeveless shirt.

"The detective looked over at the tech, and the tech shook his head no. Then the detective was like, 'So, do you know who she is or not?' 'No,' I lied, then I almost got sick all over again. That ring was the only proof that we'd been happy once. Without it, my life was one big freaking hole. Empty. I thought I was going to pass out and I reached for the side of the dumpster for support. I found out later that it burned my hand, but I didn't even flinch at the time. The tech said, 'I think he's on something, Mack.'

"I heard the detective mumble, 'shit,' and then he was like, 'Look at me kid. Can you follow my finger?' He held his index finger up in front of my face and waved it slowly back and forth. That was my cue it was time to bug out. I started back toward the crime tape and the tech stood up to follow me, but the detective was like, 'Let him go. We've got enough shit to deal with. Stupid kid…he's gonna throw his life away.' And as I ducked under the tape, he called after me, 'So, when are we gonna see you back here, kid? I want to make sure I come pay my respects!'"

"How could he say that? That's horrible!" I cried. Michael shifted around so he could look me in the eye.

"No. It wasn't," he said.

I was shocked. "But she was your mom! How could he be so—"

"Number one, he didn't know that. And number two, I needed to hear that."

"Michael, there have to be better ways to stop kids from taking drugs," I argued, but Michael was adamant.

"I don't know, Catherine. Maybe that was the best thing my mom ever did for me, you know? Letting me see her totally trashed dead body? Because you know what? After I got home, I decided I needed to lay low for a while, you know? Like stay clean for a while. I guess I wanted to prove to myself I wasn't addicted to anything. It was mostly just pot anyway, right? Maybe a little coke or booze now and then? A few pills here and there, right? *Wrong.*"

Michael turned and spat into the snow and then dropped his head and looked down at the icy ground between his knees, moaning, "I was a total head case for the next week. I couldn't sleep. I had no appetite. And irritable. Christ, was I irritable! You'd have thought I had freaking PMS."

He shook his head in an exaggerated shiver gesture, and the tips of his hair brushed back and forth against my cheek, sending electric chills across my face. Even as sick as I was, my body responded to his magic, and my heart rate spiked. He paused in his story, looked at me, his troublemaker eyes glinting, and then shook his hair back and forth again.

"Will you stop!" I cried.

"Whatever…" he murmured, stopping. But I caught a glimpse of a grin twitching at the corners of his lips, and my heart fluttered again. He glanced down at his toes and then stretched out his bare legs on the snow in front of him, crossing them at the ankles. He was like a polar bear comfortably lounging on an ice floe. It was so not fair. Despite my stadium cushion, my butt and thighs were freezing.

"So, we got the official call about a week later that she was dead," he said. "Sue didn't hug me or anything. We didn't work that way. Not yet. They were great that way, you know? They gave me my space. But I could see all this sympathy in her eyes, and it made me sick. I didn't deserve any of it."

"Yes. You did," I countered. "Your mom had just died, Michael."

He didn't agree with me. He just soldiered on, his voice taking on an ominous tone. I steeled myself for what was coming next. I'd once wondered how he'd gotten the whole world's ration of bad luck dumped on him. And I'd wondered what else could possibly go wrong in his life. My answer was coming. Like a runaway freight train on a moonless night.

The train took us deeper.

"I was still irritable when I ran into Devlin at the little strip mall near the Gardiner's house about a week after my mom died. I'd hardly seen him since I'd moved out of my mom's apartment. He'd come out to wait on a customer. It was late, past eleven, and the stores were all closed. The parking lot was totally deserted, and the black top was still hot. I could feel the heat right through the soles of my Converse." He waved the tip of his one shoe at me. "I liked to walk up to the strip mall with my guitar and mess around with it while I sat on the curb in front of the stores and smoked. It helped me relax when I was all keyed up. And I was really keyed up that night. Staying clean was more of a bitch than I thought it would be. I'd just pulled out a new cigarette when Devlin drove into the empty lot and got out of the car.

"He was like, 'Hey Mike! How the hell are ya?'"

Michael turned his chin over his shoulder to look at me. "You have to remember, we were still friends at that point." Then Michael's eyes gleamed savagely, and his lips stretched taut over his teeth. "At least, for the next maybe sixty seconds."

The timer started ticking.

"So, I lit the cigarette and offered it to him, tapped the pack again and pulled out another one for me. He was like, 'Thanks bro,' and then he pulled a small, plastic, zippered bag out of his pocket and handed it to me. 'For old time's sake,' he said.

"I flicked the ashes off my cigarette and dangled the bag up at eye level under the street light to check it out. Light brown powder. A couple of lines' worth. And it wasn't coke. It was heroin.

"And I was thinking, *oh shit, I'm gonna be sick.* All I could see was my mom's pasty face. I tossed it back to him and took a hit off my cigarette. My fingers were shaking, and I dropped my hand back down to my side. You can't let a guy like Dev see you sweat. He might not be that big, but he's got friends.

"'I'm clean,' I said.

"Then Devlin was like, 'You're fucking with me.' And he tossed the bag back at me, grinning. I bungled the throw and had to bend over to pick it up, and then I tossed it back to him again.

"'No shit, man. I'm clean. Keep it,' I said. It was a hot night. I started to sweat."

Then Michael's breathing came faster.

"Dev was like, 'Aw, come on, Mike. What, like you don't trust me now? It's good H. Your mom's been comin' to me for the last six months, though she hasn't been around this week.'"

Michael's oration came to a screeching halt as if he'd smashed into a brick wall, and then his whole body tightened up. Luke Devlin was his mom's dealer? Shit. No wonder Michael hated him. Oh crap. A whole lot of things started to make sense then, and I was ready to puke in solidarity with him right there.

Michael's next words tumbled out in an avalanche, falling all over themselves. "My hands were all over his throat in seconds, and I just shoved him backward with all my frickin' might, screaming, 'That's because she's dead, you mother effing asshole! Your effing smack killed her!' And then he was like flying backward and glass was breaking and blood was spurting out from under his armpit."

"*Luke Devlin* is the one you pushed through the plate glass window?"

He nodded his head once in answer to my question, and then he stood up and started pacing across the icy snow, his emotional lava bubbling way too furiously for him to remain motionless.

"Dev's blood was squirting out like three feet with each pump of his heart, but you know what my first thought was? Get rid of the freaking evidence. That's where my head was those days. I grabbed the bag of heroin he'd dropped and then searched his pockets and found four more plus some pot, and I buried it all under the mulch in this flower pot next to the door. Then I called 9-1-1 on his prepaid cell.

"I thought about running, but he was already going under. I couldn't leave him there to die—and he would have if I hadn't done anything. Even with the ambulance coming, he would never have made it."

Michael rubbed the back of his neck, and then he locked his hands over the top of his head and pressed down.

"Voices in my head were screaming!

"*No witnesses!*

"*No one will know it was you!*

"*He killed your mom for Christ's sake!*

"*Get the hell out of here!*"

He shook his head violently as if he were trying to silence the voices all over again.

"But I yanked off my shirt instead and tried to find that pressure point thing near his shoulder to stop the bleeding, the whole time thinking, *Crap, Michael, you really did it this time! If he dies, and they find you here, you're totally screwed! They'll try you as an adult! You are so freaking screwed!*

"I expected a squad car to show up, but the ambulance got there first. When the paramedic rushed over, I took my hand off Dev's arm, and he started gushing blood all over the place again. The paramedic pressed his hand down, and *then* I got the hell out of there!

"The medic called after me, but he was obviously too busy to chase me down, and I could hear more sirens in the distance. I slipped into one of the bathrooms at the park down the street to catch my breath. It was so damn hot! And I went to the sink to splash some cold water on my face and just like totally froze up when I saw myself in the mirror.

"My chest, my face, my hands?

"*All* splattered with his blood.

"I could smell it.

"*Taste* it."

Michael's nostrils flared as he remembered.

"At that point, I figured it was only a matter of time before the police showed up at my door, and it wouldn't matter whether Devlin lived or died. I was going down. And you know what, Catherine? I really didn't care anymore. My dad was dead. My mom was dead. I'd helped her killer deal drugs, and then I'd most likely killed him. And by then I was probably wanted for murder. I had absolutely no hope that anything in my life was ever going to get any better."

Michael sank down in front of me with his feet tucked under him, his tingling hands clinging to my pulled up knees, trying desperately to make me understand how he'd felt.

"I gave up on myself that night and I wanted to make it official. If I was going to be a psychopath, a stoner, a murderer, a hopeless case, then I'd mark myself permanently as one. And I wanted to do it before I was locked up or..." His jaw tightened, and he lost his voice for a moment.

"So I did my best to wash off the blood, which was already crusting up at the edges of the spatter marks. Then I waited. And when everything was quiet again at the strip mall, I went back and dug up the heroin. I told myself I just needed it to trade for money."

He glanced down and then back up at me, guilt ridden, through his lashes. We both knew why he went back for the heroin.

"Oh, Michael..." I murmured, and he looked away. "I still love you," I whispered.

He looked back at me, his eyes filled with doubt, his eyebrows twisted, as if it were impossible for him to believe that I was telling the truth, that he was worthy of any love at all. And I wondered if we'd reached the bottom yet.

He dropped back slowly onto the ground to sit in front of me and continued. "So...um...I couldn't go home. That much was obvious to me. Instead, I slung my guitar across my back to hide the worst of my scars and walked to the highway, hoping to hitch a ride across town. The storefront I was looking for, Ink Relic, was dark when I finally got there. I had no idea what time it was. I knocked anyway. Ian Doyle lives on the second floor above the shop.

"I saw a light go on upstairs, then something crashed and the light went out. Then Ian came stumbling out of the shadows and switched on the bright light above the door."

Michael down-shifted his voice into the deepest part of his register. "'Who the heck is it?' Ian said through the glass door. He had on his black leather pants and no shirt, and his Mohawk was all bent over. He could barely keep his eyes open, but he was raising his tattoo covered arms, trying to push his hair back in place. Ian's all about the hair. I felt a little bad for waking him up, but I had nowhere else to go, and I needed something from him."

I'd seen the guy Michael was describing. He'd been at his wake and funeral, but I wasn't about to interrupt him then. He was immersed.

"'It's Michael Casey,' I yelled through the door. Ian rubbed his eyes and opened them wider.

"'Do you have any idea what time it is?' he said back.

"I was like, 'uh…yeah! You said to call you if I ever needed anything. Ring. There. I called.' See, I was too strung out to be polite, and I knew Ian wouldn't care. He's a come-as-you-are kind of person, and he was already unlocking the glass door and pulling it open. The bells above it rang, and he flicked on the bright overhead light. The funky artwork all over the purple walls flashed in my face, and I had to close my eyes for a sec just to get my bearings.

"Ian said, 'Open your eyes, Michael.' And I did, and he took a good long look and then he sighed and said, 'You look more like your dad every time I see you. How's your mom?'

"'Dead,' I said.

"'Well that sucks,' he said.

"'Yeah,' I said. Then I walked away from him and over to the wall of art. Tattoo art. Skulls and roses and the faces of people who'd died. It was all his, and it was all awesome.

"'So what're you running from this time, Michael?' he said. Ian never beat around the bush. Ink Relic, his shop, was my favorite place to run to whenever one of my fosters got too nasty or too annoying. He'd been a friend of my dad's in high school, and he'd never turned me in. His was a place to..." Michael looked off into the frosty trees, trying to find the right word. "...just breathe, you know?"

I nodded, knowing exactly what he meant. That's how I'd felt about Lewis Woods lately. Michael hunched down farther against the tree and studied his fingers.

"I didn't tell him about Devlin, and he didn't ask me again. I just looked at all the art on the wall, and then I pointed to one, a skull with a snake coming out of its eye hole. 'I want that one, Ian,' I said. And then I turned around to see him leaning against the arm of the waiting area's zebra-striped sofa, shaking his head at me. He didn't laugh though. He always took me seriously.

"But he was like, 'Unless you traveled back in time to add on a few years, you're only fifteen, Michael. Can't tattoo you yet.' I was so mad, Catherine! I was ready to rip everything off the walls!

"'Why the hell not?' I yelled back. 'You did my dad's tattoo when he was only seventeen!'

"And then he was like, 'Sure I did. And I was only sixteen. And he was lucky he didn't get some nasty skin infection.' Then he asked me, 'Why'd you pick that one?'

"Well, Ian,' I said. 'I'm going to effing Disney World! Skulls kinda go with the whole Cinderwhatzerface theme. Don't ya think?'

"Ian rolled his eyes at me. I just couldn't tell him what I'd done or how I felt that night. There were no *words*! He told me to sit down on the sofa and then he went in the back. But I couldn't sit. I paced. I wanted to crawl out of my skin. All these thoughts were banging around in my head. The police...the drugs...my mom...Devlin's blood..."

Michael looked up at me anxiously to make sure I was following, and then he ran his fingers through his damp wavy hair.

"When Ian came back out, he was holding this black binder that had duct tape all over the outside of it to keep it together. He sat down on the zebra sofa and turned on a lamp that was on the table next to it.

He reached back behind him and switched off the buzzing overhead light. Then he said, 'Sit down, Michael. I want to show you something.'

"I didn't sit. I just watched him flip the lumpy pages back and forth. It was filled with scribbled tattoo designs on all kinds of paper. They were stuck to the pages with whatever Ian must have had lying around at the time he got them: scotch tape, staples, paper clips, gum…"

"He finally found what he was looking for, turned the book around on his lap and said, 'How 'bout that one?'

"He was pointing to a design that had been drawn on a white Post-It note with ball point pen. The paper was crumpled and stained, and the drawing was crude, but I'd have known that tattoo anywhere: a sword with angel wings behind it. It had the name 'St. Michael' inked on the hilt."

Michael glanced down at his own tattoo, and I held my breath. But instead of the sneer that he usually regarded it with, he reached out with the fingers of his left hand and traced it as if it were something holy.

"It was my dad's tattoo, Catherine," he whispered. "This was my dad's tattoo." His jaw flexed, and then he looked down at his hands again, his brows furrowing deeply. His deep-voiced imitation of Ian turned sarcastic. 'I don't think your dad would want you getting a snake-filled skull permanently inked on your arm at fifteen, Michael,' Ian said to me.

"And I was like, 'What's so *freaking* great about that tattoo? So what if it was my dad's! Big effing deal! I'm not *him!* I'll never *be* him!' He was…all good, you know? He was the best…"

And I lost track of what Michael was quoting from his past and what he was feeling now. I think maybe he was in both places at the same time right then. "I know he was," I soothed, but Michael ran his fingers anxiously through his hair again. There was more.

"So Ian waited for me to calm down, and then he told me what was so special about this tattoo. 'Your dad drew it,' Ian said. 'Woke me up around five on a Sunday morning, handed me that paper, rolled up his sleeve, pointed to his right bicep, and told me to put it right there.'

"See, Ian had already tattooed this cool shaded gray dagger above his own ankle. He said he told my dad no way, but my dad just wouldn't stop bugging him. And you'll never believe what my dad told him that finally convinced him to do it."

His next words poured out with an even mix of scorn and long buried reverence. "My dad told him, quote, 'Ian, we've gotta stop screwin' around. From this day on we're dedicating our lives to God and to helping Saint Michael with all the shit he's got to deal with here on earth.'"

I was incredulous. "The Archangel Michael?" I clarified.

Michael nodded and shifted his weight uncomfortably.

"You mean your dad pledged to help Michael, the *Archangel*, protect people from the Devil's—"

"Yeah. Yeah. Yeah. And from evil spirits, like moi, and snares and whatever. You can Google the stupid prayer if I ever stop talking and let you go home today." He wrapped his arms protectively around his knees. He started to fade.

"Please don't stop talking," I begged. You couldn't have paid me to leave. It didn't matter that I was feeling sicker by the minute, that I could barely swallow my own saliva without wincing.

Michael's now translucent gray eyes flicked to my face and appraised me carefully. I took a deep breath and tried to look...fine. He saw and felt right through me. He'd just been too wrapped up in his story to notice.

"You really don't look so good, Catherine." He narrowed his eyes and then reached out with his fingers to touch my throat.

"I'm fine, really. I'm just—"

"Sick," he said. "Your glands are all swelled up, and you *do* have a fever. I can feel it rising. You need to go home!" He started to stand up, but I hunched down against the tree.

"No," I said. "You still haven't told me how your dad's tattoo ended up on your arm."

"Ian tattooed me. End of story," he said. "Now go home."

"Bullshit. He said you were too young."

"Catherine..."

"I'm not leaving until you tell me," I said stubbornly.

He threw his hands up in the air in exasperation. "Why do you have to act like such a pain in the—"

"Because that's what I'm supposed to do. I don't know why. Now, I won't leave until you've taken me all the way down to the bottom of your cursed life and we've climbed back out again." My voice was hoarse but steady. And I tried to use the same glare my mom uses when she's made her mind up.

It worked. He flopped back down on top of the snow, but looked away from me into the trees, his outline blurring even more.

I let him stew for a few minutes and then ventured warily, "So... what do you think made your dad do that? You know, draw that tattoo? Dedicate himself to helping the Archangel Michael?"

He waved his hands up in the air in frustration. "How the hell should I know? I was only eight when he died! He didn't talk to me about stuff like that! I just thought the sword was cool." He was becoming more and more agitated, flickering and fading faster. *Come on, Michael. You can face this.*

"So he named you after the Archangel?"

Michael was already nodding, but he was flickering so fast now that I could barely make out his features. "*Yeah,* Catherine. Ian told me my dad dedicated me to God and asked Saint Michael to be my patron saint when I was born, and I was thinking, and look what the hell you've done with yourself! You've dumped drug after drug into yourself! You've probably murdered someone! You've lied and stolen and..." He clenched his jaw tight, fighting for control. He settled into a slow waver that ebbed and flowed with his breathing.

"I think Ian thought telling me all that would make me feel better. Help me realize how special I was to my dad. But it just made me feel like I'd let him down. Like I couldn't be any farther from what my dad wanted me to be. And I just couldn't listen to him anymore. I had to leave. Ian ripped my dad's drawing out from under the staple and shoved it at me as I walked out the door.

"He was like, 'Take it Michael! Your dad would want you to have it.' "But I just let it drop onto the sidewalk next to the cigarette butts and dried up gum spots. Ian wouldn't pick it up either, and we just stood there staring each other down under the street light. But I couldn't leave it there. No matter how much I hated myself at that moment—and I did hate myself—I loved my dad, and it was a piece of him lying there on the ground. So I bent down and picked the drawing up, and then I took off running for the second time that night."

Michael looked up at the shifting pine ceiling, and then he dropped his chin, leaned in close to my ear, and whispered haltingly, "You have to understand, Catherine, I had no place left to *go*. I was frozen solid inside. I felt like if I could just throw up, I could spew out the jagged ice cubes that were stuck in my gut. They were tearing me apart from the inside, slashing me to pieces, and you know what? I finally understood my mom's addiction, because all I could think about was the rush, the heroin rush that was in my pocket. I may never have used myself, but I knew what it was, and I knew what it could do. It could take it all away. All my fear, all my pain, all my hate…it would all melt away into nothing. I'd talked to enough junkies to know. The rush. I wanted it. *God,* I wanted it."

He turned his eyes to the woods again and nodded to himself. Agreeing again in his mind to the demand his tortured soul had made that night. The demand for relief.

"So I found one of those gas stations with access to the bathrooms from the outside, and I got the key from the guy at the counter, and I headed out back. I couldn't get there fast enough. It smelled like piss and flowery air freshener, and there was water all over the floor around the toilet.

"I didn't have a hypo, so I knew I'd have to snort it. That would cheat me out of the ultimate rush, and it would take longer to feel it, but I didn't care. A rush was a rush, and I wanted it bad. My hands were shaking with the need."

Michael looked down at his palms, and they were shaking now. I wondered how badly he still wanted it, and I shuddered with sorrow for him.

"I locked the door and faced myself in the dirty mirror, but I could hardly see my face, and I figured that was probably a good thing. I wouldn't have to see myself give in to the Devil. I pulled the guitar off my back, dragged out one of the bags and poured half of the brown powder carefully onto the edge of the sink, crushed the chunkier pieces with the edge of my school I.D., and then separated it into two short lines. But then I thought, what the hell, and poured the rest of the bag onto the edge of the sink and divided up the lines again. Who the hell cared if I ever surfaced again?

"I dug a dollar bill out of my pocket to roll into a straw, but my dad's drawing stuck to it, and it fell, sword side up, onto the floor in front of me."

Then Michael squeezed his eyes shut.

"God, I wanted to believe! The Angel, the sword, God's love… all of it! But the rush was *waiting* for me. And it was real. It was here. And who the hell knew where *God* was? And I leaned on the sink with all my weight, feeling like I was split in two by a bolt of black lightning. I could almost smell the smoke.

"And I was thinking: *Just do it already…Just do it already…Just do it already…*

"Then I heard that detective's voice in my head. 'So, when are we gonna see you back here, kid? I want to make sure I come pay my respects.'

"And I didn't want to give him the satisfaction of seeing me dead. I didn't want my dad to see me fall into the same hole that buried my mom and I…and I…" Michael swept his hands back and forth in front of him violently. "I shouted at the mirror, 'So if you're *real*, Michael the *effing* Archangel, then protect me from the Goddamned Devil inside me! Don't let me do this! I don't want to do this!'

"And my back was tied up in knots and my hands were locked in this death grip on the sink, but somehow I pried my fingers free and started to back away…"

I was riveted on Michael's eyes, which were nowhere near here anymore. *Please, God, let this be the bottom.*

"And then I slipped on the water on the floor and was knocked out cold." Michael sighed heavily and came back to me, watching me carefully to see my reaction.

"You think the Archangel Michael had something to do with you getting knocked out?" I asked. Michael fought to keep a straight face.

"No. The toilet did," he said.

"Not funny," I scowled, and Michael looked uncomfortable, but he didn't apologize.

"So. I woke up to the sound of the gas station guy pounding like crazy on the door. Then I heard a key turning in the lock, and I came to pretty quick and without thinking it through, I brushed the lined up heroin down the drain and rinsed my hands off. Yeah. I wasted a whole bag of good dope and was immediately pissed at myself. The guy busted in just as I was turning around. One week and counting. I was still clean. Barely.

"He was like, 'Dude, you've been in here for over an hour.'"

"I tossed the key at his chest and said 'Whatever, man,' and then I grabbed my guitar, squeezed past him and walked out into the parking lot. My head throbbed, and I felt around with my fingers and found a huge and majorly painful bump on the back. That's when I started to wonder. Yeah. I did, Catherine. Just like you. I kind of looked up at the sky and said, 'So are You freaking shitting me? Did You just answer my call for help? Because if You did, where the hell have You been the last seven years?'

"Then, I thought maybe I'd gotten a concussion or something, and I was going...you know..." And he made a face befitting the criminally insane.

"Thanks," I said acidly. "You asked me to tell you where my faith comes from, and I do and then you—"

"Just wait, okay? I'm not finished yet," Michael said impatiently. "So, at that point the sun was rising. It was reflecting really brightly off these bits of broken glass that were smashed all over the empty parking lot, and I sort of blinked a few times to clear my vision. I was just starting to think about where else I could go to rail some of the heroin I had left and nod off in private, when I saw this open pawn shop across the street." He looked away and then back again quickly. Then he leaned forward on his elbows.

"Catherine, I felt this need inside me to go and check it out. It was even stronger than the need for the heroin had been. And without thinking, I crossed the street and looked in the shop window."

It was then that I saw the embers of faith in Michael's eyes, but they were burning him.

"There was a ring in the window. A gold Claddagh with an aquamarine stone, and it was tilted so its inscription could be read from the sidewalk: 'Hope Springs Eternal.' It was my mother's ring, Catherine. It was waiting for me."

Chills ran up my spine. Michael glanced at me knowingly. "Yeah. I know," he said. "It freaked me out, too. I mean, how many pawn shops do you think there are in Cleveland, Catherine? What are the odds?" He was silent for a minute, and then he stretched out his arm and cradled my chin gently in his open hand, his eyes screwed up with tender pity.

"People see what they want to see, and that morning I saw miracles. I saw my dad reminding me I was valued, I saw an Archangel stopping me from making a huge mistake, and I saw my mom telling me there was still hope for me. And I believed. I *believed*."

Then Michael dropped his hand and shook his head in disgust. "I looked up at the sky again and cried out, 'Okay! Whatever! Just tell me what you want me to do now!' Only I didn't have to ask. I knew. I wasn't going to find hope in a line of heroin, and I wasn't going to find it out there alone on the streets, so I traded my guitar for the ring and headed home.'"

He shook his head softly again, a cynical smile playing on his lips. "When I got home a few hours later, there were two police cars in the driveway, and I thought. *Oh shit. Here we go.* And then I thought, *Crap. I've still got heroin in my pocket.*

"I stopped in the middle of the driveway and one of the cops said, 'You better get inside, kid. Your mom's worried out of her mind, and the chief's sick of the phone calls.'

"Okay, I thought. If God wanted me in jail, I'd go, but I was fine with the whole handcuff delay. And then I was like, *my mom? Phone calls? What the hell is he talking about?* But he just stared at me and motioned with his hands for me to get going. So, I went inside and

Sue just threw her arms around me, hugging me and telling me how worried she'd been, and Bill poked at the big purple bruise on my head, and I was like completely confused.

"'This your son, Mrs. Gardiner?' The cop asked her, and she nodded. She had *tears* in her eyes! Over *me!* And I was her son? And then *I* started to get choked up.

"The cop said, 'Can you call off your prayer chain buddies now? They're clogging up the police lines.'

"Sue was like, 'Of course, officer.' Then she told me that after the police refused to help find me when I didn't come home the night before, she'd had all the people on the prayer chain flood the police station with calls about me. She told me they were all praying for me all night. Then she said she'd told the stupid cops they would keep calling until I was found. That's when they sent the cars out.

"The cops left, and she made me sit at the table and fed me pancakes, and I asked her, 'Why'd you do all that for me?' And she just said…she loved me.

"And then I really broke down. I told them everything. I told them about my dad's tattoo and my mother's ring. I told them about the pot and the coke and Devlin. And I told them about the heroin. And I told them I wanted to stay clean. And they listened to it all, and they didn't judge me because they loved me."

"Michael, you are *so* loveable," I said. "Why can't you see that? Maybe you're a little prickly sometimes, but that just makes me love you more."

Michael's chin trembled a little. And he was quiet for a minute. He sniffed up hard through his nose.

"Um…" He cleared his throat. "So then Bill helped me flush the rest of the heroin and pot while Sue called the hospital to see what happened to Devlin. He was still unconscious and listed as critical. That's all they would tell her. And the three of us sat around the table to wait. And while we waited, we talked and talked until there was nothing left to say. They said they would stand by me no matter what happened."

He looked down at his hands then and brushed his fingertips absently over the icy snow. He let his shoulders drop.

"By late afternoon, the cops were back. They said, 'Your friend woke up.'

"I was charged with assault, read my rights and cuffed. Sue followed me out to the cruiser, hugged me, and told me that she and Bill would do what they could. And that I shouldn't give up hope. *Right.*

"I spent a few days in juvie, but it wasn't all bad. I had a lot to think about. It turned out Dev wouldn't testify against me because he thought I still had his smack with his prints all over it, and I didn't want to tell the police he was a dealer because he and his 'friends' would have come after me. I was better off doing time if that's what it came down to.

"Sue and Bill respected that, and I pled out in court in exchange for a year's worth of probation, a shitload of community service and a promise to go through anger management therapy." He rolled his eyes. I gathered the therapy, for him anyway, was the worst of the three conditions.

"So the Gardiners took me home and set up my therapy, and I worked out at the 'Y' to take my mind off trying to stay clean. They took me to a few twelve step meetings, which were okay except for all the hugs and stuff. Then last July, I went on retreat with the Saint Paul youth group, and I even started going to Mass every week—"

"But I never saw you at Mass last summer."

Michael rubbed the back of his neck. "Yeah...the Gardiners like to go to the 7 a.m. Mass on Sundays. They thought I would get more out of it since there were less people there to distract me." He half grinned at the memory and then went on, "After the retreat I asked to transfer to Saint Joan—"

"Wait," I interrupted again. "*You* asked to transfer to Saint Joan?" That surprised me. I'd always figured it had been forced on him.

"Yeah...well...I thought I needed a fresh start, and I wanted to learn more about my dad's faith. I'd even signed up for the Sacraments class at church and thought maybe I'd make my First Communion and

Confession this year. I had a lot to confess." He smiled ruefully, but the smile quickly faded and his eyes grew cold.

He stopped there and rested his head back against the tree with his eyes closed.

"What about the tattoo?" I asked.

When he opened his eyes and glanced down at the tattoo, the old bitterness was back to full strength. "Oh yeah…that. I convinced the Gardiners to give Ian permission to tattoo me with my dad's design. I wanted a permanent reminder of, you know, the fact that I *believed* and everything. It stung like a bitch, having it inked. The weird thing was, the Gardiners actually liked Ian, and he started coming over for dinner once a week to check on me. The Gardiners believed in me. Ian believed in me. I was just starting to believe in myself when…"

His jaw suddenly flexed hard, and he looked away.

"But Michael, you'd finally found your faith. You let Ian tattoo it on your arm," I said gently. "How did it get lost again? Did you relapse?"

"I died and…"

His lips were trembling again despite his heroic efforts to stop them. He looked up, blinking desperately, and then I couldn't believe I'd been so dense. I should have guessed what had shaken his faith to the core from the first time I saw him in the woods. His whisper was so soft I could barely hear it.

"It's easier to believe there is no God than to believe He's forgotten me."

I knew then that he'd never stopped believing.

Not for one eternal second.

And then the tears came.

Chapter 22
Missing Christmas

His tears fell like spring rain down his subtly-wavering face. They dropped off his nose and disappeared into the clean white snow. He closed his eyes, not wanting to acknowledge them, and curled up next to me like a small child.

He wasn't hiding alone anymore, and I did what I could to comfort him. I murmured quietly to him and ran my fingers over the place his damp blonde head would be if only I could have felt it. I imagined his heat warming my palm and his salty sweat on my fingers. But all I was felt static.

We sat like that for a long time, me resting my sore back against the rough bark of the tree and Michael anchoring himself close to me. His breathing slowed, his face relaxed and his mouth went slack. And I realized with wonder that he'd fallen asleep.

He gradually began to fade, and when I could barely make out his features anymore, he fell through me, dragging a blanket of soft static with him, and then disappeared into the cold winter air. I couldn't feel him at all anymore. I couldn't smell him either. But I knew he was near. I could hear his peace-filled breathing.

I was careful to stay still while I kept watch for him, but it became more and more difficult as my body fought back against its rising fever, shivering and shaking with stubborn chills. Body aches, fever, sensitive skin, sore throat, chills...there was only one affliction I knew that had all of those symptoms and came on this fast, and that was flu. Shit.

But there was no way I was leaving yet. I waited with my eyes closed, hoping I was wrong, listening to him breathe and to the soft sound of snow settling around me. Too soon, our frosty peace and quiet was startled awake by the vibration of my cell phone. And then I was startled again when Michael appeared suddenly in front of me, crouched in the snow, disoriented, his bloodshot eyes still betraying his childlike vulnerability. I wanted to take him in my arms and rock him back to sleep, but Michael would have none of that.

"You're burning up, Catherine. You need to go home."

I started to shake my head, but he pressed his lips together in a hard line and glared at me. His glare was dark, way darker than my mother's. It smoldered. Somehow he even made his eyes look sort of hollow, and I paused mid-shake and grumbled, "Okay…" then pushed myself up onto my feet. No one could glare like Michael.

My teeth chattered.

"Shit," he said.

"I'll live." I looked down at my cell and saw it was J.C. who buzzed me. I started to dial him back.

"What do you think's wrong with you?" Michael asked me. The phone started ringing.

"Flu…" I said absently.

"What? Catherine!" I looked up into his face as J.C. answered his cell. Oh crap. My mouth really needed to learn when to shut up.

"Hey, Cate. Where are you? You've been gone for three hours."

"I'm just heading out now, J.C." I said, and Michael and I started to walk.

"You must be freezing. I'm already in the parking area. I'll meet you at the edge of the woods."

"You don't have to—"

"It's fine. I'll see you in a few." And then he hung up. I guess he needed his Michael fix today, too.

"Don't they make like shots to keep people from getting the flu?" Michael asked me. My heart momentarily stopped beating. I was so stupid. Really stupid. Really, *really* stupid.

"What?" he asked. I avoided his eyes and looked down at my

boots slogging through the snow. My stomach lurched. I did feel like shit. Damn it.

"What's wrong?" he asked again.

"I was supposed to go to the doctor's office the last time I was here and get my shot, but there was a really long wait, and I wanted to see you. I—"

"*Catherine...*"

"Hey! I didn't know I was going to get grounded and not be able to drive myself back to the doctor's office later that week!" I snapped. This was all becoming a tangled nightmare.

"Why didn't you just have your mom or dad take you?"

I raised my eyebrows.

"Oh," he said. Yeah. Then my parents would have known I hadn't gotten my shot in the first place. That would have meant another lie to add to my rap sheet.

"I don't want to go home," I whispered. Crap. I really, really didn't want to go home. Everything sucked at home, and it was about to suck even worse. Michael reached out his hand and rested it on my upper back, caressing the nape of my neck lightly through my hood with his thumb while we walked. I tried to breathe deeply to let go of some of the tension, but my lungs were sore and tight, too.

"I'm sorry, Catherine."

"You have nothing to be sorry for. You didn't infect me with flu."

"Yeah, but—" He stopped abruptly and looked down at the ground with his hands on his hips.

I stopped and turned around. My momentum gone, I was afraid I wouldn't be able to get moving again. But I waited.

"Catherine..." He looked back up at me, his eyes hot with guilt. "Face it! If it weren't for me, you'd have gotten your shot. You wouldn't be fighting with your mom. You wouldn't be grounded for lying. You wouldn't have stitches in your hand—"

"Michael..." I was way too beaten down to lift his spirits one more time.

"Just...go..." He waved me down the path with his hands.

"You have to come with me," I pleaded, my teeth chattering again.

"Why?"

"Because…I need you," I whispered.

"*Right*," he said sarcastically, but he crossed his arms over his chest and started moving again. He was silent. Brooding.

J.C. was waiting for me at the entrance to the woods. He scrunched his eyebrows together over worried eyes when I arrived. "You look terrible, Cate."

"Thanks," I snapped, and J.C. took a small step backward, and then whispered conspiratorially, "Is he here?" He didn't have to specify who "he" was. But he nodded without waiting for my reply. He must have caught the scent of Higher.

"Hey," J.C. said quietly, casting his eyes about.

Michael stepped forward and circled J.C. noiselessly, leaving no trace of his passage in the snow. Then he passed his arm right through J.C.'s chest. J.C. didn't bat an eye. He had no idea.

"See," Michael said, a grim smile gracing his face. "It's always been only you, Catherine. Tell him I said, 'hey.'"

I cleared my throat. "Um…Michael says to tell you, hey." J.C.'s eyes bugged out, and I couldn't help grinning. Then he rolled his shoulders, glanced from side to side, and tried to look casual.

"Tell him to give us a minute," Michael said, walking back to stand next to me.

"J.C., Michael says he wants you to give us a minute."

J.C. just stood there with his mouth hanging open, and I tried to take pity on him, but patience was out of my reach at the moment.

"J.C.! I'll meet you at the car!"

"What?" he said.

"Go wait for me in the car," I repeated more quietly, reminding myself that he'd been an awesome friend over the last two weeks.

"Oh…OH!" exclaimed J.C., and even Michael grinned.

Michael rubbed his chin thoughtfully, then leaned toward me and whispered, "Tell him…tell him he'd be great."

I looked up at him curiously, but Michael just nodded his head toward J.C., urging me to pass his message along. J.C. was already picking his way back across the brightly lit field of snow.

"J.C.!" I called, and he stopped and turned around.

"Michael says to tell you, you'd be great."

J.C. smiled softly and glanced down at the snow. "Tell him I said… thanks," he said. Then he turned back toward the car.

Michael nodded to himself and grinned again.

"You're not going to tell me what that was about, are you?" I pressed, smiling back through a fever haze.

"Nope." he said, and then his grin receded like a playful wave retreating back out to sea.

"Catherine…"

"Don't," I said. I didn't want to hear any more apologies. He lifted his hands, palms toward me, on either side of his chest, and I pressed my hands against them. They tingled softly. Then he tilted his forehead down and rested it against mine. The pain in my head eased up as it fell under the influence of his magic.

"Just…don't like…die…or anything…" he murmured.

"It's only the flu."

"Please?" he said, lifting his eyebrows. I nodded, and he lowered his palms and took a step back.

He was started to fade.

"Michael! God never forgets." I stuffed as much conviction as I could into my voice. "Never."

Michael gave me a half smile that didn't even come close to touching his eyes.

"Merry Christmas…*Catherine*…" he whispered and then disappeared.

❧❦

My mom took one look at me when I walked in the door on Christmas Eve and sent me straight to my room. I had actually hoped that maybe I could cope with being sick on my own in my own miserable way, but there was no hiding my red eyes, cough and dripping nose from her. She'd found me in my room a few minutes later, huddled under several blankets, still shivering with fever.

"Oh, Catherine…" was all she said. She'd put her hand on my back, but even the lightest of her touches irritated my feverish skin. Waves of chills coursed through my body, my throat was on fire, and I was just so PISSED OFF AT EVERTHING!

And with that caustic mindset, I drifted off into a febrile fog that lasted right through Christmas. Yeah. After all my talk of Advent and hopeful waiting, I missed it all.

On the morning after Christmas, my mom decided it was time to call in reinforcements. Since our house now played host to hospice nurses during the day, she took me to the doctor herself. The nurses were a perk she'd received when the doctors gave my grandmother just months to live. How's that for morbid gratitude?

"Cate?" the nurse called, checking her clipboard. I hauled my miserable self out of the waiting room chair and followed her, trailing my mom behind me. Once inside the examining room, the fragile truce we'd called in honor of my trip to the doctor was dragged out onto the thin paper of the exam table and prepared for dissection. It cowered under the fluorescent lights.

Maybe I should beat the doctor to the punch line? Tell her about missing my shot?

You should…definitely.

Going once…

Going twice…

"Mom…" I began in a hoarse whisper, but the door swung open, and Doctor Fontana bustled in. He smiled at both of us, projecting his cheerful confidence into the room.

"So…" he said, flipping through the pages on his clipboard. "What brings you in today, Cate?"

"I—"

"She's been sick since Christmas Eve. Her fever won't come down. She's using her inhaler as often as she can, but she's still having trouble breathing…" My mom went on and on, doing all my talking for me. I rolled my eyes feebly.

"Let's have a listen," he said, approaching me with his stethoscope out. "Breathe."

Ha! I thought.

My breath rattled through my clogged airways. In. Out. Crap. Cough…

"Any body aches? Sore throat?" he murmured, hopping his stethoscope across my back.

I glanced at my mother and almost shook my head no. I had become attached to our current truce. But something shoved a barely-visible nod out of my head.

Doctor Fontana finished listening and turned to my mom. "I think we should do an influenza swab. Flu's already hit our area."

Confusion clouded my mother's eyes. "But she got her shot."

Doctor Fontana flipped through my chart again. He shook his head. "I don't see it here."

Confusion was replaced by stark understanding. I lowered my eyes to the black-flecked tile floor. No words were needed. Our truce was shattered.

"I'll send the nurse in," he said, then left. And then…

"Catherine…no shot?"

I shook my head, but kept my eyes on the floor.

"And your hand?" Her tone was weighed down with disappointment. She reached for my bandaged palm. I pulled it away from her, remembering the stitches that needed to come out.

I wanted to tell her. I wanted to tell her everything.

I lifted my eyes, my throat tight, but she was staring out the window now. Then the door swung open, admitting the nurse with her test kit.

I hated the flu swab. Worse than the strep test. It just didn't seem right that someone could shove a Q-Tip six inches up your nose, twirl it around, and not do some serious damage. But I sat there and allowed it. I gagged. My nose burned. My eyes watered.

"Ten minutes," the nurse said as she left the room.

Deep space silence took her place. Ten minutes. I should have cherished those minutes because, as uncomfortable as they were, they were all I had left before I started to drown.

"She has the influenza virus," Doctor Fontana announced as he reentered the room. "When did her symptoms start?"

My mom shot me a loaded gaze.

"Christmas Eve," I mumbled and then coughed violently, bringing up a thick glob of unspeakable gunk from my lungs. It sat on the back of my tongue, and I grimaced. Doctor Fontana handed me a tissue. I spat the crap out, then balled the tissue up in my bandaged hand.

"I'd like to put her on an antiviral, an antibiotic, and prednisone." My heart stalled at the mention of the last two drugs. I'd just finished a course of amoxicillin, would that matter?

"Doctor Fontana…" I interrupted, almost without thinking. "Can I talk to you alone please?"

My mom's gaze went nuclear. I glared back at her, my mouth pinched tightly shut. The doctor glanced from me to my mom and then back to me again. He set his clipboard down on the exam table.

"*Okay*," he said slowly. "Is that alright, Anne?"

"Fine," she said, then snatched up her purse and walked out the door.

Doctor Fontana waited.

I started to unwrap my hand. "I need you to do something for me," I said, pulling off the last of the bandage and thrusting my palm out toward him. "Can you take these out?"

His bushy black brows flowed together but then relaxed. He opened a drawer and pulled out a few stainless steel instruments.

"Your mom doesn't know about these?" he asked as he started snipping at the knots.

I shook my head.

"Can you tell me what happened?"

I shook my head again.

"Well Cate, you didn't stitch yourself up."

I looked away, and he sighed.

"And I…um…just finished ten days of Amoxicillin," I mumbled.

He glanced up from his work. "That won't make a difference. You'll still benefit from another course."

"And...I don't...want to go on prednisone," I stammered, still avoiding his eyes. "My grandmother—she lives with us—she's on that for emphysema. Doesn't it like have bad side effects?"

"Yes. But you're healthy. You'll only be on it for a week or so." Then he paused, concentrating on the last stitch, which clung stubbornly to my palm. When he finally succeeded in yanking it free, he looked up, a serious expression on his face. "She lives with you?"

I nodded, and his brows pulled together again.

"Cate, when you go home, you need to stay away from her and be careful to wash your hands. Flu could be especially...problematic for her." He studied my face to make sure I comprehended. My heart stopped, and then it pounded raw fear instead of blood through my veins.

Oh God, what have I done?

Chapter 23
Catastrophic Failure

Now I knew how Michael felt while he waited with the Gardiners around his kitchen table for word on Luke Devlin. Only I waited alone to find out whether or not I'd killed my grandmother.

And I waited…

And waited…

And coughed up the crap that settled in my chest into the shower drain every morning. My ribs and intercostals were bruised and sore from all the coughing, but the pounding water and hot steam helped. I don't know how other asthmatics fight their chest infections, but that's how I attacked mine. The payoff for coughing everything up was lungs that were a little clearer for the rest of the day. The payoff was breathing.

Grounded from the phone and the computer, and quarantined in my room, I had nothing else to do each day but worry about my grandmother, worry about Michael, and berate myself over and over.

You stupid bitch…you selfish brat…what have you done?

It was an insidious mantra streaming through my head in a voice I didn't recognize. And to make matters worse, I couldn't even get a message to Michael that I was alright. J.C. had flown to Puerto Rico with his family to spend the holidays with relatives.

A week into this wretched existence, I was startled out of a restless sleep by the sound of my father shouting.

"She's sick. I'm not waking her up and—"

"No! I'm not leaving until I see her! You need to—"

Jason? What was he doing here? I pushed myself up to a sitting position, feeling lightheaded.

"She's not allowed to see anyone, Jason."

The storm door springs creaked and groaned.

"You don't understand!"

"Jason, you can't—"

"Cate!"

His voice was louder. I grabbed my robe and half stumbled out of my bedroom.

"Cate!"

He was standing at the bottom of the stairs. His hair was limp, his eyes were dull, and he'd definitely lost weight. He had to be sick, too.

"Jason! What's wrong?" My call was filled with phlegm, and I coughed to clear it.

"Go back to bed, Cate," my dad barked furiously.

"It's okay, Dad," I said, coming down the stairs.

"I need to talk to you," Jason said. He was calming down, but he was sweating, breathless.

"Okay...what?"

"Not here."

"Oh for the love of..." My dad reached up to grab Jason's shoulder. Oh, crap. Think fast.

"Can we talk in your car?" I asked.

Jason nodded.

I looked pleadingly at my dad. "In his car?"

My dad shook his head no, but I was already moving toward the door. "Caty..."

"I'm not going anywhere," I promised, throwing my robe on over my oversized T-shirt and then the unzipped parka over top. What was he going to do, physically restrain me? Punch Jason in the face?

It was cold outside. My ankles were bare above my slippers and took the brunt of the icy wind. I pulled the terry cloth collar up over my nose and mouth to warm the air before I breathed it in. Jason pulled open the car door for me and then hurried around the front of the car, slid in behind the wheel and flicked the heat on high. He was shaking.

"What's wrong?"

He turned to grab his backpack off the back seat, and I grabbed his arm. "Jason..."

He stopped mid-twist. "I forgot about your stitches, Cate. They could go septic. I need to—"

Then everything clicked. "Jason, it's okay."

He'd turned around again to reach for his backpack.

"Jason, wait! I had my doctor remove them a few days ago."

He stopped, but still looked flustered, so I held my hand out to him. "See?"

He pulled it toward him and ran his thumb back and forth over the scar. Then he leaned his head back against the black leather seat and rubbed his eyes with his whole hand.

"Are you okay?"

He stopped rubbing his eyes and faced me again, nodding slightly. "Yeah...I've had some kind of stomach...thing." I leaned back away from him reflexively, and he gave me a lopsided grin. "I'm definitely not contagious, Cate."

"Oh."

"You don't look so great yourself," he observed.

"Flu," I said. Then *he* leaned back.

"I probably *am* contagious," I said. "Sorry." I rested my head back against the seat and tried to clear my throat out.

"That's not good for your grandmother is it." A statement of fact. I shook my head slowly back and forth and then met his light blue eyes. They were so sincere. "I'm sorry, Cate," he said.

My jaw flexed. Why did he keep coming back when I used him so badly?

"Jason, it's me who should be sorry."

"Because you don't want to go out anymore? I should have respected that. I should have—"

Crap. It wasn't fair. He deserved some kind of explanation for all my moodiness and bizarre requests. Some explanation for why I was so fixated on Michael.

And then I was confessing...partly.

"I saw Michael fall off the cliff, Jason." He was totally taken off guard by that, and his tired eyes suddenly focused sharply on me.

"Shawn took too much Ritalin, and he slipped, and Michael reached out to pull him back, but then he slid...God! It must have been fifty feet...and then he...he just free-fell another fifty...and when he slammed into the ground, he..." My voice cracked.

Jason reached for my hand, and I let him take it again and hold it and stroke it.

"Where were you?" he asked quietly.

"On the ledge under the cliff top at Lewis Woods. I watched him die, Jason. I watched..." My voice caught again.

"So...that's why..." he said, almost to himself. Then my outrage crawled to the surface.

"And you know what else? It was Shawn who brought the Ritalin to the park that day. He stole it from the Gardiners medicine cabinet." Jason looked up with the same look of disbelief he'd given me before. Yeah. Sure. Michael was the stoner. That's what everyone thought.

"It's true!" I cried, getting angrier. "I heard it from...someone who knows. And there was someone else involved, someone who knew enough to tell Shawn how much Ritalin to take, but Shawn tripled his dose when Michael refused. Whoever it was knows the truth, too. They could clear Michael's name..."

I started coughing, huge phlegm-filled spasms. God, my chest ached.

"Cate, you have to let it..." His voice trailed off, and he was shaking again.

Shit. I was thinking only of myself again. Jason didn't need the flu on top of whatever else he had.

"You should go home, Jason. Get some rest," I said, pulling my hand away.

"I need to go, Cate," he finally said, like he hadn't even heard me just say that. "I really don't feel well…"

His hand was already putting the car in drive, and I quickly let myself out.

"I hope you feel better," I said before slamming the door, but he barely glanced in my direction before taking off. Now I had someone else to worry about.

≈≈

My fever finally broke later that day, and my body cleansed itself in a pajama-drenching sweat. I propped myself up in bed with *The Red Badge of Courage* in my hands and Maxwell curled up warmly at my side. He kept nibbling at my hand with his sharp teeth to remind me to pet his furry, orange-splattered head.

I heard my sisters conversing softly with my grandmother through the wall. She was giving them her best poker playing tips. I wasn't allowed in. My self-imposed exile from her over the last few months seemed to have paid off though, because thankfully, she was still flu-free. With me getting better, I was beginning to think maybe she would stay that way.

But it wasn't to be.

Her fever spiked at seven that night. Her life expectancy plunged from months to days.

There was a flurry of activity in the room next to mine. No, she didn't want to go back to the hospital. The DNR had been signed before Christmas. My mother begged her, but she was adamant.

My grandmother's lungs were filling up with fluid.

And it was my fault.

I searched my mind in vain for something I could do for her, but there was nothing. I let the book fall to the floor, crumpled and forgotten, my thoughts snarled in a hopeless tangle of self-loathing, until my eyes came to rest on my Guardian Angel statue on my dresser at the foot of my bed.

She was chipped and dusty, scarred by years of being brushed aside, first by Barbie dolls and Disney Princesses, and later by flat irons and make up. I slid off the bed and picked her up. Her sapphire blue eyes were fairy-like and set wide apart. Her chocolate brown hair flipped playfully away from her face, and her gold-plated wings and halo shimmered in the lamplight. She was beautiful. A treasure.

And I didn't deserve her.

So the next time my mom left Mina alone, I crept into the hallway and stole quietly into her room. She slept fitfully in the dim light, her breathing labored, her equipment buzzing and beeping all around her. I carefully set the statue down on the table next to her bed and then, just as quietly, slipped back into my own room.

I hid under my covers then, my sleep disturbed.

The nightmares were back.

Black creatures with flaming gold eyes.

Sinuous, like smoke curling off tongues of fire.

Beautiful. Terrible. Mesmerizing.

They had come to wait with me.

And they were laughing.

❧

The next morning, I was released from quarantine, and I dressed in a black fleecy pullover and my softest faded jeans. I'd lost weight, and my jeans gapped around my waist and hung looser through the thighs. Standing in front of the refrigerator, my stomach was hollow. Nothing looked good. Not the cold waxy fruit in the crisper or the breakfast casserole a neighbor had dropped off. Yeah. We'd entered that stage of my grandmother's illness. And the food kept coming. It poured in like a rising flood, trying to put out the flames of our fear and sorrow.

As my mother walked into the room, I shut the refrigerator door and grabbed a blueberry Pop Tart out of the cupboard. It was familiar and generic and carried no neighborly sympathy I didn't deserve. She opened the refrigerator and stood in front of it, the light washing out her small face and creating shadows under her chin. Then she closed it, empty-handed too, and turned toward me.

"You look better today," she said. Her eyes were guarded, her posture stiff. She had spared me the humiliation of telling my dad about the missing flu shot, so it was just her and I who knew about the fatal choice I'd made. The sick secret hung in the air between us, the repercussions still unknown. Would her mother die that much sooner because of me? The guilty poison in my soul sloshed and burned like unruly stomach acid. I needed to think. I needed to talk to someone. I needed Michael.

I shifted my weight back and forth uneasily between my feet. "Mom..." I tried to meet her eyes.

Don't you dare lie to her again. The voice in my head was so clear that I gasped and took a step back.

My mom eyed me worriedly.

I began again. "Mom? I need to get out of here for a while. Can I take the car for a few hours?" I took a bite of my Pop Tart. It tasted like sawdust. It stuck like glue to the roof of my mouth.

She walked over to the sink and looked out the ice-glazed window. Everything outside was flat under a uniformly gray sky.

"Am I allowed to ask where you're going?"

I forced the Pop Tart down. "It's just a place I like to go to think... down in the park." I bit my lip.

She turned around and leaned back against the counter, nodding. Then she glanced around the kitchen at all the foil-covered disposable pans and said, "Be back in time for lunch."

Permission granted, I fled.

❧❧

My dad had the Demon so I drove the Honda out to Lewis Woods. It was freeing to know that I wasn't sneaking around behind my mom's back to see my best friend. I needed to see him like I needed to breathe.

I wanted to pour out my guilt and my fatigue into his heart, into his hands. I wanted to tell him the nightmares were back and that I was afraid. And I wanted him to tell me he loved me, and that he'd wait with me until the worst had passed. I wanted him to chase all my demons away.

The snow was half-melted. It wilted into the trampled grass of the field in the collapsing footprints that led back to the mouth of the woods. I was sweating and lightheaded and congested by the time my feet crossed the forest boundary, and I really wanted to sit down—*needed* to sit down—but everything was wet and muddy and cold, so I waited for Michael on unsteady feet. I didn't have to wait long.

His woodsy citrus fragrance soothed my chafed nose, but he didn't appear right away. He swept around me, slowly, invisibly, stroking the back of my neck with his fingertips, and I closed my eyes and breathed him in, savoring the relief that came with his simple presence. But then my chest began to itch, and I tried desperately to hold in the cough that fought to burst out of my lungs. Hold it…hold it…

It was no good. I bent forward with my hands on my knees, coughing uncontrollably and bringing up another ghastly ball of phlegm. I grimaced and then swallowed it rather than spit it out into the muddy snow in front of him, but it wouldn't matter, he'd know anyway.

"Shit, Catherine…" His voice flowed from thin air into my exposed ears, and when I finally stood back up, he was standing before me, his arms crossed over his chest, wincing at my weakness. He looked so strong, standing like that, with his fingers curving over his well-defined biceps and his broad back and shoulders held up tall.

"Go home," he said. "What are you doing here? You're still sick."

"You should have seen me yesterday." I rolled my eyes and forced a smile.

"Catherine…"

All of my ragged emotions were pressing hard for release. My chest trembled with the effort it took to chain them, while my mind searched for a place to begin.

"Michael, I need–"

"Just…stop," he said, looking down at the ground and then darkly up through his lashes.

And I stopped. I did more than stop. I stopped the world from spinning. I stopped time from inching forward. I stopped believing the sun and the moon would remain in the sky.

There was something in his voice.

"You can't save me," he said quietly, pushing his foot uselessly through the dirty, slushy snow on the trail.

I was drowning, and he'd thrown me a lead pipe. Please no...

"What are you saying?"

"I'm saying I'm done." He hugged his arms tighter against his chest. His jaw tensed, but he maintained eye contact.

"I won't let you give up! I love you, Michael."

His flinty gray eyes softened. I knew he wouldn't.

He couldn't...

His deep sigh was a call to surrender. "I know, Catherine. I know you do."

"You love me too," I accused, lifting my chin stubbornly.

He looked away and then struggled to bring his focus back. His jaw twitched. Then he nodded roughly, self-consciously. He took a step toward me and cupped my face within his gentle tingling hands, and his eyes softened even more as he sensed how sick I still was. "It doesn't matter how I feel," he said, "because I'm totally messing up everything that's good in you. I can't fix that. You know that—"

"NO! What about God? What about your faith? I know you believe! You can't let go of all that now and just fade—"

"Fine! Maybe I do believe!" he interrupted sharply. "But He's not here. Not for me anyway." He dropped his hands and backed away.

"There's a reason..." I had to believe that.

"I'm tired," he went on plaintively. "It's too hard! If I just let go..."

"What would the Gardiners say? They loved you, too."

"*They* would respect my decision. *They* wouldn't judge me." He tilted his head accusingly, and his eyes glittered like hard steel. That stung, and he glanced away. When he looked back, the steel had melted. "How do you know that's not what I'm supposed to do anyway? How do you know I'm not supposed to fade away? Maybe that's like, just the way it goes."

"Because," I began. "Because you'll see a light or someone will come for you when you're ready." It was true, wasn't it?

"An Angel," he said flatly, letting his bitterness infuse the word with ugly sarcasm.

I nodded, forcing a look of certainty onto my face.

"I don't think so," he said.

"Come home with me, then! Be with me always." I backed up across the boundary and into the icy field, holding my hand out to him.

"I can't..."

"Have you ever even tried?" I challenged. "Just try!" I took another step backward.

"You have no idea how many times I've tried to follow..." His voice broke, and then it resounded riotously off the trees that wanted to make him their own. "This is all there is for us!" He waved his hands at his ghostly body and then around at the forest, frustrated and angry. "I can't do it anymore! I won't..."

I held my hand out to him stubbornly, but he moved his hands to his hips and looked down at the ground again.

"Please?"

He looked up at me pityingly, but he stretched the flickering fingers of his left hand tentatively across the boundary anyway. Then he let his arm follow up to his elbow.

"See? All you needed was a little help."

The pity in his eyes intensified, but I took another step backward, and he followed me all the way out, reaching for my outstretched hand. He overlapped my hand with his, and I pulled mine in, forcing him to lose contact or take a step closer. He chose the latter, and then he leaned forward and brushed his ethereal lips against my cheek, whispering softly, "The next time you come back, take our ring off the lightning tree and take it home with you. Remember me."

Then, like a boulder that's turned to sand by the winds of time, his edges turned brown and disintegrated.

I panicked. "No, Michael! Please don't do this…"

But he closed his beautiful gray eyes, lifted his chin and gave in completely. His crumbling edges curled like dust devils back toward the forest, scattering musically among the trees. The invisible wind blew steadily, taking more and more of him away from me, until only his fingertips remained.

Finally, even they fell apart like the rest of him, falling back through my fingers into the wide-open maw of the forest.

"Go home to your family…*Catherine*…" His voice clung to me for a moment, then let go and was swallowed up as well.

A helpless fury grew in my motionless heart. I gasped in pain.

"How can you leave me when I need you the most?" I cried. I started walking away, but turned back around and shouted, "I would have walked through hellfire to save you!" I spun around a few times, desperate to reach him with my voice. Only silence echoed back.

"You can just go screw your nasty demon self! Do you hear me! So you think you're being all noble and self-sacrificing? You're just a damn coward!" A clump of melting snow fell from a branch to the ground behind me, and I turned toward it, startled. I was alone.

I wanted to give up, let the snow bury me, stay there forever, but I turned instead and started back toward the car. A voice inside me urged, *keep moving*. I focused all of my energy on that inner voice, but as soon as I slammed the car door on the outside world, the loss of him hit like a hard-packed fist. I'd failed him. I'd been too weak to save him. Oh God, no! Please no! This couldn't be happening.

Go home to your family, Catherine.

I couldn't go home. There was nothing left for me there.

The voice in my head passed me the only option left: *Find Jason. He'll know what to do. He always does.*

※

I don't remember driving to Jason's. I only remember finding myself in front of his heavy, stained glass door, knowing he'd be home and knowing he wouldn't turn me away. The door swung inward and the smell of cold marble and warm furniture polish wafted out of his cavernous foyer. Jason was standing in the doorway, barefoot, wearing his favorite black sweatpants and a soft blue flannel shirt whose cuffs hung loosely, unbuttoned, at his wrists.

His dark circles had faded, and his eyes were clear again. He was just starting to smile in greeting when I threw myself like a wild pitch into his arms.

"Mina caught my flu, and she's dying, and it's my fault, and I didn't get my shot because...because..." Jason tried to lift my face from his chest, but I wanted it buried there. "And Michael just...fell apart...he gave up...and..."

"Cate, what the hell are you talking about?" he cried. "Michael's dead!"

I shook my head back and forth, rubbing my wet eyes and nose against the buttons of his shirt. He put his hands on either side of my face and lifted firmly until I was looking up at him.

"Come upstairs and lie down, okay? Everything's going to be fine. I promise. I'll help you get through this." He slid my coat off my shoulders and then led me upstairs to his room, but I couldn't lie down. The pain in my chest kept nudging my heart into unpredictable rhythms, and I paced back and forth in front of the window while Jason looked on nervously from the doorway.

You failed... you failed... you failed...

The refrain roared in my ears like the deepest winter blizzard.

"Cate..." he called, and when I didn't answer, he pulled me over to his unmade bed and sat me down. He just held me while I shivered. "Shh," he murmured. "I'm going to get you something to drink. Stay here. I'll be right back."

Alone again, I dragged one of Jason's overstuffed suede pillows off his tangled sheets, hugged it tightly against my chest and stared out through the picture window at the frozen lake. The thick, snow-covered ice stretched out as far as my eyes could see under the bleak

January sky. Just like Michael's life and death, cold and bleak and lonely. And I couldn't rescue him from that. Not from any of it.

Jason came back into the room carrying a mug filled with steaming hot tea. "I know you like your tea sweeter, but this will help calm you down. It's chamomile," he said. He was right. It was bitter, but the bitterness brought the real world back into focus. Oh God...what did I just tell him?

"Jason, I—"

"Shh...just drink." He set more of his pillows up behind me against the headboard, and then he pulled the tan down comforter up and over me. I turned toward the lifeless lake, sipping the hot tea slowly, while he sat snugly against my back. When I'd drained the cup, Jason took it from me, set it on his antique mahogany nightstand and then crawled into bed behind me, curving his body against mine, encircling me with his arms, curling his fingers around my ribs.

He kissed my shoulder, whispering, "It must have been horrible watching him die, and now you're watching your grandmother die? No wonder you're a mess. I'm sorry I haven't been around. I've been sick, but I'm better now, and somehow I have to make you understand. I want to heal you, Cate."

He brushed my hair out of the way with his fingertips and caressed the nape of my neck with his lips and warm breath. He wrapped his arms around me tighter and pulled my hips in closer.

"Let me heal you," he murmured, and I closed my eyes. A single tear left a tender trail down the outside of my cheek before soaking into the pillow. I kept my eyes closed, inhaling the masculine scents of suede, soap and spicy shaving gel. The scent of Jason.

And I turned in to him, the salt trail still cooling on my cheek, and let him kiss me. His hands spread out to stroke the soft, bare skin of my abs, and I succumbed to the heat they generated, sliding my own hands beneath his flannel shirt and up over the lean muscles of his back. Another damp trail unfurled beside the first as I responded to the familiar call of his hands and lips. I craved their comfort. They were gentle and insistent, and they wrestled me away from thoughts of failure, and guilt, and love.

God, I loved Michael so much.

Almost as if he could hear my thoughts, Jason pulled back, leaving my lips tingling, and waited for me to open my eyes. He searched them carefully, and then settled back onto his side in front of me, propping his head on his hand.

"I can help kids like you, like us," he said. "Adults have no idea how hard teens have it, how much pressure there is." He reached out and traced the pathways of my tears with his fingertips. "But I'll take care of you now, Cate. I'll make it better. I'll help you forget." He slid his hands around my waist, under my fleece, pulling me in tight to his chest, kissing me again, long and hard, but I pushed back from him this time, my heartbeat thumping Michael's name.

I didn't want to forget.

He searched my eyes again, even more carefully this time, and I glanced away, confused by the intensity of his gaze. Then an uncomfortable waterfall of heat washed over me, and I pushed back even farther and sat up on the bed. He sat up in front of me, studying my face. Then my vision rippled, and he smiled softly.

"Cate," he whispered. "How do you feel?"

"I…" I felt heat pulse up through my chest and into my head, and then my vision rippled again. Everything kind of tilted and slid to the side.

"Shh," he said. "You'll feel much better soon."

I dragged my eyes up to his face. The tea…

My heart stopped, but the shock melted into another pulse of warm heat. My face tingled as if Michael were touching it. First my nose…then my cheeks…my forehead…

"What did you give me?"

"Not Valium," he said. "I didn't think that would win you over to my way of thinking. That just sedates you, takes the edge off. No… oxycodone is incredible. If this doesn't convince you, nothing will. Do you feel better?"

I nodded and then shook my head back and forth, and he laughed. My vision rippled without stopping for a few seconds and…

Promise me you'll stay…clean.

And then the realization of what Jason had done sank in.

"You bastard!" I cried. "I promised him! How could you do this to me? Take me home..." I shook my head hard and opened my eyes wide to try to clear my vision.

"Cate...I don't think..."

"Either you take me or..." I stood up, and the whole room swayed. He stood up next to me and grabbed me under the arms. I tried to push myself away from him, but he held firm.

"Alright...alright..." He gave in and walked me down the stairs. "But you'll be thanking me tomorrow. I research my doses carefully, and all of your pain is about to take an extended vacation. I give you..." He glanced down at his watch. "...fifteen minutes, give or take, and you'll be loving life and loving me again."

"Like hell I will."

He just smiled knowingly.

The wind outside had picked up considerably, but it kept stopping and starting in erratic fits, changing direction every few seconds, as it blasted its way across the lake under winter storm clouds. It stung my face. It helped me focus.

Jason is insane.

Yes...came the soft affirmation.

He's addicted to something that's totally screwed him up.

Yes...my inner voice confirmed.

I'm hearing voices, because I'm totally stoned off my ass.

Not yet. Baby, stay with me...

When both of us were buckled into the car and out of the relentless wind, Jason pulled out of the driveway and said, "Cate, don't you understand? You've got to stop looking for answers in some all-powerful, infinitely everywhere, conveniently undetectable, supreme know-it-all! The idea of God is a placebo. We've got to look within ourselves for answers. What can He possibly give—"

"He gives me hope when I've got nothing left."

"Hope in reality is the worst of all evils, because it prolongs the torments of man," Jason quoted.

"What miserable bastard said that?" I shot back, but I couldn't focus on his answer, because the high kept coming up stronger and stronger, and my fury was fading. I felt myself giving in. Please, no. I didn't want this...

Jason pulled into my driveway, got out of the car, and opened the passenger side door just as the last vestiges of my anger melted away, and like a powerful wave crashing over a battered break wall far from shore, an incredible rush of euphoria swamped all of my senses. It settled into the cold sand of my being, warming me all over.

"Cate..." he called softly, and I grinned at him. What was I so angry about? I loved him, didn't I? God, he was beautiful. He smiled back.

"See?" he said. "You should listen to me more often." He reached into the car, picked me up and carried me into the house, cautioning, "Your pupils are miotic. Keep your eyes closed."

My parents' overly-loud voices rushed past me as we entered the house, but I kept my eyes shut. We had a secret, Jason and I—an incredible, glorious secret. As stoned as I was, I could still think clearly enough to know that my parents would ruin it.

"I think she's just exhausted from being sick, Mrs. Forsythe," Jason reassured my mom in the front hallway. He carried me up the stairs, laid me in bed, and tucked me under my white quilt. And it was just like when I was five, only without the light. I was warm. And I was safe. And there was no guilt. And there was no pain. And nothing could touch me.

"Sweet dreams, Caty," Jason said, kissing my forehead, but when I opened my eyes, it was Michael bending over me. Tears glistened in his...silver eyes?

"I'm so sorry," Michael whispered. "They didn't tell me..." I knitted my brows together and tried to blink away the slurring of my vision so I could focus on him better. A crease formed between his brows, too.

"Catherine?"

But I had already floated away from him. He was gone, and I didn't care.

Somewhere in the woods lining the river, someone was playing music.

"Sweet Child O' Mine."

❦

Then someone was shaking me roughly.

"Catherine! Wake up!"

I peeled my eyelids open and squinted into the darkness of my room, disoriented. I'd fallen asleep early this afternoon.

"Catherine! Up. Mina wants to talk to you." It was my mom. The euphoria was gone. Vast, suffocating guilt descended.

Welcome back...

I cleared my throat and pushed myself up onto my elbows, feeling nauseated, dizzy. I coughed and my chest and back ached. My throat was raw.

"Mina wanted me to get you. She wants to tell you something."

"But I'm still sick," I mumbled thickly.

"It doesn't matter anymore." Her statement hit like a brick. It was late, but softly buzzing clouds of voices were rising up the stairs. And I knew. Mina was dying. Soon. The flu was taking her this fast?

Claws teased my heart.

Prick. Scrape. Squeeze.

You're a killer. Face it kid. Go face it.

I pushed myself up off the bed and stumbled after my mom into the room next to mine where the smell of Lysol, bodily fluids and disease hit me full in the face. The sick-room-turned-death-chamber was dimly lit by a small night light plugged into the wall. My dad got up and hugged me and then left the room. My mom followed him, saying, "She wants to talk to you privately."

I was wide awake now, my palms sweating. Did Mina even know I was the one who gave her the flu? Did she want to accuse me? Blame me?

Her face was deeply lined, her cheeks sunken and gray. Her damp, dark eyes followed me as I moved toward the bed. My eyes started to fill when I saw how much she was suffering, and I opened my mouth to speak, to say I was sorry, but my tongue lagged, and she spoke first. She breathed strategically, intertwining life's last air into her words.

"I'm sorry...*breathe*...I've avoided you...*breathe*...I couldn't face it..."

No...it had been the other way around, hadn't it? "Mina, no—"

She waved her crooked hand for me to be quiet. "Listen!" she said sharply. "Your ring...*breathe*...belonged to me...*breathe*. My constant reminder...*breathe*...of my...*breathe*...faith. I was supposed...*breathe*... to give it to you."

"You did Mina. I love it. I'll keep it safe always." I pulled the ring out for her to see.

But Mina shook her head weakly, then glanced over at the Guardian Angel statue I'd placed on her bedside table and then back at me. "It's not the...*breathe*... ring...*breathe*...that's important...*breathe*... It's the...*breathe*...the...*breathe*..."

"It's what? What's important?" As I watched her struggle to get the words out, the tips of her fingers and her lips turned blue, and I panicked. I started to stand up to get help, but she grabbed my hand and held it tightly. "Just have...*breathe*...faith. Don't ever let...*breathe*... let him...*breathe*...turn you," she gasped. "No matter what."

"Who, Mina? Who's going to turn me?"

But she let go of my hand and looked toward the window, toward the stars that had come out of the gray night mist to shine for her. "I want...*breathe*...to see...*breathe*...Father Rocci now."

I knew the importance of her last statement. It was more important than any question I might have for her, and I got up and ran from the room, grabbing the door jamb as I passed when the floor tilted under my feet. Damn Jason! Damn him to hell...

"Mom! Call Father Rocci!" I cried, but Father Rocci was already there, passing me on the stairs.

Father Rocci was alone with Mina for a while, and then he anointed her with oil and invited the rest of us in. My mom's whole demeanor changed after that. The look of utter exhaustion on her face was replaced with one of tired peace. Her mother had come home. My parents, my sisters, Aunt Julia, and a few of my mother's closest friends gathered around her bed to pray the Rosary for her.

Hail Mary, full of grace, the Lord is with thee. Blessed art thou among women, and blessed is the fruit of thy womb, Jesus. Holy Mary, Mother of God, pray for us sinners, now, and at the hour of our death. Amen. Hail Mary, full of grace...

As we prayed, my crystal beads moved quietly through my fingers, each bead a prayer for her. A peaceful death. A heavenly homecoming. I wondered if my prayers carried any weight at all anymore. Halfway through, I moved to the doorway, feeling more and more like an outsider. My nose and cheeks still tingled and my balance was off from the effects of the drug. They were reminders of the high that was past, the Hell I'd plunged back into.

...pray for us sinners, now and at the hour of our death...

And what had my grandmother been talking about? What couldn't she face? Who shouldn't I let turn me? None of it made any sense, but then she and I were both probably half-stoned when I'd talked to her. How could Jason have done that to me? I felt violated, nauseated, and I started to sweat again, so I left the room, went downstairs, and curled up under a blanket on the sofa.

My sisters joined me when they finished praying, Claire on the big overstuffed chair and Cici at the other end of the sofa. She tugged at a corner of my blanket and tucked her feet underneath next to mine. I wondered if she would have snuggled up so close to me if she'd known it was no accident that Mina had the flu. If she she'd known I hadn't gotten my shot when I was supposed to. The knowledge was burning a hole through my heart, but I couldn't talk to her about it. I couldn't bear the thought of her knowing. So, with nothing to say, we waited quietly, watching the adults come and go from Mina's room in turns. After a while, one of the adults told us she'd slipped into a coma. By morning she was gone.

So it was finally over…only it wasn't.

There was still her body to prepare, the wake to attend, and the funeral Mass to offer. And there were throngs of sympathetic people who wanted to feed and hug and console us. Console me.

Liar. Killer. Fraud.

I walked the gauntlet uneasily. I hadn't been there to share the last months of her life. I hadn't been there to fill her loneliness, hold her hand, attend to her needs, or to pray with her. And despite what she said to me, I knew it had been my choice to avoid her.

Why had I done that? What the hell was wrong with me?

You're a selfish bitch, my conscience fired back.

By lunchtime, I couldn't stand it anymore, and I begged my dad to take me to school.

I should have stayed home.

Chapter 24
Permanent Pain Relief

IT WASN'T UNTIL I stepped into the shadow of the school's covered entry, still weak from flu, that I remembered Jason would be there. There was no way I was going to Honors Geometry or Computer Lab—the classes we shared.

Instead, I went to the library, but I did more staring out the window at the falling snow than catching up on homework. My mind drifted back to the day Michael and I talked about his childhood. The day the snow had fallen lazily right through his abused body.

How could you have let him slip away?

The black hole in my chest sucked hard. It ached. God, it ached, and suddenly I needed to move. I shoved myself away from the library table, crammed my books and papers into my bag, and ducked out into the hallway, completely lost in my grief. When I turned the corner and saw Jason, I was a dazed deer caught in his headlights. I couldn't think clearly enough to get out of his way.

He was leaning against a row of deserted lockers outside the library entrance, wearing black chinos and a neatly-pressed white button down shirt whose long sleeves hung unbuttoned at his wrists. He wasn't alone.

Three pairs of eyes turned sharply in my direction. Their glare was wary, dangerous, like the warning hum of a nest of vipers deciding whether or not to strike.

Luke Devlin, Shawn Fowler and Jason stopped talking when they saw me, but they didn't bother to step away from each other and pretend they didn't have business to discuss.

I've never known Devlin to deal in pharms.

The guy I talked to told me I should take two to clear my head and study better.

Dude. He knows. Like, he knows everything.

I can help kids like you...like us.

Oh, God...

How could I have been so blind? The Valium, the Oxycodone, the packages with his father's name and address. I dropped my books and coat on the floor and took a step backward. "You're the one who told Shawn how much Ritalin to take! You've known Michael was clean all along!"

Jason broke away from his huddle, grabbed my arm and forced me back against the lockers. He caged me in by bracing both his hands against the metal doors on either side of my chest. He was shaking. He was sweating. His dark circles were back.

"Who told you that?" He bit off the words in harsh whispers. I glanced sideways at Luke and Shawn in a futile quest for aid, but found they had turned their backs on us. "Don't look at them. Shawn didn't tell anyone. Who else knows?"

I ignored his question, firing back, "So, you're not just using drugs? You're dealing too?"

"Shawn told me Michael was having trouble in school. I was just trying to help."

"You bastard! Like you tried to help me yesterday?" I inched my back down the slippery face of the locker and tried to duck under his left arm, but he lowered his hand to block me. "You have to tell, Jason! You have to clear Michael's name!"

"I can't do that, Cate. Too many kids depend on me. They need the pills I give them to function, some just to survive. Their parents won't listen. Parents have no idea how bad it can get. I do. I *won't* leave them hanging." His voice was sharply arrogant, his position in his own mind, ironclad. "That's why I couldn't let Shawn take the fall for Michael's death. Shawn's weak. He would have told them about me if he'd been caught with the Ritalin. He would have ruined everything. That's why I told him to dump the bottle."

I felt the acid in my stomach churn as I realized what he was saying.

"Don't look so surprised, Cate. Who do you think Shawn called first when Michael fell? 9-1-1?" So when I thought Shawn had been calling for help at the top of the cliff, he'd actually been begging Jason to tell him what to do, and Jason had pragmatically told him to toss the pills over the edge.

"You destroyed Michael's reputation!" I cried. "He was trying to change!"

"Michael's dead, Cate. His reputation doesn't matter anymore. There are other people to consider now. After your trip yesterday, I would have thought you'd understand that." Then he leaned in close, and whispered seductively, "We could be so good together. I can give you anything you want, anything you need. I can make all your pain go away, Cate. I've got ways to make the meds work faster. Better. You *know* you want more relief." He kissed the hollow behind my ear, his hot breath warming me despite the alarm bells going off in my head.

Don't even...

My forehead and nose fuzzed at the suggestion of another euphoric rush, another "vacation" from the black ocean I was drowning in, but I wasn't going to admit that.

"Go to hell, Jason!" I spat.

His expression hardened. "Don't delude yourself, Cate. Adults get the pills they need to help them through the bad days. Do you think your mom got through these last few months without a little help from the pharmaceutical industry?"

I glared at him.

"So you think you've suffered?" he went on. "I know you have, Cate. I've watched you fall apart. But just imagine how your mother felt. Up all night? Keeping her mother alive? Watching her die?"

I looked away, my soul shrinking from the possibility of truth in his words.

"Yes, Cate. Multiply your pain by a factor of ten and then maybe you'll understand. Check the box on the top shelf of your hall closet if you don't believe me. It was full of prescriptions when I got the bandages." But I wasn't listening to him anymore. Almost in slow motion, my eyes focused on his forearm. His loose shirt sleeve had slid down to his elbow, unmasking a line of tiny red bruises.

Blood draws?

Track marks.

Shit. He was shooting up. He was mainlining heroin.

He shrugged. "Research," he said.

"Jason…I can get you help…"

"I've got it handled," he said tightly.

The bell signaling the end of the day blasted through the halls of the school, and we both flinched—but he maintained my cage, locking his gaze on my eyes, studying my reaction to his words, evaluating his options.

"Cate!" A concerned voice from down the hall broke into our stare-down, and then Leo appeared over Jason's shoulder, out of breath.

Jason snapped his hands back from the locker and shoved them into his pockets. "Watch her, DiMaro. She's depressed," he said quietly, nodding slowly in my direction. Then he turned and disappeared into the mass of kids jamming the hall.

Leo glanced after him and then back at me. "So you and the dick are like, what, on again? Fighting already?" He rolled his eyes disgustedly at me. I stared after Jason, not wanting to believe what had just happened. The air was suddenly too thick, saturated as it was with the humid breath and sweat of a thousand students. I tried to remember when I'd used my inhaler last. It hadn't been that long ago. Could I use it again?

"Cate? Is what he said true?" Leo asked.

I had to work hard to shift my focus back to him. "What?"

"Are you like...depressed?"

"I don't know, Leo. I don't know anything anymore," I murmured. And then I pushed out into the river of students and headed for the front doors where my dad was picking me up, leaving my backpack and coat in a heap on the floor. Leo grabbed up my stuff and followed me, but he didn't say anything until my dad pulled up to the curb.

"Um...call Meri when you get home. She's worried about you," Leo said, reaching in to set my stuff on my lap and then pushing the door closed. I glanced up at him and nodded, but I'd already forgotten what he'd said. I just wanted to go home and go to bed.

I wanted to sleep for days.

❦❦

I was awake before I could move, curled up on my side with my arms tucked in close under the blanket. I could feel the mattress and the soft quilt, but I couldn't open my eyes yet. I was caught in the world between.

"Catherine..." The barely-audible hiss came from somewhere near the floor in front of me, between my bed and Cici's. My eyes opened. Just slits.

The shape rose like a black moon over the horizon, just inches from my face, painfully slow, blacker than the ambient darkness in the room—until its eyes crested the edge of the bed.

Flames danced where its eyes should have been.

My eyes split open wide, and I explosively pumped my hands forward, sending my body flying backward off the other side of the bed. The back of my head smacked hard against the edge of my open closet door as I hit the floor.

It's not real…it's not real…it's not real…

Baby, shhh…I've got you…

Oh yeah. I'd gone off the deep end, but I nodded fearfully to the self-assured voice in my head. Of course, it wasn't real either.

The bed springs creaked, and I shrunk back against the floor as ten tumbling, smoke-like fingers curled themselves over the edge of the mattress above me. The bed springs creaked again, and the blanket hanging over the side of the bed shivered. Then the creature's face appeared, black-hole black, smeared like a drop of dark, flaming oil on water.

It morphed.

Human facial features peeled themselves out of the hole that had been its head. A perfectly-symmetric nose and pair of angular cheekbones, pointed chin, huge deep-set crystalline black eyes, all framed by wild white-blonde hair that shone as bright as a morning star. His pouty lips pulled back in a wickedly playful grin.

He was the most beautiful, heart-stopping creature I had ever seen. And I was drawn to him. I stretched out my hand.

Hot! Don't touch!

I snatched it back.

"There you are, Catherine. I've been waiting for you." The creature's familiar velvet voice dulled my senses, coated my fear. He rested his chin on his delicate, now human-like hands and gazed down over the side of the bed. His eyes reached deep into my soul, and I squeezed my eyes shut to protect it, but the creature's words forced their way in anyway. "Jason was right, you know. Your mother went to pieces while you hid with your lover in the woods. Revenge is like euphoria, isn't it? It almost hurts when it feels this good. Almost…"

His whisper faded, and when I opened my eyes, I was back in my bed, curled up on my side, fighting off the grogginess of deep sleep. I bolted upright, deeply disturbed by the nightmare creature's words.

My mom hadn't needed me. She'd done what she wanted to do. Right?

My palms began to sweat, and I tried to take a deep calming breath, but my effort was cut short by a rasping wheeze and a thick, post-flu cough. I grabbed my inhaler off my nightstand, shoved it in the front pocket of my jeans and then moved quickly through the early evening darkness to the hall.

Warm light filtered up the stairs, along with a few quiet voices. Most of our grieving company had gone home. I stood at the top of the steps, undecided.

My mother was fine. She was fine.

But what if she wasn't? What if she never had been?

Check her medicine box.

Go talk to her.

But I couldn't face her, not after all my lies and accusations and recklessness. I knew my mom kept her medications on the top shelf of the upstairs hall closet in a shoebox. There wasn't enough room for them in the tiny bathroom we all shared.

I opened the closet door and nudged the box off the shelf with my fingertips, carried it across the hall into the bathroom and set it down on the counter. The only light in the room came from the tiny nightlight plugged into the wall. But it was enough.

The box was filled to the top with brown prescription bottles. I wanted to throw up. Jason was right.

I pawed through the box, reading the labels. There were pain medications and antidepressants and muscle relaxers, and there were medications for insomnia and anxiety. Was she taking them all?

I didn't have any idea! How could a daughter not know that her own mother was depressed and suffering? The answer was brutal. I had coldly abandoned her when she'd needed me most, just as she had abandoned Michael. I'd been a willing pawn in some kind of warped cosmic payback scheme.

"You used me!" I sent my soundless cry skyward, up to whoever was in charge of this mess.

You made your choice. You chose revenge.

I could almost see the flaming eyes watching, so satisfied, while my monstrous guilt sank its fangs in deep. The pain was unbearable.

You can't go back, you know. Not ever.

I couldn't breathe. I needed air. Within seconds, I'd grabbed my music player and cell phone off my dresser and was at the foot of the stairs, shoving my bare feet into my snow boots.

✦

While the demon curled around the girl, whispering, always whispering, the bright Angel followed her down the stairs, lighting the way, brighter than the Guardian had ever seen before. But he remained frozen on the upstairs landing, his heart shuddering for the first time with real fear as he listened to the demon's thoughts spill into the girl's head.

The dark Angel beside him grabbed his shoulder roughly. His eyes, too, were filled with something akin to fear. "Remember when I said she was going to need you? That she wouldn't make it without you?" he asked.

The Guardian nodded, his jaw going tight, his compact power signature flexing hard.

"This is it," said the dark Angel grimly. And then they were both rocketing down the stairs after her.

✦

I was moving toward the door before my heels had settled into the bottoms of my boots.

You did more than abandon her while her own mother was dying. You crushed her with her guilt over Michael.

I didn't mean to...

Mother's guilt is a wonderful thing.

I never said that!

Yes. You did.

Shut up! Shut up!

I snatched the Demon keys from their hook on the wall. My dad's voice broke into my turbulent thoughts, "Cate, why don't you join us for some..."

I answered him by smashing the front door open. The storm door springs shrieked in protest as they stretched way past their limit.

How could I be so stupid? God, I was so fucking stupid!

The Demon waited for me in the driveway, and I fumbled with the keys, praying the car door was unlocked. I couldn't possibly negotiate its sweet spot in the state I was in. I was lucky. The button was up.

The butt-numbing cold of the stiff vinyl seat bled right through my sweatshirt and jeans, and I wished I'd grabbed one of the coats in the hall, but I couldn't go back for it now. My dad was coming down the driveway, and I desperately needed out. I started the engine and shot back over the curb into the street.

Out on the highway a few minutes later, my temper had no one left to attack but me, and I shifted in a blind rage up through the gears.

50 miles per hour. 60. 70.

I'd failed them all. Michael, my grandmother, my mom…

Don't forget about Jason…

And Jason! Why didn't I see what was happening to him?

85 miles per hour.

I flipped on the radio and dialed the volume up to drown out the devastating judgments that pounded like sledgehammer blows in my ears.

Selfish. Reckless. Dishonest. Cold. Heartless. Weak.

Worthless…

The music, Anberlin's "Feel Good Drag," only amplified them.

> *Was this over before*
> *Before it ever began?*
> *Your kiss, your calls, your crutch*
> *Like the devil's got your hands…*

The words cut deep. I bit my lip, but it trembled anyway. Then I turned the volume up louder, letting the music do its work, seeking out my blackest emotions, drowning in them willingly. But drowning was too good for me.

100 miles per hour.

An image of the Demon tearing through the guardrail at the next overpass and crashing into the concrete below flashed through my head. A silver car crumpled and twisted beyond recognition. A hell-worthy funeral pyre.

Yeah. That was more like it.

The overpass was just five miles ahead. I gripped the wheel tighter. I pressed the accelerator harder.

110 miles per hour.

> *Prayers that need no answer now*
> *I'm tired of who I am*
> *You were my greatest mistake*
> *I fell in love with your sin*
> *Your littlest sin*

A mistake. I was just one big fucking mistake. I could visualize the steering wheel impaling my chest, my blood pulsing from my throat, just like Michael's. It could be over so fast.

Three miles to the overpass.

> *This was over before*
> *Before it even began*
> *Your lips, your lies, your lust*
> *Like the devil's in your hands*

"You were always there for me!" I cried out to my Angel, my music lover. "And now you give me this? Is it really over? Have I lost you, too? Or were you never really there at all?" My eyes brimmed with tears. I could barely see.

"I'm just some stupid...delusional...worthless..."

I buried the needle at 120, but the car kept accelerating.

One mile to the overpass.

> *Failure is your disease*
> *You want my outline drawn...*

The music cut out sharply. The thoughts in my head silenced. I was alone.

Fine! FINE! *FINE!* If that's the way I had to die…

Radio static filled the car.

Static…

Static…

And then…

> *Everything's gonna be alright*
> *Rockabye, rockabye…*

My focus shifted like a massive tectonic plate sliding home. New images exploded through my mind like fireworks…my friends at my birthday campfire…my sister Cici and I sharing secrets in our room… Claire patting me awkwardly the night Michael died.

> *Everything's gonna be alright*
> *Rockabye, rockabye, rockabye…*

My dad teaching me to drive…my mom trying to hug me… Michael's long-lashed gray eyes lifting up to plead with me. *Please don't,* they said, *I need you.*

"Okay, Michael, I love you. I miss you," I whispered, and the phantom voice in my head resumed.

That's nice. You can stop the car, now.

Stop the car.

STOP THE FREAKING CAR!

Oh shit! The instant I lifted my foot off the gas pedal, my whole body slammed forward against the seat belt. My tires hit a patch of black ice on the bridge, and the back of the Demon fishtailed left. I braked hard and turned into the skid, but overcompensated, and the car went into a full three-sixty. I fought the wheel, clamped down hard on the clutch and pumped the brakes, but I was powerless to stop it.

Once around…twice around…

The Demon finally stalled to a stop on the opposite shoulder, just inches from the guardrail, facing back the way I'd come, facing home.

I pulled in a sharp, shuddering breath, and then let it out through my mouth, my whole body trembling. Then I broke down with my forehead resting against the hard, frozen steering wheel.

"I'm so… sorry…so…s-s-sorry…" I sobbed. I sobbed for all the pain I'd caused the people I loved. My whole body shook with the force of my grief. And then I sobbed with soul drenching gratitude, because I knew I wasn't alone anymore. My Angel had found me.

> *And from the stage I can tell that*
> *She can't let go and she can't relax*
> *And just before she hangs her head to cry*
> *I sing to her a lullaby*
> *I sing everything's gonna be alright*
>
> *Rockabye…rockabye…*

Snowflakes tumbled through the glow of the street light and covered the windshield with a translucent blanket of white. The interior of the car grew darker. Cocoon-like. And I think I would have stayed like that all night, just resting my head on the wheel and thanking God I was alive, but my eyes were drawn up by muted red and blue flashing lights rushing past me on the bridge. The police car was followed a short while later by a tow truck sporting a rack of flickering amber lights.

Oh…*crap!* I wiped both my cold hands across my face and then pulled the rearview mirror down to check out the damage. My eyes were swollen and ringed by purple shadows. My hair swirled around my head in waves of cascading disarray. My sore skin told me my fever was back.

"What the hell were you thinking?" I murmured, wondering how I could have even thought about offing myself. I'd already caused my family so much misery.

I reached out and touched the radio.

"I should have known you would never abandon me, no matter what I've done." Then, exhausted, I closed my eyes and leaned back to rest my head against the seat, but when my head hit the seatback, I was jolted by an unexpected pain radiating from the back of my skull. I sat back up and reached my hand around to probe the area with my fingertips, wincing as I did so. There was a lump the size of a golf ball on the back of my head, right where I'd smacked it on the closet door as I fled from the nightmare creature in my...*dream.*

But if the bruise wasn't a dream, then...

The metallic taste of fear poured like sour wine onto my tongue. I suddenly knew that my Angel wasn't the only one trying to get through to me on the radio tonight.

And I knew that my dad was wrong.

Demons were real.

And then I rapidly crossed myself.

"Archangel Michael, protect me."

Chapter 25
The Ubermensch

MY EYES FLICKED warily up to the rear view mirror. I truly expected to see glittering black eyes staring back at me from the back seat, but there was nothing. It was empty. But maybe not down behind the seat, near the floor. My skin crawled. But I had to know.

The car kept getting darker as flurries piled up higher on the windshield. I unbuckled my seatbelt in the cold gloom, twisted around in my seat and slowly pulled myself up so I could see over the back. Just a few empty coffee cups. But that didn't mean the demon wasn't still here...somewhere...invisible.

My heart hammered hard in the frosty stillness.

I gripped the back of the seat with my hands and looked with narrowed eyes around through the darkened back and side windows of the car. All I could see beyond the few snowflakes that clung to the glass was the oddly-deserted bridge, which was suddenly pelted by a powerful northerly wind that rocked the car and threw me off balance. It blew sharp wisps of snow up and over the guardrail. It howled beneath the belly of the Demon. I might as well have been lost on some desolate tundra in Northern Canada. Where were all of the cars?

I turned around, slid back down in my seat and buried the fingers of my left hand in my hair, pulling my scalp tight, letting my mood evolve.

"Demons are real," I whispered. I felt the evidence on the back of my head again. How long had they been in my life? The urge to lie and deceive? The thoughts of hate and hopelessness? How much of that had been me and how much had been...

Crap! If I'd stayed on course tonight, I'd be dead right now, fueling a fiery wreck beneath the bridge.

But I wasn't.

And my fear gradually gave way to the soul deep conviction that I wasn't alone. Not ever. I thought of my Playlist, and then I reached under my shirt and pulled out my grandmother's ring.

"Have faith," she'd said.

"Angels are real," I murmured. And of that I was sure now. My Angel, or God, or *something*, had intervened tonight to keep me from driving off this bridge. The images of the people in my life who loved me—I hadn't come up with those on my own. I replayed them in my head, feeling more and more secure as the images unfolded—until I got to the last one. I yanked my hand out of my hair and sat up tall, my breath releasing in a quiet gasp.

"I need you," Michael had said. The images hadn't been revealed in a dream. They were more like vivid thoughts, but...

Had someone sent up another S.O.S. flare for him? Was he not gone after all? Then my heart stopped cold.

What if the demons were after him, too?

I was suddenly seething. My temper was rising. Souls are never destroyed, right? How could I have been stupid enough to believe Michael was beyond my help? That *I* was beyond help? I screw up and so...what, I go and hide under a rock and feel sorry for myself? Okay...so maybe I screwed up really badly, but bad enough to end it all?

And that's just what the demon had wanted. It wanted me dead.

I don't know how this knowledge came to me, but I could feel it in my bones now. My heart rate spiked again, but not because I was afraid. I was pissed. And I had a new target.

"I know you're here, now," I whispered, and my eyes darted reflexively to the rearview mirror again. "I don't know what you want or why you want it, but I won't run next time. I'll fight back. I won't let you destroy my life or the lives of the people I love."

And I'd start tonight. I'd go home and try to make everything right. I couldn't do anything for Mina anymore, and I'd have to live with that, but I could plead for my mother's forgiveness. I could tell her I loved her, and that I would be there for her now. God…how was I going to face her? How was she supposed to forgive me when I didn't know if I could ever forgive myself? I rubbed my hand through my messy hair, my stomach souring. I was sliding again.

Fear.

Despair.

A sense of supreme unworthiness.

They stalked me. I glanced upward at the dark roof of the car and begged for strength. I'd have to face my sisters and my friends, too. I'd hardly spoken to them in weeks. And then there was Jason, falling into heroin addiction right under my nose.

And Michael. I blinked hard.

"I'll find you," I whispered. "If you're still here somewhere, I'll find you. I'll fight for you. And somehow I'll make you believe." And with that thought, I shoved the key in the ignition and started the car. I sent the suffocating blanket of snow on the windshield flying with the wipers, revved the engine and pulled back onto the highway.

Not far down the road, I passed a semi with a blown tire jackknifed across the highway. It had traffic tied up for miles in the oncoming lane. That explained the lack of cars on the overpass. There were accidents in both directions. I shuddered to think what would have happened if I'd gone into that spin with other cars on the bridge. I could have taken out more than just myself.

I was just slowing down and checking my brakes when I felt my cell buzzing in my jeans pocket. My mom and dad had probably been trying to call me. They were probably frantic. I dug the phone out of my pocket with one hand.

"Mom?"

A broken voice answered instead. "Cate? Can you meet me at Jai Ho? The heroin, I can't stop. I thought I could, but..." It was Jason. I could visualize his sweat-drenched face and strung-out eyes through the phone.

I was torn. He was such an arrogant ass, but he'd been there for me so many times.

He's not worth it. GO HOME!

Warning thoughts roared through my head. Did the demons want me to turn my back on one more person in my life? Were they laying another guilt trap for me? What if he overdosed and died tonight?

"Okay," I said into the phone. "We can talk at the coffee shop, but only about getting you clean." It was a public place. I'd be safe there. I heard ragged breathing but no response.

"Jason?"

"I'll be there in ten minutes," he said. Then the line went dead.

The wheels of the Demon splashed into the icy parking lot of Jai Ho about twenty minutes later. I didn't see the Audi, so I stayed in the car and pulled out my phone to text my mom. Crap. She'd called three times, but I didn't want to talk to her until I could do it face to face.

Instead, I sent: **cant talk now. explain later. c.**

When I was finished, I looked up. Still no Jason. Maybe he'd driven a different car? I glanced one more time warily into the backseat, then climbed out of the car and hopped over a pile of dirty snow to the curb. The night air was damp and smoky-cold, and I hugged my arms in close to my chest, wishing again for my coat.

It was warm inside, almost too warm, and the coffee shop windows were steamed up, obscuring the view of the parking lot. I glanced around at the steel tables. No Jason. I knocked on the guy's bathroom door, but no one was in there either. Maybe he'd decided he wasn't ready for help yet.

I thought about getting some tea and sitting down to wait, but my mom and dad would be worried, so I pushed back out into the winter air. My congested lungs tightened up almost immediately, and I reached down to feel the reassuring lump of my inhaler in my pocket. It wasn't there. It must have fallen out in the car.

Shit. I was so sick of being sick. I kicked my feet crossly through the snow at the curb, yanked the car door open, and slid behind the wheel. As I pulled the heavy door closed, a flash of movement caught my eye, and then my head was immobilized by a thick gloved hand gripping my forehead and cold steel pressed against my neck.

"You really should learn to lock your doors."

My heart leapt into my throat. The tight voice came from the back seat, and my eyes flicked to the rearview mirror again, fully expecting to see a pair of shiny black demon eyes staring back at me. But the icy blue eyes I saw belonged to Jason. They were feral. Self-destructive and wild.

"Jason…you don't want to do this…" I choked out, but I reminded myself I wasn't alone, and a wave of peace and strength enveloped me.

Stay with me, please, I prayed.

"You and I need to talk," Jason said. "Drive."

"We can talk here," I countered, breathless.

He slid his hand down over my face and grabbed my chin, steadied it, and then nicked my throat with his grandfather's blade. A blast of wind buffeted the car, and my eyes flew open wide.

"Drive, Cate. Don't be stupid."

I mashed the key into the ignition, mumbling, "I'm not the stupid one." He relaxed his grip on my chin so I could see the road, but the knife remained firmly planted against my throat. I pulled out onto the wet street.

"Take a left," he said.

"Where are we going?"

His answer startled me. "Lewis Woods."

Michael! My heart leapt at the possibility that he'd still be there. But then the horror of the coming attraction sank in. He'd already witnessed so much brutality and violence, and now he would be forced to watch it happen to me? And not be able to do a damn thing about it? He'd never believe after that.

"Why Lew—"

"Just…shut up, Cate! I'll tell you when we get there."

Jason was tense and quiet until we turned onto Cedar Point Road and descended into the snowy gorge. His fingers quivered inside his glove. "Damn it, Cate! I told you to let Michael's death go! Why couldn't you listen to me?"

"I'll listen, Jason, but it's the heroin talking! You don't know what you're saying!"

"I told you. I've got it under control. When I find a connection for methadone, I'll stop." But his cracked voice betrayed his addiction. He rubbed his damp forehead roughly against the tender demon bruise on the back of my head, and a chill ran up my spine. Could demons be stalking Jason, too?

"Jason, you need help. I...I think there might be demons—"

"We're back to that? God versus the Devil?" His laugh was thick with condescension. "*Now* who doesn't know what their saying? There *is* no God, Cate, haven't you heard? He's dead!" Then he paused while he searched his mind for a quote. "I give you instead the Ubermensch–"

"*You* wrote that on the bridge?"

"You saw that too?" His tone held an out-of-place mixture of surprise and pleasure. It turned my stomach.

"So you think *you're* the Ubermensch? Some kind of superhuman? A demigod?" Shit...he had some kind of a freaking God complex.

"No...maybe...Nietzsche says, 'Man is something to be overcome. What have you done to overcome him?' Cate, *listen* to me. There are so many drugs out there now that can help us do that. Help us overcome *ourselves*, all our flaws—"

"You mean like heroin?" I asked harshly, challenging his argument. "I didn't know people used heroin to improve themselves."

"It was just a benchmark," he spat.

"Oh...I get it! All for the sake of science? How's that going for you?" He knew he was fucked. You didn't mess around with heroin without getting burned.

"It would have gone *fine* if you hadn't stuck your self-righteous nose in. There's no way I'm getting sent off to some west coast rehab center to suffer through withdrawal and have some paid-to-be-my-best-friend shrink pick apart my brain while everything I've worked for is destroyed. I can't. I won't. Now SHUT *UP!*"

I pulled into the unplowed parking area of Lewis Woods shortly after that. The Audi was already there. That scared me more than the knife. It meant Jason had a plan. It meant he was leaving here alone. He adjusted his grip on the knife and said, "Get out of the car, Cate."

I panicked. "I thought we were going to talk!"

"We did. I'm done talking," he said. "Let's go."

And it finally sank in. He was going to kill me.

"I don't have to tell anyone, Jason! I can back off…"

He pressed his lips together in a hard line and sharpened his tone. "You and I both know you won't do that. You'll never stop until you've proved Michael was innocent when he died."

I opened my mouth to protest, but he squeezed my jaw tighter.

"I found your letters, Cate. After you refused to listen to me again today, I came out here to the cliff to try to understand, and I found your letters to him in the tree. You're obsessively in love with him, though I still can't figure out how or when that happened. Now get out of the car!"

If I got out of the car, I was afraid I'd never get back in. "You said you cared about me!" I cried.

Jason winced, but then he reached for the driver's side door handle, and the blade slipped away from my throat. I knocked it out of his hand and lunged for the passenger door only to have him throw his arm around my waist and drag me back. I glimpsed my inhaler on the floor and tried to snag it with my fingers, but I dropped it in the snow outside as he yanked me out of the car.

He held onto my arm while he grabbed the knife and my cell phone off the seat, retracted the blade, and stuffed them into his pocket. "I did care. You used me," he said flatly. "I took care of you every time you came to me for help, and you repay me by wanting me to turn myself in to the cops? Tell them Michael was clean when he died, and that I know this because Shawn called me for drug advice? You want me to ruin my own family's name? Give up all that I've accomplished? For someone who's *dead?*"

He pushed me ahead of him, and I fell on my knees in the snow, my bare hands breaking through the sharp top layer of ice. The arctic air cut right through my sweatshirt and rushed down my throat to sting my lungs. They pulled in tighter. Shit. My breathing was only going to get worse.

"Get up. This is where you want to be anyway, with him." I felt the tips of his fingers reaching down and around my ribcage, and I pushed up onto my toes and heaved myself forward, up and out of the snow. My hands were wet and freezing, but my feet were warm in my boots, and when I got them under me, I sprinted sideways and tried to get the car in between us. If I could just get back inside and lock it...

Jason cursed under his breath, but he had his arms wrapped around me from behind in seconds. I was no match for him.

"NO!" I shrieked, struggling violently. "Think about what you're doing...*Jason!*"

He wrestled with me until he had his left arm wrapped around me and the knife out and pressed to my throat again. "If you don't want to die right here, you'll walk," he hissed, "and you won't make another sound." He loosened his grip and then pushed me forward across the vast silver-lit field. I kept calm by focusing on the mouth of the woods in the distance. I saw the pale translucent figure in the black sleeveless shirt and cut-offs when we were about two-thirds of the way across. He was crouched at the very edge of the tree line, tense and ready for war.

"Michael!" The strength of my emotions should have carried my voice all the way to the cliff and back, but it came out just a whisper. He needed to know we weren't alone, that we never had been. He needed to know it before the coming violence permanently destroyed his faith.

Jason was shocked by my outburst. "What the hell?"

"LET HER GO!" Michael's eyes were deep gray craters of volcanic hatred, and his voice was a cataclysmic eruption that should have blown the tops off all the trees in the forest and hurled them into the stratosphere. I thought my eardrums would blow, but Jason didn't even flinch.

"Michael! The Playlist is real! We have *Angels*. They're here. You've got to believe me!"

Jason stopped just shy of the entrance to the woods, and spun me around to face him, shaking me roughly. "Are you *kidding* me, Cate? Do you actually think you see him?" His wild glare shifted from me to the woods and then back again.

I stuck out my chin defiantly. "Yeah, Jason. I do! And he'd kick your ass if he could!"

"See, this is why I can't let you go! You're goddamned obsessed." I yanked backward with all my might, trying to pull away from him, but he was too strong. He twisted me around and shoved my arm up behind my back. I cried out in pain. Then he snarled over my shoulder, "You'll never stop until you've proved him innocent. I can't let that happen."

But I wasn't listening to him. My eyes were fixed on Michael's, which were storming with murderous rage, and I didn't know how much time I'd have to get through that before—

"What the hell is he talking about, Catherine?" Michael spat.

"It was Jason who Shawn called..." My tight chest heaved hard to fill again. "...about the Ritalin. Jason's dealing..."

But my words were choked off when Jason yanked up on my arm even harder. Damn it. Don't cry. I fought against the fresh onslaught of tears but lost. Michael's sweat-slick arm shot out across the border toward me, but it immediately began to turn brown and disintegrate. He yanked it back.

"I'll kill you, you son of a bitch!" he shouted, then groaned, "God, Catherine...I told you not to..." but he was drowned out by Jason's disturbed whispers.

"See...it will all work out," Jason explained. "You'll commit suicide by jumping off the cliff while I tried to stop you. It's beautiful, really. You want to be with him anyway. That's what you said in your letters." And then Jason held me there in the moonlight, immobile, just outside of Michael's reach, letting his plan sink in.

"He would never want me to do that," I whispered.

Michael shook his head back and forth, his jaw quivering. "Never," he said.

"Well then, it's a good thing I'm not concerned about his post-mortem opinion on that, isn't it?" Jason said.

"No one will believe I tried to kill myself," I said. But I had little conviction of that. After my behavior these last few days, I wasn't so sure.

"Ah…but they will, Cate…" Jason whispered into my ear and then pulled my right arm out from behind my back and shoved up the sleeve of my sweatshirt revealing several pale scars lining my wrists and hands. They were from the cuts I'd sustained the first night I'd seen Michael in the woods. Jason caressed them with his thumb. "Evidence, Cate. I'll tell them you've been cutting to escape your pain." He rubbed his thumb over the cut on my neck and then looked at the blood on his thumb. "And now your throat, too. Poor thing…"

I looked up to see Michael's face fill with guilt-soaked misery. Then Jason forced my hand open.

"I even had to stitch you up once. Right? See? I've been trying to hold you together all along." Then, holding my hand open, he positioned the hilt of his knife on my palm, squeezed my hand around it, and then removed it with his gloved hand. "And see? Last week you stole my knife to make your cutting more interesting. You've always liked it, this knife. My sister knows that. Then there are your letters proving how unstable you are."

"Shit…Catherine. He has you totally set up," Michael moaned, lacing his fingers over the top of his head and pressing down hard. "I'll kill him…I swear I will…"

But I knew he couldn't.

"Tell my mom…"

Michael shook his head. "Don't you start thinking that way."

"Tell her…I'm *sorry*…"

"Already thought of that," Jason assured me. "She'll get a text from your phone explaining everything right before you leap. So let's go carry out your plan, Cate. We don't want to keep your boyfriend waiting." Then he thrust me into the woods.

I caught a glimpse of Michael wincing as my flu-ravaged body was shoved over the border before he lunged for Jason in full tackle position. He had no effect on him at all, and he cried out in escalating frustration as he tried to pummel Jason over and over while I was forced farther and farther into the woods.

"Michael! There's nothing you can do! You have to accept that! You have to trust God!" I cried weakly as I watched the sweat drip from his exhausted body. Jason readjusted his grip so he could cover my mouth.

"I'll trust Him when He sends down a fucking army of Angels to save you!" Michael shot back, taking aim again, but he suddenly disappeared instead and reappeared a few inches in front of my face, his eyes fiercely determined.

"Slow him down, Catherine. I'm going to get help." Help? How was he going to get help? But I could see his face clearly in the light reflecting off the snow, and he was deadly serious. He had a plan, too. I raised my eyebrows doubtfully, and he leaned in even closer. "Stay with me. I'll be back. Be ready to run."

I nodded, and he disappeared.

Slow him down. Sure. I struggled, kicked, and twisted, but was too weak to have much impact, so I focused instead on my breathing. In…out…in…out…I sucked hard to fill my lungs with each of Jason's steps, but I couldn't get enough. I was sick, and the air was cold, and I was so tired. In the snow-strengthened moonlight, the scaly tree trunks drifted past like ships floating by in a fog. I wanted to join them. My eyes started to close.

Stay with me…just a little longer…you can live through this.

I jerked my eyes back open.

"Catherine, are you ready?" Michael's commanding voice came from behind me.

To run, right? He wanted me to run?

"Yes," I croaked, and then louder, "Yes." I twisted around just in time to see Michael finish whispering in a coyote's softly pointed ear before it lunged for Jason, gold eyes blazing, fangs snapping and snarling like a hound from hell.

I was stunned. The coyote had survived! I could see the small crescent-shaped scar in his sandy gray fur where I'd pulled out the arrow.

Jason stiffened at the sound and spun to face it.

"Now, Catherine! Run!" Michael shouted. I tore myself out of Jason's hands just as the coyote slammed into him, saliva-spitting fangs first. He hit Jason mid-chest, and they both fell backward onto the path. Jason buried his hands in the fur at the coyote's throat, struggling to keep him from ripping his face to shreds.

I dragged in more air and stumbled up the path toward the mouth of the woods and the car at a sluggish run. Michael was at my side instantly.

"Catherine! The coyote's not big enough! He can only hold Jason off for so long." I slowed down to see his face, which was calm, but grim. "You'll never make it."

I stopped and leaned forward with my hands on my knees, sucking hard. He was right…shit…I could barely breathe. I'd never make it to the car before Jason. I'd have no speed.

Michael bent down next to me, resting his tingling hand on my upper back. "You need a weapon."

I tilted my head to the side. "Where…*breathe*…where?"

"Follow me."

He stood up, but kept his hand on my back. I stood up next to him. "Come on! You haven't got much time!" The coyote was whimpering now somewhere behind us, and my heart broke for him, but I nodded to Michael, and we struck off at a fast pace into the woods. He remained just a few inches in front of me, urging me forward, guiding me with his hand on the back of my neck, soothing me with his gentle static. I glanced behind us and saw my footprints leaving a trail for Jason to follow.

"The footprints…*breathe*…Jason will…"

"I'm counting on that," Michael said. "I'll explain when we get there."

We weaved over and under fallen tree trunks and skirted several bramble thickets before he slowed down and let his hand drop from my back.

"It's somewhere…somewhere…" he whispered to himself, looking back and forth between several trees and finally pausing in front of one with several tiny woodpecker holes gouged out on one side. He squatted down and pointed to the snow in front of it. "Here. Dig here."

I didn't hesitate, and I didn't ask questions. I bent down next to him and started scooping the snow away with my cold stiff fingers. He ran his hand through his hair again. "God…you're freezing your ass off…careful…"

I brushed away the last layer of wet snow with my fingertips and lifted up the arrow that lay beneath. It was just like the one I'd pulled out of the coyote, short, with a razor sharp tri-blade tip. And I had no idea how I could use it to protect myself.

He saw the bewilderment on my face, but he didn't attempt to tell me everything would be alright.

"You're going to have to let him take you, Catherine, and then shove it in his heart." I looked down at the arrow tip. Michael was pensive, but quiet, while he let me get used to the idea. I wrapped both hands around the bolt and imagined it tearing through the muscle of Jason's heart. I could still remember how it felt when it ripped through the coyote's shoulder, the ragged tugging sensation, and I blinked hard and gasped, "Jason's sick, Michael…he's mainlining…" And then Michael was kneeling in the snow before me with both of his hands wrapped around mine. I couldn't feel the arrow anymore.

"Jason wants you dead," he said bluntly. "I don't care if he's the freaking tooth fairy on crack. You've got to take him down." Then he closed his eyes for a moment, and his brows furrowed together.

"Jason's finished with him," he said and winced. I wondered if the coyote was dead. I started to ask, but he held up his hand sharply and then tilted his head to the side and squeezed his eyes tighter. "Shit… he's following your tracks back." He opened his eyes and focused them on me.

"He's moving this way. Follow me." He stood up and looked around again and then led me forward and had me sit down with my back tucked into a hollow at the base of one of the wider tree trunks. My footprints stretched out behind me. He crouched down in the snow next to me, and held his hands up close to his chest.

"Hold the arrow like this, vertical, tip up, near your heart."

I positioned the arrow like he showed me, and he nodded tersely.

"Sit with your knees bent up in front of you like I am, so you can drive upward with your legs," he instructed. "He'll come up behind you, following your tracks. You'll have to let him grab you so that he pulls you in with your chest facing his. Okay? And you can't let him see the arrow until you're ready to shove it into his cock-sucking heart. Got it? If he pulls you in and you're facing away from him, it's over. If he sees the arrow before it's sticking out of his freaking chest, it's over." Michael flickered and rocked back and forth.

"Michael," I called to him, wanting to reassure him.

"You've done it before..." he went on, not hearing me, "...shoved an arrow through..."

"Michael!" I said again, louder, and he looked up, startled. "I'm not afraid," I said, and I wasn't, because I knew our Angels would be with us no matter what happened. He studied my face and then touched my cheek softly with the back of his ragged forefinger.

"You're not, are you?" he murmured and then looked away and rubbed his hand anxiously up the back of his neck, mumbling to himself, "She's half frozen to death, can hardly breathe, is being stalked by her dope fiend ex-boyfriend, and she's not afraid...you're an idiot, Michael..."

We both heard a twig snap and froze. Then Michael concentrated hard on whatever it was he concentrated on. "He's just left the path, Catherine. You've got time." He sighed then and leaned away from me, staring off into the ghostly trees.

"You're not an idiot, Michael," I whispered.

He turned back to me with anguished eyes, and then spilled his feelings in a rush. "You were right yesterday. I was a coward. I'd never had anyone need me or...or depend on me. I didn't like the way it made me feel...like all responsible for you...and I totally sucked at it. Shit, I'm still sucking at it. That's why I let you think I was gone." He dropped his gaze guiltily.

"Think?" I was shocked. "Think? So...you didn't actually try to fade away?"

He glanced up, and then ducked his head again. "Catherine, what you saw yesterday...that's just what happens to me when I try to leave the woods. I fall apart and get sucked back in. I don't know why. But I thought it would be dramatic enough to keep you from coming back."

I let my gaze roam over his dirt-smeared forehead and vulnerable gray eyes. He was still so lost, so afraid, and I was worried about what would happen to him if I died tonight, and he remained trapped here. I'd wanted to warn him about the demons. I'd wanted to explain to him about the lullaby on the bridge so he would understand why I was so sure that God was with us. I wanted to leave him with something to believe in, but I didn't have the breath or the time.

Instead, I pulled hard at the icy air and simply said, "It's going to be okay. Everything will work out the way God wants it to."

Michael pulled the Claddagh out from under his shirt and turned it over and over in his fingers. "What if He and I don't want the same thing?" he said under his breath. Then he stiffened. "Shh. He's coming."

Michael's breathing sped up, and he appeared suddenly crouched in front of me again, his hands on my shoulders. "You know what to do, right? Just shove it with all your freaking might into his heart, right?"

I nodded firmly and held the arrow tightly to my chest. I'd fight. With everything I had. Michael wasn't going to see me die tonight.

He nodded silently to himself and then, "God! If this doesn't work...if he...if you don't..." He struggled to finish his sentence, but gave up and went on with his thought. "I'll go over with you. Understand? You won't go over the cliff alone. We'll overlap. Okay? You won't feel anything."

I nodded rapidly, my heart rate spiking painfully. So much for fearlessness. He glanced down at my chest and back into my eyes, but didn't say anything. Then he brushed his ethereal lips against my forehead, and my whole body warmed to his electric touch.

"I'm glad I stayed," he whispered, and then he backed away and crouched down across from me so he could see better to count me down. His eyes were fixed on a spot behind me, to my right.

"Oh shit...here we go..." he whispered. "Thirty feet."

I flexed my fingers around the arrow to try to get my blood moving. Snowy pine needles crunched under Jason's feet as he came closer, and I had to fight to keep from squeezing my eyes shut.

"Twenty feet..." Michael whispered. I took a long, slow breath, concentrating on breathing quietly around the wheeze that struggled to escape.

"It's okay. Let him hear you breathe," Michael said. "You need to draw him right to you."

I took in a deeper breath. It creaked like a loose floorboard in the charged silence. I heard Jason stop and change direction on the snow.

Michael nodded. "Ten feet behind you on your right."

Michael leaned forward, the muscles in his arms flexing under glossy moonlit sweat. I knew if he was actually here, in my world, Jason would already be dead, torn apart with Michael's bare hands. There was enough white-hot hate in his eyes to vaporize an army.

"Five...four..."

I leaned forward so my weight was over my toes.

"Two...one..."

Then it was one blinding photo flash after another, overly bright, disorienting, lightning fast.

I was already pivoting and thrusting the arrow upward when Jason grabbed my arm from behind and yanked me toward him. But at the last possible second, he saw the arrow, sidestepped left and shoved his hand in front of his heart to block it. The arrow plunged into his palm, shredding and popping his tendons as it ripped its way through. I kept shoving, forcing his hand up and back, and the arrowhead sliced through the outer edge of his throat, releasing a thin stream of dark red blood that soaked into the hooded sweatshirt he wore under his leather jacket.

I glanced up into his face and saw two blood-dripping lacerations snaking across his cheek. His eyes glazed over with rage, his mouth twisted in shock.

"Run, Catherine!" Michael cried, and I let go of the arrow and ran. Jason pulled the arrow through his palm, flung it into the trees and then crash stumbled through the underbrush after me.

"Go! Go! Go!" Michael shouted. I made it maybe twenty steps before my lungs sealed themselves up almost completely. Hot, slippery fingertips scrabbled for my left hand on a backswing of my arm. They grabbed hold and yanked down and backward, stopping me in my tracks, while Jason's momentum carried him forward. He fell like a mountain on top of me from behind, shoving my left shoulder into the ground.

Something tore and then popped, and the fiery pain that exploded in my shoulder eclipsed everything else. I lay there for a long beat, with my face half buried in the snow, and then I was being lifted and dragged backward toward the cliff. My entire left arm and shoulder smarted with sizzling pain. I clenched my jaw tight and opened my eyes.

Michael was there, his deep gray eyes inviting me in forever.

"I'm sorry," I whispered, my breath barely infusing the words with sound.

"Oh, Christ!" he cried, reaching out with his hands and bathing my shoulder in soothing static. "It's dislocated, damn it!" He let go and swung mightily at Jason, and the pain inflamed my entire left side again. Michael replaced his hands on my shoulder, saying, "He's dying, Catherine! You nicked a vein in his throat! He's bleeding out, but not fast enough!" Then he shouted to the soaring pine rafters, "Oh, God! Please! Let me protect her! I love her!" He dropped his desperate, flickering gaze back to my face.

"I love you, Catherine," he said. His voice was an impotent whisper that tugged and clawed at every inch of my frozen skin.

"You won't be…" I gasped, "alone…your Angel…" But Michael was shaking his head, distrust and despair running rampant through his eyes. I couldn't let him see this.

The wind picked up as we approached the cliff. It chilled the damp curls at the back of my neck. NO! This wasn't happening! I shoved at Jason's hand, peeling his fingers away from my chest, focusing all my efforts on his pinky. I bent it all the way back, farther and farther, until he cried out in pain and lost his grip. I twisted away, but he managed to grab hold of my right wrist. I threw all of my weight backward, digging my boots into the icy snow, yanking with everything I had left.

"NO!" The trees were opening up, parting for us. "Jason! Please!"

Jason's voice rang out, absolute, but weakening, "Don't...you left me no choice...I can't..."

Michael wedged himself between us, as if he could split us apart. He glanced over his shoulder to see the edge of the cliff not five feet behind him and his own deadly precipice rising out of the dark, misty gorge in the distance.

"Oh, God no!" he cried. Then his husky voice was filling my ear, breaking softly. "I'll stay with you...I swear...all the way down..."

No! No way! I hadn't gotten through to him yet! I pulled backward harder.

"Please...Michael..." My teeth chattered with cold and pain and sorrow. "Believe."

He searched my face incredulously, and the silver embers of faith in his eyes sputtered...sparked...

Jason's good hand slid on my wrist, stretching and burning my skin. He was standing with his back to the edge of the cliff, pulling me toward him. There was no way I was going to stop him from dragging me over.

Michael's faith roared to life. He looked up and surrendered.

"Fine then!" he shouted. "If you need her, then take her! Do what you want with her. Just, please, please don't leave me here alone! Let me come with her! *Please!*"

Then his lips were rushing past mine, and all I could feel was Michael's strength, and all I could smell was Michael's scent, and all I could see was gentle light.

And then he was gone. Just...gone.

Part Four
...or something

Chapter 26
Paradise Lost

"THANK YOU, GOD," I prayed, hoping that Michael's faith had finally carried him home.

At the same moment, a burst of blinding light vanquished the darkness. It lit up Jason's face as it engulfed the entire cliff top in a blast of midday sun. There was a second of deafening silence, and then a voice like a sonic boom thundered through the woods.

"EAM LIBERA, IASON FLAMMARUM VOX!"

Jason threw up his hand and squeezed his eyes shut. A ghostly breeze followed the thunder, carrying hissed whispers past me in a language I didn't understand:

"Morieris, sed adhuc tibi est spes. Servari potes. In tuo animo eius sanguinem non cupis. Obsecro! Eam libera. Libera."

When Jason's eyes reopened, they were twisted with torment and fear. They locked on mine, and then he let go of my wrist and fell backward, disappearing over the edge of the cliff.

Suddenly free, I collapsed on the cliff top path. My left arm throbbed from my shoulder all the way down to my fingertips, and I cradled it close to my chest, shivering and struggling to breathe. I remained there, motionless in the fading light, stunned by what I'd just seen.

Jason let go of my wrist. In that split second of blinding light, that voice had broken through the insanity he was suffering, and he'd chosen to let me live. Now he was dead, smashed on the rocks below. I moved then. I pulled my knees up to my chest and sobbed. Only my sobs were soundless, starved for air. I had to get back to the car, back to my inhaler, or I was going to die.

I tried to stand, tucking my feet underneath me and pushing up with my right hand, but my lungs were sucking quicksand and my strength was gone. Who was I kidding? There was no way I was getting up. No way in hell.

No phone. No inhaler. No *air*...

And I panicked. I should have known better. But my fear rose unchecked, a crushing mudslide, obliterating all rational thought. I was going to suffocate, just like Mina. Oh please no. Not that. *Please* not that. My heart pounded. My pulse raced. I couldn't think. I let my forehead drop down into the icy snow, gasping, "Oh God, please help me!"

And then I heard the most beautiful sound in the world:

Michael's voice.

"Oh Baby, please...you have to focus..."

I lifted my eyes to find him crouched before me, completely transformed. His ragged shorts and sleeveless shirt had been exchanged for a pair of light blue jeans and a black T-shirt. His Claddagh was now double looped through a thin leather choker around his neck, and what appeared to be a tangle of windswept roots was slung across his back on a wide leather strap. His hair was longer, waving well past his ears, and he no longer flickered. He was rock steady and shone with his own pale light. Most remarkable of all were his eyes. Instead of gray, they were silver and...*God*, they were brilliant.

Those beautiful, silver eyes filled with confusion and then wonder as I focused on his face.

"Holy Christ..." he whispered. "You can see me." He glanced up over my head, and then he turned back to me, deep worry settling into his eyes. His familiar woodsy fragrance filled my nose as he bent down closer. "Baby, listen to me. You're safe now, but you have to slow your breathing down. Help is on the way." His assurance only fed my fear. It would take at least a half hour for anyone to get back here. I'd be dead.

"Listen to me, *Catherine*." He'd lowered his voice and slowed it down. "It's Claire."

Claire could run two miles in—

"Twelve minutes. She has your inhaler. You've already made it this far. You can make it a little longer." He twisted around slowly to sit beside me, brushing tentative fingertips across my upper back. They no longer tingled, but they were warm. My muscles relaxed, and I was breathing again, but barely.

"See?" he said. "You're getting more air than you think you are. Just like when you were little. Just breathe. In…out…in…out…"

He wrapped his right arm around his knees, and I was surprised to see his fingernails and forearm healed. And all ten toes were now protected by a brand new pair of white Converse tennis shoes. Had God healed him when he'd vanished at the edge of the cliff and then sent him back to me? I longed for enough breath to ask him, but it took everything I had just to keep air moving.

He answered my question anyway.

"Something like that," he murmured, his lips turning up slightly. Could he read my mind now? Deep forest shadows stretched across his face, but his silver eyes shone like hammered steel in the moonlight. Their luster was somehow more familiar than even the gray had been. They drew me in.

"That's it," he said. "Eyes on me. Breathe with me. Focus." But my ears were ringing. Black spots were crowding out my vision. I was dizzy…lightheaded…

He flicked his eyes to my hand. My nail beds were dusky blue, and I anxiously clenched my hand into a fist around a handful of snow. Then I was far away, seeing another hand—a much smaller hand—clutching a white tufted quilt in a pink Cinderella bedroom. I was a small child again, sitting on my bed and fighting for air. I looked up into the mirror above my dresser and saw Michael standing quietly behind me, a soft light beside him. He lifted silver eyes to stare at me.

Then I was slammed back into the woods, collapsed on my right side with my cheek pressed into the snow. My hair was wet, and snowflakes had collected on my lashes. Confused and afraid, I looked around for Michael.

"I'm here," he said, kneeling beside me. "I'll never leave you."

"I saw you! I..." I coughed violently. Each spasm sent exploding pain through my mangled shoulder.

"Shh," he soothed. "Christ! I know it hurts. Don't try to talk. You were right before. I can hear your thoughts now." And my thoughts unleashed themselves, desperately seeking him out.

We're mind-melded?

"Yeah..." His lips turned up a little under worried eyes. "Yeah... just like Spock and Kirk."

I saw you. You were in my room when I was little.

He ran his fingers uneasily through his hair, then reached out his warm fingertips and melted the ice crystals on my lashes. "Just...keep breathing," he said, but an anvil had settled on my chest. A thousand pounds. My eyes drifted closed, and I flashed far away again. I saw silver eyes behind bars...so beautiful...I wanted to touch them...

"No! Damn it, Catherine!" Michael cried. "Look at me!"

My eyes crawled back open, gritty, freeze-dried.

"For Christ's sake!" he cried. "You didn't fight off demons for the past seventeen years, avoid driving off a bridge, and escape that psycho- ex-boyfriend of yours just to give up and die tonight! You fight! You *FIGHT!*"

My fast-beating heart stalled. I hadn't told him about the demons or what happened on the bridge. He wasn't *there*. How did he know? His eyes softened as he followed my thoughts.

"Catherine, you've always known you had an Angel or something watching over you, right? Playing you music? Sending you dreams?" He paused and then leaned in closer. "That was me. I'm your...'or something.'"

I don't understand...

"When I disappeared back there at the edge of the cliff? God didn't just heal me and send me back *here* to you. He healed me and sent me back in *time* to you."

What are you saying? How far back? A day? A week?

He sighed softly, his eyes glistening. "Oh Baby, I was there when you were *born.*"

My eyes filled. My chin trembled. *You've been with me my whole life? My Playlist? It was you?*

He nodded. "Well, me and your Angel. And yes, you have an Angel. God, she's *beautiful,* Catherine, a pain in the ass, but beautiful. She's here now," he said. "Now hold on to my voice. We'll pull you through this."

He chose a beautiful song, a perfect song: "Lifeline" by Angels and Airwaves. Then he was singing it just for me.

> *With an urgent careful stare*
> *I see panic in those eyes*
> *If I see you lying there*
> *Hoping this was the last time*

> *If you hear a distant sound*
> *And some footsteps by your side*
> *When the world comes crashing down*
> *I will find you if you hide*

Truer and richer than before, his voice now held a resonant, mythical quality unlike any human voice I'd ever heard and yet—my heart recognized it, adjusting its rhythm to beat in time with it. And as I melted into his voice, my skin began to glow. The soft, silvery light illuminated Michael's face, and I was frightened.

Michael layered his thoughts over the lyrics in my head. *Baby, no...don't do this to me! Listen! Breathe...please...*

But I couldn't feel my lungs anymore.

> *And if you wish it, wish it now*
> *If you wish it wish it loud*

If you want it say it now
If you want it say it loud

The light within me grew steadily. A distant, symphonic humming filled my head. It grew louder and louder.

We all make mistakes
Here's your lifeline…
If you want I want to
We all make mistakes
Here's your lifeline
If you want I want to

When the light was too bright for me to see his face anymore, I heard his anguished cry split the night. Then his voice broke as he whispered, "Now? Should I do it now?" No one answered him, but Michael carefully reached beneath me, gathered me up off the ground, and pulled me in close to his chest. Utter silence descended. Peace.

"Shh…I've got you."

Wrapped together in a corona of brilliant light, he and I were bathed in balmy warmth. He'd lifted me up out of the bitter cold and pain. And his love for me…it poured into my soul like the ocean. Just like…

"…when you were five," he breathed into my forehead. And I could feel his lips and his breath mingling with my hair. I could *feel* him.

"You were there?" I whispered. "You were the one who held me when my nightmares ended?"

He nodded, rubbing his cheek against the top of my head. "Yeah," he murmured, his voice breaking.

The heat from the curved muscles of his chest radiated through his T-shirt, and I rested my cheek against him, feeling safe for the first time in months. All of my emotions came boiling to the surface, and I broke down and sobbed. There had been so much pain, so much fear, so much to regret. He kissed my temple and pulled gently on the curls at the back of my neck with his fingertips.

"Shh…" he hushed over and over, softer each time. "You're okay. I've got you now."

When I finally looked up, his eyes were brewing a bittersweet mix of joy and devastation.

"You were on the bridge tonight, too? You played 'Lullaby' for me?" I asked.

He nodded. "Catherine, I've wanted to tell you for so long, but not like this. Not now. Christ, you're only *sixteen*. You shouldn't be here yet."

And where *was* here? All I could see was light. My heart leapt into my throat. Was I dead?

"No! You're not dead…not yet. You're still holding onto my voice…still *breathing*. I don't know how."

What did he mean I was still breathing? Of course, I was breathing. My head buzzed with confusion, and I looked down. My wet, bloodied clothing had been exchanged for a white dress with a soft, stretch cotton camisole and gently flaring skirt. My silver ring lay gleaming upon my chest, my legs and feet were bare, and my skin was faintly glowing. If I wasn't dead, was I healed then?

Sorrow pulled Michael's brows together. "I'm holding your spirit, the light within you," he said. Then the circle of brilliant light that shielded us from the world began to fall away, and I could see my body lying on the ground beside us, covered in snow and spattered with Jason's blood.

"Oh, God!" I cried. "But Claire should be here by—"

His deep sigh cut me off. "Time has no meaning here. Minutes… hours here can go by in only seconds there. But there's still hope. You're still breathing." Then he brought his lips in close to my ear and whispered, "And see? Your Angel is with you."

He held me a little tighter, protectively, and nodded toward the deathly quiet me on the ground. Bending over my body was a creature of inestimable beauty. She looked up and beamed at me with an inhuman intensity that penetrated my soul, and I pressed back into Michael's arms, afraid. The Angel's eyes were huge and fairy-like, a deep iridescent blue, her hair was shorn close, the whitest blonde, and her pale, heart-shaped face shone faintly.

"It's okay, Catherine," Michael said. "That's Roshan. She's your Angel."

The Angel, Roshan, lifted her chin and vanished, leaving a cloud of tiny water droplets behind, then reappeared instantly a few inches in front of me, crouched low and up on her toes. She wore a white cotton T-shirt and ivory suede leggings. Her shoulders, chest and shins were encased in creamy leather armor, and a slender silver strap crossed over her chest, holding what looked like a sword with a twisted silver hilt on her back. One hand was resting on her bunched up legs, the other was outstretched to touch my face.

"Don't be afraid, Catherine," she said, her voice deeper and richer than I would have expected. "Michael's right. There is still hope. You may yet live."

"I have to live, Michael. My mom..." I bit down hard on my lower lip to keep it from trembling.

He held me closer. "I know."

And I knew then that he did know. He'd been there. He'd seen the whole freaking mess unfold. My mess. I looked away, ashamed. Dark memories rose from the wreckage I'd left behind—the demon's taunts, his wicked grin—and my fear rekindled. I shivered. "I think there were demons, Michael."

"I know," he said, and I looked back, startled. "I've been watching them. They've been trying to break you since I died."

"But you're safe, now," Roshan added firmly. Her tone was confident, but she and Michael kept shifting their gaze from me to the foggy light that surrounded us, as if they were watching out for something. My scalp prickled.

The circle of light continued its retreat, leaving behind watery trails of silvery blue flames that leaked into the surrounding forest, revealing hazy figures cloaked in light pacing around us. More and more of them could be seen as the light pushed back farther.

"Who are they?" I whispered.

"More Angels," Michael said, "They're protecting us. An army of demons couldn't get past them."

But someone *was* walking past them. A tall figure dressed in distressed jeans and a multi-zippered leather jacket, stepped out of the retreating wave of light. He moved toward us in slow motion, picking up speed as he approached. A shock of wild dark hair flopped down over his pierced eyebrows and sharp brown eyes, and a weathered iron cross made from two tiny nails pierced his nose. He crouched down to whisper in Michael's ear and then leaned forward on a gnarled oak root staff and stared at me, silent and motionless as a gothic tombstone. I swallowed, hard.

"Back off, Berwyn." Michael scowled in his direction. "You're seriously freaking her out."

"Ah, right," Berwyn said, settling down on the snow with his huge, long legs stretched out in front of him. He set his staff down at his side.

"You have to forgive Berwyn," Michael said, nodding in his direction. Berwyn was still staring at me, and Michael rolled his eyes. "The stare comes with the whole Guardian Angel…thing."

I looked from Berwyn to Roshan, who was also observing me carefully, and then back again. "I have two Angels?"

Roshan laughed. Berwyn snorted.

"No, Genius. Berwyn's *my* Angel," Michael said. He looked over at Berwyn and grinned wryly. "It takes a while, but he grows on you."

Berwyn's eyes flashed at me, tiny bronze flames.

Okay. Right. Sure. It all made perfect sense. My best friend was a ghost who'd been haunting me since I was born. Demons were real. Guardian Angels were real. We all had one, of course, though *some* of them were *Goth* and *Scary*. My ex-boyfriend was a closet heroin addict who just tried to kill me…did kill me…I was still confused on that point…

"Catherine…shh…" Michael soothed, but my overloaded mind ignored him. My heart started to pound, and I closed my eyes to get a grip. That's when I felt the shift. It was like my consciousness suddenly expanded. It was reaching out all on its own to explore, and I was suddenly swamped by a deluge of images filling up the dark space before me: indigo light…a silver sword…a burning palm…a flaming staff…an acoustic guitar…huge dripping, thorn-filled fangs…

"The second stage is starting, Roshan," I heard Michael whisper.

I stretched my eyes open wide, but the images remained. Panicked, I blinked rapidly until they disappeared, and I found myself still in Michael's arms. Berwyn was behind us now, his back pressed up against Michael's, scanning the perimeter of the woods, and Roshan was beside me, holding my hands. She and I were becoming brighter by the second.

Michael stroked my bare shoulder with his thumb and forefinger and whispered to his Angel, "Are you sure we're clear, Berwyn?" Berwyn gave him a terse nod. Roshan ignored them both.

"You're all right, Catherine," she said. "Your light and the images you see are part of your Luminarch."

"What's that?" The word was completely foreign to me, and their behavior was making me nervous.

She moved in closer. "Luminarch is your transition phase, your *light beginning*. Humans are hybrid creatures. They are born both flesh and spirit. During the first stage of Luminarch your spirit breaks free. In the second stage, you finally see all of the things God has done for you during your life. Humans call it a flashback."

More images were waiting, and their pull was overwhelming. I felt an instinctive urge to let go, to find out what was waiting for me, but I was worried. There was only one place all of this could be leading. I asked, "What happens after the flashback?"

"Final Judgment," Roshan said gently.

My stomach dropped. I wasn't ready to be judged, and I definitely wasn't ready to die.

Michael, I need to go back! I was so horrible! I have to make things right!

Mixed emotions crossed his face. Then he looked pleadingly at Roshan. "Can't you delay it a little longer?"

"She's ready to see what He wants her to see, Michael. It's not up to me. You know that."

Michael hesitated and then rested his forehead on my temple, spilling his warm breath like calming tea down my cheek. He pulled my hands away from Roshan and wrapped his own securely around them.

"I know what you're feeling right now. *Believe* me, I know," he said softly. "But someone once told me I had to trust that things would work out the way God wants them to. She told me I had to *believe*."

I bit my lip.

"You trust me, don't you?" He waited patiently, already knowing the answer.

I nodded, my chin quivering.

"I'm only human, Catherine. How can you trust me and not Him?" He raised his eyebrows.

You've been through all of this already? Your Luminarch? Your Final Judgment?

His silver eyes flared brilliantly. "Yeah, Catherine. It's *good*."

I looked at my beautiful Angel, suddenly torn. I'd only just met her. "If I do go back will I still be able to see Roshan?"

"Seeing Angels outside of Luminarch is a pretty rare thing," he said.

I started to panic. "What about you? I'll still be able to see you, won't I?"

His jaw twitched, and Roshan reached out and stroked my chin. "Most humans remember a light and a few images from their Luminarch," she said. "Some humans remember an out-of-body experience. Very few recall talking with those they love who've already passed on."

"You mean I might not even remember seeing Michael? Him holding me?" I looked back into Michael's face. He was struggling to keep his expression neutral. "Catherine, if you can get back, you have to go. You owe it to yourself," he said.

"But you'll still be with me even if I can't see you? Watching over me? If I go back?"

He glanced at Roshan again, and she nodded. Then he turned back to me, buried his hands in my hair and pulled my face in close, pressing his forehead against mine. "For as long as God says you need me, I swear."

"And if I die?" I whispered.

"You can't think like that."

"But...if I do..."

He pressed harder with his forehead. "You'll go *home*."

"You'll come with me?" I rubbed the side of my nose against his. It was warm and slippery wet.

"Catherine...don't..." he dropped his hands and tried to pull away, but I interlaced my fingers behind his neck and held him close.

"You'll stay with me?" I persisted.

He looked up at me through wet lashes, his breath coming in hot, ragged gasps. It puffed salty-sweet against my lips, hesitant, but filled with undying promise. "Yeah...always..."

Then Roshan's gentle voice reached in between us from far away. I felt her hand settle on my shoulder.

"Open your heart, Catherine. You're ready."

It was easy, natural, my heart opening up. Like an ocean tide rolling in and then pulling back out. I pressed forward to receive Michael's promise, closed my eyes and was swept away.

Chapter 27
The Guardian

A LIGHT AS bright as the morning sun stole Michael's face from me, and then we were free, cut adrift, blended in brilliance. Roshan said most humans remember at least a few of their Luminarch images, but who could remember or make sense of the hurricane I plunged into? My mind was nowhere near agile enough. Sound bites. Light flares. Chunks of raw emotion. They steamrolled over me too fast.

Then the next thing I knew, sharp, arguing voices were breaking through.

"You have to let go!"

"Please don't..."

The soft snick of a blade being drawn.

"Let go!"

"Cate!" Claire's voice was calling me back, but it was too far for me to go now. It was so cold out there. I wanted to stay. I was so warm and safe.

"Do it now!"

"Cate! Breathe!"

"*Please* let me stay."

The acid sting of a powerful palm blasted my cheek, and then a frozen world of excruciating pain and oxygen deprivation rushed into my body.

The light was gone. The warmth was gone. The love had faded. All that was left was pain and the overwhelming knowledge that I needed to live. I needed to live at all costs. There was something I still had to do.

"Breathe! Damn it! Don't you dare die! Mom'll kill me if you die! And then I'll kill you again! They'll have to have a closed coffin at your wake!"

And I breathed…for my mom and my dad, for Claire and for Cici, and for Mina and Michael, and for me. Yeah. For my stupid self, too. If God wanted me to live, I'd do my best to make it happen.

Claire timed the puff of my inhaler perfectly, and as the sharp, sludge-thick air squeezed into my lungs, I coughed and coughed and coughed, almost passing out again.

"Again! You stupid…" She depressed the inhaler again, and I sucked in hard. Oh God…it hurt. Everything hurt. But I pulled life back in anyway. She forced the inhaler on me several more times and then yanked her blue ski jacket off and tucked it around my chest and shoulders, spitting random curses as she did so. "Are you breathing? You better be breathing."

I dragged in another gravel-heavy breath and then looked up into her eyes. They were damp, dripping in fact, and I felt a little warmer. She cared after all.

"Yeah…she cares. She loves you, Genius." The voice, gruff but tempered with affection, came from just over Claire's shoulder. I shifted my gaze a little to the left and found Michael's anxious silver eyes shining down on me. They opened a little wider as he saw his own face reflected in my thoughts. Then his perfect lips tipped up in a full-fledged grin. My heart spilled over with relief. I could still see him.

"Hey," Michael said. "Do what your big sister says." He rubbed trembling fingers up the back of his neck. Then a black, leather-gloved hand clapped him firmly on the shoulder, and he looked sideways and grinned at Berwyn, his dark-eyed, freaky pierced Angel.

Michael whipped his face around to stare at me. "You remember Berwyn?"

My head was jammed up with pain, but I nodded my chin slightly, wincing as I sent my thoughts back to him. *He's your Goth Angel.*

Michael glanced worriedly at Berwyn. "She still sees you, man."

Then he looked at Roshan, who'd knelt down beside me, opposite Claire. "Is she still dying? Is she back in Luminarch?" His voice was controlled, but barely.

"No. She's stable," Roshan said, her large eyes calm and serene. "Just hang on a little longer, Catherine. The paramedics will be here soon." The fact that I could still see her, even though I wasn't dying anymore, didn't seem to ruffle her at all.

"Okay..." Michael said to himself, and then he looked up at the sky. "Okay...so, *now* she sees ghosts *and* Angels? I guess I can learn to deal with that." He looked back down at me and grinned.

"Cate!" Claire had to shout to get my attention. "What the hell happened out here? Where did all this blood come from? Where's Jason? He called the house. His car's here. He was looking for you."

My joy and relief evaporated. I just stared at her, dreading the next moment, and then, by way of answer, I reluctantly let my gaze drift to the edge of the cliff and back.

Her face froze. "He went over?"

I squeezed my eyes shut in reply.

"He's dead?"

"Yes."

"Oh...*shit*," she said, shivering. Then she asked point blank, "Was he trying to stop you?" She didn't have to explain her question. I glanced at Michael and saw a look of sick resignation spread over his face. We both knew what she was thinking.

"No," I said, shaking my head emphatically despite the grinding pain it sent through my shoulder.

She searched my face, weighing my shaky credibility, and then went on to say, "Cici and I were gone when you stormed out of the house. We'd left to drive Aunt Julia home. Mom was a wreck when we got back, and Dad had gone out to find you, but since you hadn't *told* them about seeing Michael die, Dad had no idea where to look." She paused and looked at me pointedly.

"Cici and I knew. She'd already guessed you'd been out here moping. But tonight...God, you've been so *stupid* lately, and we were afraid that...maybe you'd..." Her voice caught, and she paused to clear the lump from her throat. "When I saw your inhaler in the snow, I grabbed it and told Mom to call an ambulance and—"

"Mom's here?" I wanted to talk to her so badly.

"She's back at the car. She knew I'd get to you faster so she stayed to direct the paramedics. So it was an accident? Jason going over?"

I wanted desperately to explain it to her. Then she'd understand that it wasn't my fault, but with the icy air slicing in and out of my lungs, I started coughing again.

She patted my back stiffly. "Just…stay still. We'll figure it out later." Yeah. She cared. In her own way, she really did, and I'd been so nasty. I had to say something, and I cleared some of the crap out of my throat.

"I'm sorry…I've been…such a brat, Claire."

Her shivering lips pressed together, and then she looked down at her hands and said magnanimously, "Well…I guess you can't really help it sometimes."

But I hadn't said what I really wanted to say. The thought shouted out loud and clear in my head: *I love you, Claire.* I couldn't remember ever telling her that, saying the words out loud.

"You haven't. At least not for a long time," Michael murmured. His eyebrows went up ever so slightly. They said, haven't you learned anything tonight? When did he become the smart one?

He bent down close to my ear and whispered, "Seventeen years hanging around Angels. Some of it had to get through my caveman skull eventually." Berwyn choked back a laugh, and Michael shoved him, but Berwyn didn't move. He was a rock.

Michael was right, *obviously*…so, after wrestling down my pride, I said, "Claire?"

She raised her eyebrows.

"I love you," I said. The words were barely recognizable, but she understood. She added a colossal eye roll to her raised brows.

"Okay. Sure," she said. "I love you, too. Now will you please shut up?"

I closed my eyes then, giving in to exhaustion, trusting Claire, Michael, and the Angels to keep watch for me. I wasn't aware of the paramedics until they had me surrounded. They strapped an oxygen mask to my face and hooked up an I.V., then transferred me to a stretcher. Whatever they put in the I.V. took the edge off the pain, and I drifted in and out of consciousness during the long and slippery journey out of the woods. Along the way, I heard musical voices, people conferring with Michael, Roshan and Berwyn, but I could only make out some of the words—DFZ, hell of a breach, Decimus, the First Guard, monstrously huge power signature—none of it made any sense to me, and I thought maybe I was dreaming until my mom found me in the middle of the moonlit field.

Her coat was unzipped, and her lips were drawn tight. She was trying to keep up with the paramedics as they approached the ambulance in the parking lot. Its back doors were already open, throwing a mellow glow out into the night.

"Oh, Catherine!" she cried. "Oh thank God! What happened? Look at you..." She touched my face and hair, her hands like ice, trying to locate the source of the blood she found there.

Cici squeezed in next to her, fighting back tears, and grabbed my hand. "Why didn't you talk to me?" she asked. "You should have talked to me!"

"I'm sorry...I'm so sorry..." I whispered, my own eyes tearing up, but my voice was thin, and they couldn't hear me through the oxygen mask with the paramedics shouting out vitals in the background. Then the sweep of halogen headlights washed over me, and I turned my head toward the engine purr of another car splashing into the parking area. My dad? I needed to talk to him, too.

But the maroon Mercedes that slid to a halt at the curb wasn't my dad's car. My eyes went wide with mounting anxiety. They were glued to the passenger side door that was opening, to the dark-haired, icy blue-eyed woman who was stepping out into the snow in her Gucci high-heeled shoes.

My mom glanced over her shoulder at the sound of the door opening, and then she called sharply, "Claire!" She pointed at the couple stumbling toward us through the soggy snow. The woman's eyes searched the dark lot and field. Her voice cut a razor sharp swath through the night.

"Where's Jason? Where's my son?"

Claire moved to block their path while my mother whispered urgently to the two paramedics who were attending me, "Get my daughter in the ambulance."

But it was too late. Another paramedic was already walking toward the Kings, and everything slowed down.

"What did you say?" Mrs. King asked him. "No. Oh no! NO! OH GOD! *JASON!*"

The two paramedics lifted the stretcher and shoved it into the ambulance, and my mom climbed in after me. Mrs. King's screams wound their way into the ambulance after us.

"OH GOD! That filthy little middle-class *whore!*" Then the doors slammed shut, muffling but not cutting off her cries. "It's HER fault! Oh my *GOD!* My son…"

My thoughts reached out for Michael.

Michael?

He bent over me. "Yeah, baby…I'm here. We're all here. Roshan and Berwyn have just faded from your view."

Can I throw up now? Please? Can I? I need to throw up now. Michael?

One of the paramedics lifted up another vial of medication and prepared to add it to my I.V., but my eyes were on Michael. I still needed him like I needed to breathe.

He brushed his warm ethereal lips against my forehead. "We'll be here when you wake up," he whispered. Then a wave of warmth hit my forearm, rushed through my veins, and swamped the pitching thoughts in my head with…nothing. I never wanted anything more in my life.

～∞～

Sound came back first. A heart monitor. The reassuring noise wrapped itself around the sensations of cool, dry sheets, clean bandages, smooth plastic tubing. I flexed my fingers and felt an I.V.

catheter and tape tugging at the skin on the back of my hand. I was in the hospital.

I breathed in through the oxygen tubes that clung to my nose and discovered the scent of Higher. Michael was here. I opened my eyes and rolled my head to the side, sending a dull, grating ache through my tightly-bound shoulder.

Only the dim light fixture above and behind the bed was on, and it threw comforting, organized shadows of hospital equipment onto the pastel walls. And there against the closest wall, sitting on the floor with his knees pulled up in front of him, his face pressed awkwardly into his Angel's leather-bound shoulder, was Michael, sound asleep. His mouth hung slack, slightly open, and his dark lashes were soft against his cheeks. His fingers crested the summit of his knees, except for the thumb of his right hand, which was hooked through a fraying hole in his light blue jeans.

I bit my lip to steady it, marveling at the knowledge that he'd been there for me, selflessly guiding me and comforting me with his music since I was born. How had I received this gift? Why? And why hadn't he?

My eyes drifted to the pale, heart-shaped face of Berwyn, his dark Angel. He was staring at me with an intensity I was becoming familiar with, but this time I stared back. My eyes narrowed. Why had Michael been left alone in the woods these last four months? After all he'd been through in his life, why had he been trapped there, left to wonder if God had forsaken him.

The powerful creature narrowed his dark eyes back. Then without warning, he was just a puff of bronze mist rolling across the tile floor toward me. As he moved away from Michael's side, Michael fell in the direction he'd been leaning, fading until he was no longer visible.

The mist took shape again close to the bed, and when Berwyn's face reappeared, his untamed eyes were only inches from my own. I was startled, but tried not to show it. Then I saw Roshan sitting near me on the other side of the bed. She observed Berwyn with the same inhuman intensity that she watched over me, and my fear dissipated. I knew instinctively she would protect me from anything.

"Why isn't Michael waking up?" I asked him. My throat was dry, congested, my voice thick.

He looked at me as if the question offended him. "I'm suppressing his consciousness," Berwyn said. "He's been awake since Christmas Eve *worrying* about you. He finally conked out a few hours ago when your fever broke. I'm not letting him wake up yet. You humans need your sleep." He stopped talking abruptly and went back to staring at me, half his face cloaked in darkness, the other half marked by long prickly shadows that stretched from the tiny silver thorns piercing his eyebrows. The effect was unnerving.

I was furious with myself for dragging Michael into my personal emotional hell hole. I looked down at my hands which were resting on top of the clean white sheet. My blood had backed up several inches into the clear plastic I.V. tubing, and I pulled my hand up to examine it, dragging the tangled tubing with it.

"It's fine," Roshan murmured. "The nurses will be back in a little while to adjust it." When I looked back up at Berwyn, I caught the tail end of a shudder shaking off his shoulders. His eyes darted away from the blood in the tubing and back to my face.

"So you can stop worrying, kitten," Berwyn said. "Michael is safe."

But that reminded me why I was angry in the first place, and I sat up, dragging the oxygen tubes from my nose, and waving my I.V. taped hand at him. Pain ripped through my shoulder, chest and back, and I was lightheaded, but I didn't care.

"Maybe he is *now*, but what about *before?* How could you just leave him to wander the woods alone for months after he died? He thought God had abandoned him!" As I railed against him, Berwyn's eyes darkened and began to smolder. A few deep orange flames spilled from his fist and rippled down the side of his gnarled staff. He looked down at the floor, and I wondered what dangerous emotions I'd awakened within him. Roshan stretched her hand out protectively over me, whispering, "Catherine, it is not wise to question a Guardian Angel's loyalty or skill. They don't like it."

"And *you* would know about *that*, wouldn't you Roshan?" He'd snapped his head up so fast, I'd missed the movement. His wild eyes were back to brown. "Ah…but the difference between Michael and our kitten here is that *she* has no idea what we've been up against." He gave Roshan a tight grin and then leveled a dark Angelic gaze in my direction. "I think we need to change that." He stripped off one of his gloves and held out his hand to me, palm up and open.

"Berwyn, don't," Roshan said. "A human may only see her Luminarch when she is dying."

"Oh, Roshan, we won't show her the *whole* thing…just the part about the woods. God won't care." A glint appeared in his eyes—they actually flamed up a little—and he added, "Then she'll understand what we've been *wasting our time* doing."

He crouched down lower on his black boot-covered toes so he could look me in the eye. "You want to know, right? What I was doing while Michael pouted in the woods?" He nodded encouragingly toward his hand. His lips turned up slightly in what passed for an inviting grin, and despite the tiny flames in his eyes, I found myself wanting to trust him. He *was* an Angel after all. I extended my hand…

"Berwyn! Step back!" Roshan warned. Her fingers caressed the hilt of her sword. She'd gone from gentle maiden to warrior princess in the space of a few seconds. "And Michael would never—"

"Go on, kitten. Don't worry about Michael. He's—"

"Awake. And very pissed off," Michael said. I turned my head to see him leaning over the bed, his steely eyes trained on his Angel. "What're you doing, man? Don't you think she's been traumatized enough for one week?"

Berwyn shrugged and the flames in his eyes went out. "She doesn't think I protected you well enough." He shot me a sideways glance and then curled in on himself, a shrinking bronze mist, reappearing hunched against the dark, foggy window, brooding as he stared out past his reflection.

Michael looked from me to Berwyn and then back to me, at a loss for words. His eyes were heavy with fatigue, and he looked somehow… older. He reached out and touched my forehead, nodded quietly to himself, then asked, "How's the shoulder pain?"

"Fine," I said. It sucked actually, but I was sick of being the weak one. He picked up my thoughts and rolled his eyes. Then I explained quietly, "Berwyn was about to show me why he never came when you were trapped in the woods."

Michael glanced over his shoulder at his Angel, and a look passed between them that spoke of a shared past hidden from me. Michael said, "Berwyn's been with me since before I was born, Catherine. He's never left my side. I just refused to *see* him."

"He was with you the whole time?" I looked over at Berwyn, but I was still confused, and I cried out to him, "But if Michael couldn't see you, why couldn't he at least leave the woods? He could have come home with me! I could have—"

Berwyn's eyes started to flame up again.

"Catherine, shh," Michael hushed. He rubbed his hand up the back of his neck. "Baby, it was so long ago for me, I forgot you'd see it that way. I know it looked to *you* like I was trapped in the woods, but sometimes traps aren't what they seem. Sometimes they're built up around us for our protection. I was *safe* in the woods. The Angels had them completely surrounded, a whole battalion of them. Not to keep me *in*, but to keep the demons *out*. After I died, God thought I needed a safe, quiet place to think."

"So…Berwyn's the one who kept turning you to dust and sucking you back into the woods?"

"It was painless," Berwyn growled from the window.

"For my protection, Catherine."

"I'm sorry…" I murmured to his Angel. "But Michael, it makes no sense to me! Why did God leave you here on Earth to think after you died? Why didn't He just bring you home? Take you up to heaven? You'd turned your life around. You *believed*."

Michael looked down at his fingernails, then crossed his arms over his chest, his eyes twinkling with slightly less than angelic charm. "Well, it may have had something to do with the fact that I told Archangel Michael to take God's eternal afterlife and shove it up someone else's ass when I died. I still wanted things my own way. I didn't trust Him. I wasn't ready…" His voice trailed off, and he glanced down at the wide leather strap that crossed over his chest. He pulled the strap forward, jostling the roots on his back. I wanted to ask what they were for, but his last remark made me uneasy. A tiny claw teased my conscience, and then I realized what he was saying.

"Ready for what? Heaven or watching over *me*?"

"Oh, he was ready for Heaven all right, not pretty, but ready," Berwyn put in from the window.

"Be quiet, Berwyn," Michael said, but his shoulders and arms flexed subtly, just like they'd done when Jason approached me in the woods. My eyes flew open wide.

"You…you…fight those things? Those demons? For me?" I cried.

Michael set his chin, but his eyes pleaded with me. "Look, Catherine…you almost died like four times in the last twenty-four hours. The doctors had a tough time stabilizing you. We're not doing this tonight."

He was right. I was exhausted, bruised from head to toe, and the pain in my shoulder was beginning to radiate down my arm. But I needed answers. I'd spent the last four months fighting against something I couldn't see, I had Angels fussing over me, demons taunting me, and now I'd learned Michael had put himself in harm's way to protect me. I needed to know why. I looked to Roshan for help.

"He's right. You need your rest," she said quietly.

I glanced back at Berwyn, who sighed and then vanished, reappearing next to the bed. "You need to tell her, Michael. She's going to find out anyway. She's starting to *see* them now. Nasty little hell-dwellers…"

"Not tonight, Berwyn."

"At least show her the sword."

"He has a *sword*?" I asked.

"It's a good sword," said Berwyn.

"Will you shut *up*?" Michael shouted back.

"She'll never sleep until you tell her, and then *you'll* never sleep," Berwyn said.

Seeing the logic in that, Roshan was nodding now, too.

Michael looked at them both, weary and beaten. "It's hard enough just dealing with being human. Why does *she* have to worry about the rest of it?"

"Because we're at *war*, kid. And she's in the middle of it. So are you."

"What *war?*" I demanded to know. "And what does it have to do with Michael and me?"

"The war over souls," Roshan said quietly, and Michael groaned. Roshan gave him a warning look and then went on to explain. "God sent Michael back in time to be your Guardian in this war."

"You mean like a Guardian Angel?"

Berwyn coughed. "He wishes…"

Michael gave him a look of extreme impatience.

Roshan's eyes flashed at both of them. "I am your Angel," she said. "But God saw fit to give you a human Guardian as well."

"Why?" I asked her.

She pressed her lips together, considering her words. "There is a prophecy about you, Catherine. Satan and his army of demons know its content. We do not. Somehow they have discovered it, and they are guarding it closely. On Heaven's side, we have no way to find out what it says because the Angel who revealed it is bound to secrecy. We don't even know who that Angel is. But we know the prophecy concerns you, and that Satan is desperate to make sure it is never fulfilled."

"How do you know it's about me if you don't even know what it says?" I asked, bewildered. She lowered her beautiful eyes.

Berwyn answered for her. "Because Satan's been plotting your destruction since before you were born, kitten."

That sunk like a bomb down my throat. I started to shake. It was an involuntary, gut deep reaction. Nausea churned in my stomach.

So I've been targeted by the Devil himself? I looked at Michael.

His jaw flexed and then he nodded. "But Roshan and I have sworn to protect you. We even have some back-up now thanks to your call for help on the bridge." Michael sat down close to me. "Baby, you're okay now. We'll keep you safe."

But that wasn't the pledge I wanted to hear. If Angels surrounded the woods to protect him from demons, then the demons were after him, too. He was in just as much danger as I was. I wanted him to be safe, too. That's all I'd ever wanted for him. "What about you?" I asked him. My voice was thin, my airways tighter. My shoulder started to throb.

"You should put your oxygen back on," he urged.

"Michael," I said softly. "Please…"

He grinned wryly. "Well. They can't kill me. I'm already dead." I had a feeling he'd faced threats worse than death. When I didn't laugh, he lifted his chin and said confidently, "I have Berwyn to protect me."

Berwyn towered over him. "He watches you. I watch him," Berwyn said, flicking his thumb toward Michael and then tucking his lightly-flaming staff under his folded arms. Berwyn was larger than the demon I'd seen in my room, heavier, and scarier in his own way. I had no doubt he could handle himself in a fight. In fact, he looked like he craved it.

But I was still unconvinced.

"The sword," Berwyn prompted.

Michael studied me, then reached decisively up over his shoulder and pulled the tangle of roots from the leather sheath on his back. The moment he touched them, the roots formed the hilt of a weathered steel sword, twisting tightly into a shape that perfectly fit his hand. The wide blade glowed with silvery, slow-burning flames that licked hungrily at the dry, hospital air. It was marred by years of use, battle-worn, battle-ready.

He stretched out his arm, balancing his weapon expertly in his hand. Then he flipped the blade up flat onto his palms and brought it down before me. "This is Foresight," he said, regarding the blade with equal parts reverence and affection. He glanced up at me to see if I was satisfied yet. The look in his eyes was so earnest, so eager to dispel my fears, how could I not be? How could I show him anything less than my complete faith in him?

"My Guardian, huh?" I said, giving him a slight grin.

He shrugged, then grinned back, and my heart felt a little lighter knowing I had him on my side. I wondered again why God had given me these gifts—an Angel and a Guardian, and the ability to see them, and trust in them, and feel safe—when Michael had suffered alone for so long. It seemed so unfair.

Michael's eyes softened as he followed my thoughts. "Oh, Baby... don't you see? When Berwyn couldn't reach me because I was too stupid, too pissed off, too stubborn, God sent me just what I needed." When I screwed my forehead up in confusion, he leaned in closer, saturating the air I breathed with Higher, and whispered the answer in my ear:

"He sent me you."

He grazed my cheek with the tip of his forefinger, which had begun to glow softly silver, and I felt a shadow of the love I'd felt when he'd gathered my soul up into his arms.

"I love you, too," I whispered.

"I know," he said, grinning.

"Michael..." Roshan called to him, and he slowly withdrew his hand. There was a knock at the door, and it swung open with a faint creak, letting a shaft of light from the hall into the room. A nurse bustled in carrying a small syringe, which she set on the bedside table.

Berwyn and Roshan disappeared, and Michael sheathed his sword and backed away from the bed. He was quiet while he watched the nurse cycle through her tasks.

Michael? Do you think anyone will believe that I didn't try to kill myself? That Jason attacked me?

"Your family will, your friends, too, eventually anyway. They love you more than you know."

Then where are they? Why aren't they here?

I'd almost died, and I was alone. Where were my mom and dad? Where were Cici and Claire? Michael didn't answer right away, and then he said, "It's late. They were here off and on all day. They'll be back."

The nurse took my vitals, replaced the oxygen tubes under my nose, picked up the syringe and injected its pain-relieving solution into the I.V. port. "You'll feel better soon, honey," she said, patting my arm before leaving. I winced as I lay back down on the bed and shifted position. Then a gentle wave of drowsiness washed over me, and I let my thoughts drift toward Michael on a lazy tide.

They're not finished with us, are they Michael? The demons?

He moved away from the wall and sat down on the end of the bed. "We'll face them together, Catherine. You, me, Roshan, Berwyn… you know that now, right?"

Yeah…

"And we have one huge advantage the demons don't."

What's that?

"God," he said, his eyes flaring a little. Then he pulled an acoustic guitar out of thin air. The beat-up instrument was almost as battle-worn as his sword. My mellowing thoughts blended the two in my head.

What are you going to do with that?

He adjusted the guitar under his arm and pulled it in comfortably against his chest. "You haven't gone to bed without a lullaby since you were…maybe ten months old?" His eyes crinkled up at some memory, and he added, "You were an *adorable* toddler, but those preteen years…" he pretended to shiver, and then he grinned. I wished for something to throw through his head, and his smile grew wider, touching his whole face.

Then my music lover, my "or something," my *Guardian* picked out a few notes on his guitar and began to sing…just for me.

The Guardian's Playlist

"Flares"
**Written by James Barry, Daniel O'Donoghue, Mark Sheehan
Performed by The Script**

"Lullaby"
Written & performed by Shawn Mullins

"Troublemaker"
Written by Rivers Cuomo
Performed by Weezer

"Wolves"
Written and performed by Sean Smith, Gavin Butler, Bob
Davies, Matthew Davies, Rhys Lewis & Snoz Lawrence of The
Blackout

"Hold On Till May"
Written by Michael & Victor Fuentes
Performed by Pierce the Veil (feat. Lindsey Stamey)

"Kryptonite"
Written by Brad Arnold, Todd Harrell & Matt Roberts
Performed by 3 Doors Down

"The Lion Sleeps Tonight"
Written by George Weiss, Luigi Creatore, Hugo Peretti &
Solomon Linda
Performed by The Tokens

"Mirrors"
Written by Justin Neme & John Price
Performed by House of Cards

"It's Only Life"
Written by Kate Voegele & James McGorman
Performed by Kate Voegele

"Point of No Return"
Written by Dustin Bates, Robert Graves, Rob Hawkins,
& Alan Powell
Performed by Starset

"Sweet Child O'Mine"
Written by W. Axl Rose, Slash, Duff McKagan, Izzy Stradlin &
Steven Adler
Performed by Guns N' Roses

"Feel Good Drag"
Written by Stephen Christian, Joseph Milligan, Deon Rexroat
& Nathan Young
Performed by Anberlin

"Lifeline"
Written by Thomas De Longe
Performed by Angels & Airwaves

"Halo"
Written by Dustin Bates & Rob Hawkins
Performed by Starset

"Ghost"
Performed by Slash (feat. Ian Astbury)
Written by Ian Astbury & Saul Hudson

<u>*Disclaimer</u>
The songwriters listed above do not necessarily endorse the
novel, *The Guardian's Playlist,* nor the ideas contained within
it. Permission to reprint copyrighted lyrics has been obtained
where applicable.

Turn the page for a preview of

The Devil's Playlist
Book Two of The Playlist Trilogy

The Devil's Playlist
a novel

by

J. Powell Ogden

www.JPowellOgden.com
Where do your demons live?

SPARKSTREET Media, LLC.

*The brave, impetuous heart yields
everywhere to the subtle, contriving mind.*
—Matthew Arnold

Prologue

THE NEWBORN ANGEL *took his time getting to his feet. He had knowledge of this place called Earth, Heaven's most distant outpost, but he was experiencing it for the first time. He flexed his power signature—the energy field that housed his spirit. It was fast. How fast he wasn't sure, but it responded to his thoughts almost before he completed them. He grinned. There was strength, too. Not as much as he would have hoped for, but enough to take on almost any Angel or demon here on Earth.*

And which would he take on?

He had a will, too. One that teetered on the edge.

He wrinkled his nose, acutely sensing the room in which he stood. It was a small room with a drafty, paint-peeling window that let in the only light—a neon sign across the street: The Shrunken Head. He smelled the fumes of cheap beer and saliva clinging to the sides of crumpled plastic cups. Discarded, the cups scraped across the concrete as another couple stumbled through them on their way out of the bar.

Inside the room the smell of two sweat-drenched bodies lingered. He shuddered. Humans. There were two of them, tangled up in sheets on the bed. Male and Female He made them. One incomplete without the other. Surely, that was the kiss of death for their inferior, organically enslaved species.

The Angel's nearly translucent blue eyes darkened as he watched them. Janine, curled up on her side, her auburn curls dark against the pillow, and Aidan, tucked in close behind her, young and built tough, his arm flung over her in an unconscious, useless bid to protect her. They slept soundly, completely vulnerable. Another kiss of death, this biological need for sleep. The list of their failings went on and on.

The Angel knew God loved him. He already felt that love brewing in his heart. He knew what God was offering him, but he wanted more. It was his right, his freedom to choose to walk away from these humans, to live and love as he pleased, to exist on his own, answering to no one. If he left now, he could avoid the messy meeting with the Archangel in which he was required to state his intention to serve God or himself. His eyes grew darker. He could let his absence speak for itself.

But as the thought to leave took shape in his mind, an incredible pressure engulfed him. The fingers of a powerful hand twisted themselves from behind into his dark hair and an oiled blade, cocked at a deadly forty-five degree angle, materialized above his right shoulder.

"Don't say it," Archangel Michael hissed. "If you say it, I'll slash you from shoulder to hip, scattering you across the mouth of every black hole in the universe. You will never see light again."

"What is this?" the young Angel demanded. Coercion wasn't part of the script. It was against every promise God had ever made. "Why should I pledge loyalty to a God who shatters his own rules? Just because I'm the first who's dared to—"

"Don't flatter yourself, Yearling. You are not the first."

The young Angel searched his inborn knowledge of the world more carefully. Yes, another had rejected his charge, and not long ago, but that didn't mean he couldn't follow suit. Incensed, his nearly black eyes flamed up. Bronze sparks rippled across his power signature, which he knew was no match for the Archangel. "Who gave you the right to override my free will?"

Archangel Michael whipped the angry Angel around, his blade still poised to deal the Blow of Oblivion, and said quietly, "You did."

At that moment, the power signature of a brand new human sparked to life in the room. The newborn Angel fell to his knees as an indelible need to nurture and protect the tiny creature engraved itself on his heart.

"What have you done to me?" the dark Angel cried. "Oh, God…"

"It's called love, Berwyn," Archangel Michael said softly, lowering his sword.

"I know that! It's unnatural! It's not pure!" Berwyn's breath came in panicked gasps as the new human's unique traits unveiled themselves. It was courageous to the point of blind stupidity. It had a natural and unfettered willingness to break every rule. Worst of all, it had the capacity to love with reckless abandon.

The impossibility of the Angel's task was obvious. "How am I supposed to protect it?" Berwyn cried.

"Him," replied the Archangel, bestowing a rare grin. "Protect 'him.' We need him, Berwyn. His name is Michael, Guardian of the Little Light, and you were created to love and protect him. You'll figure it out. Trust me. I talked to someone who knows."

Then the Archangel disappeared.

Part One:
Under Pressure

Chapter One

JASON

PAIN. IT WAS the only thing that was familiar when I came to. That doubled-over cramping in my legs and gut. That deep ache in my bones. That stale nausea creeping up the back of my throat. Then there was that restless, panicky feeling, because you *know* it's only going to get worse. I needed to get home to my room where I had an Eight-ball of heroin stashed away inside my computer, but where was I? It felt like ice water was running through my brain. I opened my eyes and…*shit.* There was ice water running through my brain.

I was lying face down in the Rocky River.

Listen again to what I'm saying:

My face. Was completely. Submerged.

I yanked my head out of the water. The sky was black. Snow was falling. I was freezing, and I had no idea how I'd gotten there. Then the shakes hit. Withdrawal shakes you from the inside out. I started to fall forward onto my hands, but my hands were gone.

I couldn't see them.

Fear. My world was now just two elements. Pain. And Fear. That was my last thought before my "face" went underwater again. My "face" was drowning, and Fear was making it impossible for me to save it. So I ordered myself, as I often do, to push the Fear back. To master the Pain. To control that small piece of ground that exists within my head. I'd conquered that battlefield a long time ago. But the ground in my head was expanding. I could now feel the ice clinging to the riverbank clawing my skin.

That ice was fifteen feet away.

Fear won, and my head exploded with noise. It was the noise of a billion plus brain cells shouting out possible explanations for what was happening. A hallucination? A nightmare? Above the noise I heard a voice. Dark and sweet. Slow and deliberate. Ancient and beautiful.

"You're dead, Jason. You fell off the cliff. Remember?"

The noise died down as my memory came back. Just pieces. Cate's betrayal. Rage. The fight through the woods. A bright light. Then nothing.

My life was over? The concept made no sense to me. None. I was in intense pain. I was thinking. I was feeling. My life was obviously not "over." It was—

"*Jason*...I can help you focus," said the voice.

It pulled. It promised. It penetrated my skull.

That voice *wanted* me.

And I *wanted* it.

I wanted it like I wanted the heroin that would put an end to this current bout of dope sickness. I wanted it more. I'd never heard that voice before. Knew I couldn't trust it. But it offered the possibility of gaining knowledge, the one thing I needed most at that moment.

But I couldn't let the voice know that.

I pulled my face back up out of the water, more by force of will than physical power. I couldn't see my legs, arms, or hands, but I knew where they were...generally. I knew because they were freezing, trembling, cramping up in their nothingness. I wanted to crawl out of them, but instead I held still and set my jaw. First and foremost when facing the unknown: show no fear. No weakness. No *need*. Definitely not that.

I lifted my chin and looked for the source of the voice.

Twenty feet in front of me, a dark figure was standing tall and relaxed on the bank of the river. Human in form, but possessing an inhuman intensity that physically challenged me from across the river.

It pressed down on me. I lifted my chin higher. The face of the thing shone brightly. It was heart-shaped, rounded through the cheeks and sharp through the jaw. It had jet black hair that flowed out freely from its head, like it was blowing in some breeze I couldn't feel. It wasn't wearing a shirt, and its chest and abs were all smoothly developed. Indented like a human's in all of the right places. Not huge. Not bigger than me. It studied me with shiny, wide set black eyes. They were deep like the night sky. They looked *through* me.

I blinked and the thing was ten feet closer.

"Jason, I understand your needs," it said. "I can give you answers. I can take your pain away. I just need one thing in return." Then the pressure it produced, its power, began to pulse hard and fast. I almost fell back in the water the force was so goddamn strong. My ears popped. The thing's eyes got bigger. It grinned, waiting.

I'd either fallen down the bad heroin rabbit hole, or everything Cate had said was true. The ache in my bones intensified. The nausea worsened. I fought to control the shakes as best I could. And I held my tongue, because if it was true, if I was dead, I hadn't yet figured out how I was going to outsmart the Devil.

Unfortunately, the Devil held his tongue, too. And so we were reduced to a staring contest, the Devil and me. How juvenile. How effective, because…shit, I was sick.

"Withdrawal symptoms can last a long time in Hell," the Devil said.

My heart stalled, but still I said nothing, hoping for more.

"Perpetually long," he added.

No. I'd hold out this time. I would. From all the ridiculous movies Cate made me watch last summer, selling my soul to the Devil was *not* the way to go. But what did I really *know* about any of that?

Absolutely nothing.

"I'm fine," I said.

"Sure you are." This time the silky voice whispered inside my head. Teased. I staggered backward, tripped, and found myself face down in the water again, my nose sniffing shale. I pushed away from it reflexively with my mind and ended up on my knees, kneeling before him. The Devil's hot, uncomfortable pressure overwhelmed me. My stomach rolled. Hot bile scalded the back of my throat.

"You can vomit now. It won't bother me. I've seen it all before."

Could he read my mind? I attempted to douse my thoughts—memories of other nights filled with pain and cold sweat and vomit, wondering if he'd been there, too.

"No. I can't read your mind, Jason. I could lie and tell you I can, but you're too smart for that. I know what you're thinking, because I've been watching you. I watch all of you. You would eventually figure that out, and then where would that leave us? What would that do to the seed of trust growing within you? I can feel its tiny roots begging to be set free. Let them go. Wouldn't that make this easier?"

I couldn't help but laugh. The Devil thought he could convince me to trust him? I swallowed hard. "I don't think so."

"You want to trust me," the Devil said. The whisper puffed against my ear and a new wave of cramps racked my legs, cutting my mirth off at the knees. I lost my balance, but stopped myself with my right hand on the sharp shale before my face hit the water. I was already learning to function in this post-death nightmare. I didn't need him.

"Suit yourself," he said. "But I'll leave you with some music. I know how much you enjoyed Catherine's music." Then he was gone and guitar chords were licking my eardrums.

Great. The Toadies' "Possum Kingdom." The Devil had a sense of humor.

Then came the vomit. Oh shit…I hated this part.

Chapter Two

CATE

I SEE ANGELS and ghosts. They're here to protect me. You would think that would be enough to solidify my faith. It should be rock solid. I should be drifting through life in a state of unshakeable serenity.

Right.

You try staying serene with the knowledge that Satan wants you dead. *You* try finding your "Zen" place knowing that *Satan,* Ye Old Brimstone *Blowhard* himself, has been whispering his black heart out, plotting your destruction since before you were born. And that's what he does. Whisper. So quietly, you won't even know he's there until it's too late. It's over. You're either dead or broken so badly you wish you were.

I know. Satan almost succeeded with me. Three times in the last forty-eight hours.

First, there was my pitiful caving to the demon-inspired despair that almost drove me off a bridge. Then there was that little tussle with Jason, my homicidal, heroin-addicted ex-boyfriend who tried to push me off a cliff, and finally, my damn near suffocation courtesy of my own asthma deep in Lewis Woods. Without my Angel and my human Guardian fighting for me, I never would have made it. I would have given up. In the end, I fought hard to live, too. I fought because I thought maybe, just *maybe*, I could make up for all the mistakes I'd made during those demon-clouded days. But that was before I knew—

"You're spiraling again."

"*Michael…*"

"*Catherine…*" Michael said back, mimicking my whine. He had it down pat, and he should, poor kid. He'd had to listen to it since the day I was born.

Michael grinned. "*Oh* yeah. Whining's one of your specialties. You're an all-star."

Michael is my human Guardian. He and my Angel keep me safe, and right now he was leaning over my hospital bed, his luminous silver eyes not far from my own, daring me not to smile back. I couldn't let him win. I wasn't in the mood. So before the corners of my lips twitched upward, I grabbed my pillow from behind my back and sent it flying through his head. It smacked with a soft thud against the wall and fell to the floor. Michael disappeared.

Michael is also a ghost.

He died last August. After that he was trapped in Lewis Woods, and I was the only one who could see him. I spent four months trying to free him, which annoyed the hell out of him. He wasn't in the "mood" to be rescued. Then when *I* almost died, God released him from the woods, healed him, and sent him back to a time before I was born so he, along with my Angel, could protect me from Satan, who wants me dead. So now we're back to the beginning of my current rant.

Michael reappeared by the window, leaned back against the sill, and ran a hand through his shaggy hair. Michael, unlike my Angel, can also hear my thoughts. He didn't like them.

"It's true," I said, clearing my pneumonia-clogged throat. "I've ruined the lives of everyone around me, and there's nothing I can do to change that."

"Catherine, you didn't mean to—"

My cold stare broke him off midsentence.

"Irritable kitten," observed Berwyn, Michael's freaky-pierced Goth Angel who stood guard next to him. Michael thumbed the wide leather strap that crossed his chest, the one that held Foresight, his battle-worn sword, in a sheath on his back.

"Yeah," Michael agreed, not taking his eyes off me.

Berwyn fell to staring at me, too. That's a Guardian Angel's specialty. Staring with an intensity that can peel paint off cars.

Sure, I was testy. Last night I let Michael lull me to sleep thinking I could start over. That everything was going to work out. With Michael and my beautiful Angel, Roshan, on my side, how could it not? But Michael and Roshan kept something from me. They didn't *tell* me about the worst of the damage I'd caused. I knew now, and there would be no starting over. All I could do was try to prevent more harm from coming to the people I cared about.

"There has to be a way to find out what the prophecy says about me and how to fulfill it," I said. "I want it done. I want it over with. Until I do, everyone around me is at risk, including you." I looked at Michael pointedly. Berwyn snorted. Michael opened his mouth to protest, no doubt ready to extol Berwyn's many demon-squashing talents, but Roshan cut him off.

"Catherine, Angels the world over have been listening for whispers of the prophecy's content for years, but there has been nothing. The only proof we have of its existence is the fact that Satan showed up on the day you were conceived to begin his campaign for your destruction. He has devoted a great deal of resources to that end. At this point, it is impossible to guess why."

That answer wasn't good enough. I bit my lip and looked back at Michael. "What if I'm supposed to be some kind of demon destroyer, you know? Like a vampire slayer?"

One side of Michael's mouth curled up as he conjured a visual of that—me and my smallish frame doing battle with demons—but he was already shaking his head no. "Unlikely. Living humans aren't even in the same dimension as demons. There's no way for you to attack them directly."

"What about crosses and holy water?"

"Myth and myth."

"Ancient prayers? Incantations?"

The grin on his lips grew. "Catherine, there are no magic words or objects that can fend off demons. All you need is us and your faith."

"Okay, *fine*." I grabbed another scenario out of my stockpile of

Syfy channel movie memories. "Then maybe I'm going to ring in the Apocalypse? Give birth to the Antichrist?"

Michael lost the grin. His eyes met mine. Our visions matched. Me pregnant with a black-eyed, two-horned devil baby. Try thinking about giving birth to *that*.

"How 'bout *not*," Michael said. He turned to Roshan, his voice rising an octave. "That can't even happen, can it?"

"Michael, you know as well as I do that hybrid creatures and creatures of pure spirit cannot mix," she replied evenly.

A muscle in Michael's jaw twitched. Her correction stung.

"Well, Satan found out about me somehow," I said. "Someone has to know *something*. If we could find that person, maybe they could tell us."

Michael, hugged his arms in close to his chest, and my heart leapt at a new possibility. "What about Michael's dad? Before he became a cop, Aidan Casey said he wanted to help the Archangel Michael with his work here on Earth. He had the Archangel's name tattooed on his arm. Maybe Aidan actually *saw* the Archangel. Maybe the prophecy was given to him."

Roshan narrowed her eyes at Michael, who'd wrapped his fingers tightly around the sword and Angel wing tattoo on his bicep. It was identical to the tattoo his father had. "Yes. We have considered that."

"Then why haven't you investigated it?"

"Because my dad's *dead*," Michael interjected.

"Well…can't you, you know, just ask him? You're—" The expression on his face cut me off. He shook his head slightly and looked out the window, and I got the feeling I'd crossed a line I shouldn't have crossed.

Berwyn answered for him. "Michael's father is beyond our reach, kitten. He is home in Heaven where he belongs."

"I'm sorry. I didn't mean to…" my voice trailed off, and my hands began to shake. I felt so powerless.

Michael disappeared from the window and reappeared close to my hospital bed, saying softly, "Things will work out the way God wants them to. *You* told me that, remember? You gotta trust us. We'll protect you and your family from Satan's influence. That's our job. *Your job is to live your life the best you know how.*"

"Sure. Live my life. The life I've totally fucked up in the last few months."

Michael rubbed the back of his neck. "Christ, I've been a bad influence on you."

Berwyn coughed. "We can't all be Angels, Glory Boy."

"Shut up, Berwyn. You're a bad influence too."

"He is?" I asked.

"You like Butthole Surfers' "Pepper," Michael said. "Where'd you think that musical preference came from? Your mom? Roshan?"

I studied the strange Angel with the multiple body piercings, trying to figure him out, but his eyes just flashed at me, then he looked away.

I whispered to Michael, "I don't think he likes me."

"Berwyn doesn't like *humans*," he whispered back. "And just so you know, you can't whisper quietly enough for an Angel not to hear."

My cheeks warmed as Berwyn's face swung back to stare at me.

The door opened and the Angels disappeared. My mom walked into the room with a nurse pushing a wheelchair. My throat tightened, and I avoided her eyes. My mom had borne the brunt of my horribly selfish behavior over the last few months, and now she was the one who had to pay for it all. The premature death of her mother and—

"Are you ready to go?" she asked me.

I nodded mutely. The nurse explained the antibiotics and pain medication I was taking home with me. Then she demonstrated how to unwrap and rewrap my shoulder, which Jason dislocated when he attacked me. My morning pain meds were wearing off, and as she bound my shoulder back up, the sharp ache took my breath away.

Michael watched, biting his nails.

It's not that bad, I thought.

"I hate Jason," he said back. "I hope they fillet him in Hell."

Jason was sick, Michael.

"He had a choice, Catherine. Junkies always have a choice."

I let it go. Jason was dead, and it didn't matter how Michael or I felt about him anymore. I sat down in the wheelchair, and my mom pushed me to the doorway where I sensed her stiffen. "Do you want to see your father before we go?"

My throat constricted even more. I hadn't seen my dad since he'd chased me down the driveway, calling my name as I sped away in his Dodge Demon. Tears blurred my vision.

"Baby, I know this is hard," Michael said. "But you know nobody is guaranteed another day, right?"

"Catherine?" my mom said.

I nodded. Yes, I wanted to see my dad. She wheeled me down the hall. We took the elevator up two floors to intensive care. The smell of disinfectant and the sound of machines overwhelmed me. My mom maneuvered the chair around the nurse's station and into one of the tiny, glass-walled rooms. My dad lay on the bed, ghost-white and silent. Tubes sprouted everywhere. Plastic bags filled with fluid hung above him, below him. My mom pushed me in close.

"I'll give you a few minutes alone," she said and walked out.

After I'd stormed out of the house and drove away, my dad set out to find me. He was worried. I'd promised myself I'd never do that to him—leave him behind in a blind rage.

But I did.

The police found the car he was driving a half hour later in a snow bank not far from our house. An aneurysm had ruptured in his brain. Michael and Roshan knew last night, but they hadn't told me. They didn't want to upset me. That's where everyone was when I'd regained consciousness. My dad took a turn for the worse in the middle of the night, and the doctors weren't sure if he was going to make it. They still weren't.

And it was my fault.

I wasn't going to hide under a rock this time. I wasn't going to kill myself. Satan had blown his chance to convince me that was a viable option. Michael and Roshan stayed close to me. They loved me. My mom and my sisters loved me, too. In the last twelve hours they'd told me that over and over in response to my repeated, choked-up apologies.

But I hated myself.

And somehow I had to live with that.

"I'm so sorry, dad," I whispered. Then I broke down with my face on his forearm and cried.

Character Art
by
Koa Beam

Catherine
**A sci-fi spouting geek who believes she has an Angel who plays
songs for her on the radio whenever she needs a lift**

Michael
An aspiring rock guitarist from the mean streets of Cleveland with a past full of rumors and a fervent wish for a fresh start

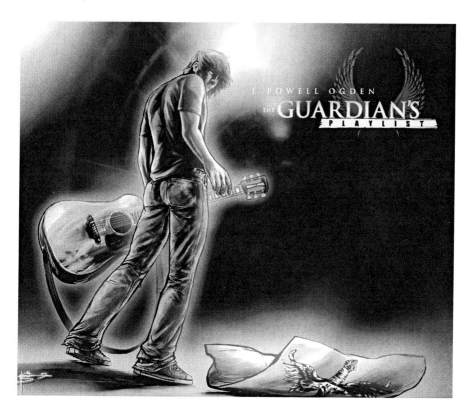

Jason
A rising high school basketball star from Bay with all the right
answers and money to burn

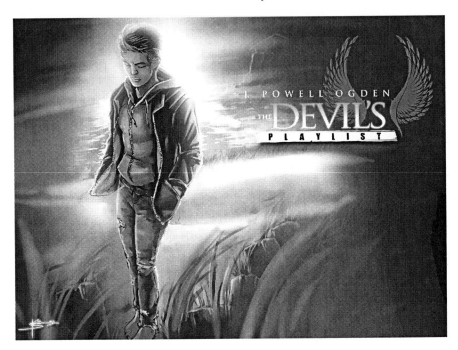

Kiss in the Snow

Deleted Scenes

Scene 1: This was the original prologue

SECOND GRADE, TWO *years later…*

I glanced up at the clock. Only a few more minutes until the bell would ring to end the year at Saint Paul Catholic Elementary School. I traced the pencil rest on the smooth surface of my desk as the student buzz got louder. The leftover scent of the bleach we'd used to scrub the desks down hung in the air. The desks were now empty and clean, and my backpack was stuffed with the dog-eared workbooks and leftover tatters of a year's worth of schoolwork. When the bell rang, bedlam broke loose and my classmates began whooping and hollering, excited for summer to begin.

"Quiet please," shushed my second grade teacher, Sister Patricia. She glanced up at the P.A. system hanging on the wall. I waited impatiently while the bus students were dismissed. When they were all pounding down the hall the school secretary announced, "Thomas Avenue Walkers are dismissed." I watched my friends, Grace and Merideth, skip out the door.

"Bye!" I called after them. "I'll call you later." I smoothed my red and gray plaid skirt and placed my backpack on my lap.

"Loyola Lane walkers are—" The secretary wasn't finished speaking before I was half-walking, half-running out the classroom door. I joined the throng of students making their way toward the front of the building. As soon as I was through the double doors, I ran. My younger sister, Cici, was lost somewhere behind

me and my older sister, Claire, was far ahead, her pony tail flying behind her. I would never catch her, but that was okay. It was tradition to run the whole way home on the last day of school.

The sky was blue and the air smelled of fresh cut grass. I ran past the baseball fields and playground, one ragged strap of my backpack pulling down on my shoulder with every step. I knew my mom would be waiting for us at home with the kitchen table set up as an ice cream sundae bar—another last day of school tradition.

Claire had already rounded the last corner and disappeared when I felt a familiar tightness in my chest. It was like a rubber band had suddenly wrapped itself around my lungs. The sensation rose up toward my collarbone.

"You're okay," I told myself and slowed to a fast walk. But I wasn't okay, and I was soon battling against my lungs for every breath.

The little voice in my head whispered, "You're not gonna make it. Run."

I forced a burst of speed into my legs. The air got thicker and thicker. I rounded the last corner and saw my house ahead. My feet were heavy and the summer air—fresh and beautiful a moment ago—was now stifling.

"Don't stop," the voice urged.

My face burned and my shoulders and chest ached as I cut across the grass and yanked open the screen door. I saw my mom in the kitchen. Her smile froze on her face when she saw me.

"I need a nebulizer treatment!" I gasped, throwing my backpack on the floor. Then I turned and heaved myself up the stairs to my room. "Hurry!"

I sat down hard on my bed, my unfocused eyes coming to rest on the dusty figurines that cluttered my dresser. My Guardian Angel statue stared impotently back as I struggled to pull in enough air...there's no air in here...where is she?

"MOM!" I called in a weak whisper, panic and anger competing for dominance in my voice. "MOMMMM!"

She hurried into the room, the ice cream forgotten, with a syringe full of Albuterol. I glared at her, helpless and impatient, as her shaking hands pulled open my closet door and attached the tubes of my nebulizer machine. She flipped a switch, placed the mask on my face and the elastic band around my head.

Too slow...can't breathe...it's not working...

The machine rumbled and cool mist billowed out of the mask's ventilation holes, steaming up my pink glasses.

"Shh…just breathe, nice and slow," my mom urged. *"In…out…in… out…"*

I leaned forward on my hands. My mom sat behind me, rubbing her fingertips lightly across my upper back. *"You're okay,"* she murmured. I looked up into the mirror above my dresser. My blue eyes squinted back at me through the mist, my frizzy blonde hair stuck out at odd angles above and below the elastic. *"Catherine… shh…"*

My panic subsided as the rubber band in my chest slowly released its hold. With every inhalation, more and more of my lungs were freed. I let my shoulders drop and relaxed my grip on the tufted white bedspread.

"Better?" she asked.

I nodded and let my gaze drift from the mirror to the window. The sheer curtains puffed gently as the summer breeze blew through the window.

In…out…in…out…

Discussion of Scene 1:

This scene was my absolute first attempt at writing the story that was growing in my head. And in my own head, the little voice whispered, "Write what you know." This scene was lifted directly from my childhood and my palms still sweat as I relive it. It is terrifying not being able to breathe.

Scene Two:

This scene took place right after Michael's wake

I SAT WITH MERI, Leo, and Leo's girlfriend, Piper, at the funeral the following morning. My body rested calmly in the pew, but my emotions ran wild. Again, I tried to get with the program of acceptance and celebration, but again, I failed miserably. When we left the church, something kept nagging at me. Something remained unfinished. I needed to find closure in my own way, and I had an idea how I could do that.

Since my parents were busy, I turned to Meri and asked if her mom could take me down to the riverbank.

"I'm sure Leo wouldn't mind taking you," volunteered Mrs. DiMaro, a small, proper woman of Filipino descent. "You can ride home with us. We just need to drop Piper off at her house on the way."

Piper, a willowy dark-haired junior, shot dagger eyes at me, obviously not happy about being cast aside, and I shot dagger eyes at Leo, still angry about his comments about Michael from the day before. Leo sighed and shook his head, but we all said, "Okay" to Mrs. DiMaro, not wanting to be impolite.

Piper kept up a steady barrage of questions directed at Leo from the back seat the whole way home. She seemed completely oblivious to the somber mood in the car. Leo walked her to her door and kissed her when they dropped her off, prompting Meri and I to groan in unison. Mrs. DiMaro gave us a warning look.

When he returned to the car, he saw the looks on our faces and his eyes shrunk to annoyed slits above his angular cheekbones. "What?"

"Oh...nothing."

After dropping off his Mom, I asked if we could stop at the grocery store. "I just need to get one thing," I promised, but crap, I'd forgotten I'd left my bag at home. "Meri...can I please borrow five dollars?" She held up her empty hands to remind me she hadn't brought hers either.

"Leo?" Meri asked, pouting slightly and tilting her chin so that her dark, shiny hair brushed the top of her shoulder. He dug his wallet out of his pocket and pulled out a ten.

"You're lending me money even though I've been mad at you all day?" I asked him.

"Cate, I've known you since you were *five*. Having you mad at me is nothing new." Then he smiled wickedly and held the ten out of reach out the window. "But... it would be nice to be forgiven."

"Come on! Please?"

"And...?" he prompted.

"You're forgiven. Just try not to be such a jerk again."

"Not possible," Meri whispered as Leo handed over the ten. I ducked into the store and purchased a single white rose while they waited with the engine running at the curb.

"Now, can you guys take me down to the bridge over the river in the park?" I asked, stroking the baby-soft petals with my fingertips.

"Are you sure that's a good idea? Maybe you need some time," worried Meri.

"No, I really need to do this today. Please?" I felt stronger now that I had a plan.

When I got out of the car near the bridge, I calmed myself with sight and sound of the river then focused on my need to finish the journey I'd desperately wanted to make on Saturday—the journey to the place where Michael had died alone, broken and afraid.

From where I stood, I could see both sides of the gorge rising straight up, stratified and crumbling, with the river flowing in between. It wasn't the shallow sparkling brook it had been last Saturday. It had swollen to a fast-tumbling stream, and the rocky beach where Michael lay dying was now under a foot of water. When I started to take off my pumps, Leo put his hand on my arm saying, "Not a good idea, Cate. What are you thinking?"

"I'm going to leave this rose where he died," I explained as I tied the bottom of my pale pink dress into a knot to lift the hem above my knees and then gathered my curls up into a ponytail.

"Why can't you just toss it and let the current carry it?" suggested Leo reasonably. I ignored him. Leo was all about following the rules and avoiding risks. He wouldn't understand. "How do you know where he died exactly anyway?"

"I…umm…think I saw it in the paper," I responded quickly, avoiding his eyes.

He shook his head, his lips pressed together in a grim line, his Asian eyes frustrated. "The river's running pretty fast. You're gonna fall in," he warned, still holding onto my arm. I looked down at his arm and then glared up at him. He let his hand fall away and clenched it into a fist.

"I won't," I said, taking the last few steps to the river's edge and dipping my toes into the water. Then I did start to feel a little foolish.

It was cold, but not like ice. The current tugged relentlessly at my ankles and the rocks were hard and bruising under my bare feet, but something urged me forward, telling me it would be okay, that what I was doing was important, necessary. I walked out toward the base of the cliff, carefully placing my feet one in front of the other with my arms stretched out to the side for balance and the rose held tightly in my hand.

Okay, yeah...you do look kinda ridiculous.

When I reached the place where Michael had fallen, I turned around and looked back across the bridge and up to the cliff top ledge I'd been trapped on. It was covered in brush and at least a quarter mile away, maybe more. There was no way he could have seen me up there. I must have been in shock, hallucinating. Then I jerked my head back around and looked up toward the ridge he'd fallen from.

"Oh my God," I whispered. It looked so high from the bottom. It was a miracle he hadn't died on impact.

The act of looking up combined with the disorienting pull of the water flowing around my ankles gave me a sudden case of vertigo, and the trees at the top of the cliff circled around as if being flushed down a blue sky drain. I lost my balance, and as Leo predicted, splashed ungracefully into the river. I cursed under my breath as my entire body was subjected to the pull of the current and was dragged against the razor sharp shale embedded in the muddy river bottom. Fortunately, it took only a few moments to right myself.

There I stood, water pouring in thick rivulets down my arms and legs from the saturated dress that was now plastered to my body, revealing every curve, bra and panty line. *Great...just great*, I thought, beyond embarrassed. It didn't really matter. It was only Meri and Leo–who'd better keep his mouth shut this time–watching. I turned to see them still standing on the riverbank. They were waving their hands for me to come back. Jerk. Where were Leo's protective instincts?

I looked back up toward the top of the cliff, slower this time, planting one foot upstream and the other downstream to stabilize myself. The leaves of the trees high above appeared black with their edges brilliantly outlined by the sun above them. I let my eyes drift down the face of the cliff and across the submerged beach, looking for signs that Michael had been there. There was nothing. Everything had washed downstream by the runoff from last weekend's storm. All traces of his lost battle with death were gone.

I lifted the velvety rose, which I'd somehow managed to hang onto, and touched it to the tip of my nose, immersing myself in its sweet floral scent. I breathed a ragged breath onto its silky surface and whispered self-consciously, "Okay…well…I just wanted to say goodbye, Michael. Thanks for being my friend. I hope you found… peace." I tossed the pale rose into the current. Just before it touched down, I saw Leo's dark wavy reflection on the water's rippling surface. He must have waded in after all and was now standing quietly behind me.

"Thanks, Leo. This has been really hard," I murmured and turned around.

The river behind me was empty.

My eyes darted back to the riverbank. Leo and Meri were still standing there, looking on anxiously. I spun around, almost losing my balance again on the slippery rocks, searching in every direction for whoever had cast the reflection on the water. There was no one. My heart beat fast and loud in my chest. I was obviously hallucinating again.

I turned then and struggled against the current back toward the bank of the river, which was much harder than walking out to the cliff. The water fought against my calves, causing white caps to form in front and sucking eddies to swirl behind as my legs pushed forward. My lungs began to itch.

Focus, I thought, as the itch spread and the familiar rubber bands crisscrossed themselves around my lungs then, *shit, I really don't need this today.* By the time I reached the edge of the river, I was taking in air through a coffee stirrer, my lungs burning slightly with each inhalation. I focused carefully on each breath: *In, out, in, out. Nice and slow.* It was bearable. But as I stepped out onto the dry rocky incline, I realized I was in more trouble than I thought. I had left my bag, and with it my inhaler, at home. I took in another breath and let it out slowly through my nose. I didn't like people to see me like this. I felt weak, defective. I'd learned to camouflage the wheezing by coordinating my words carefully with my breathing until I could use my inhaler discreetly. Staying calm was key, and after years of practice I was pretty good at it.

I looked up at Leo and asked neutrally, "Can you take me home now...*breathe*...please?"

"You can't get in the car like that. Can't you wring yourself out or something?" His tone was not sympathetic. He and I looked down at my sopping wet dress and legs together. Bits of fine gravel and mud clung to the fabric, and thin streams of blood trickled down my calves from the scrapes torn by the shale. I'd barely felt those in the cold water. Now, they stung.

His eyes and tone grudgingly softened with pity. "Shit...you're bleeding, Cate. What were you thinking?"

I was cold, wet, exposed. My eyes swam behind tears I thought I'd sent down the river with the rose. I lost my focus and inhaled too fast, freeing an audible, high-pitched wheeze.

I would have been better off if he'd stayed angry.

Meri was at my side in an instant with her hand on my back. "Can't you hear that, Leo? She's having an asthma attack. We need to get her home." He looked at me doubtfully, hesitating.

I took another careful breath and repeated, "Please?" I tried to maintain the illusion that I had everything under control. In reality, like a junkie needing her next high, my mind was entirely fixated on the inhaler that I knew was in my bag, which was sitting on my dresser under a pile of dirty clothes in my room. Leo stepped aside, and Meri and I started picking our way over the rocks up the incline. The rocks hurt my bare feet, and my shoes were several yards to my left—poor planning on my part.

I sucked in a small gasp of pain and heard Leo curse under his breath. He jogged up behind me, scooped me up and carried me to the car. I was so humiliated. The thought, *at least I shaved my legs this morning,* flew unbidden through my head, and then, *you really do have some major issues.*

Meri opened the car door and Leo dropped me onto the front seat. He looked down at his wet, bloody shirtsleeves and then back at my face. I couldn't read his expression, but I imagined he was wondering if the stains would ever come out and what his overly refined mother would say about the mess she was going to find in her car.

I averted my eyes and instead looked out the window at the river rushing away from me. As we left, I wondered how far the rose would go. Would it make it all the way to the open waters of Lake Erie? I hoped so. Then I closed my eyes and tried to relax as Blink 182's "All the Small Things" played on the radio.

I smiled ruefully. Maybe I did the right thing after all? I bit the smile back and scolded myself. *Hallucinations and delusions…you're definitely losing it.* Nevertheless, another song was added to the playlist, and I looked up at the sky as we left the park, feeling strangely comforted.

Discussion of Scene 2:

I love this scene as well. As a ghost story unfolding, I wanted the mystery to build slowly. First, the feelings and scents she noticed as she left the woods the day he died, then the dreams, then the ghostly shadow on the river then the run-in with the rabid coyote and the scent that kept her safe at the campfire, and finally him appearing to her in the woods on her birthday. Everyone who read the first draft said they wanted Michael back sooner! They loved Cate and Michael's banter and the sparks that flew between them. One of the scenes leading up to that had to go and this was it.

I am bringing it back here because it provides a little more backstory for a storyline in The Devil's Playlist. I can't say more without giving it away, so you'll just have to wait to find out how!

Acknowledgements

One day in October of 2008, I finished another supernatural fiction series and was missing my heroes desperately. I decided, out of the blue, to create my own. Without the help and encouragement of the following people, I never would have succeeded in bringing them to life. My deepest gratitude goes to the following:

To the readers of my first draft, including, Debbie Sabo, Kim Sabo, Rita Sabo, Tony and Mary Kay Powell, Brigid and Jeanette Ogden, Christie and Erin Jenkins, Greg Arndt, Julie Lacey, Brian Nutwell, Michelle McGovern, Anne Marie Neal, Bren Handyside, Karen England, Cindy Musto, Janet Ogden and Kathy Fister. Your feedback and excitement over the story was priceless.

To my sister, Donna, who was too scared to read the manuscript, but always asked how it was going.

To Amie Horan, who not only read the first draft, but copyedited it. Her results were painful to behold—there were corrections on almost every line—but not as painful as reading it probably was. Thanks for the crash course in grammar and punctuation. You're a copyediting Ninja.

To my professional, incredibly talented and amazingly intuitive editor, Erin MacLellan. She rocked the book with her honesty and enthusiasm for the story. I hope she likes the final cut.

To my book cover and interior format specialist, fellow author T.C. McMullen. You are a tiny mountain woman of epic strength, stamina, and artistic ability. Thanks for sharing it with me.

To the McMullen family, thank you for adopting me during the last four SciFi Valley Cons in Pennsylvania. Your hospitality will never be forgotten.

To Officer James Carbone for sharing his experience and knowledge of drug enforcement law with me. Thanks for caring about the kids you work with.

To Cam, who gave me the best input on weaponry and what would be cool to have in the story.

To Dan Foley for his Latin translations, Tony Mauro and Eric Adkins for their artwork, and all of the Bands for their music. You guys are awesome.

To my friends who helped me restore and keep my sanity. You know who you are. I owe you more than my gratitude.

To my family, Chris, Brigid, Jeanette, and Cam. Thank you for loving me even when the laundry wasn't done, there was no food in the fridge, and the pile of papers on the counter resembled the Leaning Tower of Pisa, all because I was "writing a novel." I love you, too. Always.

Finally, to my higher power. Thanks for loving me, too.

About the Author

J. Powell Ogden grew up in North Olmsted, Ohio not far from Lewis Woods. She now resides in Dublin, Ohio with her three amazingly talented children and one superhumanly patient, husband. When she is not writing she is thinking about writing.

J. Powell Ogden believes in the power of music to unite, strengthen and heal.

Novels by J. Powell Ogden:

The Guardian's Playlist

The Devil's Playlist
Coming May 15, 2016

Find out more at www.JPowellOgden.com

Bibliography

Nietzsche, Friedrich W. *Thus spoke Zarathustra*. Trans. R. J. Hollingdale. New York: Penguin Putnam, Inc., 1969.

Milton, John. *Paradise Lost*. New York: Oxford University Press Inc., 2008.

Publisher

Spark Street Media, LLC.
PO Box 3155
Dublin, Ohio 43016

CPSIA information can be obtained
at www.ICGtesting.com
Printed in the USA
FFOW02n0919110216
21345FF